PROJECT AGOSHA

Call of the Koteli

MT LYNX

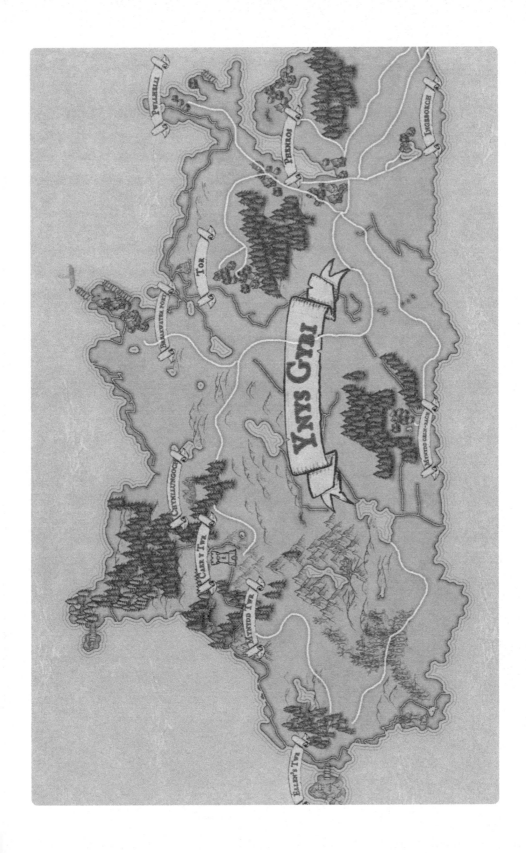

CONTENTS

Acknowledgements, Thanks & Dedications

In all the books I read growing up, I always thought this segment of a book was a bit of an afterthought. In the process of writing my own, I found that to be true. It took a long time for me to think about this part and to decide what needs to be here and why. After all that thought, I finally decided that this book would not be here without the following beneficial characters in my life, in no particular order. So here we go:

Mom & Dad:
You have enjoyed my stories for years, encouraged me to write more, and patiently vetted my initial attempts. Obviously, I would not be here at all without you. You are the only two people on this earth who have been exclusively in my corner from day one. Until recently, I never knew how much I needed that. Thank you.

My American Friends:
You welcomed me into your lives and showed me a different form of home. Your friendships are invaluable to me, and I would not be who I am today without you.

Spicer:

Sometimes you were the only one to whom I could talk. Sixteen years was not nearly enough. I miss you, little girl.

Cirilla:

There were days when you were the only reason I got up in the morning. Thank you for insisting, even when I could not dream of facing the world, that I still had to get up and try.

My Welsh Friends and Tutors:

You have taught me so much with your friendship, your patience as I navigated a new language, and in sharing your wonderful culture with me. I am immensely grateful for all of you. Diolch yn fawr iawn.

Introduction

or

Author's Comments

H ello. First, thank you for reading my book! I'm so excited to tell you this story - so thanks for reading! I have wanted to tell these stories for a long time now... well over a decade!

I really hope you enjoy this peek into the lives of the characters in Project AGOSHA as much as I have in writing them and seeing where their story arcs took the tale.

Thanks again, and I look forward to seeing you in the next story arc!

Apology

Let's get on with the story, but first, I must apologize. To all the people of Cymru, the Welsh communities, the ancestral tribes long past, and to all lovers of the Welsh language.

My story is a work of fiction, and it begins on Ynys Gybi. Some of the locations described are real as they stand today, and some I have taken artistic license in the descriptions and/or locations thereof. I have referred to some mythic figures, but most all the characters are original fictional creations.

I must also apologize to the people of Brittany. Many of the locations described later in the story are similar in region to what stands today, but great license has been taken in the distances and land descriptions. The people described in these Brittonic regions are wholly my creation and are in no way imitating any Brittonic folks I know. I endeavor, with both Brittonic and Welsh, to affect the utility of an archaic form of both languages due to the period in which this story takes place. For that, if I have erred in structure or translation despite my best efforts, I apologize. I am neither a historian, a linguist, nor a geographer. I am telling a story and shifting words/geography or access as fits the tale with what little research and historical information I have had available to me at the time of this writing.

The Charge of the Light

At the Origin of Time
The Eternal Darkness held sway,
O'er each and ev'ry Plane
And imprisoned each within its hold,
Tainted by its stain.
Until the Light bloomed forth
Shining herself into Being
And freed those of Virtue
Who embodied Righteous Feeling:
Honesty beyond reproach
Purity above measure
Veneration of the Holy
Kindness without censure
Discipline of all reaction
And, most import' of all,
Mercy without satisfaction
Thusly shall they heed the Call.

Chapter One

The Scion's Ruin

There was a small grey bird on the windowsill. She saw it as she paced down the corridor. As she drew nearer, it appeared to be lying in a pool of blood. Horrified, she veered off the carpeted path in the corridor and over to the window. No blood, she saw with relief; just a grey bird with red feather tipping. The very edges were a bright crimson hue, evoking the image of fresh claret, but the hue gradually darkened as it moved up to the body feathers, increasing in saturation and becoming a coal slate color on the body. The bird did not move, though its eyes were open.

It lay on its side, wings closed, with the feathers pooling around it on the cool brown stone of the sill. Abertha's timid hand reached for the small creature and cupped it. The limp body filled the valley of her hand, and as she lifted it, she could feel the gentle thrumming of its heartbeat in her hands. A soft vibration of life—the physical presence of a soul in residence.

She let out a sigh of relief when she realized it was not dead—only stunned. But why? She looked around for the cause of the bird's injury and found it right away. Her nose knew it before her eyes understood what she saw, as an acrid and oily smell coated the inside of her air passages and made her gasp. The response was an immediate spasm in her chest, and tears veiled her eyes as a protective response to the violence the air carried. She coughed and spat out the window, without thought or regard to the action, to clear her mouth of the taste. She dragged the heel of her hand across her face, wiping away spit and clearing her eyes as well. Sniffling and with great care, she turned the bird over, hiding the rusty brown-tipped downy breast for the coal and tar back. She returned the poor creature to the sill and squinted out across the vast seas of brown and green that surrounded her home. The forests moved like a fury, rippling and stretching into the morning sky as wind buffeted across the land. It was the wind that had brought the smell of violence into the air, wrapped in heavy smoke. The smoke must have stunned the bird.

Abertha leaned out the window, studying the billowing clouds of darkness roiling across the trees.

What is the source of this smoke? A fire, of course. But from where? A hut? A fortress within the forest proper? The amount of smoke would indicate a larger dwelling, yet—

Hasty, approaching footsteps interrupted her study.

"Your Majesty! Your Majesty!"

Male voices were calling her from down the corridor whence she'd come, bearing frantic excitement and fear. Their footsteps became clearer as they drew closer, now enjoined with the metallic sounds of armor and the rustling of fabrics as people moved with haste. *So, one of the guards is approaching, perhaps*, she mused. The noises became louder and then came to an abrupt halt, forcing her to cease her search for the source of the smoke. Turning, she saw the captain of her personal guard and the castle steward standing before her.

"Well?" Her tone conveyed that she expected this to be important.

The steward was flushed and panting from the exertion of keeping up with the captain of the brehines' personal guard. He managed to straighten himself up for a moment to answer Abertha's inquiry before planting his hands on his waist as he gasped for air again.

"Chynllungoch, Your Majesty. It's… gone!" He swiped at the sweat running into his eyes.

She frowned as she looked from the disordered steward to her capable captain. In contrast, he stood as still as a stone. He had been with her for many years and many battles, and she knew he did not startle easily. His countenance remained calm, but his eyes betrayed a worry she could not remember having seen before.

"What does he mean *gone*?" Her question was coolly directed toward the captain.

He returned her gaze, unflinching. Yes, there was worry there… and something else. Fear? Was it fear? She had never seen fear in his eyes before, not even when staring down the blades of the assassins of Ingebokch. Not even when seeing his own life bleeding down his leg as they tried to cleave his guts from his trunk at Tor. No. This was something else. Something great enough to cause even the famed captain of the Brehines' Guard and of the Koteli to be truly afraid.

Sensing her rising impatience, he answered, "The township of Chynllungoch has been overtaken by the fiends of Darkness, my Brehines." His eyes held hers. "The defenses held for a time, but they fell an hour past, and the fiends make for the castle. They will be here nigh an hour more."

"The castle walls—" she began.

"The castle walls have already been breached." His steady tone overrode her. "I know not how, but we found them open, and the fiends make their way here in haste as we speak."

As the captain was speaking, the steward had regained a measure of his composure and was attending to the conversational flow. Now he stared in amazement and shock at what he deemed a liberty that dared too far upon the personage of the Brehines.

"You dare to speak so to… to her… Majestness…" he spluttered.

"Please, my lady." The captain continued over the steward's interjections, seeming not to hear them. "We haven't much time."

She, too, ignored the steward's spluttering consternations and forgave the captain's audacity. His words had reached her, but the worry in his eyes reached her more. She had finally seen the message of resignation hiding here too, conveyed under the worry and fear in the tone of his voice.

She searched his face a final time, her look almost pleading for reassurance that it was not... could not be. What she saw there brought confirmation of what she had slowly hoped over the years would never happen. She saw the same fear, the same worry, but also compassion. He knew, and in his knowing, she felt the final resistance within her crumbling away almost before she even knew it had been there, welling up in the tears that pricked at her eyes. Quickly on the heels of the fading resistance came a weary resignation that sapped the strength that she had woken with at the start of the day.

The smoke was forgotten. The bird was forgotten. Now, it was only what came as a repulsive duty she had always known would come to her door. She'd lain with it, cheek and jowl. After all these years of stalking her ancestors and her ancestors' ancestors, the cursed ruin was brought to bear. They had come for it, and it had come for her.

She dropped her gaze so he would not see the images that passed through her mind. The horrible foreknowing of what was to come caused her skin to flush, and just as quickly she paled. A moment of lightheadedness took her, and she swayed on her feet.

The Captain, in anticipation, reached out to steady her. But as he did, the Steward (who had already been beyond shocked at the Captain's audacity and would stand for no further impropriety from a castle *guard*, even if he was the Captain of the protectors of the Brehines!) slapped his hand away with a bellow and leapt in front of him. "How DARE you... you scullery URCHIN! You... BUMPKIN!" he shrilled.

The Steward's voice had the clarity of a slap to her senses, and Abertha shook her head to clear the dread that had surrounded her thoughts and was overtaking her mind. There was no time for her to mourn, well, everything.

No time. The fiends would be here within the hour, and there was still so much to do. She grabbed her mettle and steeled herself for the tasks at hand, gruesome as they were. They were the only choices left for her.

She found her voice and, with it, the strength to rule what time was left to her.

"Steward, empty the castle of all those who inhabit it. Down to the last mongrel and rat you can find. Empty all the halls, the rooms, and the dungeons. Free the prisoners, if there are any. Not a single soul must remain. Am I understood?" Her voice dulled with the knowledge of what lay in store. The Steward stopped mid-harangue and turned to look at her.

"Why I canst… I… I… eh… um… hmm? Your… Your Majesty…?" was all he could manage.

She didn't have the heart to explain to him what the future would bring. The best she could do was protect them for as long as she could. "You heard me, Castale. Empty the castle of all living things, great and small. Take them out of here and to the Mynydd Twr… Take them there and… and…" she trailed off, unable to tell him how it would be better to be dashed into the sea than for the people to be captured by the Dark fiends. The horror that would await them if they were found.

"Majesty?" the Steward whispered, the strength of his voice draining away at the look on her face.

"And hide," she finished. "Hide them. Hide *with* them. Take nothing and leave immediately. If you do so, you may just yet have time. All of you. Now! Go! *GO!*"

Bolstered by the urgency in her words, if not the dread on her face, the Steward wheeled around and took off at a waddling stride down the corridor. As he went, his voice wailed up behind him, crying the alarm and rousing all the castle inhabitants to arms and to leave. He went on to perform the orders of his Brehines as best he could and as long as his office would allow.

Brehines Abertha, second daughter of Beli Mawr, Brehines o Caer y Twr, straightened her back and faced the Captain of her guards with a steady gaze. "We have not much time, Captain. Come."

Without looking to see if he would follow, she turned and paced her way through the north corridor, past the royal chambers, and down the western steps to the lowest level of the western rampart. It was not a large castle—her home—but it was large enough. With the many descendants of her family having lived here since the time when the Ruin was brought to their home, it had grown decently enough. The Ruin had been placed in its own room, with its own battlements, its own protective measures, its own secrets to keep, and its own way to keep others out. None had entered this place, sacrosanct of the humor of the gods, since she had been entrusted the Ruin of the Family by her father so many, many years ago. She and she alone could wield it for what it was, as her blood was the last to bear its name: Gwaedreiol.

Turning quickly down one slight hallway into another, she navigated the innermost workings of the castle until she came to the door. It was small, unimpressive, and seemed to disappear into the walls if one did not look directly at it. Cobwebs had grown over the edges of the entrance framework, but the door itself was curiously clean. It was always this way, as if the door itself could not bear to retain a mark of dirt for fear of offending what it guarded so dearly. Not pausing to check for her follower, she applied light pressure on the outer edges of the door and watched in fascination as the portal reacted to her touch, slipping away into nothingness as if a barrier had never been there in the first place. She took a deep breath and stepped through the entrance and into a room that time had left long ago.

When she had pivoted before him and begun walking down the hall, it had taken him a moment to realize that what he had always been instructed might happen one day truly was coming to pass. He had always known of the possibility, but to find it now upon himself was maddening, and the awe was robbing him of his edge. She was halfway down the hall before he was able to start moving after her. He began to jog to keep up with his Brehines, but it seemed that she was moving faster than him, and no matter what speed he added, she was always just too far ahead. Up one hallway and down another, down stairways, and across the castle in a twisting and turning path meant to lose those uninitiated into the mysteries that surrounded this family that had borne such a heavy burden over the centuries. Barely keeping her in his vision, he turned the corner at the last moment, just in time to see her step through the wall in a dead end. There was no door he could see, but he knew instinctively that he had only seconds to follow her before the wards of the castle would no longer permit his passage. As he picked up speed, his normally cadenced run became a full sprint. He ran at speed at the wall he had seen the Brehines disappear through. In the last moments before impact, as the smooth wall loomed before his eyes, he had the thought that if he was mistaken, the consequences would not only be painful but also evident to everyone. Just before his nose smashed into the wall, he closed his eyes and braced for impact.

As she stepped across the threshold, all the warmth of the castle torches disappeared. There was still light in this room, but it was cold and very dim. What little light filtered through the tiny slits in the walls that served as windows to an outside world had a cold, blue cast to it, which only served to heighten the otherworldly atmosphere. The limited furnishings in the room seemed to absorb the light rather than reflect it, which also contributed to the dimness. Pausing, she surveyed the sanctum for the last time. The room was barely wide enough for three brawny men to stand shoulder to shoulder and only high enough for a small giant to clear his head. Once, there had been torches lining the walls that never failed, but those had been removed in ages past, and now the walls were lined only with dust and empty brackets where torches had once hung. Near the ceiling and close to the tiny window slits, which were scarcely wide enough to slide a hand through, hung the emblems of the family, three on each side at equal intervals from the entrance to the back wall. On her left were three kite shields bearing the gilded, partially skeletal hand emerging from the bloom of the rose, clutching at the thorns that tore its remaining flesh as blood dripped down: the Gwaedreiol. On her right were three bucklers, with the wellspring eternal emerging from a basin and imbued with holy light. Memories of the time she was introduced to her fate flooded her, as well as memories that must have belonged to others who had also walked this solitary aisle in this forgotten room. Her father, the great Brenin Beli Mawr, showing her the door and telling her that while she could open it, she must never enter. Years later, the news had come that Anwadaledd had fallen to the Dark Ones. In the midst of mourning and the whirlwind of change that her crowning had brought, her father had taken her here and pronounced to her the fate Anwa had spurned by her traitorous act. She closed her eyes and listened to sounds of an age long past that were and were not there: footsteps whispering by her, the soft swish of cloaks and fine linens, the hushed voices of reverie or condemnation, and the flickering of absent torches. Such things were normal here, where the boundaries from one world plane to another were so thin that she could almost hear the whispers of long-gone voices discussing the Ruin that faced her now. She stepped forward another pace and was already halfway to her dimly glowing doom.

He passed through the wall as if it were no more solid than a plume of smoke. In his effort to keep up after the Brehines and with no plans to keep his pace, he tripped over the entrance stones and fell forward into the room that he just now recognized was there. The light changed from a bright and flickering orange to a cold and shrouded blue. He expected a jarring thud or a painful impact from landing on his hands and knees, or maybe his face! There was none of that. He landed on a soft yet threadbare runner that started near the door he had fallen through and seemed to end but a short way ahead. Being near the floor, despite the dimness of the light, he could see that at one point the runner had borne the emblems of the house of the Brehines. *It must have been woven together a long time ago,* he thought, as he could see the patterning had faded and worn thin with the tread of countless feet and the weight of ages gone past. He raised his head and sat up. The movement seemed slower, as though he were moving through thick water, yet it felt no different than colder and thicker air. The Brehines was halfway down the short aisle, which led to the back wall of the room. There, he could see the outline of a stone table supported by what appeared to be a single column.

"Your Majesty," he croaked.

She turned, hearing his words, as though she had not heard him stumble into the room and had just become aware of his presence. Her regal lineage was never more evident to him than now, in the slight movements as she turned and the fatally determined air that enveloped her every move.

"You're here. Good. You will find movement a bit difficult for those not of this… accursed line. Do be quick. We do not have time to dwell." She turned away and took another step towards the table.

He pushed himself to his feet with effort. It seemed everything had become more than twice as heavy in the moments he had fallen into this room. Even the air felt heavy to breathe, as though it carried a fog that made it less nourishing to his body. "What is this place?" he gasped.

"This is the place that time has forgotten. The home of my lineage's Ruin. Time flows differently here." She offered the last comment as an apologetic explanation for what he was experiencing.

He staggered forward and managed to bring himself to her side. It could only have been a few steps, but it seemed to take forever, and he would have sworn to all the Gods that he walked half a mile to reach her side. His muscles trembled on the edge of exhaustion, and he gasped as though he had the constitution of the fat Steward. Time did flow differently here, indeed, and the fabric of the space of this place was none too forgiving.

"Come," she said, closing the distance between herself and the table.

He staggered forward a few more steps, still feeling as though it had taken miles to do so, and approached the stone table. It was actually a small marble platform supported by a thin column, also of marble, that rose from the floor as though it grew there. With the age of the place, he noted that everything should have been covered with a layer of thick dust, but none was visible. The cloths that once adorned this table were ratty, full of holes, and had begun to rot some time ago. Now it was little more than faded threads held together in small bunches, with the impression of lively woven patterns worn away with the ravages of time. In the center of the table was what they had come for, and it would demand the final cost. He stared at the largish, tawny-wrapped cylinder. It stood near a cubit high, with the breadth of a large gourd. The colors of the wrapping seemed slightly brighter, as if it gave off its own light to counteract the gloomy shadows that filled the room, making the edges more distinct and vibrant. Was this the source of all the sorrow wrought and trouble yet to come?

She silently pondered the representation of the ruin of her line for a few moments, contemplating the meaning of its existence here for her. Then, with a brief smile, she asked, "Are you ready, Captain?"

He nodded. "Yes, my lady. I will be the conduit, as all who have performed the functions of this position have sworn to perform this final duty to our monarch in their time of need."

"You know, I have never learned your name." She smiled wider. "It was always Captain this or Captain that. I cannot call you Captain *all* the time. So what IS your name, soldier? If you are willing to give so much for this cause, I should at least call you by your name and not your title."

He paused, uncertain for a moment. This was untrodden ground. No monarch had ever wanted to know the names or even anything about the leader of their personal guard. The Teacher had told him it somehow made the situation easier for them both.

"Maddau, Your Majesty. My name is Maddau."

Her smile seemed to slip from one tinged with dark humor to one of more serene pleasure. "Maddau," she said, trying out his name as if testing to see how it sounded in her mouth. "I like that name. It's appropriate, you know, for what will be coming for you. And for me." With a moment of speed that he would be hard pressed to imagine possible in this place where time moved so strangely, she grasped his arm and leaned forward to favor him with the briefest of kisses on the side of his mouth. Then she withdrew, and as quickly as it had happened, it was over.

He gaped at her, unable to process what had just occurred.

She laughed a merry trill, a brief bright spark in the gloom at the brink of the end of all things for them. "You look like a fish gasping in the air for water! Very well, Maddau, I am Abertha. Now that we have a proper introduction, we might as well proceed to the last duty ascribed to us. You do know what comes next, yes?"

He nodded, closing his mouth so that he would no longer evoke the image of a fish. He did not want such a base image to be the way she remembered him in his last moments. Swallowing his confusion and shock, he answered, "You will defeat the mechanism put in place to protect the sacred relic. It requires a life's worth of energy to defeat it, and… and that's why I am here. To give my life to preserve yours as you take the relic from the pedestal." She nodded, a solemn and grave countenance chasing away the beautiful spark of joy that had flitted across her face.

"You were trained well in the knowledge of what the ultimate task of your role could be, 'tis true. What you said is mostly correct." She reached forward again, this time as gently as before when she gripped the stunned bird and enfolded his left hand between both of hers.

"Very well then, Maddau. We cannot delay further, and our time is almost up. Your duty in this matter is as clear and simple as mine. Please reach forward and take the relic from its resting place."

He gazed at her, searching her face for something else—anything else—to delay the inevitable that had brought them here to this place and this moment in time, which was not time. An answer as to why she had kissed him, a meaning behind what they were doing here, an excuse to stop this moment from charging forward into something irrevocable and permanent.

A reason to break all rank and propriety, scoop her up and carry her away with him, and free them both of this madness in which fate had bound them. It was never meant to be her. And it had always been him. So many thoughts raged through this mind, but none slowed down enough to be anything or make any sense of the surges of emotion that alternately washed him in an embarrassing need to kiss her again and then flashed into a cold horror of what was mere seconds away from being his fate. In the end, his feelings were too much, too confused, and too fast to say or do anything. In the end, in the last moments of his life, he looked into her eyes so that her chestnut depths would be the last thing he saw. Gazing into her eyes, he grasped the hands that tethered him to what remained of his world and tightened his grip. He inclined his head towards hers, words tumbling out of his heart but not reaching his lips to voice what his thoughts would not have dared or dreamed to support.

He reached out and grasped the relic.

The shock from the defensive ward, a death spell, walloped through him. He felt as though he had been struck by lightning. He must have yelled, or he thought he had. His mouth opened again and again in a soundless scream, and he could feel his vocal cords taxed beyond their capability. Energy jolted down the arm that held the relic, through his body, and to Abertha. He spasmed in a tuneless dance as the trap was unleashed upon him, and she was thrown across the room to the entrance, striking the door that had not been there an eternity of mere seconds ago and landing on the ground with a horrid thump of which his ears were unaware but his heart felt all the same. Her dress flew and fell in folds of gauzy wool around a no longer regal body in a tangle of limbs and cloth. He saw blue arcs in the air that seemed to emanate from the table, and the loudest scream he had ever heard was deafening his ears. The shrill and undulating pitch of the scream roared all around him. The world seemed to open up on all sides, revealing an inky blackness. He could hear a dark and familiar laugh and the screams of a million lost souls all swallowed in the blackest darkness he had ever seen. And then… nothing. It was gone. He stood there, holding the relic in his hand, and he was alive.

Still. Alive.

All body parts remained intact, if not in great pain, and he held the relic. He had survived, but… how? Was it not his lot to die in this exchange? In the trap that had been set to defend the relic from the hands of those who would steal it for their own gain?

The emptiness of his left hand brought back the memory of his Brehines.

"Abertha!" He gasped. His voice was gone, and there was nothing but the dry rasping as air escaped his throat. He found he could move, although each part of his body felt as if it moved on its own accord and was terribly stiff. But he *could* move.

Maddau staggered to where Abertha lay face down on the floor and fell to his knees beside her. He placed the cylinder on the ground and gently rolled her onto her back. What was left of her once polished, deep, red plaits were a smoking ruin that resembled scraggy lines of black-streaked gore. Her skin was a hideous boiled pink, far from her natural paleness. She breathed still but very shallowly, and blood ran from her mouth and nose. Her eyes were open, but horror wrenched him fully from his shock as he saw that her eyes no longer held the depth of chestnuts and the shining intelligence of his Brehines. They were glazed white orbs that showed neither the countenance of intelligence nor humor. There were no pupils where her soul once danced in her gaze. They were the pale white of poached eggs and held a similar-seeming texture. She sensed he was near, and her hand flailed in the air, reaching for something to grasp. He caught her hand with his, and she seized upon him like a drowning animal. He winced; her grip hurt, but he did not pull away.

"Maddau!" she cried, her voice barely there. "Maddau…"

"Please, my lady!" He rasped with what was left of his voice. "I'm so sorry, Abertha. I messed it up. I'm so sorry! Conserve your strength. I will find…" His eyes flitted around the room, searching for help, and suddenly his mind stilled. No. Death was close. He knew that the trap would have taken a life regardless of whose. It was just as his teacher told him during his training. But it was supposed to be him! Not the Brehines. But somehow it had attacked her, and she would die. He understood that there was nothing to be done.

"Maddau…" She struggled in his arms, gasping for air. "It… wrong. Not for you to give… for the trap… but you… must survive. It was always so… always. You must take… to… Temple… Dragon's Teeth. The sages… there… will protect… only safe place. Please… muh… Maddau… hurry. Don't forget… the… charge. My time… my purpose… served. Thank…"

Her voice faded with a crackling and bubbling sound in her throat. Blood leaked from her mouth, and her chest spasmed as she lost the fight for air. She twitched in his arms and seemed to strain against her body from the inside. Once. Twice. Three times. He heard a click in her neck and jaw as her teeth ground against each other. Then he became aware of a weight in his arms where previously there had been none. A silent and unmoving wind blew through the room.

It had become completely quiet.

Abertha, Brehines o Caer y Twr and the last of the Gwaedreiol line, was gone.

The shock of what just transpired tried to wrap around him again, but he shook it off. There would be a time to mourn. Time to grieve, even. But that time was not now, and there was more to do before he would ever be able to think back on these events.

He slid his arm out from underneath and placed her down on the floor. He closed his eyes and imagined her with all the admiration of the beauty and grace he had always seen: her shining brow, deep eyes, the line of her jaw, the plain yet mischievous mouth, which was always quick to a smirk that belied the severity below the surface, her long plaits that glimmered like fire in the sun and muted embers by torchlight, her high cheekbones, the soft curve of her neck, the gentle hills and valleys of her body, obscured by royal robes and mantle of office. Summoning that image in his mind to replace the horror of her last moments, he pressed a kiss to his fingers and lightly trailed them down her cheek, smearing the blood there.

"Goodbye, my lady," he whispered.

Before his emotions could give him cause to tarry longer, he stood, grabbed the relic, and strode out of the room, ignorant that the pressures of the room no longer seemed to affect him. He never even noticed that the door was no longer there or that he passed right through what he would have seen to be a wall without even the slightest resistance. He moved as though in a dream, driven with a purpose that, while urging him onward, he remained unaware of.

As he stepped out through the wall, time fell on him like a heavy mantle. He also strangely felt lighter and freer, as if he could leap a thousand miles or run for days on end with boundless energy. Without pausing, he moved trancelike down the corridor and up the stairs.

Maddau passed through the grand hall and out into the outer passageways where he had met the Brehines earlier that morning, what already seemed a lifetime ago. He traversed down the darkened passages and unknowingly stepped over the body of a small bird that had died some time before and was now nothing but a wizened skeletal husk surrounded by fading grey feathers that had once held a tinge of rouge on the tips. He ignored the sad presence of the once-bird and continued down to step outside the outer door that led to the inner courts. He stopped for nothing and saw no one; the Steward had done his work well. Moving with urgency but no fear, he carried the relic through the inner courts, through the barracks of the castle walls, and out the defensive gates of the Caer. He was heading to the stables, where he knew his horse waited patiently to carry him away from this place.

He reached the stables and saw that only his horse remained, tied to the feed post. The Steward had truly done his work well in removing all living inhabitants from the castle and even the outer levels. The stamping of hooves and a consistent low whinny indicated the animal's displeasure at being restrained as well as a heightened awareness that something was not right here.

He soothed the beast as he checked his equipment and prepared to ride; it would not do to be tossed from his mount when his next moves must be executed with precision. The dark fiends would be coming for him at any moment, he knew, and if he were to make it to the port, he must make no mistakes. He was out of time.

He stood atop the guardswalk, watching the lone survivor of Caer y Twr ride off from the stables and across the hill. The rider took no road and headed northeast as if he were chased by a wildfire. This was the direction of the nearest port. He knew it would be a long journey without any roads to ease the ride, but that was fine. He had plenty of time, and he knew where the rider was going and why. There was no hurry, no need to rush, and no fear. He would arrive to intercept the rider in plenty of time.

It would have been so much easier, he thought, if they had caught them before this one could escape. His men had been hungry, he knew, and he would not have been able to prevent them from destroying the place and all within it if they had not fed first. Then the silly bauble would have been lost to the ages and the location never revealed. These keepers had hidden it well for these long years, and now that it was almost within reach… Better to play it safe and wait.

The maelstrom of darkness was at his back, roiling and clashing through the air. *Has it ever been so that the darkness hungered?* he thought. *Maybe it has. Maybe it has always been this way, with the darkness' desire to feed.*

The air behind him swirled with motes of blackness from the bubbling storm of the dark, and the first in command appeared out of the writhing black, coalescing from the swirling specks of darkness that floated like black ashes in the air. Clad head to toe in the vice armor of the storm's fury, Cynddaredd stepped forward into physical being and dropped to one knee beside his commander.

"Your orders, my lord?" His voice spat across the air like an electric charge. It left a black chattery feeling in one's mind that begat all sorts of enraging thoughts to blind the reason and bend the will to the Dark's purpose. Such was his gift.

The commander of the Cotheda, the Chevaliers of Darkness, turned his head to regard the Vice Knight of his regiment.

"Regroup to the waiting point outside Kastell Paol. We will overtake them there. Take what you wish from the castle and feed with whatever you find."

"Yes, my lord." He could feel the pleasure in the chevalier's voice as the body whispered away into nothingness, returning to the roiling darkness behind him.

The black clouds began to boil and stretch as a horrific howl-like sucking sound could be heard within. It moved with a speed that belied the intelligence within and descended through the walls of the castle.

Not waiting to enjoy any elements for feasting his team would find, the Commander stepped up onto the protective ledge surrounding the guardswalk. The drop to the stone courts below was dizzying and would surely mean the horrific, painful, and messy end of any life that was so unlucky to endure such a fall.

Lucky for him, he had no life to risk. He stepped off the ledge and into the empty air below.

As his trailing foot left the stonework, his body shredded apart into wisps of blackness that swirled briskly through the air, forming a tight spiral, and made for the small town that abutted the port to the northeast.

He had a rider to meet.

Chapter Two

Hedfan y Lleuad: The Flight of the Moon

By not taking any of the roads heading towards the sea, Maddau knew he was condemning himself to a miserable ride and his horse to a difficult exercise. The roads were not the best conditions for riding in general, being no more than pitted trails that emerged into being from wear rather than purposeful creation. Despite this, the roads did allow a smoother transit than riding through the rough countryside. Thus he had committed them to a long slog across hard and rocky terrain peppered with hardy, scrubbish plantlings, shallow ponds and inlets full of silt and reedy waters, and low trees possessing shallow roots. All these minor landscape decorations made for significant tripping dangers for his mount's hooves.

His horse lurched downwards suddenly, sitting back on his rear haunches, and they began to slide rapidly down. Maddau was thrown forward onto his mount's neck and frantically pulled the reins to try and regain control and stop their descent into a low gash in the earth. Too late, he realized it was not a simple decline of the terrain but a steep slope leading to a large watershed. His horse screamed as it slid down on his rear legs, hooves splayed before it, seeking purchase where there was none. A short slide brought them a man's height down into a small ravine that was filled in with mud and dark, flowing waters.

"Easy, Brosegvah. Easy," Maddau soothed. Brosie snorted and shrilled his displeasure further; this was no place to ride a horse, and he knew so. Maddau knew so too. Furthermore, he also knew that his horse would not fare well in these streams. If he insisted on riding, they both risked a nasty fall. Their progress was slowed by the mud and the risky footing. He would need to lead his horse out of this wetted trail if they were to make any good time in a safe manner.

Dismounting splashed him into ankle-deep water, and he groaned with surprise and resignation. The shock took his breath away for a moment: it was cold! Brosie nickered at him as if to say, "See? Not so good a time, hm?"

"Alright, alright, I understand." He smiled and patted Brosie's neck as he took the reins and began to lead them through the water. The ground below the water line was slippery, and clouds of mud blossomed around his feet as they made slow progress down the flowing stream. Fifty paces in this manner brought them to a small bank that led to solid ground again. A way out at last! Maddau carefully stepped onto the prominent rocks and led Brosie up the sand-covered scree and up onto the rocks to more solid ground again. *We are lucky,* he thought, *that wet feet and being cold is all that we must suffer from such an experience.* The relief he felt curdled as Brosie completed his climb out of the ravine and out of the shadows. The light showed what he had been through. Blood covered the back of Brosie's rear legs. It was not gushing—Gods be praised!—but it was flowing with some regularity. Maddau understood that that was why Brosie had screamed. His mount's skin had been erased from his body during the slide into the ravine.

Maddau had no dressings for such wounds or even fresh water to clean them. Their only hope for help would be to make it to the Breakwater, and that was—he looked up, squinting against the reflecting light from the setting sun—at least another hour's ride northeast. He sighed in disgust. If his teacher were to see how he was treating his mount now—the creature who was his inseparable partner in battle and in life. Again, they did not have time, and there was no help for it. "Duty needs what must be done," Maddau told himself as he steadied Brosegvah and pulled himself up into the saddle. Brosie shied a bit under his weight and whinnied as he shifted back and forth, trying to settle without straining his injured legs. Maddau soothed him again, hoping his words would help as there was nothing physical that could be done at the moment.

He took a moment to adjust in the saddle as he looked towards Breakwater; time was not his friend right now, and the fiends of the Dark were on his heels. He chirruped to his horse and flicked the reins, causing Brosie to start forward at a limping trot. They made their way towards the closest building with as much speed as Brosie's injuries allowed.

The painfully slow and halting progress finally reached its conclusion as Brosegvah plodded past the low marsh fences that surrounded the edge of the Breakwater port, a smallish fishing village whose existence necessitated supporting various fishing families that trolled the coast. It had grown up over several generations from shanties along the beach and random small familial boats to a proper dock and a small town with a shop, a blacksmith, and an inn, which also served as a stop for food and drink. Maddau brought his horse to a limping stop at the intersection of the walk along the shore and the road into Breakwater and dismounted. He could tell the smith's shop was nearby from the ringing of the hammer and the smell of the fire. Based on the noise, he figured it was just after the inn on the left side of the shore and a little ways down the muddy pathways. He took hold of Brosie's cheek strap and started gently pulling him forward. Fifty paces past the inn, where he could hear laughter and some muted singing whose words were indiscernible to him, Maddau found the blacksmith working his craft. The midday sun hid behind sheets of clouds, showing its pale countenance as a white ghost of the day. It was casting little in the way of shadows and giving no discernible feeling of warmth, making the heat from the forge a very welcome feeling to the wet and stiff representatives from Caer y Twr. The smithy was a small affair, with a low overhang for a small fire and tables for a workshop. The shadowy back of the shop looked like animals had been stored there once; maybe this was where the smith worked on the village mules and managed basic medicine.

Hearing them draw near, the smith glanced up and appraised Brosegvah first and then Maddau. He grunted, "What brings y'here?"

"My horse," Maddau responded. "He needs tending. He's been through a bad landing."

The smith glanced at Brosie's blood-stained haunches and looked further at his damaged hooves. A grimace of disgust twisted across his face.

"Poor man's been through t' mill. Should be ashamed to have so treated 'im." The smith glared at Maddau. "Deserves better, 'im."

Feeling his jaw tighten at the rebuke and the open disdain communicated in the man's face, Maddau straightened his back and returned the man's gaze without flinching.

"Yes, he does. He and I both know it, and he shall have it, if I have any say. But we are moved by haste, or we'd not be at all. Duty was to be done without complaint, and he served without fail. If nothing else, he is the best soldier in my regiment, as he always executes without complaint."

The smith's frown lightened a bit. He seemed satisfied, if not accepting, of the answer. "Suppose yer part of them soldiers posted here then, being yer arm'r look more 'n same as thems at the inn. Imagine the *fancyman* will be paying for yer 'orse's work, being he pays for all other things for thems."

Maddau managed a wan smile at this derision; there was only one man in his regiment that could be described as a fancy, and furthermore, he was the only one who was authorized to pay for things for Koteli Knights.

"Yes. He will be paying for that. It's good to know he's following orders." He brought Brosie under the overhang of the smithy and to a low trough in the back. His first thoughts had been found to be true; it looked as if animals had frequented this area in days past. The trough had a small amount of straw at the bottom. Brosie needed no encouragement and began nosing in the trough, looking for a meal.

At his words, the smith looked up and seemed to take him in fully. "Y'd be th' Captain, then."

Maddau felt exhaustion wash over him. He was more tired than he'd ever been in his life; it was as if all the energy and vitality had just flooded out of him upon hearing his title again. Had it only been hours before when it had fallen so lightly from another's lips? He blinked, and in the second of darkness behind his eyes, he saw Abertha's dark eyes gazing into his and heard her voice murmur, "I cannot call you Captain *all* the time. So what is your name, soldier?" He scrunched his eyes up to hold back the water that threatened to rise up and spill out an emotion unbefitting of his duty. He wiped his hand across his eyes, more to ensure nothing showed of his feelings than to rub his face, and took his pack from the side of Brosie's saddle. After ensuring the presence of the precious cargo that had already cost them all so dearly, he turned and started his walk towards the inn. He knew his regiment was there; it was a reasonable enough assumption that the inn was filled with soldiers and sailors due to the raucous laughter and the tunes of some seafaring songs he'd heard when he had passed by earlier. As he left, the smith called out, "Wat's yer 'orse's name?"

"Brosegvah," he answered without turning his head. "He answers to Brosegvah."

Maddau pushed through the door to the inn and surveyed the room. It spanned the length of the building, showing raw beams and a dirt floor, with a set of stairs in the corner. The owner, Maddau guessed, was perched up against what served as a stove and kitchen area, where barrels and pitchers were also visible.

"Must be where the drinks flow," he mused.

Several large windows at the rear of the building provided most of the light, and lanterns burned in various corners to combat the shadows. There were several benched tables at which perched various residents of the town, sailors from the docked vessels, and a group of men wearing similar livery and various elements of armor who sat furthest from the door. *It is not hard to identify the Koteli Knights,* Maddau thought with a wry smile as he stepped across the threshold. His presence was immediately noticed by all in the room. Even when dirty and exhausted, he had a striking, if not commanding, air, but more specifically by the five men whose allegiance he would now be testing in ways for which they had never been trained. He strode across the room, ignoring the startled looks from the locals and the open stares from the sailors still sober enough to be aware of anything other than themselves. As he approached his group, the air around them seemed a little sharper, a little brighter. It was always so, he knew, due to their charges; each had accepted these gifts when they said their vows after being chosen for the duty they would now fulfill, and the change had been evident from that day forth. The only thing that was not as expected, he understood, was that he had come alone. He could see the question and confusion in their faces as he looked from one set of eyes to the next. Five faces responded with the mute inquiry: Alone?

Finally, the silence was broken by Olwygg.

"Captain, we have been waiting for you this past fortnite ev'r since the dogs of darkness have nipped at the heels of our land! What news is there? What're our orders? Go we to engage those blas'd hounds of the south'n lands?"

"Yes, Captain," replied the youngest in the group, old enough to vow over his life yet still barely more than a lad. "Are we to teach these southern dogs new tricks?" This brash boast with its unknowing innocence gave their captain pause for more than a moment, considering the burden he brought. As several more voices piped up, he raised his hand to quell their queries. They became silent, knowing well from their training what that signal demanded of them. He lowered his hand and spoke:

"I know you have waited long for this time, and it is almost here. You have been patient in your wait for the arrival... of others..."—he faltered a bit, banishing the memory of those dark eyes from his mind—"who will not be coming," he finished. He could see the color drain from their faces as they took in the meaning of his words. He took a deep breath and spoke the fated words.

"I am the rider for whom you have waited long. I and I alone."

"But, Captain!"

"No-no! It cannot be..."

"Where?"

He raised his hand again amidst the clamoring and questioning. He waited them out for many long moments, but they eventually quieted down.

"I know this was not what was foretold for us to expect." He met their eyes, one by one. "Not for *any* of us. But this is what has occurred and, as I understand, what was ultimately expected. I will explain, shortly, all that occurred. But first we must be on our way." He looked around the table, as if recognizing for the first time that he was missing one of his men. "Where is Twyll?"

The others looked around as if recognizing that Twyll was no longer among them. Burdeb spoke up. "I think he—"

"He was securing our passage on the fine vessel, Hedfan y Lleuad (*The Flight of the Moon*), and she will take us wherever we want to go," a darkly smiling voice rejoined. As if summoned by the mere mention of his name, Twyll passed through the inn's door and strode up behind Maddau to set down his bag and sword at the end of the table.

"T'was a very dear cost for them to wait for us and take us at our pleasure to wherever our winds would blow, but they did see the color of reason. It's a pretty silvery color, but they did come to understand it." Seeing that his captain had finally arrived, he strode up and clapped his hand on Maddau's shoulder.

"By the Gods, it's good to see you, Maddau!" A tired, yet cheerful smile lit his face, and his deep-set green eyes searched Maddau's pale grey ones.

"But come, man, do not delay! Where is she? You dare not make her wait. We should board the ship and be off. Come! Where are we to go? Let us be away, and for sure, with haste."

Maddau's eyes told Twyll everything before he spoke a word, and the man's smile slipped away.

"Maddau… the Brehines…?" Twyll licked his lips, trying to get his question past a mouth that felt full of unbelieving cotton.

Shaking his head slowly, yet holding Twyll's eyes with his own, he answered with the ancient phrase that commanded their duty and told them their fate. The words that had been given to each of them as part of the charge they had taken so long ago and that would tell them the time had come. Words that he had never expected to hear, let alone say.

"I am the rider for whom you all have waited long, Twyll. I and I alone."

Twyll's hand dropped from his captain's shoulder. His knees unlocked, and he sat down hard on the bench beside Burdeb. His gaze fixed on a point far away, and his lips twitched as he muttered to himself—maybe words of comfort, maybe a prayer. The words of the charge fell heavily on them. Now they understood—not everything, but there would be time for that later, if at all. They understood enough to answer their charge and take the actions necessary for them to complete the mission at hand. It was hard knowledge, but it was enough. Now it was Maddau who placed his hand on Twyll's shoulder. He addressed them all, even though his words were directed towards his First Knight.

"You say we have a ship at the ready and waiting for us to go where the wind sends us. Then let us be off."

Twyll continued to stare off into the distance, showing no sign of hearing Maddau's words. "Where?" asked one of the other knights, his voice hoarse.

Maddau squeezed Twyll's shoulder hard. The painful grip was enough to bring him around and back from whatever haunted depths had enfolded him. Twyll winced, and his lips continued to move on their own accord, but his eyes shifted up to focus on Maddau's face.

"We sail for Kastell Paol."

"When?" one of the men uttered, still shocked from the revelation.

"Tonight."

The vessel rocked hard back and forth. Hours had passed since they had set sail in the early evening, and the seas remained rough and choppy. The wind had slowed down just after they had cleared the coast. Once the sun had set, it had died completely, and with the onset of true dark; a mist had sprung up across the sea, obscuring the retreating rocky shores and enclosing them in a wet, woolish cloud. The Koteli were huddled together below decks. Despite being in the thick of summer, it had been a wet and cold season on land, and out on the open sea, it was bitterly cold once the sun set. Coupled with a fog that could wet a man through his armor, past his clothes, and straight to the skin, Maddau was not surprised that none of his regiment wished to stay above decks, even with the temptation of fresher air.

He mulled over the members of his regiment. He was no longer the Captain of the Brehines' Guard, as they no longer had a brehines. No, now they would be known by the charge they had undertaken when they were sworn into this regiment. They had each been personally chosen by the one they had all referred to as The Teacher. Even the members of the Gwaedreiol line deferred to the old man and revered him as The Teacher, but Maddau had always suspected the old man was something else. A sage, maybe. Maybe one of the Alder folk. Whatever he had been, he was long gone. He had disappeared shortly after the regiment had been sworn in and had completed their training. The last day Maddau had seen him, The Teacher had taken him aside and counseled him about the true nature of his obligations to the house of Gwaedreiol as the captain of this regiment. It was a heavy burden to know that he would one day have to give his life so the Brehines could fulfill her destiny, but he had borne it with the understanding that this was all preordained. For the Dark would ever seek to destroy the Light, and he and his regiment must stand by those of the house of Gwaedreiol and do what must be done so that the tools of the Light should never fall into the hands of the fiends of the Dark.

He remembered the day he received his charge. Five members of the regiment had already been chosen from various villages across the land. Two had been pulled from far away: a small town called Trawsfynedd and the fishing village of Pwlhelli. These two young men had been brought to the castle by The Teacher one day with funny accents and a country manner. Life in the Caer had taken them by surprise, but they had adapted well enough. The other three had come from small villages native to their island. One boy he had known when he was a young lad from a neighboring village. He himself had been taken into the castle guards as a prentice in his tender boyhood so that he could learn the trade of a soldier. His father had bound him for a better life than a farmer, and although he had hated his father then for separating him from all he knew and isolating him with men who cared nothing for boys or cared too much, he was thankful now. He never would have survived a life as a farmer. He was not built for it in the head. And in the castle guard, he had met another boy who had also been taken in as a prentice. Twyll's father had died in a mill fire, and being the youngest of six children was just one burden too much on his mother, who was barely out of her girlhood. When a soldier had been stationed in the village of Glanyr, Twyll's mother had seen an opportunity and seized it. He had been sent with the soldier to have a life of training and routine and to be out of her hair and off her hands. The only two young boys in a barracks full of soldiers, they had become fast friends who watched each other's backs with fierce loyalty. One morning, in his twentieth year, he had been praying to their patron in the alcove that served as the sacred space for the barracks. He had been wrestling with troublesome feelings that bit into his spirit, and he was working to release them. After he had finished his prayers, he had turned to leave and had seen The Teacher in the doorway. Maddau had not heard him approach, but that was the way with The Teacher. He moved without sound, as though he were made of air under his robes. Maddau remembered looking up and being entranced by the old man's eyes. They were the palest blue he had ever seen—almost as if the color was blue on the very outside and fading to a silvery white near the pupils. They had unsettled him. They looked like no eyes Maddau had ever seen before or since. But for all their strangeness, they were not unkind eyes.

The Teacher had stood before him, and as Maddau had moved to step past so he could give The Teacher privacy in the only sanctuary in the barrack, he had reached one arm out with a hand stretched before him in a signal to stay.

"Maddau, is it?" he had inquired, though he knew well enough. His voice always sounded like the ruffling of papers to Maddau. They had had several interactions across the years, always initiated by The Teacher. He was a man very much apart from the world Maddau knew, but he liked The Teacher all the more for it.

"It is, Teacher." Maddau had smiled and inclined his head in respect to the old man. "I am sorry to interrupt your time with our Patron. I should be on watch this morning and should get to my post. Can I be of assistance to you before I go?"

The old man had smiled, and Maddau had felt a bit of vertigo for a second. It was as though the world around him swayed, just a bit and just for a second. Then it was gone as if nothing had ever happened, and The Teacher had been beckoning him forward with the hand that had previously been telling him to stay. "Go? No, you shall be staying here today, young Maddau. You have a new duty that has been assigned to you."

Perplexed, Maddau had looked past The Teacher to see if the captain of the castle guard was waiting to tell him about his new duties. "I've not been told of it. Am I late to my new post? Did I miss something at the morning meal? Some orders that I did not hear?"

"No, no." The Teacher had chuckled. "You are receiving these orders from me, boy." Seeing Maddau's eyes first widen, then squint in suspicion, The Teacher had smiled. "You have been chosen, Maddau, for a special duty. You and your friend, both. He waits already, along with others who were chosen to form a special regiment. I come to bring you to the others, so we can begin." Something in his voice had soothed Maddau and made what he was saying, strange as it was, seem normal. Expected, even. As if he had been waiting all the time he had been training to be a soldier, just for The Teacher to show up and hand him this invitation to this new role. As if he had just been marking time since he came to the Caer, waiting for his true life to begin. Without even realizing that they were moving, Maddau had noticed that he had started forward and had begun walking beside The Teacher.

"Not marking time," The Teacher had murmured as they had moved down the hall from the sanctum alcove in the barrack to the doorway that led to the front courtyard. The door had swung open under The Teacher's hand, and they had stepped into the mid-morning sunlight that peeped through the clouds and speckled the courtyard in tiny pools of light. "Your time with the soldiers was necessary to give you the skills you will need in the future. You needed the training as a soldier so you would know how to defend and attack as necessary. It has all been leading to this, yes, but it was all necessary to prepare you for what is to come."

The fact that The Teacher had read his mind and just answered his thoughts no longer seemed surprising to Maddau. He just nodded and followed where The Teacher led. They had crossed the front courtyard and headed to the western wall. At the northernmost point of the wall, Maddau knew, was a small door that led to the forests that bordered the Caer on the west. It was used exclusively for deliveries of lumber, game, and herbs from the forest and, as such, was kept locked most of the time except for that day, which Maddau had seen, as The Teacher had merely pushed the door open and indicated for Maddau to step through. He had then followed, and the door had swung shut behind them with a solid metallic thud as the metal brace supports of the wood had hit the stone doorway.

The forest had grown thick on the other side of the Caer's wall, and even the intermittent pools of light that had dotted the courtyard had not made it through the interlocking branches of the canopy. A slight trail led away from the door in the wall and into the forest. Maddau's eyes had had a difficult time adjusting to the decreased light as he followed The Teacher down the path, keeping at the same speed. The way forward had been overgrown with whip-like branches and twisting roots that made keeping his footing difficult and being able to see more than five feet ahead impossible as the branches slapped back onto him from The Teacher's movement ahead. He had been reduced to lowering his eyes to avoid impacts of repeated slaps in the face with thorny branches and keeping one eye on the hem of The Teacher's robes and another on the path directly in front of his feet. Ordinarily, he would have complained about the experience as he didn't much like being kept in such a vulnerable state of not being able to see and anticipate what came ahead while constantly being kept off balance as he moved, but for some reason he had found he was at peace with the experience. He had known somehow that he was safe with The Teacher and that no harm would come to him here. For all the dangers the forest possessed, none of them could hurt The Teacher. On some level, he had known this.

The walk through the forest had been long. Maddau had followed The Teacher down winding paths that turned one way and then switched back upon themselves. The roots had caused him to trip almost every five to ten steps, and each time he had raised his head to try and see where they were headed, he endured blow after blow from the branches as if to rebuke him for not trusting where The Teacher led. Finally, the hem of The Teacher's robe had stopped moving out of his vision. Maddau had drawn up short to avoid treading on the other man's heels and looked up, expecting the path's end and some sort of conclusion to the journey, but there had been nothing. The path still stretched ahead before them into the darkness of the forest, and he could see their trail behind them, drawing back into the distance. They were so far into the forest that the vestiges of light that had played at the edge of the trees could not even be seen anymore. The Teacher had stopped on the path and peered into the woods. As Maddau stepped up beside him, he saw what had caught the old man's attention. Betwixt the tangled branches and riotous growth, the slimmest line of path appeared, seeming to dart in and out.

"Ah…" The Teacher beamed. "This is the way. Come, young man. We are expected."

The Teacher had stepped forward, and the path seemed to solidify and expand beneath his feet. Maddau could feel his eyes widening and his jaw hanging open, gawping as a rube, just like he had when he was five at a wonder-faire where a two-headed snake held court and all the little kids danced around, cried, and pulled faces at the creature so foreign to them before their tired parents pulled them away to the real business of going to market.

The Teacher had taken several steps down this new path before recognizing that he moved alone. He had glanced over his shoulder to see Maddau standing still and staring at him. Merriment danced in his strange eyes as he inquired, "Coming, boy?"

The new path was much easier to traverse than the previous one. Maddau had kept a wary eye out for roots and branches, but none had attacked him as before. This path seemed to widen to account for his armor and had given him plenty of room to move through. It was the work of another fifteen minutes of walking, and the path had opened up into a bit of a clearing. At the end of the path, the entrance to a deep gash in the earth started with a slow descent below the ground. The Teacher had not paused and kept walking forward and down. Maddau, not giving himself time to be afraid, had followed.

Despite the fact that no one knew his location, he was following a man whom he barely knew, and he had been descending below and out of the light; into the depths of the earth where deepest darkness held reign, he had felt a strange and still calm. He had known he was safe with The Teacher, even here amongst the rocks and the dark. The way down into the earth had stopped abruptly at the back of a cave. While it was deep in the earth, it was not a very long cave, and the back wall was fully rock except for a door inset. The door was a deep black, with a pebbled texture, that helped it to blend with the surrounding rocks. It had no visible handle, lever, or mechanism to open it that Maddau could see, and he had doubted that it could just be pushed open like magic. It had to be locked. *Of course, it was locked!* he thought, in derision, of his previous musing. *Doors like this, set into rock walls in a deep-earth cave, don't just swing open at the push of your hand!*

The Teacher had stepped up to the door and placed his palm on its face. Something had happened then. Time had... shivered. Maddau had thought vaguely that he had heard music. Like the soft, silvery singing of some far-off chimes. And then the door had given way under The Teacher's hand and swung inward. The faintest glow of firelight had spilled into the cave from the space beyond the door, and Maddau had heard the quiet murmur of voices that hushed at their arrival. The Teacher had ushered him forward and into the room, smiling an ever-so-strange smile. Maddau could have sworn he had heard the old man's thoughts as he passed in front of him. *"See? It did open. Just like magic..."*

The room behind the door had been dark save for the light of seven tall iron posts that had been mounted onto the floor. Each post held four huge torches that burned without making a sound. The silent torches, blazing tall in the darkened room, had struck Maddau for reasons he couldn't explain. *The fire has to be magic... torches don't just burn without making some noise! Fire makes noise, crackling, popping, and sending sparks around the ignition areas.* He had felt The Teacher pushing him forward into the room, but Maddau could not take his eyes off the torches. Their existence made no sense and offended him a little. *Fire is supposed to be noisy!* his mind had insisted, tugging and fretting at the idea like a dog worrying at a bone. His feet had been pushing back against the floor as he craned his neck around to continue to stare at the torches, yet he had still moved forward, somehow propelled by The Teacher behind him, who had been pushing him forward. They had passed through the ring of iron torch bearers, and Maddau had become aware that there were six other men in the room besides himself and The Teacher. They had formed an uneasy circle in the center of the room, and around them had ringed the iron torchbearers, encircling them in a ring of light made by the silent fires.

Maddau had looked at each of these men. He knew them all. Three had come from villages around the Caer; two were from the coastal areas;

and the last was his childhood friend, Twyll, who had given him an almost imperceptible nod of recognition. Maddau had stepped into a vacant area between Twyll and another man as The Teacher moved into the center of the ring of men. The Teacher had slowly looked at each man in the circle in turn, ending with Maddau.

"You are all here," he said, "because each of you has been blessed as the embodiment of one of the traits of the Light. I have watched you and seen the traits you exemplify, and thus these will be the powers with which you are imbued. You will each take an oath for the gifts to be granted unto you, and then you will be given a Charge that will affect the course of the rest of your lives. Life as you know it has changed since the moment you stepped into this place, and it will never be the same. There is a great enemy that stalks us at every turn: men and women who have given themselves over to the evil forces in the world and who seek to subvert the forces of the good in the world so that they can turn it for their own wicked ends: the agents of the Dark. You seven are to be the paragons of virtue in this world, upholding the virtue embodied within yourself and protecting the family of the Gwaedreiol— those who have been tasked as agents of the Light. Say you now, each as his own man. Do you understand?" The Teacher had looked upon the young men again, each in turn, ending with Maddau. Meeting those strange eyes, each man had uttered a quiet and firm "Aye."

"Do any of you choose, as your own man, to deny the gifts offered to you in exchange for the duty you will not accept and leave this place to be forever cast away from this circle?" Each man, on his own, had shaken his head or murmured, "Nay."

"Very well then," The Teacher had said, nodding to himself. "Let us begin. Kneel, all of you."

Each man had dropped to his knees and bowed his head. The Teacher had turned to the man on Maddau's right, placed his hand on the top of his head, and begun to chant quietly. The words were in no language that Maddau had ever heard before, and he could see a light, different from the firelight, that seemed to have enveloped the man beside him. At the end of the chant, the Teacher had withdrawn his hand and spoken in a voice no louder than what he had used before, yet it had boomed throughout the room, echoing off the walls and causing the silent torches to blaze brighter and higher than ever before. "Thus you are brought from the world of men into the world of the Light. You left here on the floor at your feet all your previous life. Before you now is all of eternity. You may not interfere with what man has wrought, but you must do your part to protect those who act as the agents of Light. Rise up now, Lymder, Child of the Light. One with whom discipline is strong and who can control himself."

Thus, it had been repeated around the circle, one after another:

"Rise up now, Burdeb, Child of the Light. One with whom purity is the source of his power."

"Rise up now, Haelder, Child of the Light. One whose power gives ability beyond all measure."

"Rise up now, Olwygg, Child of the Light. One whose ability respects no equal power."

"Rise up now, Gwyleidd-Dra, Child of the Light. One with whose power is given from the worthiness of his lesser regard."

The Teacher had then turned to Twyll, Maddau noticed. He placed his hand on Twyll's head and began the chant. It seemed to have gone on longer than the others, and it had taken longer for the glow to begin, or so it had seemed to Maddau. Finally, the Teacher spoke.

"Your path has many twists and turns, young man. I am not sure why you have chosen this path, but it is now upon you to follow your decisions all the way to your path's ordained conclusion. Therefore, I cannot name you as you are." He had paused and regarded Twyll, who stared up at him, his eyes wet with emotion.

"Therefore… therefore… rise up, Gonestrwydd, one whose power flows when his words ring true."

The Teacher had hesitated as if he were about to say more and then turned to Maddau. He had placed his hand on Maddau's head, and the world had gone white. A soft tinkling tune, sounding like hundreds of tiny bells playing a beautiful melody in different intonations with choruses of twinkling tones, like what he thought he had heard when the door had opened. A warmth had suffused his body, starting in his chest and spreading down his arms and legs and back to his face. He had felt a sudden power but with a quiet assumption of ability. Nothing overwhelming. No great overflow or estimation of his capability. Just a quiet assuredness that he was able to do more now than ever before. He had heard the Teacher's voice as if from far away:

"Rise up, Maddau, Child of the Light. One whose power comes from his faith and his ability to love above any wrongdoing."

Maddau had stood and looked around himself in wonder. Each of the other men in the circle had had an aura about him that had not been there before, and one by one, being in their presence, Maddau had felt the power with which each had been imbued. Absolute discipline, Purity beyond reproach, Generosity without measure, Admiration without motive, Humility in total regard, and Honesty without reservation. Maddau had found this last in his oldest friend, Twyll, who had been watching him closely. The Teacher's voice had rung out again.

"You are now the chosen ones of the Light. Knights you are all, and so you shall be charged as the Knights of the virtue of Light. Your charge is thus: In the time of great peril, when Darkness wrought o'er the land, you must protect the tools of Light from those whose lives are damned. When the stars of Light have fallen into the dragon's teeth, descend into the truth below and enter the temple beneath."

The words had fallen upon them like a mantle of light rain. Images had filled their minds: a foreign land, an overgrown rocky path, viciously high mountains, a vast expanse of ocean, a field of wildflowers encircled by mountainous spires, a desperate path clinging to the side of a sheer drop, a group of hooded and robed people in front of a cliff and facing the sea, and finally, a glowing light emanating from a seaside cave that illuminated the land surrounding it, giving way to the image of a grinning, rocky dragon and a silvery voice calling from far away. Whispered words had intoned, "I am who you have waited for…. I and I alone."

For Maddau, the images had continued. The light had given way to a darkened room, the whisper of voices and a woman's laughter. The image of the full moon sailing across the sky. He had both seen and felt himself reaching out towards a beacon of light, with a joy that elevated his soul and also brought forth the deepest terror he had ever known before. There had been an eclipsing flash of blue, and the world around him had torn itself apart in screams and shreds of black ash. He had seen flames surrounding all parts of his vision and horrible voices speaking words he had not understood, but that had caused his blood to boil in disgust. He had felt every part of himself, separately, wrenched apart and torn back together as if he had been spinning inside blades of destruction that found each of the most vulnerable and delicate parts and attacked specifically where he was most weak. He had heard someone moaning in the dark, and Maddau wished with all his heart that the person would stop. *Please… just stop.* The moaning voice had been broken and filled with pain and terror so palpable that just the sound of the moans had brought the imagery back in full force to the front of his mind. And the darkness… it was all around him. All encompassing. All enticing… wrapping itself around him in an embrace that was too familiar and more than a little exciting. The moaning he had heard had broken off into sobs of distress and he had felt the Darkness reaching for him, reaching into him… filling him from within and reaching for…

A hand, gentle and warm, lifted his chin.

"Maddau, open your eyes, child of Light." The Teacher's voice had cut through the darkness encircling him like a shining blade of reason and had brought him back to himself in the now.

He had opened his eyes, and the golden warmth of the light had come rushing back as he remembered where he was. He realized that he still knelt on the floor while all the others had been standing and were huddled around the Teacher and himself, as they were both on the ground. The Teacher's hand had lifted his chin, and then he had realized that he had been the one moaning. He had been moaning for what he had seen in the visions the Charge of Light had brought.

The Teacher had peered at him with his strange eyes. "Why did you cry out, child? What did you see that caused you such distress?" Looking into those eyes, despite their oddness, so full of compassion and a gentle kindness, it had all come flooding out in a kind of babble: the landscape images, the darkness, the room, and the fury.

He had stopped himself from saying how attractive the darkness had become in the end. Seductive, almost. He had been ashamed of how it had appealed to him as it encircled him in the visions. And it had seemed so familiar... He had been ashamed of that too, but he was not sure why.

The Teacher had peered at him a moment longer and then stood up, helping Maddau up as he did so.

"You have been gifted with the sight of what is yet to come in your Charge. This signifies that you are to be the leader of this regiment, Maddau. You alone are now aware of what will happen when the Darkness comes for the Light. Over time, we will have much to speak of to ensure that you are ready for the trial that lies ahead of you."

The Teacher had seemed a bit off balance while he spoke, as if he were uncomfortable with the subject. He had pulled from his robe a short sword whose hilt and grip were inlaid with shimmering amber stones. The moment he had seen it, Maddau could not take his eyes from the blade. It had glowed in the firelight as though it held the light of the sun itself, and he could see something etched into the blade: runes maybe or some sort of alder language that he could not read.

The Teacher had turned to face Maddau again as the other men crowded closer. He had raised the blade and lightly buffed Maddau on the shoulders.

"I commend thee to the Light, Maddau, as Captain of the Knights of the Light's Virtue. May you never falter in your duty." He had then handed the sword to him.

Somehow, a strange knowing had filled his mind, and Maddau had understood that he was to do this for all the others as they took their places in the ranks of the Knights of the Light's Virtue. He had turned to Lymder and repeated the words the Teacher had said to him, buffing the blade lightly on each of the man's shoulders. Then Burdeb, Haelder, Olwygg, Gwyleidd-Dra, and finally to Gonestrwydd, whom he would always know as Twyll. Following the knowledge that had burst into his mind fully in bloom, he had raised the sword in the air above him and chanted loudly: "Knights of the Light, we guard the line Gwaedreiol against all Darkness!"

The newly minted Koteli knights around him had begun to chant with him in unison. United in their words, they had become united in their cause and under their charge. He had felt the Teacher's eyes upon him, and he could almost hear the man's thoughts again, just for a moment.

Well done, boy. A good start is the largest part of the journey, but still, there is much to learn and more to do.

Well done, Maddau...

Well done...

Chapter Three

Treacherous Waters

"**M**addau!" There was a soft whisper in his ear, followed by a light hand on his shoulder.

He blinked, trying to shield himself against the dim light that stabbed at his eyes. His body, a mass of aches and pains, was locked into a crouching position where he had been sitting between Twyll and Burdeb. It came back to him in a flash: they were in the hold of the Hedfan y Lleuad and were sailing towards Kastell Paol in Brittany. The Dark Ones had assailed the Caer. Abertha was dead, and in his pack was… the relic.

He looked around and saw Twyll close beside him, a look of concern shadowing his face.

"How long have I been asleep?" Maddau smiled at his friend as he straightened up. His muscles complained for having remained in the same position for too long, and he winced.

"An hour on, now. You've…you've been…crying." Twyll's eyes were soothing, almost gentle, and yet there was something a bit dangerous in those green depths. "I convinced the others to let you be, as you were exhausted. But then you started to cry out. I could bear it no longer and had to wake you." He dropped his voice to just below a whisper, almost speaking without sound. "You sounded in so much pain. What made you cry out so?"

The closeness of Twyll's green eyes, the warmth of his breath on his face, and his whispering in such a way took Maddau back to the days of his boyhood. Their boyhood. When they had lain on the same rough straw pallet during the nights—it was all that was allotted to them as prentices since only soldiers were worthy of the single-framed beds—and whispered about the day's events, those things that had captured their attention as young lads: what had transpired over dinner, which lord was visiting with his ungainly daughter to try and find a match for her, and whether they'd find that lord in his own bed or in the chambermaid's bed in the morning. Muffled giggles and snorts from the musings that transpired… whether they'd have barley porridge for dinner again or if Cook would find a mouse in his trousers in the morning. Only stopping their whispered conversations when one of the soldiers woke and threw a boot or candle base in their direction and yelled at them to shut it, else they'd be whipped in the morning. The warmth, safety, and comfort of those bygone times brought fresh tears to Maddau's eyes, and he scrubbed them away with his sleeve. If he could tell anyone what had happened, it was Twyll.

"Do you remember when we were given the charge, Twyll? Do you remember what happened? Did you see anything?" Maddau dropped his eyes and studied the dirt under his fingernails. Sensing a break in the mood, Twyll sat back a little and regarded his friend.

"Yes, I remember. I saw a jumbled vision of different places and flashes of light. You, though . . . you saw something else." Twyll looked away for a second and then returned to probing Maddau.

"You saw something directly about you, and that's why the Teacher chose you as our captain. Because you have a foresight we do not."

Maddau looked up. "Something like that. You are right: I saw something beyond what you all did. I saw my death. That's all that made me your leader—the fact that I was supposed to die on the day the Dark came for us."

His words hung in the air like the clanging of a dull bell. Twyll sucked in his breath, the color draining from his face.

"Your... death? But Maddau, you are...I mean...you *are* still alive. I mean, *of course* you are. Aren't you?"

He smiled at his friend and patted his hand gently. "I'm still here, old friend. I didn't die, although I thought I was supposed to. At least that is what the vision told me."

Twyll squinted at him in confusion, and Maddau could see that this was not helping the situation at all.

"What I saw that day was my death. The images showed me that I was supposed to die so that the Gwaedreiol scion could retrieve one of the tools of the Light. My life was supposed to be given so that she could bypass the Ward that protected the relic. That is what I saw after all the places and the words." He paused, searching Twyll's face to see if his friend was understanding his words.

"I see," said Twyll, breathing out. "But Maddau, how, then, are you still here?"

"The Brehines told me that it was wrong. She said it was never meant to be my death, but hers. That it was my duty to bring the relic to those places we saw. And I was given where to go. The trap moved through me and took her instead."

Twyll looked at him for a long moment. Long enough that Maddau began to shift uncomfortably beneath his friend's gaze.

"Are you certain it was meant for her to die?"

"Why would you say that? Do you think I killed our Brehines?" Maddau was horrified at the implication. The dimness of the room felt like it was pressing in around him.

"No, not that. Not really," Twyll responded, his voice ponderous. "But perhaps she did not survive the trap because she was never meant to be

Brehines. Perhaps because it was meant to be Anwadaledd, she would have survived, and you would have met... the uh... the fate you saw."

"So you do think I killed her."

"I think you performed the task as well as you were able," Twyll said firmly. "You didn't think about Anwadaledd. Why would you? She's been gone for more than fifteen years past. She left when we were still boys, and most of the residents of the Caer don't even remember her or even know she was there."

"But the Brehines—" Maddau could barely see more than the outline of Twyll's face and his green eyes in the dimness of the room.

"What the Brehines knew or didn't know, she kept well to herself," said Twyll, overriding him. "Whether she knew what would happen or not, she did not share it beforehand, did she?" Maddau shook his head in response to this interrogation. "Then she took it upon herself, and that led to what it did. You cannot be blamed for that."

Maddau could feel Twyll's ability working on him and could suddenly see a faint glow permeating the air from the truth in his words. Maddau grimaced as he stood up, abruptly shaking Twyll's hand from his shoulder.

"Thank you for your kind words, Twyll. Forgive me, but I need some air."

Still, regardless of Twyll's soothing, it did not feel like he was blameless in the situation.

The ship rocked with the swells. The ocean was uneasy, and his feelings were mirrored in the shifting of the ship. *I should not have been so short with Twyll*, he thought. He knew the words Twyll spoke were true; the aura that surrounded them had been evidence of that. If Twyll had not been speaking the truth, the words would not have created the aura of light in the air as they had. Maddau knew this, and the logic followed. But that did not erase the doubt that crept into his heart at the questions he had been asked. Was the reason Abertha had died because it was supposed to have been Anwadaledd? Had it been Anwadaledd, would he have died in her stead? Was the true reason he was alive all down to a flip of fickle fate and a loss in the chain of succession? It had to be more than that, and Abertha had said he was meant to survive. But what if what Twyll said was true? It *had* to be true, since his gift was honesty-based. Maddau felt sick with the twisted fear that he was the cause of Abertha's death.

He should not have rushed away, and he could not pretend he had not seen the hurt in his friends' eyes as he made for the top deck. Twyll had been trying to help him, trying to ease him out of what had happened and soothe the pain that burned within him. He should apologize, he knew, but for right now, he needed air and to clear his head. A white light filtered across the deck in washes, shifting in the shadows as the ship rocked back and forth. Maddau, barely managing his legs for the sea, made his way to the fore of the ship, where he saw one member of his regiment standing.

Lymder turned at the sound of footsteps and saw Maddau approaching.

"Well met, Captain," he said cheerfully. "There's nothing like a night's watch, hm?"

Maddau grimaced. "The sea gives you no trouble, I see. How is it you have no issue regardless of the situation, Lym?"

"Self-control is my strength! And I use it well, to whatever advantage I need." Lymder laughed.

Maddau had failed to notice the silvery aura around the younger man's body, awash in the moon's light. But now that Lymder had mentioned it, it was impossible to miss.

"More truth to that. How long have you been awatch?"

"Been on two hours now. I should have relief soon, I think. I don't fret it, though. This night is fine for the time spent and not a thing to see! My, but isn't the moon a sight! It fits our trip well, don't you think?"

"How do you mean?"

Lymder smiled dreamily. "The Flight of the Moon. It's the name of our ship. And like her, we pass swiftly o'er the ocean. We fly like the moon."

Maddau gave Lymder a sidelong assessing glance but chose not to respond to this comment. Instead, he clapped his arm around Lym's shoulders and turned him in the direction of the hold. "Sounds like you've been listening to those fae-born stories with all the rhymes again and staring at the sea too long. It must have tired out your brain, I think. Your relief is here, poet! Get you back down and have some sleep before the moon finishes her flight tonight."

Laughing more, Lymder began ambling, sure-footed, back towards where Maddau had come from, with no further prodding needed. "Aye, Captain! As you say!"

Maddau turned his eyes to the ocean and began his watch. He knew that keeping watch was the best thing for clearing his head, and night watch was the best for time alone. It was unlikely he'd encounter anyone else on deck this night except the sailors, and he had seen precious little of them since boarding. He remembered meeting the captain of the vessel, a short, burly man with a greenish cast to his skin who would never quite meet Maddau's eyes. He grumbled a greeting and then, like most of his crew, disappeared amid the decks. Maddau had not seen him again. It was no matter, really, as long as the ship sailed well and they arrived at their destination. *Like as not,* he thought, *Twyll probably paid them to also leave the Koteli well enough alone.*

Glancing at the moon, Maddau thought Lymder had been right. The full moon flew serenely in the sky, keeping pace with them both in the sky overhead and in tiny flashes of light ricocheting off the choppy water below. He knew they would reach the coast of Brittany shortly after dawn, and then their travel would begin in earnest. He had no doubt that the fiends of the Dark would find them soon. It was by the Gods' grace that they had not been overtaken already and that the Dark fiends did not know where they were headed. Maddau turned his thoughts to what had happened at the Caer. As the captain of the Brehines's guard, the security of the Caer was his responsibility. *How did those scouts of Darkness take one of the larger villages outside the Caer walls with no resistance? And then, with almost no notice, they came through the locked gates and were spreading through the soldiers' barracks. How did they get through the locks? Those locks were double-reinforced, with separate barricades both inside and out. It was a necessity of security: regardless of how one got the outside lock to open, it would require someone to be willing to open the secondary locks from the inside. But that would mean—*

A light touch on his shoulder brought Maddau out of his thoughts. Twyll stepped up beside him and folded his arms across his chest. "Your watch is over, Captain. I'm your relief."

Maddau shook his head. "Two hours passed, just like that? I must be losing sense of time." Twyll grunted in response and stared out at the ocean.

Maddau turned and began walking back towards the stairs. He stopped after a few paces.

"I'm sorry, Twyll. I shouldn't have left like that," he said over his shoulder.

"You are under a great deal of stress. You just lost the woman you loved and are still trying to find your bearings." Twyll paused. "It is to be expected."

Maddau had been about to continue forward when Twyll's words made him whip his head around. His neck would hurt in the morning, but at that moment, he was unaware of the strain.

"What?" he managed to ask.

"Of course, I knew," Twyll continued, his voice stony. "You forget. I've known you since we were children. You've been in love with Abertha since your fifteenth summer. You'd never act upon it, and with her gone, now you'll never have the chance. You have yet to admit that loss to yourself, if not to others."

"Twyll..."

Twyll shook his head and raised his hand in the familiar gesture for silence Maddau used with the knights. "The day looms large ahead of us, and you need some rest that is free of dreams. I think you shall have that now, if only for the reason that your secret is known. Go on. You shall find the rest of the team is asleep, and they'll not bother you."

Chastened, Maddau faced away again and finished his walk back to the stairs to the hold. The cooler night air felt good on his reddened cheeks and helped to soothe the savage heat of the tears that ran freely down his face.

The dark embrace of the night enfolded the sleepy port town on the coast. No boats fished during the night, and all the sailors and residents were asleep in their beds or hummocks. Water lapped calmly at the shores, and the full moon shone serenely high above the land, bathing all but a copse of trees near the port hamlet in soft and silvery light. The darkness that had settled in the trees seemed to absorb all the ambient light. It twitched and shimmied as though it were waiting for something. It stamped at the roots and edged from the trunks like angry stallions that champed at their bits, ready and at the mark to race away. Where the darkness pulled away from the grove as it moved, the trees appeared to wither and dry up as though their lives were sucked dry.

A wisp of black ashes whirling in the wind came flying down the road that ran by the grove on its way to the port town. It moved faster than any wind blowing through the land—almost devilishly quick. Rounding a bend in the road, it coalesced into the shadowy shape of a black chevalier on a coal-black steed. The ghostly horse frothed grey plumes of foam from its lips, and its eyes shone with a malevolent light in each direction cast by its magenta gaze. Its hooves drew a deep rumbling from the ground, as if the very touch of its movement were the cause for deep needs to well up within the surrounding land, resulting in cracks and fissures in its passing for the want of something. As he drew level with the trees, the rider reined his horse in and stopped. The chevalier dismounted, and as his boot touched the ground, his form solidified, yet he made no sound. The chevalier's armor was covered in trinkets and embellishments. Decorative plumage erupted from the helmet and pauldrons, exemplifying the vice armor of excess. Despite all this, Gor-yfed moved in silence. As he approached, Cynddaredd's form slipped from the seething mass that had wound itself around the trunks of the trees and roosted in the branches and moved with barely controlled rage to intercept him.

"Is it done?" the first knight of the Cotheda inquired in his biting tone.

"Without fail." Gor-yfed dipped his head and raised his right hand to touch his left shoulder in the sign of fealty to the Dark, though his left hand never strayed from the grip of his flail, which hung down by his left thigh. One could never be too cautious of Cynddaredd's moods.

"Then report," the first knight said curtly.

"They never saw me coming." Gor-yfed licked his lips, delighted by his work. "It was easy to find their wants; they've had so little to sustain them these many years. T'was like picking flowers ripe for bloom. A few desires here and there, and those needs were quickly acted upon. Once the carnage started, it completed itself soon enough."

"You took care of them *all*?" Cyndaredd needled. "You are certain?"

"Easily." Gor-yfed grinned. "The only one who had not been overtaken was gasping his last as I left the site."

"For your sake, he had better be dead. Else you shall face the Commander's mercy when he arrives." Cynddaredd turned on his heel and stepped back into the molten fray of the dark mass engulfing the trees, scattering into flecks of black ash as he did. Gor-yfed rose and followed, asking as he, too, scattered into motes of darkness blacker than the night air.

"My thirst for blood is not yet slaked. When will the Commander arrive?"

Cynddaredd's rage answered him from the snake-like coils of blackness that folded in and on themselves, never ceasing movement, only slowing down to wait a bit longer.

Soon, it seethed. *Soon…*

A hard bump lurched Maddau from the deepest sleep he'd known since he was a boy and almost sent him tumbling off the wooden bench attached to the side of the hold where he had been lying. He sat up and rammed the top of his head into a support beam. He winced and clutched at the sore spot on the arch of his head—that would leave a lump. He blinked blearily around, lost in his immediate surroundings. Nothing in this grey-black forest of wooden planks, drab shadows, and salty smell held any familiarity, and he had no sense of belonging to this location.

"Get a grip, Madds," he mumbled to himself, shaking his head back and forth to clear the sleep fog from his brain. He pressed the heels of his hands to his eyes and tried to focus on his situation and not on the pounding in his skull. He slowed his breathing and concentrated on cataloging his scattered memories of the night before. Slowly it came back: he'd been sleeping for Gods know how long in the hold of a ship, The Flight of the Moon, on its way to some little coastal town in Brittany. Yes, to Kastell Paol in Brittany, with his team. They were—

Suddenly, panic overwhelmed him, and he grabbed frantically for his bag without comprehension. It was stowed securely under the back of his neck, making for a terrible and lumpy pillow and, subsequently, straining his shoulder and the lower part of his neck. But it was still there. He breathed a sigh of relief, understanding dawning only when his hand closed on the rough form of the cylinder within—the relic. Yes, that was what all this was about. They were bringing the relic to… where? He squintched his eyes tight against his hands, willing the memories to come forth. To the Dragon's Teeth… to meet the Sages there and protect the relic from the fiends of the Darkness, their pursuers.

"Maddau? You 'wake?" called a voice down the steps from the mid-decks, where the sailors' quarters were located. Someone was standing at the mouth of the hold and peering into the dim darkness below. Maddau righted himself, fixing his tunic and adjusting his clothes from the reworking sleep had wrought. He grabbed his sword and bag and headed to the stairs.

"'Ere you are! I was thinking we 'ad lost you to the sleep fae!" Burdeb was standing on the landing, smiling at Maddau. "A right good sleep you 'ad. Gonestrwydd told us all t' let you rest as long as pos'ble. 'E takes good care of us, 'e does. You, specially."

Maddau regarded Burdeb's cheerful smile with tired amusement. "Yes, he certainly does just that."

"'S'why 'e's First Knight! 'E keeps t' oars rowin' while you steer t' ship! Makes sense! C'mon now, we've docked an' all that. Boat Captain wants us to dissemble or other some such."

"Disembark?" Maddau couldn't suppress the surfacing grin at Burdeb's commentary. His first true one in awhile.

"Right! Like I said, dis-emby-ark. And we're t' go t' town. Gonestrwydd's already left to get some whadd'ya call 'em . . . supplies? Steeds, too!" Burdeb turned to head up the stairs, still chattering away.

Shaking his head, Maddau could not help but admire Twyll's ability to manage the team. *Perhaps he should have been the captain of the Koteli,* he thought. *He's already off, taking care of the men and ensuring we'll be ready for our journey... instead of me, who can never get his head out of his—*

"Captain, yew comin'?" Burdeb's voice floated back down to him, bringing Maddau out of his reverie. The other man had already ascended partway up the steps to the top deck.

"Yes, I'm coming. Right on your heels, Burb." He moved quickly, catching up to Burdeb in a few strides. Burdeb flashed another sunny smile, and Maddau followed the younger man up the rest of the stairs.

The bracing fresh air and warm sunny skies chased the remains of sleep from Maddau's senses as he stepped out onto the top deck. The sailors were busy with the myriad tasks that a new port brought: repairing rigging, cleaning, and bustling about. The captain of the ship was nowhere to be seen. Maddau saw the rest of the knights congregating near the gangplank and waiting to disembark. Burdeb started towards them, and Maddau followed. Haelder turned at the sound of their approach, and a look of relief mixed with anxiety bloomed on his face.

"Captain! There y' are! I thought ye'd be sleeping 'til time's end!"

Burdeb chuckled. "'E was sleeping prity 'ard." A chorus of snickers followed.

Maddau joined the laughter at his expense. "True enough. Yesterday, our world changed, and with all that has transpired, I was fairly tired for it. I'll answer your questions when we have a private spot to convene, but we do not have much time for delays. We have a long slog ahead of us to get to the Dragon's Teeth, so I hope you lot got some good rest during the night."

"Captain, why didn't we sail straight for the maw of the Dragon?" Gwyleidd-dra inquired. "Seems that would have saved us a ton of time." There were murmurs of agreement.

"You are quite right, Dra. And I would have much preferred to sail right to the Teeth and save us all this journey. Sadly, there's no place to dock; it's called the Dragon's Teeth for a reason. Huge juts of rock spread out into the sea to bite any ship that draws near. We'd no sooner draw close than our ship would be wrecked against those sharp jetties. Many a shipwreck dots that coast from failing to heed the Dragon's wicked bite."

"We could swim?" Lymder asked, hope glowing on his face.

"Not 'less you fancy to drown," Maddau responded firmly. "The Dragon's teeth jut far out into the water, and the distance from them to land is farther than any of us can swim with our armor and gear. It won't be an easy trip once we arrive, as we will still have to find the Temple and the Sages. I'm afraid there's no help for it, lads. We're to travel there by land."

"But why didn't we dock somewhere closer? Near the Dragon's neck, perhaps, instead of here, well past its tail and in its bloody nest?" Gwyleidd-Dra exploded.

Maddau flinched. Dra always challenged him, and the experience was for the better, he knew, as it made him reflect more on his decisions and thereby be a better leader for it, but it was tiresome to constantly have his decisions questioned. He fought himself for patience in the matter. They were as adrift as he was, and this was truly new territory for all of them. But it was a losing battle.

"There's nowhere to dock," he snapped at Dra. "The Dragon's neck, back, tail, and arse are enclosed with the lovely spines, so befitting such a beast, known as mountains. I know your skills with climbing are unchallenged, Dra. But I frankly do not fancy a mountain climb with all our gear after a long swim to reach land." He surveyed them with a harsher eye than he wished, and seeing their downcast eyes and drooping posture at his acid tone did nothing to alleviate his frustration. They needed to be bolstered; their spirits needed to be raised high for the difficult journey that awaited them, whose end was uncertain at best. *Damnit Madds,* he thought. *They need your encouragement, not your scorn. Twyll would be able to handle their questions and keep them in good spirits. Why can't you?*

The sun dipped behind a cloud, and shadows fell over them from the numerous puffs of white dotting the sky. The sound of footsteps ringing up the gangplank caused Maddau to look up to see Twyll arriving, calmly indifferent as always.

"Clever enough to have the group all assembled and at the ready, it looks like. Burb, I see you've even roused our Captain from his deathlike sleep." Twyll sampled the tense atmosphere of the group and looked to Maddau for a reason, who shook his head in disgust.

"So then?" he enjoined. "What are our plans?"

"Captain here was just telling us why we have to travel so far," Olwgg responded hollowly. "And it sounds pretty miserable, if you ask me."

Maddau gritted his teeth and continued. "We could not dock closer to the tail because there is no place to stop for supplies. No towns, no hamlets, no ports on the coast until we reached the Nest. We'd have to swim to the beach—again, we cannot get close to land with all the rocks—and then march for miles before we'd be lucky enough to find a hut in which to rest or to dry. It would take us days with no food, no water, no fire, and no horses. The Dark fiends would have us in moments." He surveyed them with evident anger. "Does this explain best for you why we are to start at the Nest?" he spat.

Twyll's look of shock and consternation at the tone of his words told Maddau every bit of how badly he was failing to handle the team as their leader, but he didn't care. *Could they not just trust him for once?*

Twyll quickly gathered that this was not going well and that it needed redirection. He clapped his hands, much as the prentice instructor had done long ago when he needed to change the momentum of a surly group of youths and provide some fresh motivation.

"Well, I've procured some fresh horses and plenty of supplies, which are being assembled for us as we speak. We've but to collect our mounts and gear from the smith's and the grocer's, and we can be off. But here's a thought: how about we stop at the tavern first and have a nice hot meal? I think we've at least time for that, Captain?" The sullen faces and defeated stances perked up a bit at the mention of sustenance. Food. They had not had any food since they left Breakwater. Although it was just the day prior, it felt like a lifetime ago, and the sailors had not been inclined to share. They'd been well paid to take the knights wherever was their pleasure and waited for them to be ready to boot. But share their food they would not, and no amount of rhetoric or pleading changed their minds, despite all of Twyll's careful verbal art and even some of Dra's intimidation. Twyll was careful to couch his words in such a way as to bring around the men while giving his Captain the opportunity to be redeemed in their eyes by conceding to the diversion of a good hot meal. They had all gone without for a night, and now the concept of food brought everyone's mood around. Even Maddau's.

Twyll's green eyes were on him, and Maddau flushed under the weight of his gaze. "Well, Captain? It's your call."

It wasn't, and both he and Twyll knew it. Maddau was just thankful that none of the other men seemed to know or understand it. Twyll had, likely as not, already gone into the tavern and paid for their meals. This farce of decision-making was just to soothe the situation and clean up the mess Maddau had made of this assembly.

He closed his eyes against the anger that pricked him inside. He knew Twyll was helping him, but it didn't always feel that way. It felt more and more like Twyll was trying to take the leadership of the group from him, and he was far better at it than Maddau had ever been. So now the question was: would he go along and let Twyll smooth everything over as he always seemed to do when Maddau blundered, or would he enforce his authority over the situation and demand they gather their supplies and leave immediately? The situation favored the latter. But… His stomach rumbled in the silence, providing an answer to him and all those around him, even if he did not like it. The decision was made, and the mood was broken as everyone began to grin and chuckle. Defeated by his own body, he had no choice but to relent. "Looks like we'll be having our morning meal at midmorn' first, lads." Maddau smiled at them, genuinely relieved that the tension was gone. Twyll's smirk of approval let Maddau know he had made the right decisions, and he smiled his thanks. Twyll had managed to smooth everything over. Again. He should have been thankful that things were leveled out again, but inside he grimaced.

The passage of two hours found them all friends again over fresh bread, hot beef-roast stew, and a finer ale than Maddau had ever tasted. *The grain must grow differently here*, he thought. *Maybe it's the air.* The taste was lighter and sweeter than the ale from his homeland. He had downed two mugs already, and it left a pleasant buzziness, reminiscent of the singing of the insects on sleepy summer nights. The men had consumed at least three pitchers worth, and they were all happily filling up on the atmosphere, the strange new environment, the unintelligible locals, and the odd customs. Maddau had visited Brittany in his youth on his pilgrimage to the Temple de la Sagesse and had taken Twyll with him. They had stayed in Kastell Paol, the Dragon's Nest, before beginning their journey and had roughly explored the area during their time with the other pilgrims. They had even picked up a smattering of Brittonic while on their pilgrimage, though Twyll's taste and skill with the language far exceeded his own. But for the rest of his team, they were in a foreign land for the first time and were as at ease as babes in the woods. It was left to Maddau and Twyll to translate and explain the local customs. Twyll had obviously retained far more knowledge of their time abroad than his compatriot, as his Brittonic was smooth, silky even, and held none of the stuttering and delays Maddau produced in his conveyance of their needs and conversing with the tavern woman who brought over their cups of ale. They'd had time for some ale and a round of stew before Twyll, having seen them all settled in and their appetites in the process of satiety, excused himself and Burdeb for having to fetch the supplies and the horses. Twyll explained that they would bring them to the tavern so they could leave as soon as everyone was ready. Maddau felt that he should have been the one to go, but he was into his third mug of ale and second bowl of stew and was starting to feel a bit restive. Olwygg had fallen asleep, head on the table, with his hands still clutching his mug. The others looked like they were not far from joining him. Both Twyll and Burb still seemed fresh, as if they had woken only moments before, so Maddau put up no complaint. They would rest here while the two men gathered what was needed for their journey. It was decided.

That had been more than an hour past, and the two had still not returned. Both Haelder and Dra had joined Olwygg and also fallen asleep, with the latter snoring quietly against the half-finished chunk of bread on which he'd leaned his head. Lymder was the only other one still awake, his self-control evident from the faint aura that surrounded him. He carried an air of meditative ease, but from the minor furrow in his brow, it was evident that he, too, was starting to notice the passage of time. Maddau frowned, his mind starting to clear a bit as a hint of worry crept in the background. *It should not take longer than half an hour to fetch what Twyll has already procured. Where are they?*

At Twyll's suggestion, they had separated to fetch the supplies: Twyll headed to the smith's for the horses, and Burdeb headed to the grocer's for the food. Twyll had given Burdeb rough directions around the small portside town and then disappeared in the opposite direction with a swirl of his woolen summer cloak. Burdeb, while dressed the same, always felt like a drabber, paler version of Twyll. Burdeb pondered, *The First Knight always looked so effortless and… regal. Almost like 'e should be a commander or some such.* Burdeb made his way down the mud-strewn lane, glancing this way and that. The people that were wandering around here looked different. They were peasants, and coastal ones at that, but their clothes looked *different* somehow in a way that he did not have the words to define. Burdeb had come from a coastal town, so he knew the types of men that made up a village of sailors and fishers and the types of women that made families with them. These peasants *looked* different, but he could not put his finger on the reason. Banishing the uneasy feeling this idea gave him, he continued until the lane ended in a round, flat area that seemed to be the center of the small town. The different dirt paths all met here, and in the center of the rounded area was a small stand that held many different foods: animal legs and fowl were suspended from the sunshield overhanging the stand; piles of different roots and fruits were in baskets out in front; and a series of dun-colored packets, wound tight with twine, were piled on a ledge attached just inside the walls. A girl was keeping the grocer's stand and calling out her wares in sweetly lilting Brittonic to the village inhabitants, with only the occasional glance from those she solicited. Burdeb stared. She was like no girl he had ever seen before in the Caer or from his hometown of Pwllheli. Her clothes, although common enough for the style of the local womenfolk in this place based on what he'd seen so far, clung to her figure. His eyes were drawn to the slip and play of the light fabric, which enhanced her shape as she moved. None of the girls at home wore clothes that fitted their forms, and he could see the side of her light-colored bodice through the lacing of her darker kirtle. He stared harder as he approached, his legs moving as if of their own accord; there was no color of fabric under her tunic, he saw. That pale colored cloth was skin! The peeping visage through the loosened upper lacings was the side of her breast and was clearly visible under her arm as she beckoned to the people.

She glanced his way and waved, beckoning him forward. Burdeb had known she would see him; it was inevitable, of course, since he was to pick up their provisions for the journey ahead from this stand. The sky was scummed over with a layer of clouds, and he was able to see her far more clearly than he had at first. Her tunic was a deep red in color, like dark clay, and her head covering was of a similar coloring with a light trim. Her skin had a pallor that was unusual for a coastal country lass, with dark feathery hairs addressing her brow and large round eyes that were a soft gold with hints of purple. Her lips were a bitten pink color that curled into a winning smile as he approached.

"*Demat Aotrou!*" she called to him. "*Ho kortoz a ran.*"

Burdeb smiled at her in confusion, having no idea what she said.

"Ah… *Brezhoneg* eu… mean… Breton… you do not?" she said, her smile turning into a grimace at using a foreign tongue. Burdeb, recognizing her broken attempts at Cymraeg, smiled anxiously at her and nodded vigorously to show he understood her.

"Ah… domaj… but… hmm… Aotrou Gaw-Nuss-Troo-Eef me told you come. Et 'ere are you!" she finished, triumphing over the strange words. "Come! Bags you are to 'ave." She motioned him to enter the side of the stall and turned to pull some of the packets and root vegetables together and place them into a sack she retrieved from inside the back of the stall. He came around the side of the stall and found a separation between the wall and the table where she displayed her wares. She had bent over to pull another sack from below a pile of potatoes and was facing the back of the stall as he entered. Burdeb stepped into the shade of the overhang, and his gaze was immediately drawn to her rear as she wrestled the bag from the potatoes. Succeeding at pulling the second bag from beneath without toppling the tubers, she turned around to grab more of the dun-colored packets from the wall and face him. He turned his gaze to her face. She was much closer now, barely a forearm away from him. He hoped desperately that she had not seen him looking at her, but he saw that she had caught where his eyes had been as her pleasant service smile twisted into a knowing grin.

A hot feeling of embarrassment flushed through him, and he had to drop his gaze from the knowledge of his transgression in her eyes. But that was no use, as now his gaze was directed at the breast of her tunic, which had a neckline lower than any he'd seen before, almost showing the beginning of her small decolletage. Horrified, he forced his eyes even lower. Now he could see the movement of her hips as she shifted under his gaze. Shaking his head, he closed his eyes and turned his face down to try and see behind him without facing away from her, as he desperately did not want to appear rude to this foreign girl.

"Ah, aotrou," she laughed. "You and my body. You see so well, no?" Her laughter increased to an almost mocking tone as blood suffused Burdeb's face. In the space of a minute, his face had already rivaled the hues of the fruits on her display.

You like, yes?" she inquired, leaning closer.

He tried to step away, but his back bumped against the display table, and she had moved between him and the exit space between the table and the wall. He felt horribly embarrassed and a bit afraid. He had never been this close to a woman before, and her incredible *nearness* was making him anxious and creating a strange sort of languid delay in his mind as he watched her, much like a rabbit watches the snake stalking it. Fearful terror and ultimate fascination with the thing inducing the terror. He wanted to get away from her and clear his head, but strangely, he didn't want to leave her presence at all. In fact, he suddenly became aware of an increasing desire coursing through him; he wanted to get closer to her, to wrap his arms around her waist and pull her close to him.

She had closed most of the gap between them and reached out her hand to caress the line of his jaw before he realized she was moving. Burdeb had thought her taller when he had approached the stall, but now it seemed she was just a hair shorter than him. Just tall enough to tilt her face up to his as she drew even closer.

He felt like a fog was moving through his mind, infusing his contemplations of her with desire. A desire of which he had been truly ignorant until just now. Oh, he wanted to grab her and pull her closer, removing all space between them. To pull her up against him, in fact, and feel her body mold to him. To grip the side of her tunic where the lacing was loose and jerk it from her body, exposing her to all and sundry. And then to…

Her green eyes had widened as she stared up at him. He stared back, entranced, and leaned forward. Their faces were now inches apart.

"Yer eyes, they're green. I thought 'em gold," he muttered, tilting his face down towards hers and reaching for her lips.

"Ah, you funny, aotrou. You want, no?" she whispered coyly, breathing against his neck. She tilted her head away and a bit out of reach while guiding his face with her hand. He leaned after her, painfully aware of the distance between them. Her other hand had slipped down to his waist and was lightly tugging on the side of his overtunic, trying to pull it up and out of his belt.

"Say," she said, having succeeded in pulling the white garment out from beneath his belt. Grasping it, she pulled him towards and against her. She could feel him pressing against her and smiled in triumph.

"Say it. Say you want."

"Yes, I…" He licked his lips, desire and lust overtaking his confusion at how this had happened. He gave up trying to understand and gave in to the directive his body had provided, unknowing and untried as it was. He reached helplessly for her, closing his hands on her waist and his eyes to what was about to happen. "I want… I… I want…"

"Trawalc'h!"

A voice exploded in his ear, and suddenly there was a gust of wind in front of his face. The grocer girl shrieked, and Burdeb was thrown forcefully back against the display table, crushing it beneath his weight and sending fruits and roots scattering. He landed on his back, feeling the squish of many things being smashed under him. His eyes sprung open to see that standing between where he lay prone and the grocer's hut was Gonestrwydd. His curly hair and cape were fluttering in the wind, and he had one hand up in a halting gesture, fingers splayed. The other was on the hilt of the long blade at his hip. Burdeb could not see his face, but he could feel an aura of absolute malice radiating from the First Knight of his regiment, and he was afraid.

"Vile puckle!" Gonestrwydd spat. "You think to take advantage of a stranger with all manner of your disgusting and diseased favors! I should end you for such a hideous and filthy impertinence."

Burdeb was slow to gain his feet, a confusion of desires and emotions clanging through his blood like the bells of the church those foreigners had built on his home island. His body was out of sorts—heavy and slow in a way with which he was unfamiliar. He felt shocked and furious at the loss of whatever had been about to happen. He did not know what that was exactly. Only that he wanted it. He wanted her and whatever came next… with her. He looked past the man and saw that the grocer girl was cowering in the back of the stall, one hand shielding her face from them and the other covering her left eye. She mewled. There was blood, from whence he did not know, splattered in the dirt between them. He started forward to stop the First Knight from taking further action. He couldn't let him hurt the girl. "Gonestrwydd! 'At's enough!"

Gonestrwydd turned with liquid speed and grasped Burdeb by the throat just as he came into range and before he could utter another word. The taller man stared down at him, fury whipping green fire through his eyes.

"You ignorant bastard." His voice crackled through the air like lightning. "You are dangerously close to breaking your oath to your charge. Did you know that, boy? Perhaps you already have, with that harlot. Let us hope not, for your sake if not for hers. Pray to all that you hold dear for thanks that I caught you in time. Lucky that I found you instead of the Captain. Gods know what he would have done to you had he seen what you were about to do!"

Burdeb gasped for air and struggled in the older man's grasp. He clawed at Gonestrwydd's hand as dark specks started to appear at the edges of his vision. The First Knight leaned forward, and Burdeb could feel the malice in Gonestrwydd's words sapping him of his strength and the will to breathe. Even with his reduced vision, he could see the dark aura that surrounded the First Knight as the words smacked into him.

"Gain control of yourself, and remember your charge whilst I deal with this disgusting Bretonnic dog."

He released his grip on Burdeb's throat and let the young man fall to his knees. Burdeb inhaled frantic gasps, kneeling in the mud, coughing and spitting. He clutched his throat as his awareness came back to him. Gonestrwydd turned and gathered up the partially full sacks in one hand while using his other arm to sweep several vegetables from the baskets at the side of the stall to finish filling them. He straightened up without looking at the weeping girl and grabbed Burdeb's shoulder with an iron grip, pulling him to his feet.

"Come. We are to return to the tavern at once before you find any more ways to try and destroy yourself."

Burdeb stumbled forward, still wheezing, propelled by the force of the First Knight. One hand still covered his aching throat, and he was using the other to wipe the tears from his eyes. He could barely make out the blurry shapes of nickering horses standing at the edge of the shop's clearing. Gonestrwydd pushed the younger man forward again. Upon hearing the cries of frustrated anguish issuing from the grocer's hut, he glanced back over his shoulder. A small group of people had started to gather around the grocer's stand, and chatter was rising in the air behind them.

"*Blys! Byddwn yn siarad yn nes ymlaen!*"

Burdeb heard the icy fury in Gonestrwydd's voice as he called back— something vicious, no doubt—and was thankful he could not understand whatever nasty thing was said to the poor wench and locals. Feeling enervated and limp, a husk bereft of the vitality that had coursed through him only moments before, he let the First Knight firmly steer him towards the horses.

The sun shone behind the shield of clouds that sat over Kastell Paol, so the fields and groves of trees were well illuminated around the town, which was covered in a small shade. All were well illuminated, except for a small grove that stood just under a furlong from the coastal town. The trees that were still standing huddled together. They had not grown that way, and several trees had aged more quickly than normal for this species and fallen into and onto the gaps between its brethren, creating deep-set shadows in lean-tos and the underbellies of trunks and amidst the snarling tangle-knots of roots. Past the edge of the trees, light fell off as though it had hit a wall. Clusters of shadows shifted uneasily around the trunks. Outside the copse of trees, a small country lane led from Kastell Paol and was the main way of travel out of the town. The lane curved near the grove as it exited the town. Near the center of the bend was a medium-sized black dog moving up and away from the town. It moved with an obvious stiffness in its back. As it limped further from the town and closer to the shadow-decked trees, it left footprints in the dusty dirt of the lane, and every few steps, several drops of blood or a small clot fell in line with the paw prints.

The dog reached the center of the turn, where the road was nearest the trees, and left the path, heading for the trees. As it stepped off the path, the dog's shape began to twist and bulk. The body began to stream out as small black flecks of night, and the chest cavity split open and flattened back into a new shape. The spine grew huge spikes from it as the back bulked out into scaly plates. A few paces closer to the trees, and the dog thing's legs elongated. Its knees bent forward, the bones cracked into new positions, and the paws stretched long into feet and hand shapes, which then bloated out into scaly gloves, forearms, and shin covers. As it crossed the tree line, it suddenly stood upright on what had been its hind legs with a horrible splintering crack, which was lost in the shrieking howl this elicited. What had, for all appearances, been a dog-like creature was now the limping shape of a knight in spine-covered blackened-red armor. The helmet that covered the damned creature's face was in a similarly blistered and blackened-red state, and the left side of the mask was caved so deeply into the unfortunate head who wore that mask that it was clear it could not be removed without inflicting irreversible damage. Blood and ichor slowly leaked out of the holes in the left-hand side of what had been the visor, and what had previously been a clear goo was now stained a thready red.

The knight waited until reaching the full enclosure of the shadows of the trees before falling down on to hands and knees, uttering a desperate howl of pain and anguish while trying to crawl forward.

The howl echoed flatly through the trees and went no further. The shadows between the trees shifted and coiled out from themselves, streaming swirling black specks to spin around into a broad columnar shape that coalesced into Cynddaredd. The sharpened horns of the First Knight's helmet and at the joint-ends of his armor gleamed a wet black in the non-light of the shadows as he stepped forward. With each step he took away from the shadow-ridden mass, the edges of his form sharpened and became more lethal until he arrived in front of the semi-prone knight on the ground, fully solid and incredibly dangerous.

"Blys...," he growled. "You were to gather intelligence on the slaves of the light bitch. Yet, I find you back here, a little more than a pathetic waste, clinging to the remains of what animates you. It is obvious you have failed your mission. We are so close now to obtaining what is rightfully ours—what has been withheld from us for these long years. Your failure, has it endangered our mission? Do they know of us? What have you done? Where have you been?" Cynddaredd reached down, grasped the edge of the visor, and pulled Blys' head up and back so he could look down into the knight's mask.

"Speak, bitch," he commanded, his voice cutting through the air like a whip.

Blys did not struggle against this manipulation, but the pain forced a whine from the mask, and she began to pant with effort.

"Mmmh... mmmph...," she whimpered. "Cynnnddaa... I... I... I haadd one... mmph... mpph of those... of... of theeeemmm..." Her voice lacked force but whined up in pitch. "He... heeeh... he was... miiinnneee... I... I had... his power... in my... grasp!" she shrieked.

Cynddaredd leaned closer, his eyes gleaming a dull, red rage through his visor. "You were put there to observe and find us a weakness! Not to engage them! How did they find you out?"

"I… heeeh… mmmph… was… haaah… stopped…" Her panting had sped up considerably.

"One of them… hhaaahhh…. struck meeeee… could… not… geeeet awwwaaaaayy," she wailed, and a fresh gout of stringy red ichor bubbled through her mask. "Huurrrtsss…," she panted, painfully. "Pleeeasee… Cyyyynnnddaaaarrrreeeeddddd…," she gasped.

He jerked her head back further, hearing the snapping of the fine bones in what remained of her neck.

"What did you learn?" he growled, the words deepening into a bass buzz.

"Use… mmmnh… use… their gifts…haah… against… theeeemm… turn… turn they…. Their gifts… to… weakness…. Mmph… nnnhhh…. Uughh… aah… ahh…" As another stream of blood belched through the mask, more and more black speckles began streaming up through all the gaps and holes in the dented and cracked remains of the armor, which was slowly disintegrating into black dust motes. They rose into the air and floated up to enjoin with the shadowed mass.

"So their gifts are their weaknesses." Cynddaredd's arm wrenched back, pulling Blys' helmet and head back in one final tearing motion, and he released the edge of the visor, allowing it to fall back against the disintegrating armor spines and glance off the plating. The helmet, with Blys' head inside, rolled off and onto the ground. From the ragged stump of a neck, streams of black specks wove and circled up into the branches overhead.

"It seems that they protect their own well and can recognize us," Cynddaredd mused, watching the remains of Blys slowly floating up to rejoin the darkness. He straightened up, wiping his hand clean of the smear left by Blys' blood. "Perhaps it's for the best, Blys," he said, turning and stepping back into the enfolding dark mass. "You've brought us valuable information and narrowly avoided the Commander's very specific form of mercy that would have destroyed you utterly had you stayed there. At least this way, you'll return to us…in time."

Chapter Four

A World Apart

Gonestrwydd moved with a livid speed as he pulled the horses he led along with him towards the tavern. Burdeb followed miserably behind the horses and watched as Gonestrwydd led them to the post in front of the tavern and began tying them there. As he finished the first horse's reins and began tying off the second, he glanced over at Burdeb. The young knight was deliberating anxiously at the entrance to the tavern.

"Go inside and see the Captain. He's awaiting our return, and we have been long."

Burdeb nodded, his face the picture of misery, and turned to mount the steps to the door.

"And Burb,"

Burdeb looked back to Gonestrwydd.

"Don't tell him. Your failing was prevented. You did not go with that whore. The purity of your gift is still alive and intact." He smiled at Burdeb as he started on the third set of reins; the slightest bit of an aura shone around his face. "Don't give him any further reason to fret or worry for you. Or your loyalty. You'll be fine."

Burdeb felt his face flush over again with shameful misery, but also mixed in was a painful gratitude for Gonestrwydd's words, harsh as they might be. Honesty was his trait, but that did not mean it had to be kind.

"Yer words are true t'that. Thanks be for yer presence... Am afeared t' think what'd happen 'ad ye not come and..." Burdeb turned abruptly and stepped into the tavern before his tongue could allow him to say more and betray him further than it already had that day.

The interior of the tavern was darker than the grey light of the world outside, and the change in lighting made Burdeb squint. A man with a large vielle had arrived at some point during their absence. He was stationed in the corner nearest the door. He plucked its strings and slapped the sides to create a beat, perhaps in hopes of receiving a coin or two for his performance, but sadly, he was much ignored by the patrons of the tavern. Burdeb was able to make out his compatriots' restive languish on the far side of the room. He saw that some were toying with the remnants of their meal, one was moodily haunting the depths of his own thoughts, and two were asleep with their heads on the table. The Captain, alone, had an air of watchfulness about him, and he locked eyes with Burdeb the moment the latter entered the room. Burdeb felt a flush of guilt begin clawing its way up his neck, bringing a rising heat and dampness along his ribs, underarms, and around his neck and hairline. The young man raised his hand in greeting and moved towards the table where Maddau held court with his watchful eyes. Burdeb could feel the intense weight of Maddau's stare as he approached the end of the table where Olwygg snored, breezily blowing crumbs off a chunk of bread with each passing breath. Try as he might, Burdeb could not meet his Captain's eyes as he approached, for the weight of his shame at being tempted cast him in far too great a quandary. If he was so easy to manipulate, so easy to tempt... was he even worthy of being a Koteli Knight? Was the light within him so easily diminished by such a tawdry and fleeting experience? Was he now a liability t' his fellows... t' his Captain... t' his charge? Was he... tainted?

Burdeb felt that his Captain, whose heavy gaze he could still feel weighing on him as though stones were being laid upon his neck and shoulders, could look right through him and read his every thought. Any moment, he would stand from his chair, illuminated in a halo of righteous light and anger, and bellow, "Burdeb! You have betrayed your charge! You have betrayed the Light! You are nothing more than a squawking worm ready to debase himself for the attention of a Dark whore! You are ejected from the Koteli Knights, banished to walk alone on this earth for your weakness for all time as punishment!"

"Burb!" Maddau's voice broke through his thoughts. He was smiling at him in bemusement, and his eyes were probing and inquisitive but kind. "I know you went to pick up the food and supplies, but did you not get enough to eat while you were here?"

Burdeb stared at his captain in confusion. "Ehh?"

Maddau gestured languidly to the boy's formerly white tunic, which was now stained with many large oblong streaks of varying pink and red hues and many darker smears where dirt had intermingled with the juices of the berries on which he had landed. "You seemed to have needed further refreshment, and by the looks of it, you... em... well... enjoyed it," Maddau trailed off.

Burdeb followed his eyes to the filth smeared across his shirt and felt the shame redouble. The heat bloomed through him again like a spreading stain that now warmed all parts of him—even his toes felt sweaty and dirty! His eyes dropped further to stare at the table, where Olwygg continued to snooze, unaware. Burdeb's mouth filled with water as his mind raced. His Captain knew. He knew not how, but Maddau knew! What could he tell him to stay judgment?

"I... well... y' see, er, I... I was pickin'... I was sent t'... t'... pick... collect... that is...," said Burdeb.

The room darkened for a moment as shadows chased their way across the table. Twyll had entered the tavern and moved effortlessly to stand beside the head of the table where Maddau sat, still watching Burdeb. Maddau glanced away from Burdeb to regard Twyll as he approached and nodded to him.

"We have all the horses and supplies. The moment to move out is simply at your say." Twyll eyed first the sleeping Haelder and Dra, the drooling Olwygg, the stone-like contemplation of Lymder, who was oblivious to the tableau, and ended with the red-faced Burdeb.

"Did I miss much? Or was watching this race of the puddle of Olwygg's spittle versus Haelder's reach the edge of the wood just too riveting for words?"

Maddau's vigilant aura cracked, and a smile burst forward as he relaxed. Twyll's irreverent and comedic disdain for the more stalwart members of their regiment and his presence were a balm to his spirit.

"I must admit, it has been all-encompassing," said Maddau, smiling. "But as soon as we solve Burdeb's issue, we should be off."

Twyll looked up at Maddau's comment and then shot Burdeb a glance. The younger man still stood by the end of the table, at an obvious loss for words, stuttering synoptic syllables as he tried to start an explanation. His eyes were fixed on a crust of bread lying forgotten on the table. "Come, Burdeb. What has you a'chittering as though your tongue is pinned in the middle and flutters in the breeze as a lady's garment on the line?" the first knight inquired.

Burdeb's face flushed further into a deeper crimson, and his throat locked up tight. Why did Gonestrwydd mock him so? He had been there. He had *seen*!

Twyll turned back to look at Maddau, dismissing Burdeb with a turn of his head.

"Upon retrieving the horses, I found that mumbling green one enduring a rather pathetic attempt at waylaying by a local farm girl. Of course, he was ever such the gentleman. She was spilling her fruit all 'oer the place with wanting him to clean it up! I had to practically tear him away as, like as not, she was thinking fruits first, partnering in a sun's course, and a young pucklet on the way by wintermas!"

Shock spanked its way across Maddau's face, and then he roared with a burst of laughter. The sudden raucousness of the sound shocked everyone in the tavern, waking the sleepers from their post-meal drowse, causing the viellist to grasp his instrument with a twanging of strings, and rousing the attention of the owner, who poked his rotund face down the hall to ensure no mischief had entered to destroy his business before pattering back to his private chamber where his mistress was attending to his every pleasure. In the moment of sound, Burdeb was released from the stranglehold of the strange shame that had infused his muscles. His legs unhinged, and he sat abruptly as though on command, squashing Olwygg's hand beneath his haunch. Olwygg jerked upright and squeaked in dismay as he pulled the offended appendage from beneath the younger man. Shaking it rapidly in the air before his face and eyeing the sore, pulsing, reddened joints where arthritis had already set in deeply, he growled, "Watch yer manners, boy." Half awake and still woozy with drink and full of stew, his voice warbled. "Peeeeples be a'sittin' 'ere."

Maddau's laughter had well livened the tavern's patrons again before it finally tapered off, and an air of good spirits rushed in to fill the gloom that had seeped in since the time Twyll and Burdeb had left to get the provisions. The candles seemed brighter, and Burdeb could feel the redness beginning to drain from his cheeks, as though with the abrupt spark of sound, a sort of equilibrium had been restored and the balance was right again.

"Well, now. I won't fault a man for helping a lady in need." Maddau's eyes glinted with mischief as he looked at Burdeb. "I'm sure you were too beset by her words to be anything other than chivalrous, Burb! But it is of little matter, and we've not time to play, cheering as it might be. We've to be off." He shifted his gaze to regard Twyll again. "It is at my say that we move, hm?"

Twyll nodded. "It is, Captain."

"Then we move now. Let's us be gone a moment before they know we've left. I'd like to not have any retinue follow us if it can be avoided."

Inspired by their captain's words, the knights all rose together, as if their minds were in sync. Olwygg, still seething over his squashed hand, herded Burdeb out in front of him with the sternest of looks and grumbled complaints about green ones not respecting their elders. Haelder, Lymder, and Dra turned with no discourse and followed suit. Maddau expected Twyll to follow Lymder in line and he would bring up the rear, but was surprised when Twyll waited for Lymder to clear the door and then turned to face him.

"Madds, there's something you should know," Twyll whispered as a dark frown crossed his face. He leaned in close.

"What I said earlier, it wasn't the whole of it."

Maddau's brow crinkled, and his smile slipped a notch.

"What do you mean, Twyll? Do we not have steeds enough for all of us? Could you not get quite enough food? I suppose that is no great loss as we could stop along the way, yet—"

"No!" Twyll hissed. "Not the provisions. *Burdeb*! I caught him, Madds! I caught him." Maddau's eyes narrowed, and Twyll hissed in his breath, realizing how it sounded.

He tried again. "I caught him with that girl, as I had said. But it was not as I said." Twyll weighed his words carefully before he continued. "He was not the innocent as I had said, Madds. I'm sorry that I misled you. I did not want to cause a scene here in front of the others. But I don't think we can trust Burdeb any longer. He... succumbed to the grocer girl and... betrayed his charge. I think she was one of the Darkness. His purity... is gone."

The light seemed to drain out of the world for Maddau at his friend's words. Burdeb? Had betrayed them? By a girl? A girl of... the Darkness?

"How?" Maddau's voice was the harsh croak of an angry crow.

Twyll shook his head in disgust. "Burdeb and I split up to cover ground faster. I was for the horses, he for the food. I had gathered the herd and expected him to meet me halfway back. But he did not come, so I went to the grocer's stand to look for him and found him there with the girl. They were... Madds... I *found* them. She was all o'er him, and he was well with her."

"The stains on his tunic then...," Maddau grunted, "I suppose those come from..."

"From the grocer girl, yes. Perhaps it was a bit rough." Twyll averted his eyes from Maddau's face and continued. "I pulled him off her. She seemed to recognize me as a Koteli Knight, as our ilk are not unknown here, and she went running from the place. Burdeb turned on me and threatened me not to tell you. I'm afraid it almost worked. He has some… some… power. Had it not been for Olwygg pushing him out the door first, I'm afraid… Madds… I'm afraid I might have said nothing. All while this has gone on in here, I felt something keeping me from speaking to you about it. I think that Burdeb… I think he's… become an acolyte of the Dark."

Maddau had thought it could not get worse than to find Burdeb had betrayed them, but indeed, to have found that the youngest and most innocent of their regiment had chosen to work against their charge and their mission. It could not be so. Yet how could it not be when it was Twyll who had told him? It was truly a heavy burden, and his heart weighed down as though pulled by the strings of a million unknown losses.

"Twyll… how could this happen?" His voice was a whisper filled with weakness.

"I dunnet know, Madds." His friend put a comforting arm around his shoulders and began guiding him up and towards the door.

"But we'll get through to the Dragon's Teeth, mark me on that. I won't let Burdeb interfere with our charge. You can trust me in that."

Maddau nodded, his mind blank, letting Twyll steer him toward the door. He felt like a confused goat being maneuvered to the slaughter gate as they exited the tavern. Burdeb's betrayal, the capable Twyll being threatened by the younger man, fiends of the Darkness about them, infiltrating and corrupting them—it was all too fast, crashing in on him like unrelenting waves. At least he had Twyll there to guide and advise—his beloved and trusted friend.

The passage of several hours brought them far down the road from Kastell Paol. The knights rode in a modified vee: Maddau and Twyll in the front, Dra,

Haelder and Olwygg in the middle, and Lymder and Burdeb in the rear. The horse Maddau rode was high-strung and skittish. He lamented its constant balking and shying. Brosegvah never reacted this way in his presence or around other horses. He considered that the relic might be influencing his horse's temperament, but Brosie had endured the presence of the relic without complaint, so Maddau felt that this was a hollow excuse at best for the antics of his steed. He felt the lack of Brosegvah in his life more sharply than he'd thought possible. When he had brought Brosie to the smith's shop, Maddau had believed that he would be retrieving his friend to accompany them all the way through the mission. Twyll, however, had dashed that belief against the harsh, honest rocks of reality: the ship they had chartered did not have enough room for his horse. Brosegvah would have to stay behind. In the rush to set sail, Maddau had coordinated with the smith to bring the horse back to Caer y Twr once he was healed and ready to return to service. He hoped that the exchange of two silvers with the name of the Steward and the promise of two more once the horse was delivered safely would ensure compliance with the task. Maddau hoped well that his judgement of the smith's character was well placed; he seemed to favor horses over people, at any rate.

Twyll had been silent for most of the ride, lost in his own counsel. His stolid horse kept an effortless pace beside Maddau's fickle mount, almost as if it was keeping an eye on the roan. The trail they traversed was wheel-rutted and well-worn, though overgrown, and the minor slipping of hooves on the long grass did nothing to sooth equine anxiety. The path itself, though, was uneventful. The land around them was populated with small farms and brooding, spotty forests. Wheat grew in the fields on either side of the trail and had not been attended to in many months, as it was tall enough to brush gently against the horses' flanks with a soft swishing sound. As the regiment approached the crest of a hill, the view of the land opened up beneath them. Maddau could see a small collection of buildings clustered together in the heart of the valley, and he marveled at this new "town" that had grown up in this tiny valley of the Dragon's breast. It was a stark reminder of just how much time had passed since he had made his pilgrimage to the Temple. Had it really been fifteen years?

Twyll's quiet voice intruded upon Maddau's reflection. "It's really been an age, hasn't it, Madds?" he murmured. "That place wasn't even a watering hole when we passed through here so many seasons ago when we were scant men. Time does pass quick."

Maddau nodded. "The regiment had only just formed and received our charge. You and I were sent to the Temple at the behest of Lady Anwadaledd, her first order as the new Brehines."

"Aye. She sent us away before we could do much to secure her. You were to reestablish the good graces of the Sages, and I was to keep you alive! And when we came back, she was gone." Twyll finished, his mood darkening.

Maddau cast his eyes onto the bridle of his horse, embarrassed.

"I was not the best with the sword in my youth, and you always bested me in practice, Twyll." He chuckled.

"Well, he always was at the practice boards for every spare minute and up before the birds' song to work his form," Haelder's voice interrupted. He had nudged his horse forward to draw in just behind and between Maddau and Twyll. "Captain, I recall you liked to sleep in 'til well after cock crow."

Embarrassment faded into a genuine smile, and Maddau tipped his head back towards Haelder. "'Tis true, and I still do. It is a mighty privilege to enjoy soft bedding and gentle rest. We should all seek to guard that enjoyment so carefully in life that we never take it for granted, else we find ourselves wanting in future days to come."

The elder knight chortled at such a return to his needling. "Well said, Sir! Well said!" He glanced at the lowering sun and then assayed the distance they had yet to travel. "I take it we be resting in yon cluster of roots t'night?"

The day had drawn long, but now the darkness of night was quickly approaching them from the edges of the wilds. Maddau could see more shadows creeping under low vegetation and clustering in congregations amongst the trees. Haelder's point was made.

"Yes. I think, to be safe, we'd best seek shelter there. Food and water for the horses, and maybe shelter for us as well."

"How long d'ye think—" Haelder began.

"Maybe an hour's passing, no more," Twyll interrupted to answer. "Calm yourself, old man. Your delicate bones will soon cease the incessant rocking from your steed's frocking if you'd be patient a bit more."

Maddau strove to keep a calm face and fought against the rising giggles that were threatening the unbiased approach he strove to keep amongst the men. He knew that laughing would reinforce the open disrespect Twyll was showing to Haelder. He must remain neutral.

"Ye'd be lucky to achieve my *old age* with such commentary, Gonestrwydd." Haelder's voice was dry. "Especially with your less than kind inclinations towards my old bones."

Twyll began to laugh, and Maddau could not refrain any longer and joined in with his laughter. Haelder maintained an offended silence for a few moments more as they continued down the road, and then Maddau heard the older man's quiet chuckle. It was difficult for any of them to keep their tempers at Twyll for very long.

The sun continued its implacable descent towards the horizon, blanketing the higher regions in a light mantle of shadows. Certain creatures travel slower in the light, as it is just more comfortable for them to move under the grace of darkness' cover. Fiends of the darkness and the Cotheda knights count themselves among these creatures. While able to move in the light, they are by no means at the peak of their skills or abilities and are often handicapped by a reduction in strength. They are also sapped of their skills in the light. Throughout the long day, a viscous black ooze welled in the hoofprints left in the soft earthen road coming from Kastell Paol, heading west. Each hoofprint welled with a dark, thinly viscous substance until it overflowed like a large puddle into the next nearest imprint. In large gaps between prints, it filled to overflow the existing imprint, spilled over into a large plash of a muted midnight dark, and then pooled together as it moved onto the next print. These snatches of faded dark moved with liquid speed and an intelligence belied by their deliberate actions, just a steed's length behind the horses they followed. The setting sun allowed shadows to take delicate touches of the landscape and then grab greedy fistfuls of their surroundings as the dark plashes that had hid themselves amongst the earth imprintings began to quietly effervesce into the air, spilling up to mingle with the drawing shade that blanketed the branches of trees and bushes, pooling under rocks and in the dips of valleys. On occasion, the spirals of effervescent darkness would pool into the shadows of the horses as they traveled, stalking too close to the riders they coveted. Whenever this occurred, the horses would take to spirit, shying and feinting as though molested by some invisible entity whose energy mixed poorly with theirs. The Koteli regiment's mounts would inexplicably bolt or begin stamping wildly, disrupting the formation with the potential to upset the balance of the riders. The anxious antics of the horses only ceased when, through the stressed running patterns or frantic rearing, would spread enough light beneath the creatures to force the spirals of darkness to find more accommodating intermediate cover. Only then would the distressed mount soothe and cease its rearing and kicking or allow the rider to slow its gait and give the trailing regiment the opportunity to catch up.

The sun had mostly sunk to the line of the horizon by the time the Koteli regiment arrived at the small cluster of buildings. The spirals of darkness were now openly pouring up into the air, spooling upwards and spreading out to join with other streams that flowed from various random covers and imprints in the surrounding areas. The darkness seethed with intention and raw need, pulsating in the last of the fading light as it began to solidify, slowly at first, then more rapidly, taking on the shapes of five riders a furlong out from the small gathering of buildings. Four Cotheda riders formed full in the deepening gloom, their armor a darker swatch of space against even deeper colored steeds. The fifth rider was indistinct in form, as though not fully there. Its outline kept shifting and pooling in on itself, with a ropey, almost liquid quality the other riders did not possess. Fully reformed, save for one, they came together as a unit in an unspoken formation that moved to mirror the group they followed, staying just outside the remaining last tendrils of daylight that held on to the land, slithering to the day's end.

Maddau had not anticipated the frenetic activity that greeted them upon their arrival at the small intersection of the hamlet that had sprung up around a mild stream. He saw that the buildings were the dwellings of the families that farmed the area—their outland shacks and covered dwellings for their livestock. Just as they arrived at the largest of the buildings, he saw there were many people flitting to and fro about: gathering water from the stream, tending to a badly injured horse, and excitedly babbling together in a group. However, the chattering came to an abrupt halt as the knights drew nigh the main house and all turned to regard the regiment. Maddau could feel many eyes upon them, some hostile, some curious, all wary.

"Ra venigo ahanout an Aotrou, ha ra viro ahanout." *Gods bless you and keep you.* Maddau greeted them carefully, without dismounting.

"Ar memestra'faot din lâr dit, Aotrou." *The same to you, Master.* The eldest of the group answered him in rough, rural Breton that sounded ticklish to Maddau's ears.

Anticipating trouble, Twyll spoke up. "Can you tell us, what is the name of this place?"

"Santus Ronanus," the man answered in a flat voice, scratching absently at the fork in his pants. "Was decided to name the place after the man who owns the land around here. Is his house and buildings that make this place."

There was still a taste of nervous energy in the air and in the eyes of the crowd, although they were beginning to draw nearer to the horses and the knights. Twyll assessed the potential danger of the crowd before responding to the elder man with the white hair. "Santus Ronanus, you say? And are you Ronanus?"

"Not I, Aotrou. I be the goatherd. He be in the house seein' t' the rider from today."

"A rider?" Twyll demanded, "What rider?" His voice arced with a sharpness of tone that made several members of the regiment look towards him in surprise.

"No idea," the goatherd said promptly. "Jus' show'd up, dragging on that 'ere 'orse. Be surpris'd if'n 'ee lives longer'n dat 'orse. N'ouzon ket, *no idea*, what caused it. They took 'im inside."

He pointed to the largest dwelling there, just fifty strides or so away from where the regiment and their horses stood.

Slowly, together, the Koteli regiment turned to look at the building. Then, just as slowly, Twyll's head turned the other way, and he looked into Maddau's eyes.

"A rider?" His voice was so low that had Maddau not been close enough to touch him, he would have missed the words in the movement of the wind whispering the last of the day's light away.

"From where?" Maddau breathed, the fear an open secret on his face.

Without further words, Twyll and Maddau dismounted and quickly made for the main house. The rest of the regiment watched them in surprise and then began to dismount. Lymder assessed the assembling people and the conspicuous departure of their Captain and First Knight and then spoke in a calm tone to the rest of the men. "I'll stand post here at the house. Why don't you help them, Olwygg? Dra, Haelder, perhaps you should see to the horses. Burb, could you do patrol and the watch?"

The firm control in Lymder's voice instilled a level of calm obedience in the other knights, and they immediately broke for their individual tasks. Olwygg turned and vanished into the building, following Maddau and Twyll. Dra and Haelder collected the horses' reins and began leading them towards a smaller outbuilding where a couple piles of straw had been stacked for the animals. Lymder walked over to stand by the door and watched as Burdeb turned reluctantly away and began to walk towards the beaten track that circled the outside edges of the grouping of buildings.

Olwygg stepped through the rough-hewn door to find himself in a sparse and neat main room. Everything had been wrought from the materials provided by nature and the farm, and therefore were all the lovely colors of oak and ash, flower and bloom, horn and hoof. Olwygg saw that nothing went to waste here and nodded his approval as he entered. The room was furnished only with windows, a large table on the eastern side of the room, and two chairs near it. There were stairs to the upper floors set against the western wall, and there was a door in the back that ostensibly led to the rear kitchens. Maddau, Twyll, a man, and a woman had taken positions by the table, on which lay a man's body, with the Captain standing by the man's head. Twyll stood beside him at the prone man's side, and the two others mirrored the knights across the table. The injured man's belabored breathing punctuated the quiet murmurs of those surrounding him. Several candles had been placed around the room to provide light, and their flames danced in the draft, belying the seriousness of the situation. Olwygg approached the cluster of people around the table, and as he did, he saw the legs of the man. They hung off the end, too long in his body for his feet to rest comfortably or even be somewhat supported. Olwygg initially believed he saw a pair of red hose that ended in brown, muddy boots. He soon realized that was not the case. The boots were muddy, to be sure, but the original color of the hose was lost as they were soaked with blood. So fully wetted through, were the man's hose, that they dripped with regularity to puddle below the table. *The man's legs are hanging down from the thighs, so at least his shoulders, head, and trunk are supported,* Olwygg thought. He could see several long gashes that had been sliced into the calves and inside thighs of both legs. *To bleed him out yet leave him alive,* Olwygg surmised. *A battlefield move used to get answers from a captured foe while he still lived but not allow him a long enough life to escape.* As Olwygg drew closer, stepping next to Twyll, he could see more of the man on the table. The unfortunate wore a white tunic, similar to what the knightly regiment wore. But where the knights of virtue wore short tunics with a blue crossed star on their breast, this man's tunic—what remained of it—had been long so that its hem, red with blood up to the man's hips, trailed in ragged ends near his feet. Whatever had been embroidered on the tunic had been destroyed by huge tears from some encounter—with a sword, Olwygg guessed—that had cut open the man's guts. Red, clotted blood stained the man's belly, and wet bubbles appeared with each strained breath around the purple and blackened protrusions from the holes. Drawing up to Twyll's right side brought the man's face into view, and Olwygg gasped. It was clear that the man had been one of the Sages. He bore the mark of Wisdom, burned into his skin over his left eye. Where the eye had once been, though, was a ruined horror: a blackened-reddish hole that oozed yellow pus-like tears. The other eye was there, crystalline gold in hue, and aware. It fixated on Olwygg as he approached, and he felt an unmanning fear whip through him, cutting his movement and rooting him to the spot. He *knew* that eye… and the man to whom it belonged. There was but a single person in the caste of the Sages with eyes that hue, and he was the Keeper of the Mystery of Veneration. Olwygg had studied under him to understand the mysteries of his charge over the years and had become quite fond of the elder Sage. It had been his hope, long ago when he was but a naive lad, to train to one day succeed the Sage as a Keeper of the Mystery that carried his charge in life.

The man on the table became agitated, his remaining eye fixed on Olwygg's face. Frothy, foamy blood collected at the sides of the Sage's mouth as he gasped hoarsely, "*Haa… Owww… guggck!*"

Observing the Sage's obvious distress and the direction of his limited gaze, everyone around the table turned to look at Olwygg. Seeing the frozen, panicked shock on Olwygg's face, Twyll reached out to grasp the older knight's shoulder, simultaneously steadying him and providing a stoic form of comfort. Maddau, placing a gentle hand on the Sage's upper arm to restrain him, spoke in a voice just above a whisper to Olwygg, though his eyes never left the Sage's face. "We know not what happened. Master Ronanus here said his horse just rode up, lamed in the leg and bleeding, with this poor fellow hanging on him. From the looks of things, he's spent himself and his horse just to get this far.... But he has been unable to tell them what happened with any clarity. He's been in and out of his head since he arrived." Maddau glanced up at the man standing across the table from him for confirmation, who nodded without responding. "And he seems to be fated for worse."

"I'm not sure he'll last the night with those wounds," Twyll murmured, averting his eyes from the bubbling, frothy mess of the Sage's chest and belly. "The miracle is that he's lasted this long to get here. I wonder how he managed to get away from whatever... did this."

Olwygg could not speak. The Sage's remaining eye continued to fix-ate him, unable to look away, unable to turn from the horror this man had endured. He was being forced to bear witness to the indecency of his old mentor's reduction to this vexatious state. The brilliant wisdom of the Sage's mind was wiped clean of its auspices and attentions. Focused only now on the single imperative to survive. To prolong life, moment by moment, just a little longer by brutally clawing breath back into his ravaged lungs that had been disinterred from his body and now floated somewhere between the two worlds of within the body and the outside world: somewhat removed and outside the body, and still yet trying to remain in the ribs' embrace.

Maddau caught the farmer's eye and nodded his head towards the door. Ronanus nodded and reached his hand over to catch the edge of the woman's apron. She had been watching Twyll in wary awe, and the farmer's movements made her jump. Maddau turned and walked through the door in the back of the room, confident that the farmer and his woman would follow. He stepped from the main room of the farmhouse into a long, rectangular room that ran the length of the back of the house. It was easily wide enough to accommodate two able-bodied people beside each other and consisted of several containers of root vegetables and small apples.

"*Digarez.* I apologize," Maddau murmured when they were out of ear-shot of the ravaged Sage and the others. "He is one of us. Whatever happened to him, thank you for your kindness in caring for him."

Ronanus nodded stiffly. "Our people have known the Wisdom Keepers of the Temple for many lifetimes now. They have always been good to us, helped guide us, and helped the land. But never did they leave the Temple; always we went to them. Why is one here alone? Why is one hurt so? We do not know. This troubles me."

"Troubles us all," The farmer's wife stated shortly in her rural Breton. "What'ver that did t'im… did for 'im but well. Soon he'll be food for the land, with the blessing."

"Silence woman!" Ronanus hissed in fury, cutting a quick glance at Maddau and then glaring at her.

She narrowed her eyes at the farmer without paying any attention to Maddau. "Be it so, whether they want it or not. He be not long on this land; none come back from those wounds."

"Be it so or be it not, ye'd not have to speak it to be, woman!" Ronanus chastised her and then looked apologetically at Maddau. "Forgive us, Aotrou. We speak with mind most times."

Maddau gave the farmer a tired smile. "*Rien eo*, it's nothing, friend. Speaking plainly is sometimes best. Could we trouble you to stay the night? We are on our way to the Temple and can look after the Sage in his duress."

Ronanus frowned. "I can put up three in here, but I'm afraid the rest must stay in the outrooms. We've not spare room in the house, Aotrou. Sorry. We can feed the lot, though."

Maddau nodded to him. "It will be more than enough, and your kindness will be well received. I thank you, Ronanus, and your lady for your hospitality to us and to the Sage." He bowed to them and returned to the large room, where the Sage continued to articulate his distress. Twyll and Olwygg were conversing in low tones as he approached, and Olwygg turned toward him as he arrived.

"Captain," Olwygg's voice trembled at the edges but had the undercurrent steel of conviction running through it. "Gonestrwydd and I 'ave talked, an' it's been decided. I will care for the man."

Maddau stared at the elder knight. He could feel Twyll's eyes on him, studying him, yet he stayed focused on Olwygg and kept his gaze. The elder knight was road worn and tired. His age betrayed him in body in most ways these days, and he could use a good meal or three. Yet a conviction burned in the man's eyes that told Maddau that, should he argue against this, it was not a fight he would win.

"Y'er certain, Ols?" he asked, though the answer rang clear in the posture of the elder knight's body and the stricture of his face.

"Aye be. 'Tis all I can do fer the man, an' I owe 'im as much an' more. Much more."

Ronanus and his wife had returned to the room and now stood behind Maddau, overhearing the discussion.

"You can stay in this room, Aotrou knight," Ronanus said in a quiet voice. He then looked to Maddau. "And you can stay in the over-room." He then turned his eyes to Twyll. "And you—"

"I'll be staying with the others," Twyll interrupted. "There's not room in here for all of us, and someone will need to oversee keeping guard. Whatever harmed this Sage... mayhap is still out there."

A silence descended on the group; they had not considered this. Whatever had attacked the Sage might be stalking them yet, just outside the safety of the buildings. The farmer stared around at the structure of the building as if evaluating the robustness of the design. The woman covered her mouth with her hands, and her eyes grew large as she, too, stared around the room, conning the shadows for monsters hidden in the furniture or the cracks of the base or floorboards. Maddau closed his eyes in resignation. He had been so focused on the Sage, Olwygg, the Farmer and his wife that he had neglected to think about the potential threat still out there. And what of their mission? And the Darkness? He had lost sight of these things while focusing on the Sage's predicament. Yet Twyll had easily anticipated concerns far beyond the immediate. Of course he had. He always did. And in doing so, he reminded Maddau again how ill-equipped he himself was for the job of being captain of the Koteli. Maddau sighed to himself, thinking again that it should have been Twyll as their Captain...

Maddau followed the Farmer's wife up the stairs to the over-room. The farmhouse was well made, and the craftsmanship was sound. However, the finishing was only for the lower floor and the main rooms. The stairs were left unfinished with rough wood edging, and while the pieces were crafted with attention, more than one splinter caught in Maddau's hands as he tried to guide himself by touch in the dimness. There were no recesses for lighting or natural light, and he was glad for her company to guide him, as moving through the darkness was disorienting. The trip up to the shallow hallway was brief, and Maddau soon found himself at the head of a short hallway with two rooms branching off. She gestured to the room on the left side of the short hallway that faced the front of the farmhouse, overlooking the stables and the small front yard. He stepped past her and entered the small room. Across from the door was an overhead window that let in the fading traces of the day. On the left side of the room was a small pallet of straw, bound loosely together with scraps of cloth and heavy twine. The right side of the room boasted a small stool, low to the ground and worn in the middle, and a rough container fashioned from the remains of old tree stumps, on which was a worn-looking earthenware bowl with several chips missing from the rim. This room looked well used, and Maddau surmised that he was taking someone's normal bed for the night. He looked back towards the Farmer's wife, wondering how he could suggest staying with the others without offending her.

"We shall sleep in t'other room. Guest has best place to stay." Her terse voice, already choppy from using a strange language, matched her pinched face and gave away what Maddau suspected. He *was* taking someone's bed for the night. Most likely hers. The look on her face was none too pleased for it.

"I'm sorry to trouble you…. Wait. What are you called?"

Her face twisted, her nostrils flaring as if she smelled something odious and offensive, and her eyes squinted into slits so close they were almost shut.

"Jantielle." Her rough voice was stern in the passing quiet. "I call myself Jantielle Ronanus."

He smiled at her, more in relief than good humor, and tried to imitate what he thought Twyll would do to put her more at ease.

"I am Maddau, Captain of the Koteli Knights. *Itron*, Lady Jantielle Ronanus, we are most indebted to you and your husband for hosting us this night and for caring for one of the Sages of the Temple in his duress." He dropped his head slightly forward, bowing at the shoulders, and swung his sword arm wide. It felt foppish and more than a little grandiose, but he hoped it would communicate his appreciation in a way that would convey that her hospitality was an honor for him and his regiment. She made no response. After a few moments of awkward silence while he held the pose, he glanced up at her. One look at her face told him the overture was ill-received. He had not thought it possible that her face would crinkle in on itself any further, but indeed, that is what it did. She now looked as though whatever odious smell had previously besieged her was now coating the inside of her nostrils, and she was twisting her face to relieve it. Her upper lip had pulled upward in disgust, causing her lower lip to jut forward in a moue, and her eyes were completely squinched closed. She fanned her hands, one before her face and the other back at him, almost in a warding gesture as she stepped, without looking back, backwards down the hall and towards the stairs. He could hear her stomping down the stairs back to the main floor, muttering to herself in a garbled mixture of Breton and something else. He could scarcely make out anything through the echoing banging of her feet on the stairs, but there was one thing he thought he heard clearly enough.

"Knights... k'telly... knights..." He was sure she was muttering the words over and over, her voice tripping over them as though through a mouthful of rocks.

Maddau let his arm drop to his side and felt the reddening flames of shame creep up the sides of his face and neck. The gesture, something he was sure would have been acceptable, even laudable, had it been Twyll, had come across to her as pretentious and "Lord o'er Thee." Not at all what he was trying to convey. Now that he had insulted her, she had fled him out of hospitality rather than put him in his place. He breathed out a long exhale and waited for the sounds of her retreat to die away after she had reached the main floor. He did not want to agitate her further, and it was probably best to not engage in any further behavior that she might find insulting while Olwygg was tending the Sage in the main room. Goodness knows they did not need to prolong the Sage's suffering by enacting an encounter with the locals in his presence. Maddau glanced down at the pallet in the corner. Its presence deftly reminded him that a day of riding was behind him, and he felt the weary pull of exhaustion from his back and at the base of his neck. It had been truly a long day, and the pallet called to his weary body with a siren's soliloquy of the desire for comfort and release from the day's cares. The small square of window in the room showed now the overcoming inky darkness of night. Maddau's stomach gave a small grumble, further reminding him that food had not been forthcoming during the day's ride. A rueful smirk twisted its way across his lips as he reached for his bag, hanging beneath his cloak. He doubted that a well-stocked meal would greet him this eve. Not after how he'd insulted Jantielle. He would do well to satiate his hunger with whatever remains he could pull from his personal bag and replenish that on the morrow before they rode out. It was doubtful that the Sage would endure this world much longer, and Maddau suspected that the dawn, or shortly soon after, would bring an end to his suffering.

A quick sorting of his pack brought to his attention the roughened canvas-wrapped relic, his spare shirt, a roll of bandage cloth, and a small provision pouch, tied loosely with a leather thong. He pawed through the small pouch and came up with a rind of bread that had the tiniest bit of green around the edges, a few wilted tree nuts, and three shriveled berries from a local vine. Meager as it was, he suspected it would quell his stomach before he rested for the night. Maddau labored for a moment in his thoughts over the wisdom of eating his provisions all in one go or parsing them to delay the moment of ending this scant feast. The truth, he knew, was that it mattered little in the end. His stomach gave another growl, a little louder this time, and his guts twisted in a pang. The debate over the wisdom of process was set aside for the necessity of satiation. He scooped the nuts and berries together into his mouth and began to chew them over while he pondered the bread rind. He ran his fingers along the more colorful edge of the crust, using his thumbnail to scrape away the powdery little circles of mold bloom. He swallowed the macerated lump of berry and nut mixture in his mouth and quickly took a bite of the rind before he could think about the fact that it had had mold bloom there just moments before. The crust was hard and stale beyond mere crunch, and it hurt his jaw to bite into it. He bit down forcefully on the crust, mashing it into smaller pieces and swallowing them quickly. The bread chunks slid slowly down his throat, sticking partway down and settling uneasily in his gut. His stomach contracted at the lack of moisture in his meal, but he knew it could not be helped.

With the pouch empty of its contents, Maddau placed everything back into his pack and placed the pack on the pallet. He wrapped his cloak tightly about his body and sank down onto the pallet, placing his head carefully on his pack and kicking off his boots.

He closed his eyes and tried to get his body to relax. The tension of the day had nested in the hard-to-reach spot in the middle of his back, between his shoulders. His upper back was aching, and no matter how he shifted, he could not find a comfortable position. Using his pack as a lump pillow did little to provide comfort, but it alleviated his fear of losing the relic. After much tossing and turning and finding no satisfaction, he eventually found a position that was not too disagreeable. His mind settled, and his body finally quieted. Time passed, and he could feel his thoughts slipping away to more agreeable topics than the discomfort of his body or the fatigue the day had brought.

In his last moments tethered to consciousness, he thought he heard a merry, laughter-tinged voice whisper "Maddau" in the darkness.

Chapter Five

Blood Sacrifice

Flickering candlelight played across the room, playing catch as can with the shadows it chased around. Olwygg's forehead rested on his knuckles as he leaned wearily into the prayers that rocked his wizened frame. He mouthed the words entreatingly to the Almighty of the Light on behalf of the Sage over and over again. Begging for healing. Begging for a return to health. Begging for the soothing of his mind. Begging for a calming of his soul.

Begging. Just… begging.

Like a dog.

Hours ago, his mouth had attained the quality of roughened sand, and his swollen tongue grated against his lips as he tried to spread any moisture left in his mouth against his lips. Shadows flitted around the room; Olwygg prayed in entreaty and in veneration.

The silence was pierced by a strangled cry. Olwygg opened his eyes to a horrific sight: a pall had set upon the old Sage's skin, and his features had settled into a stony laxness. Belying the peaceful aura of death that draped him, from his throat came an agonized mewling like that of a small animal caught in a trap it could not survive or escape.

Olwygg desperately wanted to quit this vigil for fear of what was to come. Yet he was unable to remove his eyes from the perfect display of liminality before him. Olwygg regarded his charge miserably. The mewling grew in volume and then died off to a soft chuffering from deep within the old man's throat.

Only when this, too, had trailed away did Olwygg finally stretch forth a trembling hand to seek for signs of life. The Sage's skin had attained a marbled cast, and it chilled Olwygg's hand. No stirring of life could be felt in the silent body that lay before him. Olwygg rose to do a breath check, and then hesitated. The stillness of the man was profound, but...

But what? he chided himself. The old one was dead. He had seen dead bodies before, and this was no different. He should be deep in prayer for the man's spirit to commend it to the Light.

Except that it was. It was different. This was the body of one he had revered—one he had hoped to emulate one day. And it was a body badly destroyed by something dark—something of the Dark.

A deep chill settled just below his stomach, and its cold spread through his body, setting off an unquellable shiver. Olwygg stared at the Sage's mauled face. He must do the breath check, he knew. It was necessary to ensure the man's spirit had parted ways with the world of life. It was of no consequence to him to lean over and place his cheek near the poor body's nose and mouth to ensure no breath yet dwelt within, and no harm could come of it. He knew that, and it was the least of the actions to take for the poor body. Olwygg knew all these things, and yet...

The candlelight flickered again, dimming a bit as shadows chased across the walls. The brief halo of light the candle provided encapsulated Olwygg in its aura and shrank ever so slightly with each passing moment. In the corners of the room, shadows had begun to pool and deepen.

The breath of air in the room had ceased to move as life fled the ravaged Sage. Olwygg could feel the closeness of the room pressing in; drawing breath became more difficult, and a dimness was starting to eat away the light at the edges of the room. He knew fear was irrational at this moment, but the presence of Death here with him—Death caused by the Dark in such a savage way—unsettled him.

The presence of Death was so profound in the darkest moments of the night that Olwygg almost felt he could see the Specter in the Dark. A coalescing shape of deeper darkness amidst the shadows; man-like in form yet made of gently swirling darkness. As the swirling specks of shadow-form became more pronounced and the Darkness more distinct from the pale shadows that painted the walls, the Specter seemed to move forward at a pace towards Olwygg and the dead Sage. It seemed Death had come in person for the venerable old man.

Never taking his eyes from the new presence in the room, Olwygg's desert of a throat found the ability to give voice to the formerly unfounded terror that had turned out to be well-founded after all. He began to pray.

No moon shone in the ratty circle of standing stones five hundred paces from Santus Ronanus. A circle of dry earth, devoid of any greenery, where five large stones, a man's height and width in form, were placed. Equidistant, and with a stone at each point of a man's body around the borders of the circle, this had been made a special place by the inhabitants of the area for sacrifice and thanks given to the spirits of the land, sea, and sky. It had fallen into disuse over the years as another form of worship moved through the land, but people still came to venerate the Old Ways and keep the elder customs by and by. In the darkness of the standing stones, a form lay on the ground. With his head facing the headstone and arms and legs pointing appropriately to the others, Cynddaredd gazed up at the midnight sky, where not a single star glimmered. A heavy cloud fall had set in during the night, and neither the moon nor stars could be seen.

"I call upon the Walker. You who trods the planes of Dusk." Cynddaredd's voice lanced sharp through the night, hissing and spiky. "I call upon you, Walker. Come!"

At the edge of the circle, between the stones toward which Cynddaredd's legs pointed, the air began to move with a restless anxiety as swirling motes of blackness began to dance in the space.

"Walker! Come!" Cynddaredd commanded again, his voice no louder than before and yet sharper and spikier than ever.

The swirling motes of Dark spun faster, and then faster still. The fabric of the air began to shred between the specks of the Dark. A thin, blood-red scream emitted into the night as the veil of reality was ripped apart as first the charred and blackened pommel of a great sword and then a pair of spike-mailed gloves protruded into the air. Next, the ebony scales of the armor belonging to the Lance Knight of the Cotheda and the vicious death's head helmet appeared. Cenfigen stepped through the veil between the worlds and into the circle of the standing stones. Due to its length, his great sword took the longest to move through, and the end of the blade dragged through the dust in the ground, scoring a deep gouge in the earth as it moved from one plane of existence into the next.

As Cenfigen passed into the circle, the shredded remnants of the atmosphere between the worlds fell together to reseal the hole torn by his passing. The feathery edges of the fabric between the planes of existence that clung to his armor as he passed through fluttered down to dark dust on the ground, disappearing as it came in contact with the earth and leaving no indication of the violent force that had just rent its way into the world.

"I call upon the Walker, Dusk Treader from the Planes of Pain, Limnalist from the Razor's Edge of the Veil, to heed my call!" Cynddaredd's words spit into the night, shredding the ominous quiet that surrounded him again. "Heed, Walker!"

Cenfigen stood at the edge of the circle, gripping the hilt of his great sword, and made no movement. His voice was the deepest echoing cry of despair at life's end, the wailing bespectered misery of errands unfinished, and the reluctant relinquishing in the final moments of life as breath fled the body and wrested the final tethers of the soul from their anchors. It was a hollow, defeated sound that luxuriated in its own weak-kneed acquiescence.

"I HEED."

Cynddaredd's wizened, blackened lips writhed in the delicious anticipation of a dark deed and a darker result. "Walker," he hissed, spittle flying, "I call upon you to step into the decaying world of another who yet lingers beyond their time. Seek him out and transgress the Veil. Do my bidding, and you may have the pure spirit of a Koteli Sage that hovers nearby as your reward. Heed, Walker!"

Silence was the only response to the hissing voice from the center circle of the standing stones. Cynddaredd's armor scraped and ground against the earth as he shifted his arm to his waist and gripped the short handle protruding from the joints in his mail. A hard tug pulled a sharply serrated dagger from its hidden sheath. The anticipation of what the next few moments would bring quickened his blood and breath, bringing a dark elation and a rising bloodlust.

"Heed, Walker!" he panted. "You are set by my words and bound by my blood! You will answer my call and do as I demand. Feed upon the pure spirit of the Koteli Sage. Inhabit the decaying world it left behind, and destroy all who surround it and set themselves against you! Come! Walker! HEED!"

Raising the dagger above his chest as his malice-fueled whispers fulfilled the invocation to the psychopomp of the Dark, Cynddaredd pulled it down at the last moment. The forked tip of the blade easily pierced the gores of his armor above the second rib and slid down. The pain did not announce its presence in the first moments; it was just a minor feeling of discomfort, as with a stubbed toe. It was the spreading warmth, contrasting with the chill of the night air and the ground below him, that informed his senses the blade had cut true. And deep.

Cenfigen, bound in the ritual of blood, stepped into the circle with slow and measured steps. He approached the wounded Cynddaredd and continued moving forward, bypassing his feet and stepping over Cynddaredd's prone form until he stood astride the commander's chest. The long greats-word's end was planted between Cynddaredd's legs.

Suddenly, he dropped violently to crouch above the commander's chest, letting the poleyn covering his knee impact the hilt of the dagger, jamming it further into Cynddaredd's torso, twisting it down at an angle, and slamming the tip of the blade into the earth below, pinning him there. The violence of the blow's impact forced Cynddaredd's shoulders and hips upwards reactively, and Cenfigen caught the edge of Cynddaredd's helmet before he could lay back down. Blood sprayed up between Cenfigen and Cynddaredd, coating their armors in the swirling darkness.

"I… HEED!" Cenfigen rasped, the ichor of his breath flaring out from his helmet, engulfing the commander's helmet in a miasma of the blackest impending doom. The foul air of his words spread about, encircling the standing stones. As it moved, it transformed into swirling shadow fragments that danced about the circle. Once, twice, and three times, it transgressed the starless night. And when the final act of the parade of shadowlets had completed its arc through the standing stones, Cenfigen was gone, and Cynddaredd lay alone in the circle in a spreading pool of his own lifeblood.

Flickering shadows danced above Olwygg's bowed head. All the other candles had long burned out in the room, and only the one beside him was left, and it was no more than a finger's width in span. The urgency and fervor of his prayers increased in measure with the growing presence in the room. Over and over, he repeated the prayer of Veneration to the Light, chasing it with the prayers of Forgiveness and of Purity. These were the standard prayers at the end of life, and they were ones he had known by heart and mind since he had joined the regiment. Over and over again, hailing the life of the Sage, giving thanks for his service to the Wisdom of the Light, begging forgiveness for his transgressions in body, mind, and spirit, and hailing the purity of his actions. Olwygg repeated this until his voice ran out and until his mind ran a rabbit's race around and around the track on its own plan. As his lips mouthed the words and his heart mouthed the pain of the loss of his mentor, the unmanning terror that had built in his heart began, little by little, to slip away. The presence of the specter seemed to have lessened a bit, and his awareness of the presence had fled without any indication of its passing. Quietly, and with a gently growing sense of complacent peace, the old Knight's thoughts started to wander into the dreamlike trance brought about by fully submersing oneself in prayer in the small hours of the night. His head remained bowed low over his hands, and as he prayed, his upper eyelids slid down to meet their mates.

The dancing flame guttered, bringing the shadows ever closer to the table, the corpse that lay upon it, and the dozing Knight that sat beside it with his bowed head and folded hands resting fully upon it beside the body. The tiny spark of light clung to the crumbling wick and then skirted across the liquid offcut of the wax that pooled on the table's edge, dancing around the few fibers left protruding from the pool of cooling wax before dimming to a soft bluish glow. The final circle of warmish light that surrounded Olwygg had faded away to a soft, grey, enfolding shadow that finally winked into darkness as the last blue spark disappeared. As the embrace of the dark filled the room, a soft snore issued from the mouth of the sleeping Knight. His heart still quietly mouthed the prayers his lips had abandoned as sleep claimed him.

A few moments passed, with the faint breathy wheezes of air passage through the old Knight's nostrils being the only sound in the room. Then the farmhouse settled creakily as the cooler outside air caused the rough-hewn wood to contract into its joints and supports. Mild skittering noises came from below the floor as the inevitable field mouse set about in search of a meal.

The first tattered scrap of shadow bled from the tiny gap between the floorboards and cartwheeled around the room. Another followed, boiling up from the gap and following the first as it danced and spun in the air. Soon more followed, exploding from the floor gaps in a flood of ragged shadowlets, spinning and flowing until they began to merge into a puddling pool in the corner of the room nearest the table upon which the once-Sage's body rested.

The pooling shadows frothed and draped, hanging in darkly gossamer webs as shadowlet additions continued to attach themselves to the ponderously rising form. Amorphous and indistinct, the flowing, wavy form rose higher and higher, up to the full height of a tall man's measure. More shadowlets fled from the walls to join the apparition as it filled out in form; dark points began to expand out from beneath the flowing lines of shadow. First, the harsh lines of the shoulders, with wicked points spiking up into the air above where the shoulders jutted. Next, the rounded shape of the head elongated upward, and the profile firmed into hardened points above the crown of the head. The rest of the body was draped into the shadows, with no noticeable protrusions, save for a long expansion in the rear of the shadowy form to which the last joint shadowlets clung, forming a ridge like that of a weapon that drug along the ground.

With the arrival of this specter of shadows in the room, a deep chill began to permeate the farmhouse, and a soft rustling sound could be heard whispering in from the eves. It was as though the presence of the shadowy form leached the heat from the very fibers of the building and pulled all the warmth of life out of the air, leaving behind in its wake the coldness of absence.

Olwygg shivered in his drowsiness, unconsciously hunching his shoulders closer and pulling his knees up against the roughened stool between that and the table his sleeping form slouched against.

The shadow draped figure approached the table in silence. Each movement it made, though without distinct articulation due to the webbish draping of the shadowlets at its base, brought it more and more from the realm of the intangible shade into that of the physical being. As it drew near, the movements were pronounced steps, and the still subtle form of the body shifted with each step. The right shoulder moved, and the bloom of an arm appeared below the draping darkness. The arm raised higher, and the shadowy webbish draping began to fall away, revealing first the spiked ridges of a gauntlet-enshrouded hand. The hand stretched and splayed the fingers, articulating smoothly despite the pointed, metallic, blackened joints in the armor. The hand rose further, with more shadowy draping falling away, revealing an armored forearm and mailed upper arm. Drawing closer to the once-Sage's body, the hand hovered above the ruined face, covering the upper left section of the head in a darker shade of night. The middle finger of the hand descended to point down. With ponderous slowness, the hand and its pendulously rigid finger descended to the once-Sage's face, paused for a moment as though considering, and then continued to descend.

The finger slipped into the reddened and raw hole once occupied by the Sage's left eye, violently scoring the flesh around the eye socket and erupting watery yellow pus from the inflamed ducts. The brand of Wisdom over the Sage's eye was torn asunder by the rough, mailed digit's relentless descent. Thin blood welled around the finger joints in the gauntlet as it descended further into the eye socket, piercing the thin membrane that had once been behind the eye. As the gauntleted finger penetrated the once-Sage's skull up the third knuckle, light began to emanate from the orifices in the skull, streaming away from the remaining eye, the nostrils, the ear channels, and the mouth as though it fled the presence of the intruding digit. The body began to shiver, emitting a hollow rattling from deep within the spaces between the joints and bones.

Moments had passed since Cenfigen's discorporal form had streamed into non-existence. Cynddaredd lay on the soaked earth, panting against the pulsating ache in his side. Little sprays of blood and ichor flew from the grill of his helm with each passing breath and dotted the collar of his mail in a fine bloody lace pattern. The night had gone quiet again with the Planeswalker's departure, and now the silence was broken by the distant call of a bird.

Cynddaredd waited, the flesh in his side still roiling against the blade that yet pinned him to the ground, and continued the physical part of the invocation to the Lance Knight's services. The pain was maddening, but he needed confirmation that Cenfigen was nowhere near before he could move. He wanted to ensure the pact was sealed and that the work would be done.

The pain was a distraction. He had to focus on the matter at hand and avoid any distraction that could scatter his attention further. Giving Cenfigen the pact and thereby giving orders for him to attack would anger the Commander, and Cynddaredd did not want to be the target of the Commander's anger.

Just look at what happened to Blys. Cynddaredd needed to achieve his goals without delay.

Another bird call broke the heavy hold of silence in the night. Sweat pooled at the collar of his mail as Cynddaredd started to move. He grasped the handle of the dagger with both hands and began to heave it upward, but it did not budge. He looked down in disbelief, gripped the handle more tightly in his right hand, and pulled upward again. The force of pulling up and at an angle caused the scalloped edge of the knife to cut another line as it twisted into the meat surrounding it, yet it still did not budge. Fresh warmth oozed against his back as frustrated panic caused him to yank at the knife's handle and hilt. It still did not move.

A footstep behind his head finally caused Cynddaredd's yanking at the pinned blade to cease. He rolled his head back, twisting it bonelessly to the side as he did so, and started straight into the baleful and pridefully malicious magenta eyes of Malchder.

"I see you are incapacitated, Cynddaredd." He stepped to the side and began to walk slowly around the prone Cotheda First Knight, regarding him with an intense, gleeful study. His eyes shone in the moonless darkness, creating pinkish halos on his face. "Or napping while I do all the work!"

Cynddaredd spat bloody phlegm at Malchder's words.

"I would rather have sacrificed your blood to the pact for Cenfigen's work had you been here!" He hissed, his words splitting the darkness in his fury. "But as always, you were late."

Malchder had completed his circle around the prone Cynddaredd and now looked askance at the First Knight's predicament. "Well, well, then. Looks like you have managed to get yourself into quite a bit of trouble there. Caught, are you? Mmm…. And it would be nothing for me to fix it, of course."

"Enough of your preening. Aid me before I scatter your bones to the depths of the planes beyond!" Cynddaredd's voice dripped with the acid of disdain.

Malchder drew closer and leaned down to where Cynddaredd lay.

"What of it if I don't?" he inquired, his eyes glowing brighter in the dark. He reached forward and grasped the handle of the blade, carelessly knocking Cynddaredd's weak hands away in the process. With a grunt, he yanked the blade out in one convulsive heave.

When it separated from Cynddaredd's flesh, the blade's metal began unraveling into thousands of tiny red sparks as the pieces that made up the blade in this world boiled into un-being. In moments, the blade had ceased to be, and the handle had fallen away into shadowy withers. Where seconds before Malchder had held the horrible woe-slung blade of Cynddaredd's charge, now there was nothing to show it had ever been there at all.

The First Knight rolled weakly to his side and attempted to get to his knees. That attempt failed. He had lain pinned to the ground for long enough that his bloody shape had soaked into the ground where he had lain. His side was split from the blade's work, and although the shadowy trails of his life were dripping out of him still, the wound was beginning to close now that the blade no longer pierced his flesh.

Malchder looked on with disdain as Cynddaredd tried again and finally succeeded in gaining his knees. "You should be more thankful for my assistance, Cynddaredd." His voice grated in Cynddaredd's ears.

Cynddaredd clenched his arms, causing muscle twitches below his armor and making fresh blood spill from the fast-closing wound. The desire to reform his blade and rend Malchder's mocking face in two whipped through his thoughts, yet he held himself still. Now, while he healed, was not the time to test his body in a fight with the prideful sot. It would not advance their cause.

"Shut yer wyrm-infused gob! We are to take the lambs of the Light tonight to the slaughter. It is the Commander's will, and we shall see it bring an end to their world. Take Gwanc and encircle the place with your wolves. Kill any who dare to oppose you. Ensure none escape. The Commander wishes to take them there tonight."

Malchder's glowing eyes regarded the Cynddaredd for a moment longer, open disdain staining his face. He gave no acknowledgement to the First Knight of the Cotheda before he melded back into the shadows of the surrounding stones from whence he came.

"You'd not be free if not for me, remember." His words floated back to Cynddaredd in the cool night air as he departed.

"Oh, I'll remember." The bleeding had ceased, and now that he was able to stand, Cynddaredd reformed his blade in his hand and tucked it back into the joints of his armor. "I'll remember well when your boastful throat is choking on the steel of my wrath. I'll remember this, indeed, Malchder. And a memory is all you'll be."

The slavering mouths of the two of the wolves of the Dark hung open as they raced through the night. The pads of their feet beat the earth with each step, sending any small life that dwelt near their runs away and causing it to flee in search of a place for respite throughout the night. Far and away through twisting fields of grain, across muddied rivulets where creekbeds had scarcely run dry, and into and around each small hovel and hidden wild run, they plundered and claimed whatever lives they could find. Encircling the huddled buildings of Ronanus, they found the small barn where the smell of ripe, plump piglets sleeping with rich dreams of warm sun and feed as they snuggled against the sow, amid the riper scents of sweat and roadwear of adult menfolk in the adjoining stable. The two wolves skulked silently inside, tongues hanging out as they chuffed in the breath of the sleeping livestock. They nosed about the hay bales for a moment, drippy ropes of saliva hanging from their jaws. The sow grunted in her sleep as she rolled over, causing small squeals of indignation to erupt from her side. The wolves stilled, tasting the air before them, and together they turned to look towards the quieting pigs.

As a unit, they approached the pen.

Burdeb paced around the slight track that surrounded the collection of shambling buildings. It was clear from the patchy growth encroaching into the furrow that this was only used during times when predators assailed the livestock or the inhabitants needed to guard against miscreants. The moonless night allowed little room for error; one misstep guaranteed an injury, and he could ill afford such distractions when his job was to be on guard. He strove for vigilance, to redeem himself for his weakness, so that his Captain would not have cause to doubt him ever again. Yet his heart was not in it. He could feel dejection setting in; being the only one sent out for patrol whilst the others rested or saw to the urgent situation in the farmhouse did not give him confidence he could redeem himself in the Captain's eyes. He was unreliable to Gonestrwydd and Maddau because of his personal failings, and as such he could not even be trusted around the group, so they sent him away. To the periphery of the situation, where he could do no harm to the regiment's mission.

He methodically placed one foot in front of the other, watching his step to ensure equal footing while scanning the shadow-strewn landscape. He looked towards the hamlet, where the buildings slumbered in the darkness, darker shadows against the landscape of the night. Only one spark of light broke the surrounding darkness, coming from the corner window of the farmhouse. As he watched, it winked out, and shadows flooded into the swallow where the light had been. He paused midstep, still looking in the direction of the farmhouse, his mouth going dry. The way the light had just been swallowed away by the darkness, something about that sudden extinguishment of the last bastion of the Light in the night opened a gnawing and bottomless feeling of dread below his stomach. It felt wrong.... Somehow, it felt... portentous.

A frenetic scream of terror split the night. Burdeb startled, his feet tangling together as he turned suddenly in the direction of the sound. Several more screams erupted into the night, creating a cacophony of horror that painted the shadowy landscape in shades of terror, anguish, and fear. And it was coming from the direction of the stables.

He waited only a moment before jolting into a run towards the stables. He kept his eyes on the low-slung building on the far side of the path he had so recently traversed. As he ran, there were more screams, repeating brays that evoked terror over and over.

A grey-brown shape darted across the path just in front of him. He pulled his chest back, trying to avoid a collision. His left foot came down wrong on one of the overgrowths that had reached into the trail, and his ankle rolled underneath him. Burdeb toppled forward, landing hard on the outside of his shin, and the splintering crack of yielding bone overrode his terror from the screaming stables. A white flash of pain exploded, engulfing his attention in the raucous fire that shot up through his ankle, into his leg, up the fork of his crotch to his chest, and dancing-stepped up the back of his neck, lighting up his body in pain as it flew around, alerting his body to the major event. An unwitting screech tore its way out of the side of his mouth as he went down with his mangled ankle slithering underneath his still forward-moving frame, and he braced himself on the palms of his hands to keep from landing on his nose. His forward trajectory dragged him along the path, scraping and bloodying his hands and forearms.

The screams fell suddenly silent from the stable as if in response to his cry of pain, and the surrounding silence seemed very loud in their absence. Burdeb was ignorant of the silence, as he was wholly engulfed in the microcosm of his own pain and all the facets of that world therein. So engrossed was he in the assessment of the physical that he also failed to notice the large wolf just a few paces off the path.

Perhaps he could have been forgiven for missing a lighter shadow amidst the cloaking gloom, but the sparkling magenta glow that emanated glee from the beast's eyes would have caught Burdeb's attention had he not been so focused on his own pain. The wolf tilted its head to the side and listened to the bleating mewls coming from the broken Knight as he lay on the ground. Its mouth opened wide, showing many rows of sharp teeth that seemed to go all the way back into the throat of the beast. The wolf heaved himself back onto his rear paws, and as he did so, he planted his paws more firmly in the dense vegetation. The rear legs twisted, cracking and grinding as they elongated, and the knees forced through to flex the joint, closing in the rear instead of the front. The pelvis separated and spread open to retilt upwards as the spine thinned and curved upwards, with the ribs reshifting to sit squarely above the hips. The cuffs of the shoulders opened up and back, opening the chest and allowing the neck to raise further. With a final cracking and a loud pop, the wolf had now contorted its body from its original form and taken on the form of a man. The blood clotted and matted fur fused together to form the shape of the armor of the prideful Cotheda chevalier, Malchder. His baleful eyes glowing with contempt, the newly transformed chevalier strode towards the bepained Burdeb.

The crunching of the weeds off the path cut through the curtain of pain ringing in his ears and brought Burdeb's head around to the approaching Malchder. In the darkness, he thought he saw two glowing eyes set into the shaggy form of a wolf's head. Burdeb shook his head, trying to clear the fog in his brain from his mangled leg. He knew it couldn't be right what he had seen—glowing eyes set into a wolf's head at a man's height? That wasn't possible. It might be the pain that causes phantoms to dance before his eyes.

He shook his head again, grinding the heel of one palm into each eye in turn, smearing the blood on his palm across his face, and turned back to look right into the glittering eyes of Malchder, who had crossed the distance without a sound and now crouched beside him, not a hand's span away.

"Hello, Lightbringer," Malchder purred, his voice dripping with malicious disdain.

Burdeb felt real fear. Without any introduction or foretelling, this man knew him as Koteli. As he stared into the sparkling and dancing eyes before him, he understood that this was an agent of the Darkness. And he was at a disadvantage. None knew that he was out here, save Gonestrwydd. None knew of the danger that now perched right beside him. None knew of his injury out here, far from the stables, and with the slaughter-born screams still trailing in the darkness, none would mistake his screams for anything different. Or come to his aid.

Burdeb licked his lips. "Yer one of Them." He croaked. "One of th' Dark."

Malchder's smile widened, again showing many rows of teeth. Too many for anything…human.

Burdeb recoiled from the chevalier's grin and signed himself against the Darkness, muttering a fervent prayer of preservation to the Light. At his words, Malchder's grin seemed to widen even more.

"Come now, Lightbringer," he cooed. "There's no need for that sort of whispered nonsense to stain the air with toothless spite. You are one of us now. I'm just coming to bring you home." A long, thin tongue slithered out from between the teeth on the left-hand side of the chevalier's mouth and dropped several inches below his jaw. It unrolled into two the prongs of a long, flaccid fork, as if a banner declaring the degradation this being brought.

Burdeb cast his eyes away, raising a hand as a shield between himself and the demon of Darkness. "I am nothing like you!"

"Oh, but you are…." The rotten egg air of his breath eased through the teeth and hung about Burdeb's hand in a knowing caress. "You chose one of our Order by your own volition. You consummated the relinquishment of the Light by owning your own lust for her. You belong to the Darkness, and it is already inside of you!" Malchder threw back his head and cackled in mad glee. Burdeb shivered as terror dropped his will through his stomach and cast it somewhere out of his body.

So it *was* true. His charge had been betrayed with the grocer girl. He was no longer pure…. He was no longer of the Light. Tears welled in his eyes, and a muffled sob escaped as he tried to draw breath. It *had* been a wolf's head he had seen. This was a demon dog of the Darkness, sent to claim him for his impurity. He was tainted, and the Darkness had come to claim its own.

Malchder tilted his head to the side, opening his jaws wider, and reached up to grab one protruding fang from the back of his jaw. The tooth broke off into a jagged spike with a crumbling crack.

"Come now," he cooed again in a soothing singsong as he wrapped one arm around Burdeb's back, nestling his hand in the hair of his neck.

"Do not take on so. You chose your pleasure over the Light…. It's only natural."

He gripped the boy's hair with a vicious strength and yanked it down, forcing Burdeb's head back. Burdeb squeaked at the sharp pain in his neck, and this jerking motion awoke the angry murmurs of pain in his ankle, sending the clarion call of agony reverberating through his body again and causing the trembling tears that had heretofore been dancing on his lower lashes to overflow onto the planes of his face.

"Why, what has the Light ever given you except pain and denial and solitude?" Malchder reached forward with his other hand, bringing the wicked edge of the tooth up to the hollow where Burdeb's jaw reached his neck. "Who could blame you for wanting what only comes naturally in a man's life? The caress… the touch… the… *heat*…"

The tears were flowing with some consistency now. The burning at the back of his skull, the alarm bells of agony in his lower body, and with all this also the burgeoning knowledge that, despite what Gonestrwydd had said, he had lost his purity. Now, he had been overtaken by this demonic dog of the Darkness in a moment of weakness, and it would kill him. His spirit would be cast out to wander alone in the Darkness between the worlds for all eternity… and none would bear his name. None would cry for him in sorrow. Forgotten amongst all those traitors to the Light, he would not even be a memory to anyone.

Malchder pressed the points of the tooth's edge into the boy's neck, drawing thin blood. "That's right. Release yourself to me and embrace your new place in the Dark order. You gave yourself to the girl. Now give yourself to me, and we shall begin."

Burdeb turned his eyes away and closed them against the scalding of more tears. He could not move away from the grinning heat of the chevalier's breath and his impending death that had now begun, for the chevalier's grip on his head was tight. Still, he tried to escape his fate. He could not believe that Gonestrwydd had been wrong…. Had not his words been true, as that was his charge? No… Gonestrwydd had been in his power when he had said that he had not betrayed his charge… that meant….

Burdeb brought both hands up to grip Malchder's arm and opened his eyes. They rolled to see the rows upon rows of teeth opening up to caress his cheek. The Cotheda chevalier intended to eat of him what he could after extinguishing his life, Burdeb understood. He used all his strength to force the hand cutting into his neck away, but it was a losing battle. "I am NOT of you," he grunted. "I did nothing with that… that… *girl* in the market square!"

"Oh, but you DID!" The jagged sharpness pressed further in on him.

"I did NOT!" he panted. "I have NOT betrayed my charge. I am Burdeb, Koteli Knight of the Light! And…," he gasped, forcing the chevalier's hand back even farther. "I AM pure…. Purity is mine!" A faint light began to radiate from his body as they grappled.

"You are tainted, Lightbringer!" Malchder squealed with histrionic glee. "Tainted! Tainted! Tainted! Betrayer of your charge. Befouler of the accursed Light! Now you are owned by the Dark. Impurity and Darkness be thy Fate!"

So intent were they upon their struggle that they neither saw the swirling of shadows nor heard the approaching footfalls or the quiet clinks of shifting mail ringlets.

Twyll stepped onto the path directly in front of the struggling men and gazed at them. It was clear that Burdeb was disadvantaged in the fight.

"What is the meaning of this?" Twyll's voice was a low, thunderous rumble, splitting the foreboding night air and causing both struggling men to freeze and turn towards him.

"Gonestrwydd!" Burdeb shouted. He could not believe his eyes. The First Knight of the Koteli had found him out here. He knew not how, and all would be right!

Malchder rolled his eyes at the new arrival. Impossible as it might seem, his grinning mouth opened even wider. Seeing Burdeb's concentration broken by the disturbance of their test of wills, he took the opportunity. He put in a force of speed and shoved the points of the tooth deep into Burdeb's neck. Burdeb's body jerked and became still as stone. Blood erupted around the tooth, flowing in heavy rivulets down his neck and soaking into his shirt and mail. Malchder released his grip on Burdeb's hair and slid from the boy's side in one fluid movement, yanking the tooth out as he did and allowing Burdeb to fall backwards onto the ground. Burdeb clutched frantically at his neck, heedless of his falling, as he tried to keep his life from draining out of his body.

Twyll remained motionless, regarding the tableau before him in resignation.

Malchder gained his feet and made a clumsy bow, dropping to one knee. His joints, still somewhat in the wolven form, cracked and ground as though filled with rough gravel.

"Commander!" He bowed his head. "'Tis always a pleasure to be in Your presence!"

"Begone, Malchder, Chevalier of Pride," Twyll said in a monotone voice. "Your work tonight is not over, and there is more blood yet to shed."

Malchder bobbed his head in acquiescence; his long tongue slithered out to wrap around the tooth in his hand, tasting the blood. His tongue wrapped around the tooth and pulled it back into the socket it had come from, sliding it home with a deliberate sucking sound. The tips of the forks of his tongue pinched between the surrounding encroaching bone and were ripped off in the process. Black drops of shadow welled around the tooth and then sealed it into place.

"I heed your orders, Dark Commander, with most faithful speed! I hear and I heed!" Malchder dropped from a bow to prostrate himself on the ground. With a whirl of darkness and hideous cracking as though the rending of green timber, his body had reformed as the magenta-eyed wolf. It sprang to its feet and began backing away with a reverence shown to no other of his regiment; Malchder rejoined the surrounding darkness and sped back towards the stables, where the stink of blood and terror still hung heavy in the air.

Twyll never took his eyes off Burdeb, and the boy gazed back at him with shocked eyes, still holding the wound on his neck. Twyll stepped forward until he had reached the side of the youngest of the regiment of the Koteli knights. A faint aura still flickered about the boy's chest, but it shone in fitful inconsistency in the darkness of the night.

Twyll knelt down beside Burdeb and put his hand over the ones holding the wound at the boy's neck. Burdeb's eyes were wide with shock and fear, but he was aware for all that. He opened his mouth to speak to Twyll, to demand why the demon of the Dark had called him Commander, to know how the demon had known him and spoke so to him, to gain a reason as to why Twyll was so accepting of the demon's talk, to ask a hundred more questions, perhaps to plead for comfort in his distress. But he was only able to articulate a gargling groan.

"Burb," Twyll said with some tenderness, "You were always so dedicated, yet so easily led." He tightened his grip on the boy's upper hand and pulled it away from holding pressure on the hole in his neck. Burdeb twisted away and tried to place his hand back, but Twyll easily held it at bay. Twyll took his other hand from the hilt of his blade and gripped the other hand, covering the wound on Burdeb's neck.

Burdeb's eyes widened in understanding of what was to come. His mouth opened and closed like a fish out of water, making strangled gurgling sounds, and his struggles redoubled.

"Easy now, Burb." Twyll's gentle whisper spread Burdeb's fear. "It will end thusly and soon. You were right, you know. Purity was and still belongs to you…." He gripped the fingers of the remaining hand covering the wound, crushing them in his grip, and pulled it away from the bloody hole with inexorable strength. Blood gushed out of the ragged hole and down across the stained skin. "It is an unfortunate thing that this knowledge will die with you."

Burdeb struggled, twisting his body first left and right, yet Twyll held his arms away and pinned him to the ground. Burdeb heaved his body, trying to free his hands, his eyes rolling in fear. His gaze grew dim as his consciousness began to flee for the release of sleep, yet in his last moments of awareness he could see a faint shimmer of golden light around Twyll's head as he whispered: "Go well into Darkness' embrace, Knight of Light's Purity."

Twyll watched with some detachment as the blood dribbling from the hole in Burdeb's neck slowed in frequency and grew weaker in flow until it was no more than an ebb, then an ooze, then a trickle. Burdeb had lost consciousness well before the flow of his life's essence had stilled, so Twyll knew he felt no more pain and would not be returning to this world now that his life's flow had ceased. He waited a moment more before placing the boy's hands upon his stomach. Burdeb's skin was cold to his touch as the heat fled, chasing the life that left.

A bird called in the darkness from far away. Things had been put into motion that would move to put the last fragment of the Light's hold on this world in their hands this very night. Twyll stood and looked down again at Burdeb's still form.

"I'm sorry, Burb. I wish you could have joined our cause… but your insistence on the Light kept you from us, despite our entreaties otherwise. It could never have ended other than thus."

Twyll placed his hand over Burdeb's nose and mouth, sensing the fleeing traces of the Light. He closed his eyes and began to draw forth the Light from Burdeb's body, calling it towards him. Another scream erupted from the hamlet, this time from one of the main buildings. Twyll stopped feeding on the Light and looked towards Santus Ronanus again.

"It seems we've only just begun," he murmured.

Turning, his woolen cloak swinging in a limp arc in the shadows, Twyll stepped back off the path and into the darkness without a glance back. As his foot broke the line of shadows, he exploded into tiny trickling streams of dark fragments that spiraled across the air, circling for a moment around the dead knight before snaking across the fields, heading towards the farmhouse.

The golden-warm light of the afternoon stretched across the anteroom in the ancient temple. Small bookshelves had been carved into the surrounding stone. Tables and seats had also been carved from the surrounding rock, further reinforcing the air of ancient solemnity and the atmosphere that this was a place of learning—a place of knowledge. Despite solemn reverence scenting the air, Olwygg always felt a quiet joy in the presence of his old masters and the place of learning where he had trained. He gazed contentedly around the room. Scrolls of paper lined the shelves, each tied with a leather thong. He was the only student in for lessons today, so the others must be away on the sea or seeking to learn of life's experiences in the countryside. He was in lessons today for… for…. He gazed around the room again, feeling foggy from sleep.

"You fell asleep in class again, boy!"

The hearty voice of his master cleared the sleepdust from his eyes. Olwygg looked about and saw the rotund shape of the Sage of Veneration standing by the window. Light shone in and wrapped around the Sage, making most aspects of his personage and outline indistinct and difficult to see. His face became clear for a moment, and Olwygg could see the man's golden eyes twinkling in the afternoon sun. In his hands, Olwygg saw, the Sage held a thin reed of instruction. He tapped the bookshelves and the walls with the heavy end of the reed as he spoke. *Tap... tap... tap-tap....*

"You always were a slow study, Olwygg."

The Sage smiled down at him. Olwygg looked blearily at the Sage of Veneration. The halo of light that had engulfed him, slanting in through the window behind him, had dulled away, yet still Olwygg could not clearly see his teacher of old.

"*Of old...? How can that be?*" His head was so fuzzy, and he felt so tired. Nothing seemed to make sense in this experience.

"Master..." he tried to say, but his lips only formed the words of an oft-repeated prayer, venerating the Light.

Oh ye Host of Holies, illuminating that which hides. In our hour of need....

Olwygg could not hear any movement, yet he knew his old teacher was approaching as the sound of the reed the instructors used to rap the knuckles of misbehaving acolytes rebounding from the shelves drew closer and closer yet. *Tap... tap... tap-tap-tap....*

Old teacher?

His befuddled brain worried at that thought like tugging at a hangnail. How, though? The Sage was perhaps mid-life. Not so old as all that... and neither was he. He was a spry student of the Mysteries in the Temple de la Sagesse, here at the Maw of the Dragon. It was only his third summer there, learning of the charge he bore to the Light... and, as was common to occur on warm summer days when the oppressive heat blanketed the classrooms during private study, he had fallen asleep when he was supposed to be focused on pondering the mysteries of his charge.

Tap... tap....

He looked down at his hands, folded in reverence on the desk before him in preparation for prayers. Why was he ready for prayer? Surprise gripped his lungs, stealing his breath in shock. These were not the supple hands of youth.... They were the wrinkled and time-scored hands of age and experience.

Tap-tap… tap….

This was a folly-dream! In the heart of his mind, he knew. He knew that he was not the youth in his dreams at this school of mysteries in a bygone time. He was an elder member of the Koteli Knights, charged with bringing the Relic of the Light to the Temple… and… the revered master of instruction whom he had honored…. The same Sage, as the tapping drew nearer and nearer, who now approached him was… was….

Dead.

Tap… tap-tap…. Tap….

The tapping, which had been right before him, had ceased.

The fog in his head had cleared. Olwygg raised his eyes from where they had rested upon his hands to the face of his revered master and cherished mentor, the Sage of Veneration.

The light had faded completely from around the Sage. The once vibrant and life-infused folds of the man's face had sagged into hanging jowls with the ravages of time. Yet now those folds of skin were hanging in strands from around the column of the neck as though a tattered scarf of body. The dancing golden eyes of the Sage had been reduced to just one faded, yellowed eye shot through with large scarlet threads and flattened after death, hanging loosely in the socket. Where the other eye had been was a craggy, irregular, perforated cavity. Olwygg should not have been able to see anything inside of this skull cavern in this benighted room, yet there was some faint flicker of luminescence in that hollow. He could see… movement… in there.

The face of the dead Sage hung before him, a handspan of breath separating them. The blood-caked lips of the corpse separated into a cracked grin. The foul stench of decayed air that had been trapped in the Sage's lungs released as a slipstream of high-pitched, shrieky, menacing giggles that blew into Olwygg's face.

Bile crawled up his throat, and Olwygg gagged, turning his face away from the apparition before him yet keeping his eyes locked on the ravaged horror. The rotted, cloying smell of high-speed decay boomed out from the corpse and wrapped itself around Olwygg, cloaking him in its heavy miasma.

"Still the slow study, even with all this time."

A low whisper filled the room, blaring from all the corners and yet seeming to whisper up from the seams in the flooring.

Spittle dripped out of his mouth as the slight remains of his last meal ventured a return visit. Olwygg's hands had risen to cover his mouth and nose as he tried to avoid breathing in any more of the befouled perfume of death that hung around the corpse. But it was in vain.

The outline of the Sage's ghoulish visage hung before him, seeming to glow in the darkness, and Olwygg realized he could somehow see in this dark cavern of a room. The corpse was giving off an otherworldly light that emanated from within the flesh and cast a faint illumination around the room. Still retching, Olwygg managed to push himself away from the table upon which the Sage had been previously lying and started to stand.

Two bloody hands shot forth from the darkness, closed around the thin bones of Olwygg's wrists, and squeezed. He heard a visceral snapping noise—small yet somehow very, very loud in these short moments. Though it was mere seconds, it seemed to take an incredible amount of time from the sounds of those delicate bones snapping reaching his ears to when the white-hot pain danced down his arms. He sucked in air reflexively as the pain yanked away all the breath from him and immediately began gagging again upon the repulsive, odorous stench. Tears spilled from his eyes.

The bloody hands jerked downward, yanking Olwygg close so that he was eye to eye with the remaining eye of the ghoul that had been the Sage. A noxious giggle filled his ears. "Ol… wyg…." Its lower jaw dropped down, and its tongue rolled forward and fell out of its mouth to hang below the lower jaw in slaverous glee. The ghoul stretched its maw wide as it leaned in towards Olwygg and fastened the broken teeth around his throat.

The scream that had been clawing its way from his lungs and up his throat finally made it out of his mouth. Olwygg gave voice to the repressed horror and despair that had taken over his spirit since he'd first laid eyes upon the monster that had once been his mentor and most cherished tutor in life. As the ghoul pulled him closer and its jaws began to tighten, Olwygg screamed.

Wrapped in the warm embrace of a soft, ethereal darkness, a soothing numbness of spirit flooded his senses. The laughing mouth and deep eyes he had never truly known, yet had dreamt of for half his life, echoed through his enchanted dream. He had slipped into unconsciousness with eagerness and a desire for respite from the horrors of the day. His relief had given way to a darkness that numbed his senses for a time, and then an even darker awareness. He was neither awake nor completely unaware of the comings and goings of the world around him. Instead, he was submerged in a deep cocoon of unrest. Unable to wake and affect the world around him, yet neither could he rest and be ignorant of the depravity of the actions of the Dark. His spirit clamored in its unrest as noise made its way into the misty depths of his mind. His heart stirred despite the seductive depths of his dreamlike state, quickening. He began shedding the confines of sleep, twitching as he rose through the reluctant waystations of consciousness. Rolling over into the harsh pinpricks of stiff straw stabbing his body in angry response to his movement, Maddau opened his eyes to a foreign world.

Moonlight blanketed the sterile roomscape in soft blue tones. The normal rough, handwrought state of the room was smoothed over into soft lines and blurry edges. He did not know this place, and the feeling of unbelonging and wrongness was thick in the air. He was unsure of what had brought him out of his state of rest, but he could feel a jarring sense of displacement. This was not the familiar paddocks of the Knights' barracks in the courtyard of the Caer, with the comforting presence of Twyll nearby. Nor was this the isolated and suffocating silence of the Koteli Captain's quarters in the main building, just down the hall from the Brehines, where he had spent many a night pacing, emotions conflicted and heart unsure. Of both of his duties in this world and of what he wanted in life.

No… this was a new place, and its unfamiliarity was unnerving in equal measure to the heavy silence that seemed to add weight to the moonlight did nothing to alleviate his unease.

The relentless prickling assault of straw on his body brought around his focus: it was late at night, and he was… where? He gazed blankly at the open door, leading into the shadows.

A wavering, high-pitched, and squeaky moan broke the stranglehold silence held on the moment, floating up and across the air to him from below, freezing his movements in shock at the sound.

And fear of what made it.

With the sound, remembering filled his mind with memories that were always there, just buried under the thin veneer of sleep. This was the farmhouse of the man Ronanus. He was here because he had to bring the relic to the Dragon's Maw… the temple… where it would be safe. They had to move it because… because…..

Because the Dark had attacked the Caer. The Darkness was coming for the relic.

And the Brehines…Abertha…was dead.

Abertha…

This terrible knowledge slowed everything to a crawl, and the unspeakable last moments of her passing replayed in his mind, heedless of his desire to stop them. Her straining to pass on the things he must know. The charge of the relic… her suffering… those beautiful eyes that had been robbed of all their soulful spirit as well as their sight…. her dying…

The sound came again, stuttering stoccato… jolting him back out of his memory. His eyes returned to the doorway, this time perceiving a little of the adjoining hallway within the shadowy depths beyond. The sound had come to find him from there, and outside the door was the hallway that led to the other rooms in the house… and the stairs that led to the floor below.

Where the Sage was…. The memory of the savaged Sage bloomed large in his mind.

And where Olwygg was…!

The thought of the steadfast, resigned elder Koteli Knight got Maddau's limbs moving. The noise could only mean one thing: something had happened in the rooms below, and Olwygg needed help. Maddau rose, but his left knee did not support him, and he staggered left to keep from falling over back onto the hundreds of needle-like straw pricks that waited to greet his tender flesh. He righted himself, shaking the feeling of bugs racing up and down from his left knee to his foot until he could find feeling in his toes again, and grabbed his sword as a matter of habit. He made his way to the door in only his tunic, leaving his armored shirt and other dressings behind.

The shadows of the hallway cut the blue moonlight where it fell. The hallway was in almost total darkness, and only the sparse inroads of light from his room gave any dimension to the rough shapes. Maddau could make out the faint outlines of the man Ronanus' room, and with that came awareness of a faint wheezy sound that he recognized. Ronanus was snoring. Below the infrequent and almost too quiet sound, he could also hear a whispered and unintelligible muttering in the darkness. Maddau guessed that Ronanus's woman, Jantielle, as he remembered, spoke in her sleep.

He moved with deliberation down the hallway, placing his feet with care so as not to cause unnecessary flexing of the floorboards. Creaks and groans accompanied his progress all the same, and by the time he had made it into the deepest depths of the hallway and reached the stairs, he was sure the farmer and his wife were wide awake and listening to his passage. He paused to see if they were awake. Still hearing the reassuring honks and mumbles indicating continued slumber from their room, Maddau began making his way down the short flight of stairs. The darkness at the top of the stairs was almost absolute, so he gave great care to the placement of his feet, ensuring stable footing on each step before shifting his weight. Halfway down, he realized he could see more of the steps themselves and the doorway into the main room of the farmhouse. When he arrived at the bottom floor, a wavering, reedy, moaning noise came again… ending in a horrific squeak. An ominous silence filled the air with the sudden cutoff of the sound, giving Maddau a dreadful sense of foreboding.

His hands moved of their own accord, following the orders of instinct so deeply ingrained from years of training that he had drawn his sword before he was even aware he intended to do so. A threatening aura bled into the air and caused him to hesitate at the threshold of the main room in the farmhouse. Fear was an emotion he knew and understood well, but this feeling of dread was something else. It was a feeling of aversion. To what, he did not know. But it was to something so wholly unnatural that it bubbled in his blood, and with that aversion came a surprising anger at the existence of such an affront to nature itself. This was his natural and instinctual reaction to the presence of the Darkness. Much like his instinct to draw this sword, Maddau assumed a battle stance and stepped forward into the room before his mind had half realized that he had moved. Instinct, while highly valued amongst warriors for keeping one alive despite oneself, came with a price.

He stepped into the room and saw a thin light surrounding the table across the room. In the center of this light, which seemed to emanate from the body of the Sage slumped on the table, was the figure of Olwygg. He hung like a limp rag in the gripping fists of a semi-transparent, shadowy form of what appeared to be a man in the armor of a knight. One of the shadow-knight's fists was locked around Olwygg's wrists, and his hands bulged limply from either side out of the top of the shadow-knight's gauntlet. The other fist was mostly closed around Olwygg's neck. Olwygg's eyes bulged in their sockets, and his tongue lolled out the side of his mouth. Maddau watched, frozen in shock. The shadow-knight tightened his grip on Olwygg's neck even further. There was a horrific *crick* sound. Olwygg's head slumped further to the left, and the elder knight emitted a spray of spittle and articulated a brief "Pthapck" as he sagged bonelessly forward. The shadowy armored figure released his grip on Olwygg, and the elder knight fell to the ground in a heap, his head bouncing with terrible finality on the floorboards. Maddau screamed and hurled himself forward, his sword arm rising to strike at the shadow-knight.

Cenfigen turned his head at hearing Maddau's cry but had no time for further movement before the Captain of the Koteli was upon him. Cenfigen was corporal enough that Maddau's blade made a glancing blow against his armor, but still consisting mostly of shadows, the deflected blade passed mostly through him without major injury, although it did sting.

Maddau, blinded by the pain and fury of loss, had overcommitted to his attack and stumbled when his blade passed through Cenfigen. He landed hard against the wall and pushed back quickly to reform his attack. Everything seemed to slow down as he focused on the flickering image of the shadow-knight and readied his sword arm again to swing.

This time Cenfigen had a longer window to defer the advancing Maddau's attack and was able to discorporate quickly enough that when Maddau swung the blow, it landed on naught but air. Maddau stumbled through the shadowy, cold spot the Cotheda chevalier had left in his wake and tumbled to the floor. His hands splayed as he attempted to catch himself and scraped along the wood. Blood welled on his scraped palms. His sword went spinning out of his hand and landed an arm's length away. Maddau pushed himself to his knees to spring forward after it, when a crushing weight landed between his shoulders, knocking him down onto the floor and crushing the air from his lungs. Cenfigen had partially reincorporated behind and just a bit above him and had thrust his knee forward and then kneeled down onto Maddau's back, pinning him to the floor.

Maddau could hear the rusty scrape of air across the bladed guards of the shadow-knight's helmet. He knew not whom he fought; that this was one of the minions of the Dark was enough for him. That he was Olwygg's murderer made it more than personal; it was an attack on the Light and it was no accident that it had happened here and now. Of that, he was sure. He squirmed beneath the pressure on his back, trying to roll or squeeze out from beneath the shadow-knight and regain his sword.

Swarms of patchy black shadowlets swirled into Cenfigen from all corners of the room as he fully incorporated. With the increase in his physical presence came the increase in his weight. Maddau had lost most of his breath when he'd been knocked down; now he ceased to be able to draw breath at all as the crushing weight of the shadow-knight increased. He gagged, his face reddening as he tried to draw in a breath. Desperation started to take over, and he planted his hands more fully on the ground, heedless of his wounded palms, and tried again to lift his chest far enough from the floor to breathe. The pressure was too much, and he sagged back down. Shadows flickered at the edge of his vision, and a rushing noise filled his ears. Something popped somewhere. He felt, more than heard, the noise, but it was faint now... no longer important. He wished he had been more of a fighter. He wished he had taken more care in this attack.... But that wasn't so important either.

He wished Twyll was with him. He did not want to die, and he did not want to be alone. He wished he could tell him...

Large shadow flowers of grey and black bloomed across his vision, obscuring the floor. The rushing noise was now a deafening roar, but his chest didn't hurt so much anymore. He still could not breathe, and although that hurt, the pain was dimmer now. He kept trying to find something to grip to be able to pull himself out from underneath the crushing weight, but the smooth wood gave no handholds, and even that didn't seem so important anymore.

Cenfigen peered down at the man, pinned to the floor beneath his poleyn, hands and fingers scrabbling for purchase on the ground, trying to seek freedom like a bug stuck beneath a boot. The faintest aura seemed to pulse about the man; Cenfigen could *smell* the Light on this creature, and it disgusted him. He leaned down further, studying the reddened face and bulging eyes of his trapped quarry. A cracking noise beneath his knee told him he had just broken a rib or two belonging to the suffocating man. Cenfigen smiled, the slow draw of his breath quickening in anticipation; this one would die much like the old man had. Slow and in excruciating intensity. Perhaps he would even denounce the Light if Cenfigen promised to let him live. He wouldn't, of course, let him live.... But it might be fun to get in one last deceit before this one's life was extinguished. Increase the despair, which was so delicious to the Cotheda Planeswalker.

He leaned down and hissed, "Give in to me, Worm of the Light. Give in to me, and I'll let you live."

Maddau's mouth opened wide as his lungs began to pound for air. The shadow-knight above him, not so shadowy anymore, was saying something, but Maddau could not hear him. All he heard was the rushing noise of the wind in his ears and a loud buzzing sound. His vision was going dark. He opened his mouth to try to pull in air and relieve some of the pressure that was building in his chest.

He understood that he was dying. He would die here, with Olwygg, in this farmhouse.

Maybe that was alright, he thought. *Twyll could take over now...and maybe that was alright, too. Twyll was always better at leading.*

The darkness started to recede away from him, and Maddau could feel the world becoming fainter. He was becoming fainter... dimmer.... His grasp on the world was slipping away.

He fainted.

A rivulet of shadows spilled through a crack in the door from the outside. His form rising out of the liquid pool of shadow, Twyll stepped into the room without a sound. The brutal scene displayed before him snatched a startled protestation from his lips: Olwygg was lying crumpled on the floor beside the table where the dead Sage lay, and to the right of this was Maddau lying crushed beneath the form of Cenfigen, the Cotheda Planeswalking chevalier, fully formed in this world. Cenfigen had pinned Maddau to the floor and was crushing the life out of him. Twyll knew only one thing could have brought Cenfigen into this world: the blood sacrifice of one member of his own regiment. Twyll had given no leave for anyone to summon Cenfigen, as he acted as his own force and did not carry orders from another without blood payment. Yet here he was.

And he was killing Maddau.

Cenfigen leaned down, his voice hissing something that Twyll did not hear. His attention was riveted on Maddau, who did not move.

A red haze suffused Twyll's vision. He crossed the room in the span of one breath. With no thought to his mission—their capture of the relic of the Light—or consideration for those he commanded, he acted. Olwygg's form was of no greater import to him than a squall of dirty clothes kicked off on the ground, and he cared not for the remains of the Sage that were spreading back into the table as the rapid decomposition continued its course. He never liked the Sages much, anyhow, with all their mysteries and their rules.

He saw only that Maddau was hurt.

And that Cenfigen had hurt him.

Twyll drew his blade and leapt forward, moving with feline grace that was as much a part of him as his eye color or his bladed eartips. Despite his nature, Cenfigen never heard the Commander of the Cotheda chevaliers coming. Twyll was at his side before Cenfigen even knew of his presence. He thrust his blade forward into the gap where the Cenfigen's gorget offset from his breastplate. Fully incorporated, the blade struck true and knocked Cenfigen sideways, tumbling him off Maddau's back. Twyll followed him over, forcing the blade further home to its hilt. Cenfigen stiffened beneath Twyll's blow, the fight going out of him, and he began to discorporate with swirls of shadowlets spilling out of him in unorganized streams. Twyll leaned into his blade, muttering, "If he dies, I'll send you to Planes from where you could never return. You'll think a second and third time before I catch you fully in this world again, acting without my leave!"

The pace of the shadow streams increased, and the form that had been the chevalier faded into a dark shadow stain on the floor of the farmhouse that lingered for a moment. Then it was gone.

Twyll dropped his blade and spun around to stare at Maddau; the Koteli Captain lay unmoving on the ground. He approached with great care, as though a sudden movement could act for good or ill, and gently rolled Maddau onto his back. Maddau's face was red, and small purple patches had erupted across the skin of his cheeks. Flecks of off-white foam caked his lower lip and the sides of his mouth, and though his eyes were rolled back in his head, Twyll could see blood coloring the whites of his eyes. He was not breathing.

Twyll leaned forward without hesitation and sealed his lips over Maddau's, breathing into him. One full breath, then another. He paused, listening, and began breathing into his childhood friend again. One full breath, then another. Maddau gave no response, and his chest did not move on its own accord.

Images of their life together flitted through Twyll's mind: Madds giggling with him over their snail races and the slow way the snails climbed the fruit trees outside the Caer, sunlight gently glowing on his face before Maddau woke up in the mornings on days they shared a paddock together in the barracks, a thousand whispered conversations passed across the hallway when they had to clean swords as punishment for sneaking out after lights out, the bruised look in his eyes when Twyll had bested him in training with swords and he had told Madds to stop staring after girls instead of training, or else he'd never get good with a blade, the trusting way Maddau's eyes had always slipped up to meet his when there was work to do and they knew they could count on each other to get it done. The comforting way Madds had dried his tears after their pilgrimage to the temple was over and he had told him of his experience with his mentoring Sage.

The way he had looked at Abertha when she became the Brehines.

The same way he never had looked at him.

Twyll realized he was crying only when he saw the tears fall onto Maddau's face. Shadows began to twine around his frame, brought into being by the intensity of emotion as he sucked in another breath and breathed again into Maddau's slackened mouth. One full breath, then another. He paused and listened; there was no response.

"Breathe, damn you!" Twyll cried. A dark aura was growing around them. He'd thought himself incapable of crying after all this time and after all he'd done—all he'd *caused* to be done. This was not supposed to happen—not this way. Maddau was supposed to be his to deal with, *to handle,* so that he could bring him into the fold. Make him understand what he, Twyll, had achieved for them. For the *both* of them.

More tears ran down his face, interwoven with the streams of shadow that emanated from his pores, dripping into the corners of Maddau's gawping mouth and pooling there. He clasped his hands together, raised them, and slammed them down onto Maddau's chest with all the force he had left and all the energy he could summon from his own Dark power.

"BREATHE!"

A harsh cough erupted from Maddau's mouth, spraying bits of dark-flecked foam across his face. Twyll stilled, listening, unconscious of the spittle on his skin, as a ragged gasp emerged from Maddau's mouth. His chest spasmed.

Darkened tears fell faster now, bathing his face and Maddau's as Twyll breathed for his friend again—just one breath this time. Maddau coughed it back out, spraying his face with spit this time instead of foam as his lungs breathed on their own, but Twyll didn't mind. This time, the ragged gasps for air continued, and as Maddau breathed more regularly, the redness began to fade from his face, leaving it with a splotchy pallor.

Twyll kissed his forehead and cradled Maddau to his chest, rocking him back and forth as the Koteli captain struggled for air.

"You're coming back, Madds," he whispered. "I have so much to tell you, but you're coming back. Don't leave me, Madds. There's so much still we must do… and so much more to say…."

As he was rocked back and forth in Twyll's arms, tiny black flecks of darkness slowly flitted up across the whites of Maddau's half-open eyes and crept up under his eyelids.

Call of the Koteli

Knights of the Light's Virtue
Heed the Call
Return to the Plane of Bywyd
Ride forth ye One and All
Embodiment of the Light
Manifest upon the Plane
To Venerate the Right
And Thwart Darkness' Gain
Thusly you are Charged
Against the Eternalia - you will Ride
To Fight for Light's true cause
And stop the Evil Tide
But should you not succeed,
If you falter or you fall
Whence summon'd you shall return again
To always Heed Her Call.

Chapter Six

The Hidden Village

The sun had set, and the various farming families had retired for the night. Lymder had left his post at the main farm house to settle in with Dra and Haelder in the stables. He'd passed Burdeb, ranging around the hamlet on patrol, sullen in his countenance and without even glancing in his direction. Lymder entered the cool shadows of the stable building.

Much use Burb is on patrol; not even seeing him as he passed by, Lymder mused.

Haelder and Dra had done their work well. The horses were all brushed down and fed, with scant hay left in their collective stalls for a possible late-night snack.

Lymder found the other two members of his regiment in the smallest stall reserved for straw storage and tack. Haelder was sitting on the ground with his back propped up against the thin slats that formed the building enclosure. His head leaned back against the wall, his mouth hung open, and soft, chuffing snores issued forth with some regularity. Dra had found a soft pile of straw and made himself a sort of pallet against the far wall. He had stretched out, and his snore was reminiscent of dragging sopping wet clothes along the dry pan on laundry day. Lymder sighed with resignation upon realizing that he'd get little sleep tonight with this musical number keeping him company in the stables.

As was his life practice, Lymder made it a rare occurrence to complain about the things in life with which he was given to work. His lot in life had always been a simple one, and rarely did extravagantery or lavishness appeal. He did not envy Maddau his accommodation in the farmhouse; that elevation came with a great deal of responsibility and worry, things he did not desire to endure. Additionally, he would have to entertain the worries of the people of the house, a burden Lymder did not wish on anyone. Neither did he regret assigning Burb as lookout; the boy had a waywardness about him that was well acknowledged within the regiment. The Captain was more than kind to the weaker member of the regiment, and Lymder often wondered, in his lapsing moments of judgement, when their leader would force the boy to toughen up and cease to be a liability.

Gonestrwydd, however, Lymder did wonder about. The first knight had been long absent that eve after dismissing the team to their appointed duties. The captain was with Olwygg in the farmhouse. Dra and Haelder had attended to the horses in the stable. Burb was to patrol around the hamlet until sunrise, and he had stood a-watch outside the farmhouse until dark. Gonestrwydd had left the farmhouse shortly after assignments were made and headed away from the stables towards the outer edge of the farming community.

Lymder had assumed that Gonestrwydd had headed after Burdeb to assist in patrol, as the youngest was not much to be counted on. But now it was much, much later, and he had not seen the first knight return. Gonestrwydd was the most skilled swordsman amongst them, leagues better even than the Captain, yet Lymder fretted momentarily for his safety. Even a skilled swordsman could be overtaken when outnumbered.

Lymder made a brief survey of the storeroom before settling himself against the entryway support pillar. His usual smooth countenance creased into a frown of worry. It was rare for the First Knight to be absent for so long. Perhaps he would stay awake just a little longer to keep a watch for Gonestrwydd's return.

Lymder had just started to relax when a frenetic, braying scream jerked him to full attention. He grasped for his blade and stood as a barrier in the doorway to protect the sleep-vulnerable and prone knights inside. More screams erupted from the barn attached to the rear of the stables. Lymder gritted his teeth and hunched his shoulders. The screams were loud and particularly aggravated, tinged with tones of terror. They continued on and on, intertwined with other animalistic noises, for several minutes.

Horrific blood-curdling screams, rapid panting, and angry squeals.

It was the pigs.

Lymder collapsed against the doorway, his back against the frame, relief weakening his knees. He had been around enough livestock to know that scuffles over territory could often result in injury or even death. These screams, while riling and disturbing, were likely of the territorial scuffle variety or over the ownership of food.

He forced himself to relinquish his grip on his blade's handle with some work as he sagged back into a sitting position, his face twisting into a rueful grin. The regular log sawing from the Haelder and Dra had come to a brief pause when the scuffle from the barn erupted, but with the return of silence, it had also resumed. Lymder had not realized he had been holding his breath until he exhaled in a gust of shaky laughter that came out more of a croak.

Dra's grumpy voice floated ponderously out of the darkness to him: "Keep't down a'bit, Lym, ma lad. Be try'n tae rest 'ere."

Lymder stared at the vague shapes of the other men in the darkness before rolling his eyes in incredulity and settling back. There had been enough excitement for one night, and riling up two elders over scuffling pigs was a pig's scuffle in the making. He'd rather take this scolding than the argument that would come from his rebuttal any day. Keeping it down, indeed!

Shaking his head, he felt the work of the day sink into his bones and felt truly weary. A long voyage with little in the way of routine was exhausting to him, and sleep was the only remedy for such. Still, the thought of the absent First Knight nagged at his mind. He should keep a'watch... just to be certain Gonestrwydd was safe...

So thinking, he leaned his chin to the left against his shoulder and wrapped his arms around himself, shifting his eyes towards the door. His eyelids were ever heavier, yet he kept them open just a bit, watching the slightly lighter rectangle of open night in the darkness of the stables, where full night held her moonless court.

The wind made a brief whooshing noise as it rounded the buildings of the hamlet and scraped against the corners of the stable doorway. Time marched onwards with deliberate slowness, and the hooting cry of a bird echoed in from far away. Although he still thought himself a'watch, Lymder's eyelids had long slipped closed. Soon, the regular log sawing of the elders was joined by a quiet coo as breath passed through Lymder's pursed lips. Despite his best attempt to watch for Gonestrwydd's safe return, sleep had claimed him in the end.

The wind continued its travel, sighing across the land. Its passing raked the trees for any loosened leaves.

A silent specter of brief shadowlets cartwheeled past the doorway, then paused to spiral together. Soon, more shadowlets fell together and into place, creating a lumbering shape: a huge quadrupedal shadow. Two pinpricks of wild magenta flared in the darkness, low and near the ground. Then they began to rise in height: two feet, then five, until they reached a height of seven feet from the ground. The dark shape eased forward with simple liquidity, a flowing of the shadows, and approached the threshold of the stable to hover by the entryway.

The night stilled, and the far-off calls of the nocturnal fowl grew quiet. A hunter—a predator—had arrived, and the creatures of the night listened for its presence.

Malchder breathed deeply, inhaling the fragrances of the stable as if sampling the atmosphere of a zephyr buffet. There was the stuffy yet warm scent of hay, the roiling growl of animal scat, the slow and fusty fragrance of herd beasts, the rank tang of pigs, the essence of unwashed men, and… the spicy smell of the Light.

Malchder's mouth began to water. The essence of the Light was a delicious treat, and he had been denied his previous meal by the Commander's arrival. He had willingly relinquished his meal to his Commander—a deferment he would not have endured with Cynddaredd—but now he was hungry, and there was the essence of the Light nearby. In the stables, right before him, in fact. Minor salivation became an anticipatory drool, and a low whine issued from deep in his throat. The wolfish shadow, now stretched into the monstrous malformity of a wolf-shape on two legs, leaned forward and placed its hand on the outer wall of the stables. In touching the wall, the shadow solidified into a misshapen paw-like hand, and the enveloping shadows unzipped from around the hand and were snatched away by the night air. Malchder, in his anthropomorphic wolf form, leaned forward, farther still, and breathed in the stable air once more.

His unmasked panting alerted some of the stable's inhabitants from their sleep, and they began to roll over, uneasy and aware of the presence of something unnatural nearby.

Malchder's jaw dropped open in a ravenous grin. His tongue, loosed from its cage, unrolled between his teeth to hang out in the night air, dripping his hunger in heady drops onto the ground. His elongated and tooth-filled muzzle broke the plane of the doorway, and he inhaled the new aroma of fear generated by his presence. The somewhat awake, yet not fully aware, inhabitants of the stable began to shift away from him, trying to put distance between themselves and the unnaturalness of the new presence.

The spice-filled aroma of the Light was here. Faint, but there nonetheless. It suffused the stable room, heady and swirling like the drug-riddled smoke of sweetflowers.

One large paw-like foot, arched high over the footpad, stepped into the stables. The magenta lamps in his eyes glowed in the darkness as he gazed at the sleepy and confused stable dwellers. Malchder's jaw dropped open even further, landing on his chest, as he dialed in on the splayed legs of the nearest, delicious victim. He raised his claw-tipped paw-hands and lunged forward, pouncing on the nearest sleeper. His jaws snapped closed on the helpless belly at the same time his paw-hands raked into the inner thighs and upper torso, and a thrilled scream of triumph tore its way out of his throat.

A sliding scrape of footsteps on the stairs intruded on his fixated focus and roused Twyll from his fugue over Maddau's limp body. He quickly wiped a hand up and across his eyes and nose, smearing away the crust of mucus and tears that had dried there and into his sweat-soaked hair as he pushed it back and out of his face. He turned his head, and irritation flared when he spied the long, dour face of Ronanus' wife. She met his eyes and first she bowed her head in respect, then raised her head to survey the carnage of the room: the still bodies of knight and sage, the table having fallen to its side during the tussle for Maddau's life, and in the middle of the room, Twyll cradling the unconscious Maddau. He saw her looking around and swiveled his head to see what caught her attention. His eyes came to rest upon the mangled body of Olwygg, and he quickly shifted his gaze back to her face.

"Aotrou..." Her tremulous tone scratched across his raw nerves.

"Clean this up before anyone else sees." His tone was flat and dismissive. "Burn the bodies. Leave no trace."

"Yes, Aotrou." She bowed low in obedience, reaching her hands forward and depositing a crumpled, dun-colored bundle on the ground near his feet.

Twyll did not notice her reflexive, fawning emote. With great care, he laid Maddau's shoulders on the ground, letting his head roll back onto the floor, then stretched his legs to stand. His rise came up short with a sudden spasm, jerking a strangled cry from his throat. His back and leg muscles had locked into place from sitting so long while holding Maddau, and they had seized when he'd gone to stand.

Twyll hunched forward, bracing his hands against his knees for support, gasping in harsh, jagged breaths. A hot, fluid pain ran from his lower back up along his spine and back down through his lower regions to spike down the back of his leg all the way down into his left heel. Sweat shined on his brow and dampened into dark patches under his arms and around his belly as the pain made its way through his system. He wiped the moisture from his eyes with absentminded irritation as he tried again to straighten to his full height. He knew he would never be able to lift Maddau to carry him out.

There was no time. They had to leave. Now. Before Cynddaredd arrived with the rest of the Cotheda.

He turned his head to look at Maddau. The Koteli Captain had always been fond of his food, and while trim enough for duty, he was apt to keep an extra stone or two of weight about him. Still, Twyll could see that the recent voyage had provided some slight definition to his face and collar where there had been none before. Twyll crossed the room in a stilted cadence to retrieve his blade. As he rehomed it at his side, he glanced back towards Maddau, and his gaze fell upon a familiar rumpled pack. He reached down to grasp the pack and dropped it with a whistling gasp. His senses buzzed on high alert, and all manner of dark foreknowledge flooded his thoughts with what lay within the folds of burled cloth.

The relic. The accursed cup of Light was the reason for all he had set in motion: the attack on the Caer, the deaths of Burdeb and Olwygg, the ruination of the brehines, Maddau's near-death state, and even Anwadaledd's removal had all brought them here to this point. To this moment. For that damned bauble.

"All because the Light desired to control everything," The dark voices in his mind hissed. "Maddau chose all that… over you."

Fury welled up in his throat, closing it in a hot wash of tears at the demands placed upon him all these years… the demands placed upon them all…. For what? A simpering, self-serving ideal that only took and never gave in return? That fragile and useless toy that had cost them all so dearly? That had cost him so dearly?

He reached for the bag again, intending to smash it. Intending to crush it until even the traces of dust that remained were naught but memories to the wind. Dark, wispy twinings of shadow bloomed from beneath his nails as he stretched forth his hand again towards the bag.

A deep, shrill buzzing filled his mind with the chattering excitement of the forces of the Dark.

Here!

IT IS HERE!

Done WELL boy - you've done WELL

Here~ DONE well BoY!

HERE! OURS! HERE! OURS!

BOY well, You've DONE!

BRING… to US…. NOW boy…. BRING IT!!!

HERE! BOY! HERE! WELL!

NOW NOW NOW NOW NOW NOW!!!!

The heady mixture of screaming Dark ecstasy in his mind swirled intoxicatingly through his senses. Twyll splayed fingers touched the strap of the bag, and as his mailed hand caressed the roughened burl, his eyes flicked guiltily to Maddau's face.

Twyll froze.

Maddau's eyes were open. They were aware. They were accusing, and they were focused on him. His outstretched fingers faltered, then drooped;

his reach wilted, faltering. Maddau's eyes were hollowly socketed in his face, with threads of red still easily visible along the bridge of his nose, yet they were the sharp and battle-hardened eyes of the true Captain of the Koteli. They shone with the presence of being fully aware of everything at play in the moment, and they were focused on Twyll's face.

Twyll gazed at him in disbelief. The yammering of the Darkness in his mind receded and then ceased to be important, pushed to the side in the knowledge that Maddau was awake.

Maddau's slackened jaw shifted slightly, and his chest hitched a bit. A dry, barking cough exploded in the near silence of the room, and his throat twitched as he tried to swallow past the swollen tissue that did not move when requested, as before. His eyes closed in pain as he tried again, yet they remained on Twyll's face.

"Too… thooo… eh…. Ee… eellll."

"Madds!" Twyll, the aches and strains forgotten, scrambled over on his hands and knees to where Maddau lay limp on the floor and scooped him up as though he weighed no more than the pack that had so recently occupied him.

Maddau's eyes rolled to look at Twyll's face. They were still wide, yet they had relented a bit from their silent accusation.

"Madds!" he gushed, pushing his guilt deep inside. What Maddau had or had not seen…. If the mask had slipped enough that Maddau now knew…. Well, all of these things could and would be dealt with later, when Twyll had endorsed the relic to the Dark masters. For now, he would play on as if he worked for the Light, as he always had.

And he would ensure Maddau recovered to join them, as had been the plan, of course. His plan, anyway. A big, booming smile arced across his face as he supported his Captain in his arms.

"Madds! You're alive…. You're awake! And you can talk! Tell me. Tell me what happened."

"Twuh…. Eell," Maddau wheezed again. His eyes had clouded a bit, and he suddenly looked tired, as though old age had crept into him in a moment's time.

Twyll spoke the truth of the situation with his usual dry precision: "You cannot speak yet. Your throat, possibly your voice now, is damaged."

Maddau opened his eyes again and regarded Twyll with bleary understanding. The outline of Twyll's face was bleached out in a soft white glow that made it difficult to focus, yet he made the effort.

"Tim… temp… plh…" It was too much, and a rattling cough seized him.

"Yes. Indeed." Twyll nodded tersely and licked his lips. "The Temple. We must get you there to fulfill your destiny. Indeed, to fulfill all of ours."

Twyll whirled to scoop up Maddau's pack, balancing supporting his friend with great care, the knowledge of the presence of the relic seemingly forgotten for the time being. He strode out the open farmhouse door without so much as a backwards glance to where the farmer's wife still stood, forgotten.

Jantielle stared at them in confusion. The Dark One had taken the Knight One and left. Why he had not been killed in his weakened state was beyond her. Much of the machinations of the Dark masters were beyond her. It was only her place to do what she was bid. It was the agreement after all their help in getting her man's farm to prosper.

She turned her attention to the task at hand, remembering the instructions from the Dark One. The room was a mess, and it would be easier to start afresh than to clean it all again with no one to know.

Resolved to her decision, she stepped into the small storage room, where the ashes and cinders of the day's fire still brooded in faint tones of blood in the darkness. She reached for the dry husks of vegetable skins for kindling and pushed them into the coals.

Twyll carried Maddau from the farmhouse and hurried towards the stables, heedless of swirling shadowlets that floated minutely through the air, flitting ebony patches in the dark of the night. His footfalls were hushed against the grassy ground, moving faster and faster through the grainy weeds and grass plants that grew between the muddy farmyard areas and the farm-land and stables. The surrounding night had gone eerily quiet, as though something had been suddenly rendered irrevocably mute. Twyll's instincts informed him of the unnaturalness of the silence of the night, but he pushed on regardless of the feeling of predatory danger. Being of the Dark himself, he was a far more dangerous predator than anything out there tonight.

Cynddaredd approached the small outcropping of buildings that stood silent and unprotected in the clutches of the night. The telltale smell of blood car-ried on the wind brought knowledge that carnage had already taken place there. More would be coming, he knew, and for the momentous lull between the occurrence of the rapacious violence and the resounding human response to such outrages of the flesh, Cynddaredd reveled in this knowledge of things to come.

A furious grin split his face, showing the blackened, ground, and flattened teeth. Blood… it was sweetly let and ever so more sweetly taken.

The scent of blood brought by the wind was overlaying the air in a heavy mantle and stoking the coals of his underlying rage from a slow glow into a frenzied burn. As if in response to his change in emotional state, the darkness was split by an orange glow that shot into life, illuminating the inte-rior of the largest building. A dwelling, he surmised, that was now glowing in a malicious and gleeful light. Tongues of flame were lapping within the lower and upper structures, and a sick and sweet charring smell had added itself to the wind, infused the with scent of blood and carnage.

In the growing light that was spreading around the area, Cynddaredd saw a stealthy shadow move from the larger building and pass towards the outbuildings. The pulse of a Dark aura surrounded this shape, and Cynddaredd's eyes slit in recognition as he watched the Commander of the Cotheda. The Commander's shape paused at the entrance to one of the smaller buildings and looked around, scenting the air.

He senses me…, Cynddaredd mused, his anger glowing in tandem with the spreading fire.

As if reading his mind, the eyes of the Commander turned and locked eyes with Cynddaredd. The greenish-dark glow emanating from the sheer power of the Knight Commander's eyes cut across the grassland between them and pierced through the First Knight's fury, filling his mind with the booming voice of his Commander as he communicated his orders.

Finish here and feed as you will.

Kill all who oppose you.

Then follow me.

Then it was gone, and he was gone. The echoing clanging of the Commander's voice faded in his mind, and when Cynddaredd looked again, the Commander had vanished. It mattered little: he would seek the Commander wherever he traveled so that the Dark Eternalia would prevail. For now, though, he had his orders.

Twyll shook his head as he ducked into the stables. He should have known that Cynddaredd would arrive to see the fruits of his labor and to feast in the revelry of destruction. Such was his way, and such was the way of all the Cotheda. It should have been no surprise that he would find them there; Twyll was just relieved that the intoxication of the violence being wrought upon the farm was distracting enough that Cynddaredd was not inclined to approach him directly. It would have been difficult to explain Maddau. Twyll glanced down at him as he continued to stride towards the open door of the stables, but if Cynddaredd's senses were keen enough to detect the presence of the relic, things would get… messy.

"Er…," he murmured to himself. "Messier. Things are already quite messy."

The sharp and pungent smell of blood greeted his arrival, causing him to pull up short. He eyed the silent and sleeping barn with suspicion. His senses were heightened by the presence of the relic, and something was not right here.

There was no evidence of the carnage that the smell of blood implied… and yet…

A muffled snore crashed through the silence, causing him to cry out in surprise, almost dropping Maddau's limp form. Twyll's head whipped to the right and found the huddled form of Lymder crouching in the doorway to the adjoining room, from where the sound issued.

Twyll's startled yell roused Lymder, causing him to shift on the floor and raise his head. He scrubbed a fist across his sleep-crusted eyes and blearily gazed around. He focused on Twyll without recognition at first, seeing only a dark outline in the orange light spilling through the doorway to the stables. Then the blurry lines sharpened into the face and forms of the Koteli's First Knight. And in his arms was the unconscious form of their Captain.

Full knowledge of the wrongness of the situation bloomed in Lymder's mind, and he was rising to his feet before he was even aware he intended to move.

"Gonestrwydd! Captain! What has happened?" Lymder demanded.

Twyll stared at him in a mixture of amazement and confusion.

"You are here? But *why* are you here?" He demanded, unthinking.

How could it be that Lymder was here? Did that mean that Cynddaredd and the others had not completed their task? What of the scent of blood then? And whose blood was it?

Lymder shook his head. "We rested in the stables, as you ordered, Gonestrwydd. Now, what has happened? Tell me, man!"

Twyll continued to stare at him, his mind desperately reaching for its moorings. "*WE???*"

Lymder squinted. Gonestrwydd's confusion was troubling to him. The Koteli's First Knight was always so in control and collected. To see him confused and scattered in such a manner indicated that something was truly very, very wrong. And the Captain...

"GONESTRWYDD!" he roared. "WHAT HAS HAPPENED TO MADDAU?"

Surprised and scared voices sputtered to life in the other room, and the metallic sounds of weapons and armor moving brought Twyll around from his shock at finding Lymder there and still very much alive. In a moment, Haelder and Dra appeared in the doorway behind Lymder, swords drawn and wary.

Twyll licked his lips. He needed to react well in this moment. Lymder was already alarmed, and now he had these others with whom to deal. If he did not soothe them and bring them back under his control, their outcry would alert the Cotheda, and a true massacre would be on his hands. He would be unable to keep the opposing forces apart, and all his careful planning would be for naught. He could still sense Cynddaredd's wild fury nearby. Too close for comfort. And if he could sense Cynddaredd, then it was likely Cynddaredd could feel him as well.

Hoping his distress was not more evident in the shadows, he tilted his head down and looked behind Lymder at Haelder. "Forgive my confusion. So much has happened and so fast. With what has gone on, I thought you all dead." He gestured back towards the farmhouse with an indifferent shrug of his shoulders.

He could feel Cynddaredd's attention on him now—a crawling, wrathful feeling that started at the base of his skull and began creeping along his brain like tendrils of fury and hate that brought the Darkness more fully present in his mind.

He must remain cool. Must remain calm. Should Cynddaredd sense his distress, it would bring him along in mere moments, and Twyll could not risk it. Above all, he must master his emotions and remain calm.

"Dead!!" Dra exploded. "Wotcher mean, *dead*?"

Haelder had now seen Maddau. "What happened to the Captain?" He babbled.

Their yammering voices were causing him to want to lash out, if only to give him a moment's silence, but he knew he needed to think. The rising anxiety was bringing his heart to his throat. Maddau weighed ever heavier in his arms, and the knowledge of the relic's presence weighed even more on his soul. The Dark's delight in his mind, Cynddaredd's presence was growing nearer, and now these men—men whom he thought already dead, men who trusted him—were now inconveniently still alive and demanding answers to questions for which he had not prepared answers!

And in the face of all this, he must remain calm, no matter what.

He knew what he had to do. He had to gain their sympathy.

Twyll sank to one knee, careful to hold Maddau still close to his chest as the hand holding the pack released and let it fall. At least, with it gone from his hand, the presence of the Dark was receding from his mind a bit, giving him space to think.

Lymder was there without a sound, supporting him on his right, taking Maddau effortlessly from Twyll's sagging arms. Dra had appeared wordless and with sword sheathed to support him on the left.

Twyll murmured his thanks absently, eyes closed and focused only on maintaining internal calm. He must remain calm—soothed and calm—or else Cynddaredd would come and bring the wrath of the Cotheda down upon them all. There would be time for this long-foretold epic clash, and as foretold, the dark would attain the cursed relic. But just… not here… not yet.

It was all getting away from him… and he still needed time to tend to Maddau.

He felt lighter somehow. That seemed ironic in light of the present situation.

"Madds," he whispered.

"I've 'im. Gonestrwydd," Lymder said from somewhere on the right, his even voice stoic despite the events. "'Ee breathes yet, but 'e looks terrible. What happened, man?"

Dra was holding his left arm and supporting him. Twyll sank onto Dra's arm and let himself be supported for a moment. When he opened his eyes, he saw Haelder kneeling down to peer at him.

"Tell us." The simple command cut through Twyll's riotous thoughts like a knife cutting cleanly through soft cheese.

Twyll began to talk.

The frantic sound of footsteps reached their ears just as Twyll finished recounting the night's events. They turned as one to see Ronanus running into the stables. His body was covered in char, and he reeked of soot and smoke. He stumbled to a stop and bent over with his hands on his knees, his face reddened with exertion, and began to wheeze. The wheezes turned into coughs until, finally, he retched into the straw a mixture of blackened char and spittle. When the farmer's breathing had eased a bit and his face had ceased to resemble bloodwine, Haelder offered his hand to help the man stand. Ronanus continued to cough.

"Aotrous, you must…run! Jantielle… she… she's not herself. She's set the house afire. I saw her dancing in the house and screaming about her Dark Master is here. I… I can yet save her… but I…. I…" He trailed off, looking towards the main house, panting.

"There's a man…" He started again, his eyes flicking from Lymder to Dra and then to Haelder. He seemed ignorant of the presence of Gonestrwydd kneeling by the hay pile or Maddau's limp form lying nearby.

"Walking around the house. I think 'e's a man… he has a man's shape, anyhow. But he's… I thin…I think he's the Dark Master she called…"

Ronanus licked his lips and looked directly into Lymder's eyes. "He doesn't look human…. And … I saw him… and… I ran… I could've gone back in to save her but … I ran." He finished and burst into tears. "Saints of Light, what have I done?"

Haelder held the farmer's shoulders as he wept and looked up at Dra and Lymder.

"The Lords of the Dark are here," Dra said quietly. "The Cotheda have found us."

"We must leave. Now," Lymder replied and glanced at Gonestrwydd. "We've little choice. If we stay longer, all at this site are doomed."

"As like as not, doom is their destiny, regardless of our actions now," Haelder said. "What of the Captain and Gonestrwydd? They are in no shape—"

"Gonestrwydd will be fine to ride," said Lymder, cutting him off. "And we'll tie the Captain to his horse. We must be gone before this Cotheda Dark Lord finds us here, or none of us will escape!"

Dra looked at Lymder. "You know the balance of the scales, Lym. You know the purpose of the mission. Like as not that none of us will return from this, regardless."

Lymder scowled at Dra. "We all knew when we accepted our charges what the outcome could be."

Dra looked away. "But it dunna 'ave t'be this way. We dunna 'ave to…" His voice died off, as he tried to find a way to say it. "We could just…"

"No. We cannot *just*," Haelder interrupted. "We made our oaths and took our charges, Dra. That is the choice we made, knowing full well what the price could be. We've been called to play our parts, is all. And we *will* play them, Dra. All of us."

"Yes, of course. Right, you are." Dra looked down as he stood and headed out the door. "I'll just bring the 'orses around front, yeah?" He was gone before any of the others could reply.

Lymder looked back at Haelder, then at Gonestrwydd and Maddau. "Come on, we've not much time, and these lot will take a bit of convincing."

"What of the farmer?"

Lymder glanced at Ronanus and then shook his head at Haelder. "He's got no part in this and has already paid far too much for the dubious pleasure of our company. His life will be forever changed after this night is over, if 'e survives it at all. His and all the others, those that're left, depend on us leaving this place quicker than th' wind now. And drawing that Cotheda Lord after us."

"So we leave him here?"

Lymder grimaced. "If he comes with us, he will die. Here, he could survive. It's as simple as that, Haelder."

The sound of hooves and horses nickering stopped the conversation there. Dra had brought around six horses, saddled and ready to go. Dra poked his head inside the stables entryway.

"We should be off."

Lymder looked around. "Six horses... so that's you, Haelder, Gonestrwydd, Maddau, Burdeb, and myself." He paused a moment, and the realization dawned upon him. "Light preserve us! Burdeb is still out on patrol!"

This knowledge splashed across Haelder and Dra's faces, rendering them pale and mute.

"We have to warn him! We have to get to him before—"

"Burdeb is dead," Twyll's hoarse voice interrupted.

Three sets of eyes swiveled to stare at Twyll.

"What did you say?" Lymder's voice was barely above a whisper.

"Burb is dead, Lym." Twyll's socketed green eyes turned to stare at him. "He died a'fore I could get to him in the fields. The wretched dogs of the Darkness tore him apart like an animal on the table of sacrifice. I saw it happen across the field and could do nothing."

Lymder shook his head at Twyll's words.

"That makes no sense. You are the First Knight. The fastest and best swordsman among us. How could you not defend him or render aid?" He railed. "Burdeb was the least experienced swordsman. He should have been protected!" His voice cracked over the last word, spilling emotion into his tone and belying the calm facade of his face.

Dra flinched, stepping back out to busy himself with the horses.

Haelder winced and turned towards Ronanus, who stared off in the distance, oblivious to their infighting.

Twyll's eyes glinted darkly at Lymder's accusation. "What would you have had me do, Lym? He was set upon before I got there. When I arrived, he was already being torn apart! Had I intervened, I would be dead as well! I had just time to arrive at the farm house to intervene on Maddau's behalf and save the relic from the Dark Ones! Would you have chosen better in my stead?" he hissed.

Silence held between the two men as they stared at each other. Lymder chewed on his cheek as he stared. Twyll glared into Lymder's eyes, an icy aura of contempt wreathing his countenance.

Several minutes passed before Lymder dropped his gaze. "I am sorry I shouted, Gonestrwydd. It was a difficult position to be in, and none can know the right choice until they are in the heat of the moment." He sighed.

"Then we've lost Olwygg and Burb," Haelder whispered. "Saints of Light preserve us."

Twyll got unsteadily to his feet. The long hours of crouching in the straw had stiffened his legs again, and electric tingles ran rabbit races in his feet. "It's not to be helped now, nor ever. We must be off." His voice had resumed a modicum of the gait and authority reminiscent of his old self, yet still it was a shadow of before, lacking the normal tone, ease, or strength.

Haelder looked towards Twyll. "Where we be off to, Gonestrwydd?"

Twyll set his teeth and started towards his horse. The tingles in his feet made his steps falter, but he pushed through to grip his mount's reigns. "We have to get the relic to the Temple de la Sagesse. It is the only place it…we… will be safe from the Dark Ones."

He looked back at them and managed a grim smile. "Quickly now, we must be off before that Dark Master here knows we're gone."

He looked at each of them in turn, and one by one, they nodded.

Lymder was the last, and he did so almost reluctantly. The stoic air that normally surrounded him had fallen again like a heavy curtain, keeping his thoughts and inclinations masked.

"Right, Gonestrwydd. Well said." He stood and reached for Maddau. "Help me with the Captain, then?"

A scattering of light across the hills heralded dawn's coming, but it was a heavy and hollow arrival. Mist had filled the valley during the night, composed partly of the moisture transition from warm valley night to cold mountain morning and partly of the clouds of smoke and soot from the still-smoking ruins of the farmhouse. The result was a chilly, white ground cloud that enveloped them in an obscure light. It had helped their escape from the farm, unheeded by any of the other residents or the Cotheda that stalked them. Yet it also clung to them as they moved, dampening their clothes and slowing their progress with no real ability to see ahead or forecast their path. All shapes were obscured into dark blobs until they were almost underfoot, which made any movement beyond creeping in single file on the long-abandoned road to the Temple treacherous. The road itself was barely a road at all anymore. Having been long out of use and with no one to keep it clear, roots and rocks had crowded the old grooved path, unhindered.

Twyll rode point in the procession, with Haelder immediately behind, carrying the pack with the relic. Dra rode tandem with Maddau, who was tied into his saddle as he was still too weak to keep himself fully upright for long, although he was aware. Lymder brought up the rear, keeping an eye on Maddau in case Dra needed help and watching their backs for signs of the Dark Ones.

Maddau's improvement both relieved and troubled Twyll. He was, of course, thrilled that Maddau had survived the encounter with the Dark Planes Walker, Cenfigen. Twyll knew that few who had encountered him lived to speak of it, and it's possible Maddau would never speak normally again. Yet his old friend had regarded him with an odd wariness since his awakening that Twyll could not reconcile exclusively to almost dying. That *did* change a person, to be sure. Twyll knew that personally. However, this was something more, and he could not put his finger on what the catalytic issue was. As far as he knew, Maddau was still ignorant of his true nature, and thus there was no issue on that end. He had seen Twyll reaching for the pack that contained the relic, but he'd made no indication of his intent. So what could it be that had set his friend so on edge?

The slow progression up the trail gave him time to fret, time to muse, time to plan for each and every contingency of which his tortured mind could conceive, and time to scheme.

The whisperings of the Darkness plagued him still. The relic was so close—within arm's reach. It would be nothing to kill them all and take it for himself. He could have it. He *would* have it. Soon. But not yet.

Not *just* yet.

But soon. When Maddau saw the truth of things, he would give it to him willingly. And then all would be right in the world. And the Darkness would rule over all. As it should be.

It brought incredible relief to Gwyleidd-Dra to see Maddau awake and aware again. Sometime during their flight from the farm, with the light of the flames consuming the farmhouse at their backs, Dra had looked over to see Maddau staring around at their procession. He had met Dra's gaze at first with a blank lack of recognition, and Dra had feared that the battle with the Dark Lord had sapped the Koteli Captain of his senses. Then Maddau had smiled a lopsided smile at Dra and tried to nod, but his neck was barely able to bend. Dra smiled back in relief and nodded in return. They needed to move in silence so as not to alert any Cotheda that could be following or searching for them in the fog. Else, Dra would have alerted all that their Captain was awake.

The long procession out of the valley took most of the day. The slow pace and enveloping wet and woolish fog did little to alleviate the sense of impending doom that hung over the group. Thus, it was of little surprise that their spirits were lifted when they finally crested the surrounding hillside and made a quick release from the billowing cottony fog. Twyll brought them up close, regrouping into a circle to ensure what remained of their regiment was still present, his eyes counting each in turn.

The reduced regiment looked back down the valley. With the waning light of the day broadcasting shafts of golden light across the land, they could see the whole of the valley was still cloaked in the fog's soft embrace. The last kisses of the sun's light danced across the mist but did not penetrate, leaving all in the valley below shrouded in shades of darkness and shadow.

The little farming village was completely hidden from sight, and no trace of it or any of the pursuing Dark Lords of the Cotheda was to be seen.

Chapter Seven

A Field of Worries

The trip up the mountain was not long in distance, but it was very steep. The knights were often forced to dismount and climb alongside the horses for fear of slipping. Twyll knew it was two days' worth of trip up the Dragon's Spine, a mountainous ridge, to the Holaf Tavern, if it was even still there, but the going was hard. He hated to force Maddau to make such a steep climb on foot, but he knew one misstep could send them all tumbling down a steep cliffside and bring a premature end to their journey. *It was lucky,* he thought. *Maddau had seemed to regain some of his strength during the journey out of the valley.* He could ride without a tether now and was even able to converse in halting bursts with the men. Dra, Haelder, and Lymder's moods were all heartened by Maddau's recovery, and Twyll knew it did yea things for their morale.

It was only between them that things were still strained.

Maddau had resumed his place beside Twyll at the head of the regiment, and Twyll did his best to resume the old banter that had always come so effortlessly before. Maddau did not react to Twyll's quips and stories, grunting in response only on occasion. Twyll was at great pains to pretend that nothing had passed between them. Yet when he took the opportunity to cast a subtle glance in Maddau's direction, he often found the latter staring blankly at him, as though unsure of Twyll—or as if he did not know him at all.

They had reached the midpoint in the Dragon's Spine by early eve, a flattened plateau scraped clear by centuries of pilgrim travels into a large, empty, shield-like shape. The perfect location for letting their mounts rest, with space enough for them to stretch out and have a fire. The day had come over cloudy after the morning's sun, and the increase in altitude had brought on the shivers as they traveled. The difficulty of the terrain kept them warm if they were moving, but once they stilled, their lack of preparation for the environment became evident. None of the knights had anything more than a woolen cloak in addition to their armor, and Twyll had even less as he only wore a lightly mailed shirt, eschewing the normal protective gear in favor of ease of movement. Or so he had claimed in the past when questioned or chastised for being too lightly geared.

Maddau was not himself.

His last sure memory before awakening to the rocking motion of a horse pacing slowly through a cottony white cloud was of intense pressure on his back and being unable to draw breath. His stomach and chest had hurt, and his head had felt like it would explode. Then it had all gone dark. He did not know if he had fainted or how long he had remained insensible to the world, but he did know he had not been wholly unaware. In the darkness that had overtaken him, there had been sounds... and *dreams*.

Words whispered incantations of the monster that had killed Olwygg. Horrific intimations of death and what lay beyond that veil in the realms of the Cotheda, awful gloating over his fate, and terrible, maniacal laughter that seemed to emanate and echo from all around him, regardless of where he turned.

Then things had changed. He had seen the scene of a grand battle. Knights with the symbol of the Light emblazoned on their armor were clashing with the Chevaliers of Darkness. The Light Knights were enveloped in a holy aura, and he could see that their counterparts were likewise engulfed in a seething dark aura. They clashed again and again, behorsed knights fighting against the rabid fury of the dark anthropomorph lords. But something was wrong. Though the battle raged on, he could see the knights had pained looks on their faces. And while they did defeat their adversaries, the knights, too, fell in the battle; their holy light was extinguished as the dark aura from their slain foes enveloped them regardless.

Maddau was forced to witness these horrors, and then a new terror emerged on the battlefield. A lone knight, bedecked in the vice armor of a Commander of the Cotheda. He paced with slow deliberateness onto the field, kicking a Light-emblazoned helmet out of the way and regarding the carnage strewn around him with little interest. The aura of the Dark Ones pulsed around him like a living thing. He reached the center of the battlefield and paused. As Maddau watched, he reached up to remove the horrid spike-and-hook festooned helmet that covered his head. It took both hands and skewered the armored gloves the Cotheda Commander wore, leaving trails of black ichor oozing down the gauntlets.

With the helmet off, a cloud of steam erupted into the cold darkness of the battlefield. Maddau recognized the sweaty, dampened hair plastered to the badly scarred forehead and the deadened grey eyes as their gaze turned his way.

Maddau stared into his own eyes and felt a scream of abject denial, horror, and despair claw its way up from his soul and struggle out of his throat. Darkness had flown to him from the corrupted version of himself then and entered his eyes, his nose, his and mouth, sliding down his throat with slimy speed and filling his stomach with a coldness that emanated throughout. The coldness of the Dark brought with it a knowing. An intelligence. And he could hear the wild mania of the Darkness' exultation at its conquest of him as a resounding and lunatic laughter.

Then that was all there was. Darkness within. Darkness without. Darkness was all there was and all there could be. It had won, as it always would. For Darkness always falls ravenous and insatiable upon the Light, extinguishing that which seeks to fight. And in this Darkness within his mind and soul, he understood that the Cotheda had won, as they had obtained the relic and now would rule over all.

And he had been the one to bring it to them.

Soft, shaggy, mottled white, bespeckled brown hair. The hair was filled with dust, and it moved back and forth a little faster than the slow roll of a ship on an even sea. He watched this gentle, undulating landscape for several rolling shifts before he became aware of the sound that accompanied the shifting vision. Ba-bock, Bock, Clop, Clip, Clop, Bock, Ba-bock, clop, clip, clop.... On and on. The sound took awhile to penetrate the still-strong yet supple stupor of fog protecting his mind from itself.

Sounds like a horse....

Clip, clop, bock, ba-bock, clip, clop....

Then the smells made their way into his fuzzy awareness. The warm and bright smell of straw, the grassy and gassy aroma of farm animals, and the comforting scent interwoven between the two stronger scents of a large, mild, and friendly animal that was at ease with its surroundings. This comfort smell's familiarity soothed him on a level inexplicable to conscious thought yet spoke to his spirit of humdrum daily work, with nothing out of place in the world.

Brosie....?

In these minor mundanities, Maddau came back to himself. After many moments of listening to the horse plod along and watching its neck and shoulders shift, he became aware that he, himself, was moving with this horse.

Little by little, he began to look around. There was not much to see. It was mostly white and mostly cold and damp. But he could see, and he was on a horse. And he and this horse were moving. He did not know if this was what came after death, as he could not see any others around or nearby.

If this was death, he thought, *he could do worse.*

At least he had a mount, and a fairly sweet-smelling one at that.

It was not Brosie, though. Somewhere, he understood that.

He did not know why he was staring at the horse's neck and shoulders and did not think to change his position. He was still tired after that battle with the Dark Lord.

He was not sure if one was supposed to still be tired in death. Perhaps that was normal.

He would think on it after he rested a bit longer, perhaps. After all, if he was dead, he had a long time to muse and peruse the oddities he discovered in this plane.

Maddau's eyes slipped closed as the movement of his mount rocked him back into a stupor-like rest. Clip, clop, ba-bock, bock.

Clip.

Clop.

Ba-bock....

Things were fuzzy for a time.

"boc...bok...boc..."

The soft rocking motion was soothing, almost hypnotic. The swaying was kept in play by a soft nudge at the extreme of each shift.

"bok...boc...bok..."

The soothing sway was soporific in the heat of the day. Maddau opened his eyes. The room was a cool oasis of shadows in the heat of the summer, and the hummock he lay in swung in a gentle breeze that danced through the open window and cavorted around the room. A day of rest was rare under the tutelage of the Sages, and Maddau neither knew nor cared for the cause of this uninterrupted leisure time—only that he was at his whims with this freedom. And his whim was to do naught but sleep. His eyes slipped shut.

The breeze danced another round in the room, bumping into his hummock and making it sway again. He was dozing, warm, and sleepy in the summery heat of the day.

Hurried footsteps echoed in the hall. They sounded furtive. They sounded…sneaky.

Maddau opened his eyes and looked at the opening that led from the main chamber to the pilgrims' quarters. Twyll was hunched against the carved stone of the doorway. His dark hair had hung in a smooth plait down his back when he had left early in the morning. Now it had begun to unwind, and many strands had been torn loose from the intricate plaiting. His smooth and tanned complexion was reddened from the sun, and his cheeks were splotchy with vigorous exertion. As if he felt Maddau's assessing stare, Twyll raised his eyes to meet Maddau's.

The two men stared across the small span of the room.

Emotions communicated the silent query and the responses that followed. Maddau's inquisitive stare became too much, and Twyll's face twisted in anguish as a hoarse sob tore through his throat, rooting him where he stood, not quite in the room with Maddau and not quite in the main hall of the Temple. As though caught between the two worlds of private contemplative desire and prayerful duty. Twyll's misery distressed Maddau, who climbed out of his hummock and crossed the room in one reflexive movement.

"Twyll…," Maddau whispered, his eyes searching his friend's form for some obvious injury.

"What happened?"

Twyll covered his mouth with his hands to muffle the noise. His bloodshot eyes seemed to finally see Maddau, as though for the first time.

"Madds…" His voice was a tiny whisper in the suddenly enormous silence of the room.

"Twyll, what is it? What's happened?" Maddau repeated as he reached for his friend.

Twyll cringed away from him, pressing himself against the entrance frame. Maddau's hand faltered mid-reach, then dropped. He stared at this person before him—so different from the strong, confident, and brave Twyll he had always known. This person he did not know. This person was scared—that much he could see.

"Maddau! Please, help me!" A single, searching claw of a hand shot up and grasped Maddau's shoulder. The pain was immense, but he could not move away from the strength of that grip. He stared at Twyll. His friend's red-rimmed green eyes stared back at him through the wild, dark tangle of hair that had fallen across his face.

Maddau gazed back at Twyll. Those penetrating green eyes froze him to the spot.

"Madds!" Twyll panted. "Forgive me!... Please..."

Twyll leapt forward in a sudden lunge before Maddau could respond and wrapped him in a stifling embrace. Maddau gasped in surprise, inhaling the strange scent of sage and lavender in Twyll's embrace. Twyll was always the taller of them, but somehow Maddau found his friend's head nestled against his shoulder. Though Twyll faced away, Maddau could feel the secret coolness of his friend's tears against his arm.

Maddau raised his arms in a tentative gesture of comfort. After a few moments of tears and sobs, the story came in halting chunks and scarlet whispers about the ocean breeze, the bright summer sky, Gwirionedd's intense and scornful laughter, and the lonesome cry of a solitary gull. How he was flattered for the attention. How good her touch had felt against his skin. The conflict in the heat of the moment—and how it had all turned to ash. Then, her scornful laughter... and oh, how she had laughed.

Maddau held his friend as the painful secret came tumbling out. Twyll bared his shame to him, and Maddau held his friend, rocking him in a gentle rhythm in the cool sanctuary from the summer's heat.

As he rocked Twyll, soothing his friend's tears, the edge of Twyll's sword guard knocked a gentle pattern against the ground.

"Bok...boc...bok..."

The gentle rocking soothed him as well as Twyll. Maddau closed his eyes against the ugliness of Twyll's shame and drifted away again.

The white, cottony haze had given way to swathes of gold and greenish brown.

Strange noises—like animal cries but in the tones of men.

"By the Light! HE'S AWAKE!"

"Captain!"

"GONESTRWYDD! He's awake!"

"Captain, can you hear me?"

"Captain!"

"Captain?"

"Let me see…Dra! Hold us here! Maddau? *Madds*?"

Bleary spots of color bled together for a minute as the brightness stabbed his eyes. The voices were distorted and jagged to his ears, booming one second and then hissing the next. For a moment, he was afraid he was hearing the wailing voices of the Dark again, calling his name and calling him to join them.

Maddau's loosened mouth pursed, and a faint wail slipped from his lips. He turned his head away from the offensively loud noises, squinching his eyes shut against the stabbing colors that attacked his vision. A cold hand gently cupped his jaw, holding his head up, and Maddau squinted his eyes open just the tiniest bit, tears leaking out against the jagged pain from all the colorful brightness. He strained to see who was around him and who was touching his face.

"Maddau." Twyll's voice was like liquid velvet on the raw nerves in his ears. As though a balm were applied to the screaming frenzy of a fresh wound, Maddau's fear melted away just a little bit. He was still uneasy about the situation, but the overmastering fear had receded.

"Twa… Twy… Twyll," he rasped.

"Madds!" Twyll exclaimed in joy, but on seeing Maddau shrink away from his yell, he immediately lowered his volume. He reached to hug his friend, overwrought with relief that Maddau had rejoined them. Upon seeing Maddau's face, the excited fire of his joy became a steaming pile of ash, and his arms dropped from their encircling hug to rest on his thighs as he regarded Maddau's recoil and pained expression.

Twyll saw that it was too much for his senses. It was all too much, too fast. One could not come back from the Dead Plane and expect to return to normal life right away.

Twyll knew that those who walk the plane of the Dead are insulated from all the cacophony of life, as it is a plane devoid of all sound and light. It was a plane where the shades of the dead could congress without the fear of being burnt by the light or bruised by the noiseful acts of the living. Thus was the reason all new children, just born, wailed so much—living was painful. It was only after one had lived in the Plane of Living for awhile that one became used to the sensory assault.

Some sensitives never did recede, though.

And Maddau, newly returned to the Living Plane, was much like a freshly birthed babe.

Twyll raised his fist for the attention of the other knights. Their excited babble was silenced almost at once.

"Easy now, Madds." He dropped his tone and carried his voice in all but the softest of whispers. "You need to adjust back to this plane. Come, open your eyes a bit."

Maddau squeezed his eyes open a bit more. They were watering heavily, and tears tracked their way down his cheeks. Unconsciously, he wiped the heels of his hands on his cheeks to scratch their tickling progress down his face.

Twyll moved his horse closer, in between Maddau and the Light that sprayed the mountainside. His shadow stretched over Maddau's face, relieving the pressure of the light on his eyes, and Maddau relaxed slightly. Twyll kept his voice low and gentle. "Open your eyes fully, Maddau. Come on, now.

What is it that the Captain of the Koteli fears to see from the Light of day?" he chided gently.

Maddau opened his eyes and looked blearily around him. He saw Haelder's gentle brown eyes, so full of concern. Dra was there, holding the reins of both his and Maddau's horses and watching this all unfold with knitted brows. Lymder sat stoically upon his mount, having brought up the rear and using his horse to corral Maddau's horse in the grouping so that it would not wander. Maddau tried to see Lymder's eyes, but it was a blur—too far for him to see just yet. He turned straight in his saddle again, and there was Twyll, whose familiar face and warm green eyes were so well known and loved.

"Twyll." His voice was like jagged splinters to his ears. He did not sound himself. "It's you?"

Twyll's face had grown haggard in the later days with worry and a lack of nourishment. Now it split into a sunny grin Maddau had not seen since they were boys before their pilgrimage. A white halo burst into existence around him, and its light was both soothing and scorching to Maddau's eyes.

"It is indeed, Captain." His smile could not get brighter. "And your return to us is the Light's blessing in form. Nice of you to finally grace us with your presence. I knew you liked a good nap, Madds. But that was a bit extreme—you missed out on all the fun!"

As was custom, Twyll's irreverence fell on the group with all the gentleness of a wallop across the face. In the silence of the following moments, all stared dumbfounded. Then, the peace of the moment was shattered as Dra began to giggle.

Haelder gasped and then also began to chuckle. Even Lymder cracked a smile. Maddau, used to Twyll's humor and not shocked at all, just smiled tiredly.

That smile was worth gold to Twyll. How sure he had been just hours before that he'd never see it again.

Hours into their trek up the Dragon's spine, morale had remained high. Maddau's energy was limited, so conversations were stilted and one-sided. Twyll spent most of that climb filling Maddau in on what had happened outside while he was fighting for his life and everything after he had begun walking the Death Plane. The mood had held well enough until the subject of Burdeb's death was reached, where a solemn air descended. Lymder, Dra, and Haelder had heard the news the night before and were somberly reliving the painful knowledge of the loss of the youngest member of the knights. For Maddau, the news was devastating.

His relationship with Burdeb had never been very good; the latter's immaturity had always gelled poorly with the Captain's need for competent execution. This had led to frustration for Maddau and low morale and self-defeating behavior in Burdeb. The poor match between Maddau's inability to be an empathetic teacher and Burdeb's need for instruction led to a rocky relationship. In the past few days, Maddau had been even more on edge with the advent of their task and therefore had even less patience with Burdeb's antics, which had made his remarks more cutting and shorter than usual. The last real interaction between them had been in the tavern. Maddau knew he had not been particularly patient with Burdeb, and after Twyll had informed him of what had really happened with the grocer girl, he had become suspicious that Burdeb was set to betray them to the Dark.

Maddau winced at the memory. Of all of them, he no longer had any right to be suspicious of anyone's motives in relation to the Dark. Especially since he was fated to be the one who would hand the relic over to the Darkness…

NO! he chided himself. *That was just a phantom trick of the Death Plane! It was not prophecy! Not real! That was not me—will not BE me! It's NOT prophecy!*

"Not prophecy…," he mumbled to himself, staring straight ahead at nothing.

"Hum?" Twyll trailed off, glancing at Maddau curiously. "What was that?"

"Nothing. Con… continue."

Twyll nodded. "And then I heard a horrific screaming coming from somewhere near the farm buildings. I rushed back and saw lights in the farmhouse. I ran there first… and thank the Saints of the Light I did, as I walked in on your murder!"

Maddau turned his head with slow care to stare at Twyll. His face, void of all emotion, had grown pale, and his countenance was distant. He stared at Twyll as though he did not know him.

Twyll, in comparison, had become more animated. His normally alabaster skin had erupted in large, ruddy blotches under the stress of the memory. His eyes sparkled in anxious fear, and his normally calm and self-contained mannerisms were cast aside for sharp and energetic actions, though still concise. Maddau could sense fear bubbling off the man in waves. A part of him wanted to exploit that—to taste Twyll's fear. Twyll, who was never afraid of anything.

I'll bet it tastes good…..

He recoiled from the thought in horror and dismay.

That was not the thought of a Koteli Knight of the Light's Virtue, and definitely not of the Captain of those Knights. That was a thought more suited to the Cotheda, with their evil designs and twisting of men's thoughts and desires.

It's NOT prophecy! he told himself, desperate in his aversion. *I'm NOT like them! I will not BE like them. It's not prophecy!*

At least not yet… his mind whispered back.

Now that they had arrived upon the plateau of the Scale, Twyll scouted the best place for their camp while Dra and Lymder began unloading their horses, and Haelder helped Maddau dismount. There was really not much in the way of coverage on this flat part of the mountains. The wind blew fiercely and without restraint across the clearing, scouring the land of all but the hardiest of lifeforms. At these elevations, it was already incredibly cold, and with the added force of the wind, the cold now cut through their skin as though they were bare-bummed bumblers in the wild. Lymder and Dra worked in earnest to create a shelter from the remains of their blankets and gear, while Haelder, having settled Maddau, foraged for what little provisions could be found around their site: fodder for a fire, anything edible, or rocks that could be used to buttress their shelter.

Despite Maddau's return to them, Twyll maintained command of the group, and he bade Maddau sit near where Dra had begun building a fire while Lymder finished their rudimentary shelter. It was not much, Twyll knew as he tended to the horses, brushing them down as best he could and ensuring their blankets covered as much of their bodies as possible to protect them from the long, cold night ahead.

It would have to do. He resigned himself to this knowledge.

He attached their reign tethers to a lead and then the lead to one of the blanket stakes. He was at pains to ensure the stake was well forced into the rocky earth so that the horses would not wander off the side of the mountain in the night and, in their misadventure, leave them to climb the Dragon's neck by foot.

Maddau had been silent for the last of that day's travel. Knowledge of the Burdeb's loss and the reminder of Olwygg's murder weighed heavy on him, and Twyll's tale of the fight against the Dark lord to save him had silenced what little responses he had made until then.

Twyll had tried to rouse him to respond several times as they had drawn nearer to the Scale, but Maddau had been unable or unwilling to respond.

"Here now, Captain. This should get us warmed!" Haelder said from over his shoulder. Maddau, taking great care to shift his head just the slightest of turns to look to his right, saw Haelder approaching with both arms full of the reedy growths that were this mountain's attempt at grass. Haelder plopped down beside Maddau with a grunt and dropped half of the puckery branches into his lap. "We'll be making applets, like so." He explained, showing how to wrap the reedy lengths around the width of his hand several times, then switching the orientation of the wrapping to make a ball. "Much like the hay balls our horses yield t' us. This'll burn, just as well."

Maddau watched as Haelder began another ball and then took some of the reeding himself and began to attempt a wrap of his own. The motions taxed the muscles in his shoulders; the process was difficult, and he had to stop to rest several times. In the end, though, he had completed a fire apple. He favored Haelder, who had been watching as he worked, with a wan smile, and Haelder returned the smile with his own tired one.

"'At's a good 'un, Cap'n."

Dra, who had been gathering their supplies, also obtained what had been available from the horses, both previously and currently. He now brought out their fire starters and began the laborious process of creating sparks in the sawdust and shavings.

Lymder had finished securing their blankets and bedding and now began rifling through what Haelder had foraged. "Not a' much t'work with, Hael," Lymder observed.

Haelder shot a dismissive glance in Lymder's direction and kept wrapping fire apples. "Not a'much t' *find* up 'ere, Lym. Dunnae like what'E got? Find more on yer own."

Lymder shook his head, exhaustion painted clearly across his face.

"I've not the energy to fuss wit'ye, Hael. We've just not got much t'night."

Twyll had reappeared in his usual silent manner and seated himself beside Maddau. Dra had finally gotten the fire started and had begun building a large enough flame to keep them warm. Lymder handed out what passed for their meal that night on scraps of cloth: a handful of berries, a piece or two of gummy root, a few scraps of root vegetables, and a hardened crust of bread.

Then men ate without conversation.

By silent consensus, the men had given their Captain, back from the Plane of the Dead, the largest share of the food. The irony, Maddau realized, was that he could barely eat it. Chewing was painful, and swallowing was worse. It felt like a large metal clamp had been fastened around his neck, and each time he sought to swallow, it was like trying to move a congealed lump of curd through a pinhole. The going was slow, and he had to take tiny nibbles of food and ensure it was well chewed and wholly soaked in saliva before he could attempt to make it past the invisible choke point that had set up barricades in his throat.

After a few moments, he understood the futility of his predicament and, despite the arguments made by his stomach, passed the uneaten food to Twyll to distribute back to the men. He had not the energy to explain, but somehow, he thought, Twyll understood all the same.

Taking the majority of food that had been apportioned for Maddau back, Twyll softly remarked, "Well now, Madds, save some for the rest of us!" Twyll's gentle chiding still felt like a slap to his cheeks, and Maddau's eyes watered. He glanced away as Twyll split the remaining berries and roots between Lymder and Dra. Haelder passed, claiming he was sated. The knights pretended not to see Maddau's embarrassed exhaustion as they finished their meager dinner and began pulling their cloaks around themselves and readying for sleep. Maddau took great care to tuck his cloak around himself as he lay down in the makeshift shelter of the extra horse blankets. Twyll and Lymder had bookended him in silence, and without conversation, Dra and Haelder had bookended them, creating a protective wall around their Captain.

The fire had burned itself out, and only the glowing coals of the fire apples indicated where the Koteli camped that moonless night. In their sleep, the knights had spread out from the tight and almost smothering group around their Captain to their more natural sleeping postures. Lymder remained perfectly straight on his back and slept without moving. Dra was also asleep on his back, but with his legs akimbo, and while one arm supported his head, the other was thrown across Lymder's upper body, resting on his far bicep. Haelder had rolled onto his side, stretching out in the space between himself and Maddau, and slept with his jaw agape, snoring softly. Maddau lay on his back, his right side pressed against Lymder's arm, with his hands folded on his chest. His breathing was weak but steady, and a faint growling sound emanated from his chest as he exhaled.

One of the knights was not peacefully resting in the horse-blanket enclosure. Twyll had waited until the breathing of all the other knights had settled into a routine pattern and their movements had stilled into the postures of deep sleep before extracting himself from the sleep pack. It had been a slow process, and his body had tried to betray him into rest several times as he had waited for all the knights to first relax, then still, then sleep, and finally for that sleep to deepen into a trip to the Dreaming Plane. The side of his cloak had been caught under Haelder's arm and knee when Twyll had finally begun to slip out of the pack of Koteli knights, so it had been necessary to leave it in the pack of sleeping men and venture out without protection from the cutting cold of the night's wind.

The temperature had further dropped once night had fallen, and the wind that howled its way through the mountaintops had an icy breath. Twyll shivered. His exposed skin puckered, with a million tiny hairs jumping to attention as he stepped outside the enclosure. A faint frost had overlaid the ground surrounding their campsite, and nothing remained of the fire but a few cherry-red eyes winking at him in the night. He rubbed his hands briskly up and down his arms and chest, trying to create some warmth from the movement, and his breath plumed out in front of his face. His mail shirt had stiffened with the cold and moved roughly against his body, chafing his shoulders unpleasantly in the chill air.

He slowly weaved his way through the encampment to where the horses were huddled by their tethers. The hungry beasts had scavenged any possible vegetation around them in a circle of excavation as far as their tether allowed, and as he passed, they looked up at him with naked hope and anticipation. Twyll absently patted the flank of his mount as he walked by, sparing just the briefest of movements of his arms before wrapping them around his body again to conserve warmth. Past the tight grouping of horses, he made his way to the outer edge of the clearing, where the side of the mountain dropped sharply to the sea. In the darkness, Twyll could barely see the outline of the cliff's edge, yet he could hear the crashing of the anguished waves below with ease. He squatted down, feeling around for the edge before lowering himself, with great care to avoid sitting on pointy rocks, to settle into a restive state with his legs hanging over the edge and swinging in the wind's bitter gale. It was but a matter of time now. All he had to do was wait.

The gloomy landscape was marred by darkened streaks of ashy earth and puddles of black water, with a garnet spiral of bloody shadowlets floating on the surface. Maddau trod carefully on the former and stepped around the latter. Somehow, he was assured, there would be no benefit to walking through that water. It held memories he did not want to know about. Each streak upon the ground was life's remaining cares and worries that could not be carried over into the next plane. Each puddle represented the regrets that were anchored in this plane when Death had ripped them from this world and spirited them past the veil, never to return.

This knowing pooled in his mind, and Maddau understood that this must be the Plane of Difaru, where each soul went to release their remaining tethers to the world before Death claimed them. The cacophonic silence of this plane made Maddau want to cover his ears. The unsounding was intense, and he could not bear it. His senses were becoming unmoored with the lack of any sound. The landscape seemed to upend itself and spin around him as though he were the center of a wind column. He turned his eyes, searching for a way out of this place, and saw standing a pace behind him a lone figure of a knight.

The knight's armor was ancient beyond all knowing. Any heraldry or insignia that had previously branded the metal had long worn away, and each segment of the plating was smooth, though long discolored with age. Maddau eyed the other knight across the span of terrain, studying him. The knight did not look at him but seemed to be staring off into the distance. The plumage of the helmet had been cut close to the hackle, and all that could be seen were brushy bits, faded grey with the ages. As Maddau stared, the knight's helmet turned to face him. The visor had been cracked in many places and was missing a chunk over where the nose ridge should be. Despite the distance, Maddau could see that there was a dark hole where the nose bridge would have covered it. The hole sloped upward at an angle and was between two pale red-brown shelves of bone.

He understood that whatever was in that armor was not alive and had not been for a very, very long time, if it had ever been. Nothing on this plane stayed alive long, as Death came for all.... Then this must mean....

"Death..." Maddau's voice was a croaky wheeze. "You are Death."

It was as though uttering the title, the knight's identity was realized, and it gave force to form. The body of armor turned to face the same direction as the helmet, and the knight took one measured step towards Maddau. He had only taken one step, yet despite the expanse of ground between them, Maddau found himself jumping back as the knight was less than an arm's distance away in a single moment's breath. He could see clearly now that there was nothing filling out the mailed shirt, and the overtunic hung loose in grey rags of no discernible symbology. There was no stalk of a neck to hold up the helmet, which rested open-front and sitting on the pauldrons. He could see one hollow socket peering down at him, where light intruded through the inner corner of the hole in the visor.

The mailed fist of this Death Knight reached forward, and Maddau was sure—more sure than he had ever been in his life—that if the Death Knight touched him, he would be reduced to another smear of ashy dust and a puddle of bloody shadowlets decorating this accursed plane. He cringed away from the hand, which had reached forward and grasped his shoulder with a clamping force.

A stream of images flashed through his mind: scenes of his boyhood, chasing after Twyll in the fields, kissing the goatherd's sister under the festival harvest moon, becoming a soldier, the flush of heat in the entangled moments after his first kill on the battlefield, the grave cold knowledge of his life's ending when he'd accepted his charge, Abertha's dark eyes, the relic's obtainment, his journey over the wide sea, almost dying at the feet of the Dark Lord, the Other Planes, waking up on a horse, the campground….

Then, with speed that moved faster than the crack of a whip, the images reeled back, and Maddau also found himself reeling backwards, the claw-like hand having released him from its grip.

The Death Knight regarded him for a moment that seemed like an eternity, and Maddau could feel a frustrated confusion emanating from the Guardian of these liminal spaces.

An echoey whisper that seemed to resonate from somewhere inside the hollows of the armor hissed at him:

"You… Interloper… You are a Planes Walker…Not readily in your plane…. But not ready for this one yet… This is not your time… Leave this plane… Do not return until your appointed time." The withered, mailed arm lowered to its side again, and the Death Knight stepped a single step backwards. As it did, its body separated into dust that flew away on an invisible breeze. So quick was the process that by the time it had completed its step backwards, nothing was left to mark that it had ever been there.

Maddau tried to find where the Death Knight had gone, but a roaring gale had begun to blow across the plane, kicking up sand and ashes into a whirling column of confusion. It spun around him, obscuring everything until there was no visibility left. This spinning storm surrounded him for but a second, and when it cleared, he saw a familiar hellscape.

This was what he had seen while unconscious after his encounter with the Dark Lord. This dream? Vision? Didn't matter… this place …. Was where he had seen the battle between the Light and the Dark… and where the Dark had won. And it was because he had been the one to betray the Light.

Was this truly another Plane? Was it a vision? He could not tell. Maddau closed his left hand into a fist and thumped his chest as an experiment. He felt a hollow thudding from the impact, but little else. He felt no stirring of the air here, but he did hear a dull, hollow roar in the background, implying the presence of the great storm that had shifted him from the Plane of Difaru to whatever place or plane this was.

Or Time....?

Something was different: this time, there were no bodies of knights fallen mid-clash and no warring knights moving around him mid-fight. This time, he was alone on the battlefield.

Maddau turned, craning his neck to try to look in all directions at once. He was, it seemed, indeed alone.

Except now there seemed to be something with him here; he squinted at the strange stone shapes installed in what appeared to be the center of the battlefield. They were unmoving, in the way statues were. Yet they looked as though they could spring into action at any moment. With nothing else visible on this desolate ruin of a field, Maddau began walking towards the statues. In the absence of any other option, they had to hold the answers.

The moonless night had gotten colder as time dragged on, and Twyll's regular shivering had given way to an uneasy stillness. He had a sense of time passing, but with no moon in the sky, he lacked any visual way to measure it. He crossed his arms over his chest, hugging himself. Tonight would be the last chance he would have to bring this epic farce to a conclusion on his terms. He wished things had gone differently, that he had brought this about differently, that he'd had more time. Time to explain things to Maddau—to explain and to bring him to the right side in this battle of universal wills. But now, it was all a mess. He just needed a little time with Maddau, alone...

To explain... and to convince...

Lymder, Haelder, and Dra would not betray the Light—not on their own. If Maddau were to join the Dark, however, the others might come around; with some convincing. Twyll leaned his head back to face the looming, faceless night sky and began to whisper, starting slowly but building in speed and fervor. He whispered his plea to the Guardian of the Planes, a soft cajole to be allowed to walk the Planes as an emissary of the Dark in the land of Dreams. At the end of each refrain of the incantation, he paused for a moment and waited for a response. Despite the full incantation of six individual invocations, there was no answer—not one he heard, at any rate. But there was also no denial, either. Twyll took that as implied permission, and a little sliver of a smile slipped across his face as he began to dissipate into tiny scraps of shadowlets that slipped and slid on the icy breeze and disappeared into the nothingness that marked the borders between the Plane of the Living and its sister, the Plane of Dreams.

Maddau approached the statues in wonder. They were like nothing before in his experience: the light shone on them from whatever angle he looked, and the quality of the material the statues had been carved into gave the supple impression of the natural hide of mortal people, yet as cold and still as the stone beneath its base. The two statues faced each other, mirrored in pose. The statue to his left was of a divinely graceful being with beautiful tendrils of light emanating from its back and rising from the joints. These tendrils were of a different material than the base or body, translucent in appearance and seeming to glow with an inner, smoky light. The statue's right arm was raised, hand facing away, as though in imperious command. The left arm was lowered, hand facing upward, as if offering something. The body was held in a rigid and constrained pose of authority. There was no indication of clothing carved around the body, and the base of the body melded in a swooping spiral to become the base of the statue itself. The face of the being was shaped as though of a person but gave no indication of its gender, and the body was, while slender in nature, was also without indication. While the being of light seemed divinely imbued with an air of grace, the face, while featureless, communicated an air of cruelty. A single symbol was carved into the base of the statue in the direction it faced. Before Maddau's eyes, the symbol seemed to fold into itself and then break back out into a word that he could read: *Light*. Maddau mumbled the word to himself and looked again into the face of the statue. It had not moved, as statues do, but it seemed that the cruelty embodied within the carving had intensified and the subtle glow emanating from the tendrils at the joints had gotten brighter.

A small fear blossomed in his chest. The presence emanating from this statue was horrific, and he did not like to have this entity, or whatever it was that was housed within this statue, so nearby. He also did not want to take his eyes off the Statue of Light. He had the irrational fear that when it was out of his line of sight, the statue would be able to move and would reach forward to grasp him.

That was silly, he knew. Statues could not move. He chided himself for such childish fears. But still…

With some difficulty, Maddau turned his eyes to look at the other statue.

The opposing statue's base was labeled with a similarly shaped carved symbol, in a manner similar but unique. As he regarded the symbol, it shivered against itself and flowed into the shape of a word he could understand: *Darkness*.

He lifted his gaze from the base of the statue to the figure depicted above. The body, while mirroring the statue of Light, was also androgynous in nature, and the face held no distinctive features. Unlike its Light counterpart, it seemed to emanate an aura of deep quiet and peace. The angular, blank planes of the face held an impression of gentleness and compassion.

Maddau felt a stirring of longing within his spirit. Longing to be understood, to be forgiven for his personal failings, for his failing as the Koteli leader. An understanding of his needs, his wants, and his dreams. An understanding and a forgiveness that he wanted to be something more than what had been thrust upon him before he even understood the true meaning of his Charge.

His hand, of its own accord, began to reach up to take the proffered hand of the Statue of Darkness.

But most of all, a longing for permission. Permission to lay down his unfair war in which he was just a pawn. Just a pawn that did not matter one whit. His life would be laid down at the base of the altar of the Light, and it would not matter one bit. It was a waste, really. A waste of his life. A waste of his potential. A waste of *him*.

Wasting your potential….. Because you could be… so much more….

Maddau jumped and pulled his half-proffered hand back to nervously rub the back of his neck. He was alone here, on this Plane between Planes. Of this he was certain—in this moment, at least. Yet he would have sworn someone had spoken those words in his ear. A whisper a bit sinister, yet all the more compelling for the compassionate current that ran underneath the hissing syllibants.

His eyes strayed back to the Statue of Light, and in horror, he saw that the cruelty of the figure seemed to be lancing out towards him now. It was as though in looking at the Statue of Darkness, he had infuriated the entity that dwelt within the Statute of Light. An ominous miasma of malice permeated the air and wrapped itself around him, instilling true fear in his heart, which shivered in response. He did not understand the fear all the way to his mind, but his body understood it well and the menace that was the cause of this fear. In a moment, it would percolate all the way up into his brain, and he would bolt. But for now, he stood there torn between the decision to take the hand of the Statue of Darkness and the fear of the repercussions that would follow from the Statue of Light if he dared.

But We shall protect you, if you choose Us. By choosing Darkness, you choose yourself. And isn't that what you always wanted…? The ability to choose? To have a choice?

The ability to be chosen? For once? To be the First Choice of another… if not of yourself?

Yes. He wanted to have a choice. He wanted to BE chosen first. Most of all, he wanted to LIVE and not serve as a sacrificial lamb in some Other's war. He was worth more than that! He MATTERED!

Of course you do. You and you alone can make a difference in this world. Choose Us, and we will ensure that your name is heralded for centuries to come and that all will speak of you. You are the Chosen, of course.

Eyes glued to the blankly menacing, yet still, face of the Statue of Light, Maddau's hand reached out of its own will and took the hand of the Statue of Darkness.

Twyll had been searching for some time. Maddau's dreams were shrouded from him, and Twyll could not feel him on the Plane of Life, so he began listening within the other Planes. He thought he heard an echo of Maddau's heart in Difaru, but there was no reason for his spirit to be there. He was still alive. Twyll's consciousness searched on, listening for the soft musical refrain that signified a soul of the Koteli. After a cursory check within several other Planes, Twyll heard the gentle, chiming refrain coming from the Breuddwydion: the Plane of Dreaming. Twyll willed himself into this Plane, knowing it changed when each person entered to reflect their dreams. Since he was awake and outside the influence of the Breuddwydion, he would not see what Maddau was dreaming. Only what would be affecting him in the Plane itself.

He arrived at the gates of the Plane and found that the Guardian of the Plane was strangely absent.

"That's unusual," Twyll muttered.

Each Plane had its own Guardian who kept the law of Rule within their respective realms. To find a Plane unguarded was indicative of meddling.

None should be interfering with Breuddwydion on his side, though. None of the Cotheda were in the area, and the only other one who could Planes walk was Cenfigen. Twyll had banished him far to the Outer Planes; it would take him a lifetime or more to return close enough to even reach out to mortals in their dreams, much less enter this hallowed liminal place between death and sleep. He carefully entered the Plane and gazed around. His senses were on high alert.

At first, the Plane appeared empty. The ground was strewn with hazy bursts of sand and some odd deep-sea plant life that were lying clumped together. The air was filled with an ethereal mist that shifted to and fro, both revealing and concealing the stage dressing of Dreams. Twyll could see a hazy outline of the Temple de la Sagesse in the distance and seemed to hear a soft and deep feminine chuckle coming from that direction. He deliberately turned his head from these mirages and listened for the chiming of Maddau's heart.

There, off to his left! The mist cleared a bit, and he could make out three forms standing in a line. The two forms on the outside were swirling vortexes of Shadowlets, and Maddau stood between. He could see the Swirling Shades clearly: two messengers of Deceit. One who seemed to be posturing menace towards Maddau, leaning over him in a manner befitting aggression and dominance. The other Shade was offering its hands in a manner most enticing. Twyll could feel the alluring glamour the Shade emitted and was even attracted himself for a moment. He could picture himself reaching Maddau's side and joining him in reaching for the Shade's hands, to be spirited away to whatever delightful fantasy with which the Shades were sent to distract, much as he had done in the past.

But no, this was not his dream. And he was not here to play in fanciful delusion. He was here to speak with Maddau in a way that he could be clear of his intent and direct without interference or ambiguity. He had to remove Maddau from whatever temptation had been sent by the Darkness and get him to listen to what he had to say. But... how to say it?

This was the crux of his problem—how to tell Maddau of what he had done and what he had become. Surely Maddau would understand why he, Twyll, had made the choices he had and what had driven him to the actions he had taken. It would be hard, especially given the losses of Olwygg and Burdeb... especially Burdeb. But he was confident he could make Maddau see...

Yes. He would make him see. Maddau, alone, knew all that he had endured at the hands of his mentor from the Temple. He would show Maddau what had been done to him—to both of them—in the name of the Light.

Twyll nodded to himself, certain that he could convince Maddau here in the Dream Plane. It was the only place he could both show and tell his truth to his only and dearest friend. With his resolve solidified, he began walking towards Maddau and the Shades.

Movement bolstered his resolve even further, and Twyll finally gained the courage to raise his head and regard Maddau and the Shades again, hoping he would look over and see him approaching.

He raised his eyes just in time to see Maddau reach forward and take the hand of the enticing Shade of Deceit.

"NO!" Twyll roared and began to run.

Lymder never slept deeply, even in exhaustion. He had always been a light sleeper, and despite the conditions of their travel, or perhaps because of them, even while treading the edges of the Dream Plane, he remained aware. As such, when Maddau began thrashing in his sleep, Lymder was awake and aware almost from the first frantic kick. His eyes sprang open as something moaned in the darkness. He stared up at the blanket roofing of their enclosure with some trepidation, unsure of where the sound had originated and further anxious for its meaning. When the moan came again, this time with a blow to his calf, Lymder sat up and looked around at Maddau. His Captain had scrunched himself into a protective curl, holding his head with one arm and the other wrapped around his lower stomach. Lymder could see that Maddau was kicking randomly backwards with no awareness of his situation.

"Dreaming?" Lymder wondered. He looked around for Gonestrwydd but could not find him in the dimness of the sleep enclosure. "Probably on guard," Lymder muttered to himself as he tried to position his lower half away from Maddau's erratic kicks. "But why now…? Was there a noise or something?"

It occurred to Lymder that they had not discussed a watch schedule, which they always did before resting. Especially with the stakes as high as they were.

Maddau moaned again, and this time it was followed by the wet sound of weeping as he began to thrash his arms and kick his legs wildly.

Haelder rolled over, partially alerted by the sounds but mostly still asleep.

"'Ere now. What's all…?" His movement coincided perfectly, Lymder saw, with Maddau's thrashing arm to get an elbow in the nose. Haelder's voice squeaked to a halt. Fully awake now, he sat up and covered his face with his hands. Lymder could barely see Haelder in the dimness, but he could hear the snuffling noises he made as he began to crawl out of the enclosure and surmised that Maddau had cracked Hael's nose a good one. Might've even broken it.

Dra was saying something in the background, but Lymder could not really hear his words. He was focused on curtailing Maddau's movements, which were becoming more pronounced as though he were trying to fight Lymder for his freedom.

"Where, in the Gods' names, is Gonestrwydd?" Lymder shouted at Dra.

Dra said something, but again, Lymder could barely hear him in the scuffle. He had managed to get his hands around Maddau's wrists and turn him over onto his back to prevent any further damaging kicks from Maddau's old boots.

"C'mon, now, Captain!" Lymder grunted as he worked to hold Maddau still. "WAKE UP!"

All at once, Maddau became still. The wild swings of his arms ceased, and he went limp in Lymder's grasp; all the fight had gone out of him.

Lymder was reluctant to let go of Maddau's wrists, should this just be an interlude in whatever dream fight his Captain was facing. He leaned forward and brayed in Maddau's face: "WAKE UP, MADDAU!!! IT'S JUST A DREAM!"

To his shock, Maddau did not awaken and instead began to weep.

Haelder came back into the enclosure, lifting the segments of the blanket overhang as he did and allowing brief bits of starlight to cut through the darkness of their sleeping enclosure. Lymder could see that Maddau's eyes were open, and he gasped.

In the pooling wetness of tears on Maddau's face, he could see swirling fragments of benighted Shadowlets.

His hand touched the statue's, and Maddau watched with some fascination as the stony stillness of the statue's hand wrapped itself around his own like a glove made custom for his fit. As soon as the material of the statue's hand enveloped his, he saw the material at the edges near his skin begin to flake and scale. It began spreading, as thin as a paste, along his skin, flowing up his arm to the hinge point and further up to his shoulder, taking his breath away in its speed of transfer.

And everywhere the material flowed, it began to burn.

There was a horrible, echoing laughter boiling about his ears, as though he was encircled by giants guffawing at the most hilarious jest of all time. The stone's skin continued to flow across his body, down his chest, and to his hip. The burning was as though his skin were drenched in acid while already on fire, and this acid had only made the fire burn hotter.

Maddau finally caught his breath and began to scream.

Twyll's legs pumped as fast as he could manage, but as was customary in the Dream Plane, he knew he was moving yet seemed to draw no nearer. When Maddau touched the Shade of Deceit, it had wrapped itself around his hand and begun spiraling up his arm. Maddau screamed, writhing in the grasp of the Shade while the other Shade swirled around them. Twyll thrust forth his hand with a shout, a command in the Dark speech, demanding that the Dark Shades cease their attack.

Nothing happened. The Shades continued their attack on Maddau.

Twyll put on a burst of speed and finally reached Maddau, intending to attack the Shades and rend them asunder.

Only as he arrived did he see that the Shade wrapping itself around Maddau had reached his mouth. It forced his lips ever wider, and then shoved itself between them and into his still-screaming mouth.

Twyll pulled up short, horrified by what he had just witnessed. The Shade continued its violent entrance into Maddau's muffled, screaming throat, and Maddau began to gag. He fell to his knees, with the other Shade still swirling protectively around him, overrun by the Shade of Deceit's violation. Twyll's hands crawled up to cover his mouth of their own accord in shock and revulsion. Within moments, the Shade of Deceit had completed its entrance into Maddau's body, and Twyll watched as the last bit of its tail slipped between Maddau's slackened lips. The second Shade had disappeared sometime during the assault, but Twyll had not noticed.

Maddau remained kneeling, having fallen back on his collapsed legs, and stayed with his head lowered, panting and drooling in turn.

"Maddau," Twyll whispered. He felt a deep revulsion at what he had just seen.

Maddau did not respond. He continued to drool and pant, his chest hitching and twitching with the errant cycles of breath.

A low, rumbling sound began to emanate from the ground around them. Twyll looked away from Maddau for a moment and down at his feet. The ground there had split, and a black ichor bloomed and bubbled from the crack. All around him in the field of the Dream Plane, the ground had split and pools of black ichor were bubbling forth. As Twyll watched, the bubbling dark sludge formed a probing extension and wrapped itself around his calf. As the ichor touched his skin, a forceful impact-thought shoved its way into his head as though from his own consciousness in Maddau's voice: *"I'M NOT WORTHY TO BE CAPTAIN!"*

Twyll shook his head and staggered backwards, away from the darkened pool.

In stepping backwards, he stepped squarely into another tar-like ichor pool, and the thought form of Maddau's voice smashed its way into his knowing: *"NO ONE RESPECTS ME!"*

Shaken, Twyll jumped away again, this time on more stable ground. He shook his head to clear his mind of the words... the *worries* he was hearing.

He stepped carefully, stabilizing his stance and avoiding the pools of worry that were blooming all over the Dream Plane field. Why were Maddau's worries manifesting like this? It was like he was no longer in control of his....

Twyll looked up to where Maddau continued to kneel. The roaring landscape of turbulent emotion erupted with his friend's deepest fears and desires. He had given himself over, or been taken over, by a Shade of Darkness.

As if sensing Twyll's attention, Maddau lifted his head to gaze back at Twyll.

The eyes that gazed his way no longer held the gentle grey steel of his friend. They were devoid of all spirit.

They were the dead eyes of a servant of the Dark Eternalia, completely blank and entirely veined through with black. Shadowlets had seeped into the irises, staining them with a darker ichor.

Twyll looked into Maddau's eyes, seeing that his friend was gone and that only the keening, mad rapaciousness of the Dark Eternalia was there, and began to scream.

The dream fell apart.

Maddau heard screaming. Was it his? Was it another? He could not tell.

The Dream Plane began to rip apart around him in swatches of color and swathes of sound. His mind held the repulsive memory of something enclosing him in a dark embrace. He felt *violated* and that this violator was with him still. An alien force that had its own agency. Its own *goals*. And he was now one of them. He had been its goal.

This was all very troubling, but he had no time to worry about that now. The ground had disappeared, and he was falling—tumbling down, down, down, nose over bootless heels as he went. His body ached. His throat and jaw hurt. His mind felt as if it were on fire. He smelled roots.

Roots?

"…a dream!"

Was that… Lymder?

"MADDAU!!!"

And where was Twyll? I could have sworn….

Senseless in his screaming horror of what Maddau had become, Twyll backed away.

His heel came down in one of the black pools as he retreated and splashed up to his ankle in memories. As though a curtain had dropped before him, separating him from Maddau's ruin, the scene before him altered.

The barren and ruined dreamscape of the plane morphed into a dark and cramped little room. Shadows clung to every corner of the little stone lined alcove. He could see two darker, person-shaped shadows in the artificial gloom. One shadow was hunched over the other in an almost comforting manner. The scene clarified as if he was drawing closer to the event, and he could make out the armor of a Koteli knight. The knight's mannerisms were familiar, and he recognized Maddau—not in the cloak and pauldrons of the Captain, but in the regular regiment's gear. A soft tug at his memory brought this moment into light. Twyll remembered that this moment had occurred just after the regiment had been formed but before Abertha had become Brehines, the Brehines. This was from the time when Anwadaledd was gone—having disappeared without warning from the Caer one night. An assassin had been caught in the Caer on the eve before Abertha was to assume the throne. Maddau was bleeding from a wound to his leg. He had slain the traitor who had come for their new Brehines, but the Dark's assassin had injured him in the fray. Twyll could hear their whispered conversation—more out of memory than sensation.

"You're safe, Madds. Breathe!"

"He's…he's dead? You're sure?"

"As sure as can be. You ran 'im through!"

"Yes. But I… you're sure?"

"Deadly sure. As are you. Now, breathe!"

Without warning, Maddau began to cry. Twyll busied himself wrapping the wound on Maddau's thigh.

"None of that, now. They're taking the body to be hung outside the gates."

"Where's—"

"The Brehines is asleep in her chamber." Twyll cut him off. "You can see her—you *will* see her in the morning. Right now, you need to rest."

"But I—"

"Rest, Madds. You've been through a lot today, and you are injured."

"Aye, but—"

"What now, Madds?" Twyll broke in again, his voice testy as he probed the wound to see if it would bleed through the bandage. Perhaps it was a bit too much pressure, as Maddau winced and pulled away.

"Had I been a better swordsman, he might not have nicked me, so."

Twyll's brow furrowed. "You should practice more. Get out into the yard with the others."

"I need to be by the Brehines's side, Twyll."

"You need to hone your skill. That much is evident." Twyll's voice was curt.

Maddau looked away, chastened by the tone.

The moment froze, and the image began to fade. A howling of wind raged across the Planescape with the receding of the memory, and after the howl came an anguished sob in the tones of Maddau's tears.

Why? Why can't I be good enough? Like Twyll? WHY? When will I ever be good enough?

The force of the anguish rattled him, and Twyll staggered back out of the pool of memory. His foot came down funny, pitching him forward. He overbalanced and, unable to catch himself, fell, landing on his hands and knees. His right knee plunged directly into another memory pool.

This one was sludgy and not wet at all—almost forgotten then… relegated only to the recall of Dreams.

Twyll braced himself as another scene bloomed before his eyes. Out of the ether, a group of young knights, the newly formed Koteli, were seated in a circle in the enclosed grove behind the Caer. The young men regarded the Teacher, who sat ensconced in the center of the group, waving his hands in the smoke from his double-bowled pipe. The old man's white hair matched the color of the smoke. He could not hear the words of the Teacher; they had always been in a lower tone that Twyll found difficult to discern. Unlike the other memory, when things had become clearer to him and he could see the emotive memory he had been able to hear along with the words in his mirroring memory, this time he could not hear the Teacher's voice. It did not matter, he knew. He had been there that day, and he knew what the Teacher had been doing: telling the story of the Dark and the Light and how the Great War came to be. Twyll knew this story by heart, and as he watched the memory play out, the words played forth in his mind.

"You are all here," he said, "because each of you has been blessed as the embodiment of one of the traits of the Light. I have watched you…."

The Teacher trailed off, looking into the distance away from the group of young men. He seemed to be looking at Twyll, who stood away, watching the memory.

"The traits you exemplify will be the powers with which you are imbued," he finished, still staring at Twyll. His lips continued to move, but Twyll could not hear him well.

"Say you now, each as his own man. Do you understand?" The Teacher looked at Twyll for a final moment, as if asking him alone, then turned to look upon the group of young men again, including the younger Twyll.

The hazy curtain of memory fell across the image, but the imprint of the Teacher's intense eyes remained in Twyll's mind. He felt the rancid ground of memory's emotion give way beneath him, and then he was falling into the grey haze—a greyze—of lost thoughts and feelings in the Dream Plane.

Chapter Eight

The Dragon's Maw

Someone—it sounded like Lymder—was braying his name over and over again. Maddau opened his eyes and looked to see that it was, indeed, Lymder. The normally stoic knight was now near hysteria with worry and fear.

"Lym," Maddau croaked. He reached up and touched the other man's face.

Lymder had not yet realized his goal had been achieved. "MADDAU!" he bawled into his Captain's face. "IT'S JUST A DREAM! WAKE UP!"

Maddau flinched away. The sudden movement caused his neck to constrict, and he began to cough.

Lymder realized Maddau had come to. "Oh thank the Light!" he gasped. His voice had roughened and fried with overuse, and now he could barely raise it above a whisper. "Maddau, you were crying out and weeping."

Haelder snorted from somewhere behind him and to his right. "Yer fightin' be as'good awake as t'wer asleep, Capt'n."

Maddau tried to crane his head to look back at Haelder but could not make it.

Haelder seemed to understand his difficulty, because he continued on: "Yer arm made a right go of me face. I'd not be pretty again for that."

Dra coughed softly. "Ye never were, Hael."

"Feck it, Dra," Haelder continued, unphased, "yer not'un t'talk 'bout looks."

Dra snapped at Haelder, but Maddau had lost track of the banter. He looked around the opened enclosure, seeing in the low lighting the blankets, their packs, and some lumpy shapes gathered against the far wall. After a moment, these shapes resolved themselves from the shadows to be Burdeb's and Olwygg's packs. Maddau's heart hurt at seeing these reminders that two of his teammates were no longer walking this plane. He felt around behind his head with his right hand and felt the reassuring presence of his pack, with the form of the relic easily felt within.

His eyes roamed around the enclosure again, and then found Lymder's face.

"Lym," he croaked, "Where…where is…Tw—"

What Lymder would have said in response was lost to the ether as the covering of their enclosure was pulled open as Twyll strode in.

"There ya be!"

"Where've you *been*?"

Lymder rounded on Twyll and snarled, his voice so raw from all the yelling that it was a seething hiss of a grater removing wood chips from a barrel.

"Where were you?" He opened his mouth to begin a rampage of fury, a complete contrast to his normal reservation. He drew up short upon seeing Twyll's face, all of his ire bleeding away.

Twyll stood before the group huddled around Maddau, who still lay in the mess of blankets. He raised his hands in response to the bracing demands from the other Koteli.

Maddau remained silent and simply gazed at him. Twyll felt the weight of Maddau's stare and stared back into his eyes, unabashed. When the others finally quieted, Twyll spoke. His tone was low and even without being rushed.

"They have found us."

"No!" Dra hissed as Haelder sucked in breath. Lymder and Maddau said nothing. The former looked down towards Maddau, while the latter only stared up at Twyll.

"Gonestrwydd," Haelder murmured, "Are ye sure?"

"There is no time." Twyll said, his voice flat and cold. "Gather all your things that you must have, and prepare to ride. It's almost dawn, and I saw the smoke from their campfire on the next crag over. They've heard us already. It'd've been impossible not to, with you lot screaming all over the land about yer dreams." He cast his eyes to the side at Lymder.

Lymder's mouth dropped open in indignation. He was about to fire back at Twyll's comment when he felt Maddau's hand on his arm. Maddau sat up, and in his best Captain's voice, which was still weak and quavering, he answered Twyll. "Then we must go. They cannot catch us here, where we have no defense and are as vulnerable as newborn babes. We have to get the relic to the Temple!"

Maddau looked around, meeting each of their eyes as he had before to ensure their comprehension. He met Twyll's last, and Twyll acknowledged his understanding with a slight nod. "Lead us, Gonestrwydd. Get us out of this."

Twyll dipped his chin to his chest in acquiescence to Maddau's orders. "Yes, Captain."

He raised his head, and his eyes blazed as he looked at each of the others in turn, mirroring Maddau. "We ride now! Gather your things and go! But quietly. Else, they'll know we've spied them! Utter silence! Go!"

It took no more than a few moments for the knights to gather their meager belongings, mount their horses, and set off with as little noise as possible, one by one, in the pre-dawn darkness, so as not to alert the Cotheda. Maddau moved the slowest, but Twyll would not let him fall behind, gathering his gear and boosting him up onto his horse before gathering his own equipment and mount to follow at the rear. Before, they had ridden grouped together and whiled away the time up the mountain trail with idle chatter and a breezy confidence. Now, they skulked like sought-after thieves in the broad light of day. It chilled Maddau's heart to think back on how careless they had been while the Cotheda had eagerly stalked them.

How was it that the Cotheda were able to track them with such ease? Maddau wondered. Perhaps they could sense the relic, sure, but how had they followed so surely under the cover of night and the obscuring fog?

Without sight of their pursuers, the Koteli Knights had become complacent in their journey and had forgotten the threat that had taken two of their number. They would not get the chance to be so carefree again.

The passage of another two hours brought dawn and the return of light to the land. Maddau twisted round in his saddle as best he could, looking for any sign of their pursuers, but there was none. No indication of the Darkness that pursued them. No signs of the Dark Lords. Of course, there was also the matter of the Darkness that pursued him. From within.

He turned to face forward, avoiding Twyll's searching look, to see that the path had finally begun its descent into the Dragon's Maw. From this angle, Maddau could see the reason for the way the mountain range had been named. It truly looked as though they were climbing up the spiny back of a dragon and entering the back of its head to descend between its jaws. The mountainous range that had surrounded them on their path now split to become the back of the dragon's head, the upper jaw, and the lower jaw. Between the two jaws was a small plain of grassland that had managed to flourish despite the inhospitable elevation. In the center of this plane, he could see a small grey hump of what he remembered as Holaf Tavern. The last place where people who were wholly of this plane lived, or congregated, before the descent to the Temple de la Sagesse, wherein resided the Sages of the Light.

Where the relic would be housed and protected.

Maddau fixed his eyes firmly on the Holaf Tavern as the next step in their journey. He felt certain they could find some aid and supplies to sustain them a bit longer in their journey and that they would be safe there.

The sun had mounted to the highest point in the sky by the time they reached the Dragon's Maw. The path opened out into a small clearing, and the knights were able to ride again as a group. The plain area was not huge, but it was deep enough into the mountainous peaks, rising high on either side, to make them feel small by comparison. The peaks encircled a cove of windswept and rocky land where large patches of lemony-golden grass struggled to survive. The rocks were piled in small, indiscriminate mounds, and at some interval, small towers of rocks had been constructed with delicate care to indicate a long-treasured life or various momentous occasions of import. Maddau looked down the path of memory and saw all that had changed. There was no longer a well-cared-for path from the entrance through the clearing. Now, all that remained was an old, worn groove in the dust from the passage of many feet and hooves. The tavern remained unchanged with the passage of the years: a squat dwelling supported by large wooden beams and a steeply angled roof, shingled with flat clay plates forged with the soil from these mountains. Once there had been an open section to what had been an outdoor kitchen, now a chimney merrily bloomed smoke into the still, cool air. The riders had stopped as if waiting for a cue to begin their descent to the tavern. "Or for permission," Maddau murmured to himself.

"Permission for what?" Twyll turned a curious eye towards his Captain.

Still much in his thoughts, Maddau spoke his feelings aloud: "To take the first of our last steps." As he spoke, he edged his horse with his heels, and they broke forward.

Twyll and the others watched him for a second, the symbol of leadership from their own Captain not lost on any of them: the Captain of the Koteli Knights, on his horse, leading them forth down the path. Taking the first of the last steps, as he had said.

Twyll spurred his horse and followed. One by one, the others fell in line as they made their way down the short, yet very long, trodden path. No rocks hindered their horses' steps. No dips or swales marred their travel; it was smooth and serene until they reached the side of the tavern, where a hitch pole had been erected just outside the eastern corner. They dismounted, and Maddau surveyed the ancient building. His eyes flitted across the stony walls, supported by the thick wooden posts at the corners and wooden beams at intervals between. The clay-tiled roof had many small collections of hollow wooden sticks and shells hanging from the edges, which clinked against each other as the wind blew around the eaves. The stoning of the walls had long stood the test of time as the tavern weathered its life and varied in color from the reddish hue of the rocky path to the brown-grey of the peaks that spired up above them. From the far side of the building, faint noises flitted back to them on the breeze, like shadows of life, raucous in the vivacity of the sun.

Maddau's mind sensed something off before his eyes had accounted for it. "Twyll, is it that...."

Twyll, who had been watching Maddau inspect the building again, as if for the first time, said, "Aye, Madds."

"Are you sure?"

"It has no windows."

Maddau turned to look at him, misunderstanding evident in his demeanor, his eyes pleading, "But I thought it used to..."

Twyll shook his head. "No."

Maddau persisted. "Are you certain, though? I thought—"

Frustration crept into Twyll's voice. "It never did."

"Oh."

Maddau looked down at the sparsely growing grass. His emotions were in complete turmoil, strangely, over this variance in his mind—in his memory. Somewhere, his heart was keening over a lack of windows, but he felt uncertain as to why. What did windows matter? What did it matter if they were never there? Why were windows, or their lack, of any import to him in this hidden place that did not matter except that it was on his way to the end of his charge?

He shook his head, trying to clear away the clutter of these useless thoughts and emotions.

Dra watched the silent blanket of confusion descend on Maddau, who just moments before had seemed so purposeful and decisive as he led them through the clearing. And now, after this terse point of tension with Gonestrwydd, he seemed lost again. Dra stepped to the captain's side and cleared his throat.

"Not sure what'n cut'uts 'ave t'do wit it. But am sure a good drink'll do fer what'ver ails, Capt'n," he said, his voice a soothing balm to Maddau's distress. Maddau turned his grateful eyes to Dra and nodded.

"A drink would be good, Dra. Very good."

Dra wrapped his arm lightly yet firmly around Maddau's shoulders and began steering him towards the front of the tavern, from where the faint sound of voices floated towards them. Lymder looked at Gonestrwydd, whose frustration had migrated from just overlaying his voice to twisting his face as well, and felt somehow saddened by the exchange, although he could not pinpoint why. He took Gonestrwydd's arm and began steering him towards the tavern's entrance as well. "C'mon Gonestrwydd. A drink does, indeed, sound like med'cine for what ails us all. Haelder, the mounts?"

Haelder, who had been on his way to follow Dra and Maddau, froze midstep. He saw that Lymder was escorting a tense Gonestrwydd, and he did not want to risk the First Knight's vexation after getting almost no sleep the night before. Dra and Maddau were already at the front of the building, leaving him with all the cleanup and preparation of their horses.

Cursing under his breath, Haelder turned to gather up the reins. Those horses needed a good brushing after their hard trek, and he reckoned a few more minutes of his time to treat these poor beasts well would not hurt. But he'd see that Lymder would be well set to pay for his drink when he got in there! This caused a smile to creep onto his face, and he began to tie the first horse onto the tether pole.

There had been clear sounds of voices, laughter, and the clinking of dishes being moved coming from the front of the building as they drew near.

But when they rounded the corner, the door to the tavern was shut, and there were no people outside.

Dra frowned at this. Where were those sounds coming from if'n there were no people here? The door was closed, and there were no windows, so how had there been noises? He saw the confusion writ clear upon Maddau's face and the growing worry in his eyes and quickly shifted his frown to a sunny smile, quite unbecoming on his craggy face. "'Ere now, Cap'n. Let's jist git inside for a good drink, like all 'em people we heard." He steered Maddau to the door, where the faintest sound of voices could still be heard. Gonestrwydd and Lymder had just come around the corner to see Dra, gripping the door handle in one hand and with his other arm wrapped firmly around Maddau, pull open the door.

For a split second, the sounds of voices talking and laughing got louder, then fell away to silence. Dra stopped at the entrance and looked around. The interior of the tavern was shrouded in darkness, and only two small lights burned in the interior. Little could be seen inside except for what seemed to be a shelf that supported the lights on the far side of the building. Silence prevailed for a few more moments as the knights peered into the tavern with a sense of anticipation.

A voice called out to them from the darkness, enticing and full of warmth.

"Welcome strangers! Familiar strangers in a land that never changes are always welcome. Come! Enter! Drink for the thirsty—the best medicine for what ails ye! Come in and close the door after ye!"

Dra hesitated, and he could feel the hesitation coming from Lymder and Gonestrwydd as well. Maddau, however, felt no such reservation and marched right into the shadowy depths of the building. In his unease, Dra's hand reached forward to grasp Maddau as he passed, but he missed his grip, and Maddau slipped through.

The three knights stood there for a second, frozen, as they watched the dark, broken only by two pinpricks of light, swallow their Captain.

Maddau stepped into the cool shadows that swelled through the tavern and let his eyes adjust to the darkness. Had he taken the time to consider it, the speed at which he was able to see clearly would have proved a point of oddity to him. Despite being in the sun and light of the outdoors for hours, his eyes adjusted with no pain and an almost welcome relief to the darkness. If he even gave it a thought, it was just the barest flicker of acknowledgement as he stepped through the door before consideration of the interior of the building took over the forefront of his mind. He surveyed the interior and saw that the tavern was wholly dark and empty of any other patrons. There were several tables with benches or stools pulled up to them, all without occupants. The far side of the building hosted a bar that consisted of a board atop two tree trunks that had been carved into some bestial shapes. Which beasts they were was impossible to tell. Time had worn the identifying angles to smooth curves, and the edges that were left had been darkened by the oils of many, many hands. This was an ancient place yet looked no older than the knights themselves.

Two lights, candles with their bases rammed into small bottles and metal pans to protect the flames and divert the light surrounding the wicks, were set upon the bar, and between them he could see a pair of hands. From just behind the hands, the voice emanated, calling again: "Welcome to the Holaf Tavern: the Last Tavern here in these mountains!"

Maddau began to advance: the first step was unsure, but he found the sound of the voice warm and reassuring, and each step thereafter was easier. As he approached the candles, the outline of a man distinguished itself from the shadows behind the bar. The man, who seemed familiar to Maddau in a way he could not place as he was sure he was a stranger, smiled at him. The man's eyes were a silvery grey in color and reminded him vaguely of the Teacher. They seemed kind. His hair was long and flowed across his shoulders and down his back in dark waves. The length of the man's hair was indeterminate, but Maddau could see it went well past his elbows. The stranger stood at his height, and his complexion, while pale, seemed to glow with an inner light of good health. He wore simple yet well-made robes of a style that, while appearing to be very old, were in excellent condition.

"Greetings," Maddau stated with an awkward smile. "We are—"

"Here to rest on your pilgrimage to the Temple De la Sagesse?" The man's already expansive smile widened and, seeing the shock on Maddau's face, laughed in an equally expansive manner. "'Course I'd know that! All who come through here on your plane are Temple bound! It's just natural! What can I get ye?"

"What do you have to drink?" Maddau asked. He could hear some movement behind him, but his focus was on the man operating the tavern. He did not know if this man was the owner, just worked here, or even how he should address him. Still, he did not want to be rude and assume, but he also did not know how to ask without being rude.

"Ye can call me Barkeep, if that'll do ye," the man murmured, as though Maddau had asked the question aloud. "And I have water, ale, and the waters of some of the fruits that grow in a village near here. What tempts ye?"

Maddau felt neither surprise nor shock that the Barkeep could read him so easily, and the man's voice fell soft upon his ears with none of the spiky accenting from his homeland nor with any of the lilt of the Bretonnic tongues. The Barkeep's voice was melodious and of a dialect that he did not recognize. *He must be from far away*, Maddau thought absently.

"I'll take water with thanks."

"Very far away, indeed," the Barkeep answered as he reached for a cup, and the jar where he kept the water. "Planes and planes away."

"Oh." Maddau's voice came out low and unsurprised. He felt a bit like a child during lessons when the instructor demonstrated a skill with the well-practiced ease of nature that he had yet to learn. There was another rustling sound behind him, and he thought he could hear, very faintly, the murmur of voices just off to the side. He wanted to turn to look, but the Barkeep's eyes held his with a compulsive strength. Besides, he knew that there was no one else in the tavern; he would have seen them when he entered.

But would he have? It was very dark in there, and his eyes had been sun-dazzled. Hadn't they?

"Of course there's plenty others here," the Barkeep said, his voice even. He could have been describing the color of the walls.

The rustling noise was louder now, and Maddau's ears prickled with the closeness of the noise.

"Others? Here?" he breathed the question aloud, although he could have just wondered in his mind as the Barkeep seemed to be able to answer him with ease either way.

When Maddau had disappeared into the shadow-festooned building, Twyll, Lymder, and Dra stared after him, dumbfounded. As they watched the looming, dark, rectangular door, they saw the two tiny spots of light inside the tavern wink out and then reappear, first one and then the other, as Maddau's body passed in front of them on his way through the room. Twyll watched intently for a moment. The two points of light had blinked out into darkness again, first one and then the other. He heard Maddau's voice say "Greetings." Then Twyll shook off Lymder's restraining arm from his bicep and strode forward into the darkness. He moved through the shadows with liquid ease, approaching the figure standing in front of the bar with a speed that was both silent and full of menacing intent.

Dra looked at Lymder, and the other man met his eyes. They nodded to each other and both stepped forward into the darkness, with Lymder leading the way. They could hear Gonestrwydd's movements in the darkness ahead of them, and they could see the burning lights at the other end of the room, but even though they moved through the entryway of the shadowy tavern with quickness and care, they could not seem to catch up to Gonestrwydd. After they had crossed the entryway, the door listed back to rest on its frame, closing off the outside light that had penetrated the shadow-infested room with thin rays and engulfing them in darkness.

"Gonestrwydd! Wait!" Lymder called as he jogged after the first knight. His hip banged into an unseen table on his right, pausing him for a moment long enough that Dra pushed into him, pushing the edge of the table into the newly forming bruise deeper, and then bouncing both their shins off a bench hidden behind the table in the dim light.

Lymder squinted to see the shadow-blurred form of Gonestrwydd receding from them as he followed Maddau. Dra grabbed Lymder's arm and hurried him to stand. The room seemed blurry in the dimness. Lymder wiped away the water swelling at the corners of his eyes caused by the impacts to his hip and shins, but the inside of the tavern got no clearer. It was like the air inside the tavern was… thick.

Maddau could still hear the fervent rustling of the knights behind him, but it sounded a world away. His eyes remained fixed on the Barkeep, even as he brought the cup of water to his mouth to drink. The water tasted sweet and cool as it passed through his throat, and he would have sworn he could feel it heal the remaining damage done by the Dark Knight. The sweetness was not a taste of the water but a function of the cool liquid itself, and every tissue in his body responded. He could feel vitality brimming over and a fullness and vigor he had not known since his childhood returning. The Barkeep's eyes smiled at him, and he opened his mouth to say something when a hand fell on his shoulder.

Twyll could see Maddau drinking something at the bar, and there stood a shadow behind him—so close that it was almost upon him. Twyll could see the outline of armor, something like a cloak or a tunic, and a helmetless head. The outlines of the armor in the flickering light looked sharp and jagged, like the elements of the Cotheda's armor. He reached his mailed hand forward to grab the shadowy form sneaking up on his Captain, but somehow grabbed Maddau's shoulder instead. As his hand passed through the shadowy armored shoulder, it melted away into the air. Twyll got the briefest impression of a face turning to look at him: all pale, bony facial planes and hollow-socketed eyes that were all whites with no awareness. Then the impression, the vision, whatever it had been, was gone. He was roughly grabbing Maddau's shoulder and jerking him back, causing him to spill his drink on the bar. The Barkeep immediately turned his focus away from Maddau, his mouth still open as he began to speak, and Twyll froze when he got a good look at who was tending the Holaf's bar. The man was old. He must have been in his latest years and looked well wizened for it. His balding head was covered in age spots and scabs, indicative of a poorly functioning body, and he was clad in filthy, bile-spotted rags. His eyes were clouded with the fog of old age, and Twyll's gaze could not field even a single tooth in the ancient crone's gaping maw. He turned to Twyll, who was bewitched by the man's gaze.

"Here, now!" the Barkeep cackled at Twyll. "What brings ye on so fast in here, Brother?"

Maddau, freed from the Barkeep's gaze, was brushing the spilled water off his tunic and turning to look at Twyll in annoyed reproach.

"Twyll! Really! What was that all about—making me spill the first cool water I've had this age? Barkeep, my apologies for my friend's rude haste. Please, another?"

The Barkeep, without breaking his stare at Twyll, handed Maddau another cup of water.

Twyll felt his mind go completely blank. It sounded like a wind was starting to blow behind him. His eyes felt hot, and sweat was starting to pool in between his shoulder blades and at the base of his spine. Those eyes. Those cold, colorless eyes were boring into him, and yet his mind felt totally empty, as though he were walking the planes between the worlds and there was nothing there. Nothing but emptiness. The sands of time, devoid of all meaning and value, nothingness, minutes left empty of all purpose. The howling of the wind was closer now. Closer. It was closing in on him. It sounded like some monstrous, shrieking specter had come for his spirit. Maybe it's already there, between his ears and behind his eyes, in the emptiness of his mind.

"More like the emptiness of the Heart, Brother," the Barkeep croaked at him and pushed a cup of water towards him. Twyll stared back at the Barkeep, unable to look away. Unable to move, the hand that rested on

Maddau's shoulder hung there like a dead weight. Maddau did not seem to notice, drinking his water in restive complacency.

Twyll's mind stuttered only blankness, refusing to think. Those eyes held him still as stone, yet his right hand moved of its own accord, grasping the cup of water on the bar and lifting it to his lips. His mouth opened in reflex as he prepared to take a drink.

What flowed over his teeth and tongue was foul and fetid. The pungent smell of growing mold in stagnant ponds filled chock full of rotting fish and plants flooded the passages of his nose and the back of his throat. He could taste the wriggling life of a hundred tiny tadpoles and wormlings crawling across his tongue and teeth, heading for his throat, making their way to his gut, where they would latch on, grow, and feed.

His stomach clenched, and his throat tried to spasm, trying to retch up the worm-infested water. He could not, though. His mind was empty. His gaze was fixed on the Barkeep. He could only observe, in a helpless and detached way, that he must swallow. Or choke. The feeling overwhelmed him. He was unable to move. He was unable to think. He was unable to spit. And still the slimy, semi-congealed fluid that passed for water in this hovel welled in his mouth, burgeoning at the back of his throat, cutting off his air, and starting to tickle his throat with the dancing of the worms.

He could not breathe.

He could not breathe!

Could NOT swallow this foul miasma!

Could. Not. BREATHE!

The muscles in his neck and jaw twitched as he fought the reflex, fought against the strain in his lungs. Fought against the need to remove his tongue from blocking the back of his throat and let the air in with the wormy liquid.

A trickle of water spilled over his lips and ran in tiny rivulets from the corners of his mouth.

A lightheadedness was starting to creep into the blankness of his mind, and Twyll understood that falling unconscious here, at the mercy of the Barkeep, would have dire consequences for him.

His chest pounded for air. His head pounded with blood as he tried to keep from swallowing the water. His chest seized; he could fight it no more. He must breathe. Or die.

Twyll choked on the worm-ridden water, coughing and spraying the air with a fine mist of water droplets as his mouth and throat opened and he heaved in the blessings of the air.

Under the watchful eyes of the Barkeep, Twyll swallowed.

Maddau had finished his water and felt ready for another. He opened his mouth to ask the Barkeep for yet another, but before he could form the first sound, his jaw sagged open. His head tilted back on the stalk of his neck, and his eyes rolled back into his head and closed of their own accord. His hands splayed limply on the board of the bar and then slipped off to hang at his sides as his body relaxed into a standing stance, mouth agape. A petrifying sleep overcame him, quelling all motion and thought instantly into rest.

Lymder and Dra had been making their progress through the moist, thick air of the tavern. To Dra, it felt like wading through body-temperature water that was chest-deep but not buoyant enough to make him float, even without armor. To Lymder, it was like trying to wade through waist deep mud, like the thermal springs near their homeland. Only that was a pleasant, if not distracting, experience that warmed the body and soothed the spirit. This was… something else. Something not so pleasant or distracting. Something bothersome. Something worrisome. Something uncomfortable to the spirit and a difficulty to which to bear the sensation.

Lymder squinted. He could no longer see Gonestrwydd at the other end of the tavern, where two small orbs of light glowed in the darkness. He had no idea where the Captain and the First Knight had disappeared to, and he was starting to worry.

"Captain!" he called in the darkness. "Gonestrwydd!"

Dra took a struggling step forward and planted his foot on the ground. He panted with movement. The air felt thick in his mouth, and his chest strained to draw breath; it seemed like though he pulled air into his lungs, it did not satisfy.

One more step further, Lymder thought with grim determination as he stepped forward again. *One more.*

The outline of the bar looked a little clearer. There seemed to be something standing in front of it—maybe that was the Captain? Lymder shook his head in stubborn frustration and stepped forward again, squinting at the outline as he struggled to pass the table closest to the entrance. Why was it taking so long? The building was no longer than fifteen stride lengths of a man of average height. Gonestrwydd and the Captain should be within arm's length by now, yet Lymder could not seem to get any closer to the bar, despite his struggles to progress forward.

One more step. His grasp on Dra's arm clenched tighter as he pushed to move forward, communicating the difficulty of making each step intertwined with the frustration of the process. It should not be so hard to walk across a room!

A soft wind whistled across the clearing, chasing the scant cloud cover away and causing the scraggly grass to briefly dance in the early afternoon light. Haelder had finally finished tying all the horses to the hitch pole, giving each in turn a brush down, and ensuring they had water from the hidden well beside the hitch pole. Now to ensure they would have something to tide them by as they rested. He grabbed his pack and looked in it for the packet of horse grains. It did not present itself with ease, so he stuck his hand in his pack to root around. After sifting through several different small packages, some wrapped in cloth, others in a thin, papery material, he felt the leather packet of horse grains. He pulled it out with a triumphant cackle and released the leather thong that held the packet closed.

It was empty.

He had expected the rations to be slim. The Koteli had fled from the Ronanus farm to escape the Cothedan attack with naught but their packs and their horses; no rations were afforded them, and they could not take the time to procure any in the heat of the attack. In the same vein, they had been forced away from their campsite on the Dragon's scale before they'd had full rest or even had a chance to do a proper forage—not that there had been any real rations to be foraged out.

Now they were at this tavern. Holaf tavern. A proper tavern for resting before they descended to the Temple. Haelder had been there only once before, many years ago, for his training, but he remembered the way a bit. He knew they would have a bit of time here to recuperate before the long climb down the steep and rocky mountain path to the sandy shores below, where the Temple rested in the Dragon's teeth. *The Cotheda would not dare to pursue them there.* He thought. *That was hallowed ground, and no demons of the Dark could step foot on hallowed ground!*

Still, they'd had no chance to forage or procure supplies. For them or the horses.

Haelder looked at the empty packet in resignation. This just would not do. The horses needed something to eat as they rested. Just as he did.

He would soothe his spirits with some alder food and drink in this remote tavern soon enough. First, he had to keep the horses in good spirits if they were to carry them back to the port town when they had, well, finished whatever they were to do in the Temple.

A whinny and a chuff brought his attention back to the task at hand: horse feeding. The mounts were impatient to eat and had begun to nip and chuff in their hunger-induced bad humor.

He tossed the empty packet back into his pack, neglecting to re-tie the leather thong. It was as useful as tits on a goose, he thought. He'd have to forage here, in this clearing, for something with which to feed the horses.

Haelder gazed around, searching for potential horse fodder. There were scant resources in this sun-dappled and windswept mountain clearing that played host to piles of rocks, craggy grass, and not much else. The grass would have to do.

Minutes of bending and twisting around the perimeter of the tavern brought the rewards of an aching back and a few small handfuls of grass to Haelder's hungry horses. He'd no sooner opened his hands below their mouths when the horses had eaten the proffered grass and were bumping into each other to grab more portions of the scant meal and any others they could steal.

Haelder gently rubbed their ears and pushed down any pushy noses that bumped him for more grass. "Alright, alright, yer bossy nags," he murmured to them. "I'll see what I can find else. Mayhap the tavern hast somet'in t'feed yers." He patted the flank of the closest horse as he walked around them and stepped out of the shade from the side of the tavern where the horses were hitched up. He glanced around as he stepped clear of the tavern's shadow and stopped. There was something glowing between the rock spires at the entrance to the clearing. Haelder shaded his eyes for a minute to study the glow.

At the edge of the clearing, where they had entered from the mountain's path, a bright sun spot erupted from the rock. Haelder stared. It was as though a star had settled on the entrance to the clearing and was twinkling there, emitting a white, bright light. But it was the middle of the day, Haelder thought, rubbing his eyes and looking again. There were no stars to see at this time of the day, and anyway, stars do not land on mountains and shine here.

He felt his relief and restful mood slip away, only to be replaced by a gnawing anxiety coupled with a dread that bubbled up from his guts. He knew that that glow had an ominous source. He knew that though it twinkled and glowed like a star on the ground, it was not. Haelder knew what else twinkled and glowed like a star in the sun's light: armor.

He backed slowly and with great care towards the front of the tavern, never taking his eyes off the light coming from the entrance to the clearing. One foot back, shift his weight, next foot back, shift his weight.

The Captain had to be warned.

Gonestrwydd had to be warned.

The Cotheda had found them again.

Twyll had no sooner cleared the worm-ridden fluid from his throat and breathed in a huge gasp of air when he felt the stinging of the worms biting his tongue and the inside of his mouth as they made their way down. He coughed forcefully, trying to dislodge them, but to no avail. He bent over the bar mid-cough, bracing himself on the wood. From far away, he could hear the Barkeep saying something. Something about emptiness. Something about darkness. Something… something…

Twyll rested his head on the bar, feeling the rough surface press into his forehead. It seemed splinters rose up to meet his skin and stab at him, yet he rested his head regardless. He was sapped of strength, as though the worms had sucked him dry of any will to proceed with his tasks. He closed his eyes, feeling listless. Feeling tired. He had not slept well the night before—not at all, if he was being honest.

"And how often *are* you honest anymore, Gonestrwydd?" a voice from nearby inquired.

Tears welled below the lashes of his closed eyes. His cheek had sunken onto the roughened bar board to join his forehead, and he collapsed into a bending position as the petrifying sleep spell took hold upon him, with one hand sprawled on the bar and the upended earthenware cup lying beside it, empty except for a drop of crystalline pure water clinging to the rim.

The Barkeep regarded the surrender to sleep of the First Knight with some bemusement.

Maddau looked around the tavern in shock. The place was filled with warmth and light. Several lamps hung down from roof trusses, and each table had one or two candles in potted holders on them, creating little islands of light in the room. The benches and stools around the tables each held a familiar body. As though his attention had called to them, when Maddau looked upon these personages, they each turned to look at him and smiled, waved, nodded, or winked at him. The conversations filled the room with a low din that made eavesdropping on individual conversations impossible. He could not believe the difference from one moment to the next in this room. He turned to Twyll to ask if he saw this too.

But Twyll was not there. Not beside him on a stool at the bar. Not behind him in the tavern proper. Not there at all.

"No, Gonestrwydd's in another tavern," a sultry voice cooed in his ear.

Maddau whipped his head to the right, spasming his neck in the process, and gazed into the cool green eyes of a lady standing behind the bar.

Maddau stared at her. "Who.."

"I thought I told you to call me Barkeep." She smiled back at him.

Her smile seemed familiar—almost the same smile as the man Maddau would have sworn was standing behind the bar just moments before when Twyll had bumped into him.

"It should be the same. It's one of the few things that does not shift around here." The Barkeep displayed her dazzling smile again. "Not many things that don't shift around here. But that should be one of them."

Maddau noted that this version of the Barkeep could also seem to read his mind.

"Of course I can. That also doesn't shift."

"What do you mean by 'shift'?" he asked.

"Planes, of course." She giggled, tilting her head to the side and smiling at him.

"You mean we're…"

"That's riiight!" She sing-songed the words, nodding her head. "We're in a different Plane here. I prefer this one, and so do the people who come to drink and rest!" She gestured to the others in the tavern. "It's much more agreeable than the Plane you are on." She lowered her voice and gazed into Maddau's eyes as she finished her statement: "Although there are other Planes this tavern exists in that are not as pleasant as this one. Your friend is visiting us there."

Maddau stared back into her eyes, burning with questions and confusion. "What do you mean 'visiting there'?"

The Barkeep favored him with a brilliant smile and picked up the tipped-over earthenware cup on the bar. She grabbed a rag that had been draped over her left shoulder and began busying herself with drying it out. "I'm not really allowed to discuss others' experiences in different Planes. Maybe the other guests can explain it better." She gestured towards the tables with the hand that held the rag, causing the end to flicker outwards in a flourish.

Maddau's eyes followed the waving end of the rag to look at the crowded tables, where a few people were looking back at him and the Barkeep.

"Alright," he said, more to himself than the Barkeep. "I'll go see if anyone here can give me more information. Thanks—" He turned back to thank the Barkeep for her help and to hand her back the cup he had used, but the space behind the bar was empty. There was no Barkeep in sight, and since there was no planking below the top board of the bar that rested on the carved pillars, he could see she was not crouched down below the bar board. She had just disappeared into the air behind the bar.

A large, blank, grey-brown wall filled his view. It was covered in striations and deeply worn grooves from years of impact. Tiny feathers of light bled in around the edges of the wall and stabbed at his eyes. With the stabbing of the light came a sleepy, creaking ache in his temples, informing him of unpleasant pains yet to come. Probably resulting from whatever that excuse for water had been. His mind felt muddy and heavy. The little feathers of light were painful prickles against his eyes.

Edges of the wall...?

Twyll slowly tilted his head up and saw that the height of the wall before his eyes was only a short journey to clear air and a boarded and beamed roof far above. There were sounds—some hollow and muffled, some precise and also sharp to his ears. They came in patterns and cadences, but he could not distinguish any recognizable flow. Even with his battle-honed senses, the sounds felt so blurry to his ears. The surrounding noises acted as though, rather than climbing into his ears and announcing themselves, they merely stood on his shoulders and commented on their presence.

Large, pale reddish cylinders covered in a river of cracks and shiny weals flooded his vision suddenly, causing a startled Twyll to jerk his head back and stand up in a singly sharp movement. The dull pain that had been sleeping in his temples flared like an angry cat, making him suck in breath and wince in response. He opened his eyes to see the gnarled hand of the Barkeep encircling the earthenware cup that had been directly in front of his eyes when he awoke.

"I see yer up, boy," the Barkeep cackled and pulled the cup closer. He peered into it for a moment and then looked back at Twyll. "I'd wondered when yew'd be back amongst us."

Twyll peered at the Barkeep. Something about this situation was, well, different, but his dulled sense could not quite perceive the change. The wizened old man looked blurry, and his face seemed fluid, as though his features kept shifting ever so slightly.

The Barkeep began to dry out the cup with the rag he held loosely in his left hand. "Haf you fig'red out yer predicament yet?"

Twyll shook his head with great care, trying to calm the hissing and spitting pain that throbbed behind his temples.

Another cackle: "Well, then I'd best suggest yer look 'round fer some 'elp!"

Twyll squinted at the shifting figure of the Barkeep and, using his hands to steady himself on the bar and turn with glacial slowness, moved his whole body around to see the tavern.

The Barkeep shrieked his leathery laugh again. "They've been waitin' fer yer these long years! Go an' haff a see!"

At these words, the murmuring noises in the room fell silent, and Twyll could feel the weight of many a gaze fall upon him. He looked out into the dim tavern and saw many shapes turning towards him.

The cup the Barkeep had been cleaning fell onto the plane of the bar with a hollow "*pling!*"

He glanced back instinctively over his right shoulder, causing the pain in his head to roar again, and saw that the Barkeep was gone.

Maddau stared at the space the Barkeep had occupied so recently behind the bar that was now devoid of her presence. He had the creeping feeling that he was not alone in this immediate space, yet he clearly saw that he was.

He looked fixedly for a moment longer, willing something to move, to change. Nothing did, and after a few minutes he began to feel foolish, silly even. He placed the cup down, landing on the rim of its foot on the bar, and turned back towards the room, muttering his thanks even though he knew there was no one there to receive the words any longer.

The cup, which had fallen from its footer and rolled slightly to the edge of the bar, righted itself as if moved by an unseen hand and scraped back away from the edge.

A hollow whisper, too low for human ears to register, echoed softly: *"Twas my pleasure, Cap'n."*

Maddau approached the nearest occupied table. Around it, he could see three figures, each dressed in the garb distinct to the Sages of the Light. When he first approached, he would have sworn that these people were the Sages he had known in the Temple when he had trained there years before. But as he drew nearer, he could see that these were not the Sages that he knew at all. Yet they were, indeed, Sages, for each had the symbol of Wisdom marked upon their face above the left brow. Each Sage's robe held the insignia of the Temple on the chest, and within that was the symbol of the Virtue these Sages embodied. When he approached, all three had ceased their discussions and turned towards him, observing his advance. The marks of Wisdom on their faces seemed to glow a tiny bit in the reflection of the candlelight.

"Well met, Maddau, Captain of the Koteli," offered the man closest to him. This Sage bore the symbol of Veneration on his robe. His well-lined face wore a good-natured smile that seemed to glow from within, and his amber eyes were kind.

"Come. Sit with us here."

He indicated an empty seat across from him and beside a reedily thin, distinguished-looking woman. Her robe was adorned with the symbol of honesty, and her face was very smooth. Her green eyes sparkled with childish mischief, yet her white horse-tailed plait belied her age. She gave Maddau a cheerful grin and patted the empty spot beside her but did not speak.

He stepped around the edge of the table to sit beside the Sage of Honesty and across from the Sage of Veneration. As he did, the third Sage's face and the front of his robe came into full view. The man who sat beside the Sage of Veneration was grizzled, dark of countenance, and regarded him with eyes of the deepest brown, almost a darkened red in color. Maddau studied the symbology on this man's robes and saw that he was also in the presence of the Sage of Mercy.

"Your presence was foretold." The Sage of Veneration smiled at Maddau. "We have long awaited your arrival."

The Sage of Honesty sighed. "Too long." Her voice was so low, she might have been whispering. "And for you to come here means both the end of the beginning and the beginning of the end."

Her quiet words seemed to clang through his body with the alacrity of an alarm, and for a moment, the cheery lights of the tavern seemed to darken. He heard an ancient creaking noise from the bench beneath his body, and the wood of the table seemed to become slick with the dirt and grime of ages past. He looked down at his hands in the darkness, and when he looked back up to the eyes of the Sage of Veneration for answers, all had righted itself again. The tavern was warmly lit, and the tables were well oiled and in good, clean condition.

The Sage of Veneration's smile had shortened a bit, and concern had furrowed his brow, causing a cascade of wrinkles to emerge on his face.

"It's a tenuous grasp that you have on this Plane. You are the Captain of the Koteli, but something draws from you your full ability." He stopped and looked towards the Sage of Mercy, who looked back at him. Some communication passed between the men, Maddau could see, but he could not catch the nature of it. After a long moment, they looked back at him, and he could see real fear in the Sage of Veneration's eyes. The Sage of Mercy's eyes held disgust and contempt as he regarded Maddau.

"Give me your hand!" the Sage of Mercy barked at him, shocking and compelling Maddau. His right hand thrust forward, and the Sage wrapped his hand around Maddau's wrist, holding it down to the table. Maddau stared at the Sage of Mercy, who regarded him with his burning, reddening eyes.

Hadn't those eyes been dark brown? Maddau wondered, alarmed.

The Sage of Mercy grabbed Maddau's smallest finger with his other hand and scratched deep into the skin just before the first knuckle.

Blood began to well up in the groove of the scratch. And with it flittered a tiny, black scrap of a shadow wisp.

The Sage of Honesty gasped at this sight, and the Sage of Veneration sighed.

"It is as we thought." The Sage of Mercy shook his head. "You have been tainted."

Understanding their words missed Maddau completely, but the feelings they evoked hit home and brewed a despairing mixture of anxiety and shame.

"I... I'm sorry...," he whispered, his voice faltering. He licked his lips and tried again. "I'm so sorry. I don't know how. Why?"

The Sage of Honesty looked askance at him as the lights within the tavern dimmed again and his home plane bled through where they were for a moment. Her eyes glowed like green emeralds in the flash of darkness. The light flickered and then came back to the warmth of the tavern.

"What can I do?" he whispered, his words seeming faint even to his ears.

The Sage of Veneration placed his hand over Maddau's on the table, holding it down on the wood. He looked at Maddau, and his eyes, though still very kind, were grave.

"You'll have only one opportunity to avoid the future the Darkness has planned for you, son of the Light." The words floated across the table to him. Maddau was dimly aware that the Sage of Mercy's other hand was now holding his smallest finger, and it was beginning to ache. The green glimmer of the Sage of Honesty's eyes seemed to have turned into a brighter glow off to his right, but it was the golden glow of the Sage of Veneration's eyes that held his gaze.

"You've only one chance, so you must get it right! The treachery visited upon us is not yet over, so you cannot fail. The Darkness cannot ascend to the Hallows. Make your stand there."

The Sage of Honesty gripped his shoulder hard, and Maddau found he could tear his gaze away from the Sage of Veneration. He turned to look at her. She was much stronger than her willowy build implied. She leaned forward to whisper in his ear, "We cannot heal what is within you. Once there was a time when we could, but that is long past now, and our effect on your Plane is no longer. We can help, though it won't be easy. Would you like our help?"

Her eyes glowed even brighter, making it hard to look at her, but Maddau found himself nodding.

She cut her eyes to the Sage of Mercy and nodded.

"Do it then."

In the moment of her words, Maddau's eyes also shifted to the Sage of Mercy, and he saw that the man's eyes had become the red of a molten furnace. His hand had completely enclosed the smallest finger of Maddau's right hand, and his face was that of immovable marble. His hand closed into a tight fist, crushing Maddau's finger in its grasp. Without warning, the Sage of Mercy yanked his hand backwards and, with it, went Maddau's finger.

In its place came a tearing, rending pain that felt as though fire crawled over his hand and up his forearm. His shoulders tensed from the pain, and he screamed.

The bond across the planes shredded itself, wrenching Maddau back into his time, snuffing out the lights of the tavern, and erasing the presence of all the others in the room.

Nerves scorched by the fiery grip of agony and his body spinning with the nauseating gut punch of a Plane warp gone horribly wrong, Maddau began to scream.

Twyll backed away from the bar, trying to look everywhere at once. There were no lights in the tavern aside from the two candles at the bar, and the shifting shadows seemed to dance and spin in the darkness. His eyes shifted back and forth, keeping watch for any incoming attack. Nothing was perceivable in the dimness, yet there was an underlying feeling of menace in the atmosphere of the place. He wanted to get to a side of the room—preferably a corner—to provide some sort of defense for his back and flank, so he began to move with deliberate slowness to his left. He felt like his head was spinning on the pole that was his neck, as he kept trying to see in all directions.

The ache in his temples was long forgotten in the rush of adrenaline that the anticipation of battle brought.

Two steps.

Eight steps.

Ten steps.

More than a dozen.

Twyll felt a slow throb of anxiety. Could he have so misjudged the room's size? It could not have been more than ten strides across, and by now he should have found the inner wall. Yet he kept moving and came into contact with nothing but the swirling dark shadows.

"Gonestrwydd…," the clicking purr of a familiar voice whispered from behind him.

He spun around, his eyes frantically searching for whomever had whispered that.

"Gonestrwydd," the voice sighed again, this time from his right rear flank.

Twyll spun around again, his right hand dropping low and his left arm raising up to ward off any blows that could come from above or below. But there was nothing. Nothing around him but the dancing shadows in the dark.

His anxiety was growing, with an undercurrent of rising tenseness beating to the rhythm of his pulse. The uncertainty of the situation brought with it a frustrated anger that lashed its red arms around his mind. He could see the cloud of anger reddening the edges of his vision and pulsing with the beat of his heart. He tried to cool his reactionary impulse, but it had already pulled too far into his mind, and, with it, his heart rate was beginning to rise.

Twyll jerked himself fully erect and, with the snarl of the Dark Lord's power that rested within his spirit and the fury of the First Knight of the Koteli, whose orders had been disobeyed, shouted into the darkness that danced around him.

"Show yourself, vile shade!"

"Oh… Goooonnnnneeesssttrwyyyydddd….," the voice sighed again, drawing out each part of the word with syllabic hisses.

Before him, the shadows swirled a bit faster, forming a spiraling and spinning column of darkness that began to coalesce into shapes that formed a female figure.

Two deep-set, almond-shaped, dark green eyes opened in the darkness.

Twyll's anger was quenched in a rising pool of fear. He knew those eyes. He had known those eyes. He would never forget the last time he had seen them: bulging in terror and unreleased pressure, with the cognition of ultimate betrayal in their fading light as life fled them.

The spinning of the shadows ceased, and out of the darkness before him, a woman with long, white, plaited hair, deep green almond-shaped eyes, and dark golden skin stepped forward to stand in front of him. A wicked knowing slid the curve of her lips from a normally beautiful smile to an arrogant smirk. Her eyes squinted at him in that familiar way that had always made his legs feel a little weak, especially when her brow furrowed a little over the left eye, causing the wisdom branding to ripple. Her long robe also bore the mark of the Sages, with the worn and almost indistinct symbology of Honesty on the crest.

It hung open, and he could almost make out the silhouette beneath.

"Gwirionedd," he breathed. His jaw hung open as he panted her name. "Is it really you?"

She leaned in closer, smiling into his eyes, and rested her forehead against his.

"It's been a long time, Gonestrwydd."

Twyll closed his eyes against the intimate conversation of her gaze and tried to slow his breathing. His heart raced. Sweat dampened his brow and chest, causing his shirt to stick against his ribs, and rolled off his temples in beads of cold fear.

Between panting for air, he inhaled deeply through his nose and smelled the scent of sweet lavender that had always graced the air whenever Gwirionedd was nearby.

He also smelled himself—a rotten stench that was a mixture of sweat, fear, and betrayal.

The heady mixture made his stomach turn: sweetness and rot, willingness and force, wisdom and betrayal. He felt he would soon vomit.

He could feel the smile of her lips against his mouth as she tilted her head back to kiss him while keeping their foreheads pressed together, as she had done before, and his mouth closed to meet hers as if of its own accord.

He felt her move closer as she deepened the kiss, her body pressing forward to reach him: left hand against the woolen cloak on her shoulder, right hand against the robe on her hip. The aroma of her scent engulfed him, but still below that was his own scent of rot and betrayal. The urge to vomit was stronger now.

"Gonestrwydd," she whispered against his mouth, twisting her lips to encircle his. "It's been so long, so long since you visited me. So long since those days in the Temple."

The scent of rot was stronger now. Was it him? Her? Both of them?

She was close now, just a breath away, pressing against him.

But there was no heat from her body. Just... cold.

The coldness of space. The coldness of the embrace of the Dark.

Bile was inching up his throat, and his mouth was filling with spit.

"NO!" His hands clamped down on her bony frame with sudden fury, and he pushed her back while turning with violent speed and bending over to his right. She fell backwards into the gentle cushion of the shadows as he braced his hands on his knees, his mouth open wide. Saliva and bile spewed forth in ropey projections as what little he had eaten in the past day made an efficient exit.

Tears fled his closed eyes to make their runs down the planes of his cheeks and dripped after to meet the vomitous mess on the ground.

The stench of rot boiled around him again. It was him. Of course it was. It had always been him.

He shook his head, the most natural denial of something.

"No," he sobbed weakly, still crying with his eyes closed. "No. You're dead. You can't be here. You're dead."

A hand ruffled through his hair with the gentle caress of a lover.

"But Gonestrwydd, I am your Truth." The quiet smile in her voice whispered through the darkness to him. "I'm always here," it added, with a slight lilt of sass.

The room seemed to be spinning around him, and the stench of the rot of his own betrayal, his own lies, and the taint of his own spirit rose up around him. "NO!" Twyll screamed out in the swirling darkness of the air. "NO! YOU'RE DEAD!"

"But how can you be certain of that, Gonestrwydd?" her voice asked from within the dark cage of his own mind, echoed by the even darker beat of his own heart.

"BECAUSE YOU'RE DEAD!" Twyll howled against the empty shadows of his heart, wiping his hands fitfully against his face to smear the tears and spit away.

"How do you know?"

"YOU'RE DEAD AND YOU ARE NOT HERE!"

"But how can you be sure?"

"BECAUSE…"

"BECAUSE…"

"BECAUSE I KILLED YOU!"

Dra had been edging forward, dragging Lymder with him, when a terrified and defeated howl echoed through the tavern, stopping them in their tracks. Dra stared around the shadow-festooned tavern, looking for where that howl could have originated. He turned to look at Lymder, and he found the other Knight staring back at him with equally puzzled and fearful eyes.

"Was that Maddau?" Dra whispered.

Lymder shook his head. "It sounded to me like Gonestrwydd," he whispered back.

"It didn't sound human to me," Dra responded.

"Dra, where's Gonestrwydd and the Captain?" Lymder asked, his voice still very hushed.

Dra shook his head and kept edging forward. Each step took more courage since they had heard the howl. The room was empty. Of this much, Dra was certain. *So where was the Captain? Where was the First Knight?*

He edged in a little further, approaching the bar where the Captain had gone just moments before. There was nothing else in this place that indicated any life, so it seemed the best place to start searching for answers. A little closer, and he'd be able to see beyond the bar itself. For sure, there'd be something there to tell them what happened.

Dra felt a sharp pull on his arm, holding him in place. Fear and anxiousness became irritation at the additional delay: first it took forever to move through the room, then they kept bumping into the tables and stools in the dark, then they kept falling into each other.

"Now what?" he hissed. But when he turned to look at Lymder, he saw the man had become still as stone, staring fixedly at the table at which they had just drawn abreast.

Dra followed the line of Lymder's stare and saw what had transfixed his fellow Knight so: there was an outline of a man, in the faintest of greys, sitting at the table. He was slumped over with his head resting on the table. His left hand dangled down against the bench, and his right hand was splayed on the table.

"Lym… what is it?" Dra whispered to him.

"I think…. I… that…" Lymder could not fully articulate the horrific thought that was more knowing of the heart than realizing of the mind.

Dra changed his course and began inching towards the table. Drawing closer, he realized what Lymder's heart already knew, despite his mind's refusal to see it.

"It's the Captain," Dra breathed out.

He could see the outlines more clearly now, as though Maddau was coming into focus. But something was wrong with the hand on the table. It looked as if his hand was melding into the table.

Lymder stepped noiselessly up to stand beside Dra.

"He looks as though a ghost," Lymder breathed out.

Dra jumped. He had not heard Lymder move, and the man's presence had startled him.

"'E looks PlanesWalker," he said with quiet reverence.

"Is he alive?"

"Not sure. But that we see 'im here is a good sign. I think."

"A good sign?"

Dra sighed. "As good a sign as any. We need to bring him back to this Plane."

"Maybe that's where Gonestrwydd….?" Lymder didn't need to finish the question.

Dra nodded. "Aye. Maybe so."

Lymder reached forward. "D'ye think we could?"

Dra nodded again. "Nothin' lost in trying."

Lymder went to place his hand on Maddau's shoulder.

His hand went slightly through the grey outlines, then landed on the firm slant of the Captain's shoulder. He gripped Maddau's shoulder hard and felt a measure of relief to feel the reality of the man's body.

"He's real!" Lymder gasped to Dra, who also reached forward to grasp Maddau's shoulder and moved further to give it a rough shake.

"Captain!" Dra hissed in Maddau's ear. "Captain! We need you to WAKE UP!"

Another howl erupted nearby, this time from the empty space where they had just been standing when Lymder had seen the Captain's form at the table. Dra and Lymder froze, and together, their heads turned to see that the empty space beside them was no longer empty but was filled with the pulsing silver outline of a person. This figure was crouching on the ground with their hands over their head.

"Lym… do ye see…?" Dra managed to choke out his inquiry through the unmanning fear that was making its way up his throat.

"Aye, Dra." Lymder's voice was low in the swirling shadows within the tavern.

"I see."

"Auugch." Maddau felt a rough shift back and forth. There was a pounding in his head, and his body felt disconnected, like it was no longer attached to his head. He could still feel a burning in his right arm. Coupled with the ache in his head was a loud, keening whine ringing in his ears and some equally loud whispers. Whoever was whispering was doing a poor job of being quiet, he thought as he opened his eyes. Sprawled at eye level were the thumb and first finger of his right hand, resting on the plane of the table. Through the hazy blurring of his vision, he could see two human-like shapes move into his field of vision. Each seemed to have several versions of himself swirling about them.

"Curse my eyes," he grunted, squeezing his eyes shut and shaking his head. He opened them again, groaning as his shifting head caused the fire in his arm to announce itself with greater stridency. With the pain came a moment of clarity; all the floating shapes coalesced into two figures, revealing themselves to be Lymder and Dra, and they were walking away from him. He could almost see the faintest outlines of the Sages, who had recently occupied the other seats at the table, around the shapes of the knights. Maddau squeezed his eyes closed again, clenching his fists, and trying to anchor himself in this Plane. He had to rid himself of the disconnected and floating feeling of being between the planes. Else, he could not be wholly vested in either world.

Another ear-splitting howl erupted in front of him. Maddau jerked upright from the table and gained his feet, his internal focus shattered. The planal overlays had disappeared, and he could see with a crispness to his sight that only came in the heat of conflict: Lymder and Dra were standing over the hunched figure of a man, crouching on the floor with his hands over his head. Wails were coming from this man almost without cease. Most were soft, piteous cries that bespoke grief and remorse in their tones, but some were full of anguish and fear. Those were the loud shrieks that had brought Maddau out of his reverie.

Drawing closer, he could see the crouched man had several images of himself shifting in and out of the main man-shape. Each image mirrored the main shape but had its own movements. One covered his eyes with his hands and wept like a child. One raised his face to the heavens and howled; it was this one that they would intermittently hear. One was prostrate on the floor, arms flung out in front of him. The main man-shape was the croucher, who also wept. The shadows swirled in and around these minor movements of the man, causing them to flicker and twist in and out of vision.

"What is this... what is *he*?" Lymder whispered.

Dra shook his head. "I'd not be sure."

"Is he Planeswalking... like... like the ... Captain?"

"If'n 'E is.... 'E did't stop jest 'a *one* Plane." Dra shook his head again. "Not like any ah've seen... not that ah've seen much."

Maddau stepped up behind them. He could see something through one of the man-shape's movement—a strangely elongated and whitened face peering at them. This face held no eyes in its sockets, and something seemed to be wrong with the placement of the features: they looked... *shifted*.

Lymder reached forward towards the crouching man-shape, intending to shake him back into this plane as he had done the Captain. As he reached forward, Maddau saw the elongated face roll forward through the different images of the crouched man. It loomed over Lymder's arm, opening its horrific mouth, which was placed above its eyes, wide and showing off a rack of jagged, broken, and spiky fangs. It poised itself with its teeth over Lymder's arm, ready to bite into him the moment he touched the crouched man.

Maddau began moving. He had to stop Lymder from touching the crouched man.

The rotting stench of the decay of the Dark rolled through the air to assault his senses, more in his mind than in his nose. Maddau looked at

Lymder and Dra in shock. Did they not see the horrific, leering face of the Dark Lord? Were they unable to smell the rot of its despicable stench?

Lymder continued to reach forward, his fingers a handspan from the crouched man's shoulder.

He would not reach them in time. The jaw of the leering Dark Lord's head had swung open to encircle Lymder's arm, and drips of shadowlet saliva were falling out of the corners of its mouth.

"NO!" Maddau shouted.

His voice was drowned out by a massive booming noise. Golden light flooded the room, blinding the three knights as they stood over the man crouched in front of them. The shape of a man filled the doorway, with the golden light of the afternoon sun streaming in around him. Haelder strode into the tavern, squinting in the dimness. After a moment's pause, he was able to make out the Captain, Lymder, and Dra standing in a semi-circle, half turned towards him, their eyes blinking owlishly in the light. He could make out that the room was furnished, with only one table and two benches in front of a makeshift bar of one wooden plank on top of two roughly carved logs.

"Captain!" Haelder's voice was rough with urgency. "We've t'go. Now. They've found us!"

The impact of the light ricocheting through the low lighting of the tavern had the effect of a collative slap upon the crouching man. The different versions of the crouching man coalesced into one. He lowered his hands and saw the three men standing before him, looking over their shoulders at the voice telling them to leave and the emptiness of the room around them. He stood up, checking himself for wounds or damage as he did so. A cursory review found him to be without injury, at least of the physical kind.

He looked around for a moment, as if to ensure they were alone... that there were no other occupants around them.

"What?" Maddau started.

"How?" Lymder demanded at the same time as Dra gasped, "No!"

Twyll, having finally regained his full height, looked over their heads to Haelder.

Haelder saw Gonestrwydd stand up behind the knights and felt a flood of relief rush over him. The First Knight was here. He would know what to do.

"Haelder..." Twyll's voice was husky and fried from exertion. "How much time do we have?"

At the sound of Gonestrwydd's voice, Maddau, Lymder, and Dra looked back to face him in surprise.

"Gonestrwydd!" Lymder and Dra gasped in unison. "It was you!"

"Twyll...," Maddau whispered in disbelief.

Twyll did not acknowledge any of them. His eyes were on Haelder. "How long?"

Haelder swallowed. The First Knight's gaze was hard and full of fear. "Ten minutes... perhaps a mite more?"

"Then we haven't any time at all, really. We must go!" Twyll's voice trailed off as he started forward. When he passed by the others, his gait faltered. The change in Planes and having knelt for so long made his muscles weak, and his knees felt primed to give way at any moment. He steadied himself on the edge of the table as he moved past. "We must go," he repeated, the quaver in his voice gone.

Haelder looked past him towards the Captain, started to speak, and then looked back at Gonestrwydd. The words dried up in his throat, and he just nodded.

"Of course. Of course. Let us be off then."

Maddau stared at Twyll's back as he and Haelder walked out the door and then ran to catch up with them.

Dra and Lymder stared at the Captain, then looked at each other. Dra shook his head at Lymder, and Lymder nodded. Without a word, they followed. Neither noticed the line of small grey bones that were lying on the table they passed on their way to the door. The three little bones, decreasing in length, were very old in appearance and had tiny webbings of dust connecting them, but little else. They looked as if they had been there for many ages.

Having left that tavern without seeing the bones lying on the table, they also failed to notice the faintly glowing silver eyes that peered after them from behind the bar, marking each step they took and noting all that had taken place.

When the tavern was empty, the Barkeep came out from behind the bar and approached the lone table in the room. It carefully brushed the bones off the table with the side of its hand and deposited the dusty collection into its pocket.

"Paid in full," a soft voice sighed in the shadows of the room.

Chapter Nine

Blood on the Steps

"Gonestrwydd…" Haelder trailed off as he followed Twyll outside. The man's face was drawn and pale. He looked as though he had been through a harrowing experience. Twyll opened his mouth to speak when Maddau ran up and accosted them. He grabbed Twyll's arms, ignoring the burning in his hand, and shook Twyll.

"Twyll! You're safe! You're alive! What happened in there? Where did you go?" Question after question bubbled out of him in a frenzy of excitement, worry, and fear. He could not shake the image of the drawn, white face with empty eye sockets that had stared at him over the crouched man's head.

Twyll stared at Maddau blankly for a moment, as though he did not recognize him. For the barest of seconds, instead of Maddau's face, he saw the angular planes of the Sage of Honesty looking up at him, full of reproach and accusations. He pushed Maddau away from him and turned away, muttering, "Not now, Madds. Not now… not… *you*…"

Maddau stared, mouth agape, as Twyll turned away from him.

Twyll looked at Haelder, ignoring Maddau's stare, and put his hand on Haelder's shoulder.

"Hael," he said, his voice full of quiet resolve. "We'll not escape them. They've come too close, and we've not the time. I want you and Dra to hold them off. Give us enough time to make the entrance to the Temple. It's quite a bit of a path down the cliffs, but I think we can make it with some distance. Do ye ken?"

"Twyll! Listen to me!" Maddau spluttered. Twyll gave him no notice.

Lymder and Dra had drawn close while Twyll spoke. Haelder looked over Twyll's shoulder to Dra, who nodded back at him, then started to turn to Maddau but averted his eyes back to Twyll.

"Aye, Sire. We'll hold the fort here. Per'aps we can use the tavern to…." he trailed off.

"Good man." Twyll's voice was soft, almost gentle. "You were always the obedient knight, Hael. Goodluck. And… Fare ye well t' the Light." His grip tightened on Haelder's shoulder for a moment, then he looked back. "Maddau, Lymder, we must go! If we are to evade the dogs of the Dark Lords, we must run. To the Temple! Now!"

He released Haelder and took off at a run towards the western edge of the clearing without looking to see if the others would follow. In the intervening years, scraggy grass had grown over to mask the footworn path to the descent down the cliffside, but even after all this time, he could clearly see the opening in the rocks that hinted at the way down.

Maddau, whose face reddened in embarrassment and fury, took off after him. "Twyll! Wait!"

Lymder turned his eyes from the retreating forms of the running men to meet Dra's gaze. This was the goodbye he had always known was a possibility but never really believed would come. Not really.

"Dra…"

The corner of Dra's mouth lifted in what would have been half a smile as he looked down into Lymder's upturned face. Had the situation been different, it *could* have been a smile. Now it was just a crease in his cheek.

"I know it, Lym. Always have." He wrapped his right arm around Lymder's shoulders and gave him a quick squeeze. His half smile curled into an emotion-filled grimace as he squeezed Lymder's shoulders, but he was careful to attempt to put the smile back into place as he leaned back.

"Dra, I—"

"Never you mind now," Dra said. "We've no time for it, anyhow. Not sure it'd be good to say t'either way. Go on. Protect the Captain. Protect the relic! It's all we 'ave, now. It's all we're left for," he finished, his voice roughening with emotions that would never be expressed.

Dra shoved his arm forward hard, forcing Lymder away from him. Lymder had to run forward to catch himself and keep from falling. He ran after Gonestrwydd and Maddau and ran away from his friends and the doom that was slowly advancing on them.

He ran towards the location where he had just seen Maddau disappear through the gap in the rocks down to the cliffside path, following Gonestrwydd. He ran, and he did not look back.

He did not want to see.

He could not handle seeing what was to come, though his heart already knew.

In the casting light of the afternoon sun, he could see several silhouettes break away from the larger outline of the building and dart towards the far end of the rocky enclosure surrounding the field. His senses, honed by countless battles across the ages and brought to a heightened peak by the proximity of the accursed bauble of the Light, immediately picked out their Commander. Though he was in his field of sensory perception for but a moment and then gone, Cyndaredd could tell it was him as though a giant green beacon descended from the sky upon the man. *Not that there is much left of the man part any longer,* he mused in furious delight.

The Commander was in the lead, but he was being followed by two of the Koteli knights.

"He must have the bauble of the Light!" Cyndaredd seethed to himself. "And those slavering Light whores are after him!" he snarled. "Cotheda! To me!"

Gor-yfed stepped into presence from the swirling cloud of shadowlet specs that buzzed around behind Cyndaredd and dropped to one knee at his side. "Sire."

The twin wolves of the Dark, Malchder and Gwanc, padded into existence behind Gor-yfed and sat down, their magenta and orange eyes glaring baleful disdain upon the scene.

Cyndaredd did not spare them a glance. He could see two more silhouettes standing beside the structure, and it did not seem like they were attempting to hide.

"Malchder! Gwanc!" he spat. "Dispatch the two by the building!"

Malchder sniffed and began trotting into the field. Three steps, and he discorporated into a swirling mass of shadowlets. Gwanc stepped forward and then paused, turning his huge, shaggy wolf's head to look back at Cyndaredd.

"Sire," he barked, slavering, "may we feed upon these slaves to the Light?"

"Devour them if you wish!" Cyndaredd raged. "Just dispatch them quickly! Our quest to obtain the faltering bauble of the Light is almost at an end...And I will tolerate no further interruptions! We go to ensure the bauble of Light is OURS! Join us when you are finished here."

Gwanc chuffed and took off at a run, spiraling into shadowlets in order to catch up with his brother, who was already streaming across the field.

Cyndaredd screamed his rage at the sky and stepped forward into the clearing, immediately spiraling into his own stream of shadowlets and streaming towards the spot where he had seen Twyll descend through the rocky enclosure. Gor-yfed followed the Vice Knight, streaming into a swirling menace of shadowlets as they pursued their Commander, the Koteli, and the bauble of Light.

Dra watched as Lymder ran after Maddau and Gonestrwydd until the men had dropped below the rim of the rock partition that surrounded the clearing. When he was sure he could no longer see the shape of Lymder's back, he turned to look at Haelder and found the man watching him.

"Yer all right then, Dra?" Haelder inquired, his voice stony.

Dra flushed and nodded. "Ye'll not fault me fer regrettin' nuthin'...."

"Oh, no... no... not 't'all," Haelder said in a mild tone.

"Hael—"

"Tis not any't'one's mind 'cept yours, Dra." Haelder smiled at his old friend. "T'was well known, and none cared."

The flush spread further across his cheeks and deepened to a darker red. Dra found himself studying the ground with intense scrutiny. "Thank ye, Hael...," he trailed off, not knowing how to finish.

Haelder looked over Dra's shoulder and stiffened. The milling shapes at the entrance to the clearing were gone. The Cotheda had vanished.

"Dra! The Cotheda... they're...."

"Well, well now!" a slavering voice interrupted from behind him. "What a sweet moment between two.... good friends... here." A voice emanated from behind the side of the tavern.

Haelder and Dra spun around to face the creature—a wolf larger than any they had encountered before. It was the size of a bear, mottled with green and black patterning on its mostly dark coat, and had shining orange eyes that gazed at them with greedy fervor. Its mouth overflowed with rows of dull, spiky teeth. Too many rows to be a normal wolf, not that anything about this wolf screamed of normality.

It drooled as it gazed at them, hungering.

Dra grabbed the grip of his sword and, in a quick move, unsheathed the blade. Haelder mimicked the movement and armed himself as well.

So focused on the wolf before them, neither heard the soft padding of paws behind.

Malchder was within an arm's span before he stood up on his rear legs and, with grinding of bones and popping of tendons, stood up to full height and sprung at Dra with a roar.

He swung one claw-tipped paw-hand at the back of Dra's neck. The claws caught Dra's cloak, tearing it from around his neck and yanking him backward. Dra landed heavily on his back with an "Ooof!", knocking the wind out of him and causing him to drop his sword. Then Malchder was upon him, raking his claws upon the Dra's mailed shirt, searching for a weak spot to attack.

Haelder had spun around when he heard Malchder's roar and saw Dra go down. His mind registered the wolf-man thing attacking Dra, and he raised his sword to swing at it. Before he could begin the swing, Gwanc leapt forward and fastened his teeth around Haelder's left arm. His teeth tore through the flesh of Haelder's arm as though it were soft creme, and the crunching of bone as it broke made Haelder shriek in pain and terror. Holding Haelder's arm between his almost closed jaws, the Wolf Gwanc began to pull.

It was now a tug of war with Haelder's forearm as the rope. Haelder pulled forward, screaming in pain, though he really could not feel his hand and forearm any longer. It was now so much mangled meat in the beast's jaws, and all he felt was the agonic, electric buzzing at his elbow where nerves still railed. He raised his right hand and began slamming the pommel of his sword down upon the wolf's head, raining down blow after blow, all the while the wolf pulled on his arm, continuing to bite down and chew. One. Two. Three.

By chance, the pommel hit the wolf's left eye socket, blinding it with the force of the blow. Gwanc howled deep in his throat, clenched his teeth, and whipped his head away.

Haelder was flung to the side. There was a horrific tearing feeling in his arm, and then the world went white.

Gwyleidd-Dra was in the fight of his life. He could sense, peripherally, that Haelder conflicted with the wolf that had surprised them, but once he had lost his air all other fights had ceased to be important. He'd lost his sword and his breath in the same instance, and a drooling, snarling, half-wolf-half-man was scrabbling at his mailed shirt. The claws were catching in the rings of the maille, lifting him up and dropping him each time the wolf-beast freed itself. It had already done terrible damage to his thighs, where the maille did not cover, and he could feel the hot blood running down his legs. When the thing tried to free itself again, Dra was finally able to catch a breath and looped a wide-swung punch at the thing's mouth. His swing was too wide, and it managed to hit Malchder's temple instead with the full wallop of impact.

The world shuddered around him, and Malchder went limp on his chest, blowing hot air into his face. Dra rolled the wolf-beast off of him and quickly stood up, trying to look in all directions and get his bearings.

The wolf-man-thing that had been attacking him lay prone before him, breathing heavily. The wolf that had been attacking Haelder was facing away from him, pawing at the side of his face, and Haelder was lying a few feet from it, in a spreading pool of blood. His sword lay near his hand. Delirious with the hot, jagged pain that railed from his lower half, Dra grabbed his own sword from where it lay but a foot from him. He grasped it firmly in both hands, raised it above his head, arched his back to get the full range of motion for the swing, and swung it down in a bludgeoning arc on the wolf-man-thing's neck. The blade was not overly sharp, but with the force of the swing and Dra's excitement at the moment lending to it, he managed to mostly sever Malchder's head from his body.

Dra turned on unsteady legs. He was beginning to lose feeling below his knees, and the rags of his pants were blackened with the steady flow of his lifeblood. He staggered over to the wolf, Gwanc, who had yet to notice his presence. Gwanc continued to paw at his eye, shaking his head to clear it.

"Who... *what...* are ye?" Dra panted.

Gwanc, hearing noise, turned to look. There were three fuzzy, man-shaped figures standing before him that kept moving in and out of each other. He could not see Malchder, nor could his senses pick up the Dark Lord of Pride nearby. Had he fled? Gwanc was confused and shook his head again with a high-pitched whine.

Dra raised his arm and pointed his sword at the incapacitated wolf. "I ask again. What ARE YE?!"

Gwanc shook his head again, still whining. The man-shaped things were making a groaning noise that sounded as if they were underwater. Everything moved as if it were underwater, with slow-dragging shapes that would not keep to their original structure. The light was too bright, and he could not see out of his left eye. It was just Dark, but his face hurt. Oh... it hurt so... *much.*

Dra shook his head. He would get nothing from this one; it seemed to be in shock, and the other was done for. He dared not get close enough to be in reach of the beast. Else, he would fare like Haelder. It could still be dangerous. Instead, he raised his arm, aimed his sword at the wolf's throat, and leapt forward as he stabbed with all his might towards Gwanc's throat.

In the last moments of his charge forward, Dra lost total feeling below his waist. His feet tangled, and he fell forward against the wolf. His sword found purchase, and though his aim was true, his fall thwarted his attack. The sword pierced Gwanc through his ribs rather than straight through the heart, as Dra had aimed. Instead of killing him, the sword ran deep into his chest, puncturing and skewering most of what was left in there. Gwanc was pushed back with the impact of the blow, away from Dra, who lay face down on the earth, panting. The giant wolf, skewered by Dra's sword, flopped on the ground, trying to roll over. His head whipped back and forth, trying to reach the hilt of the sword and, alternately, trying to push himself up. Gwanc began to change. His legs began to pop and elongate, his spine clattered and ground as it straightened itself, and he became more human-shaped. Too late, he resumed a mostly human form, though still covered in rough patches of fur and with far too many teeth that protruded from his far too wide mouth. He rattled out a staccato whine as the pointed tongue seeped out of his mouth and lay on the ground beside him. Shadowlets had begun to pool underneath his chest as he flopped around, trying to remove the sword that pierced his chest and pinned him to the ground. Once he had turned man-shaped, the shadowlets poured out of him in earnest, leaving him in streams and rivulets. A few moments passed with flopping attempts to free himself, and then the beastly Gwanc stilled.

Dra felt the coolness of mud on his cheeks. It was soothing—nice, even.

Inside, he felt cold all over and could not feel anything below his chest any more. He could not even feel his hands. Was he still holding his sword? His mouth felt really dry, as though he'd inhaled a desert during his fight with the fox.

Fox…?

No… it was a wolf.

Was it a wolf, though? It had been so big. Too big for a fox, surely.

Yes… it had been a wolf. One wolf, though? Or two? He couldn't remember anymore.

His chest was starting to hurt, and his head was aching like he'd been drinking for too long. He groaned.

Why was the ground so close?

Was that mud? Yes… mud. So…. am I… lying down… *in* the mud? Why would I do that when there was a fox-wolf to fight?

Stop it with the foxes! That was sloppy thinking. It had been a wolf he fought. He knew it!

Was it dead, though?

Dra shook his head, smearing more mud across his forehead, nose, and cheeks. The beast was dead. Had to be! It just had to be!

It had to, because he was tired now.

Was it, though? What if it wasn't?

It would come for him… it would come for Haelder, if it had not done for him already.

He could not let that happen, no matter how tired he felt.

He spat out a curse into the mud, which curdled a bit at his words.

He lifted his shoulders and maneuvered his elbows to curl up underneath him. He placed both hands on the ground and endeavored to push himself up. One hand placed palm down as it was supposed to, but since he could not feel them, the other splayed helplessly, facing the wrist. When he put the pressure on his upper body's weight, a weight he could barely feel anymore, there was a quiet cracking sound that came from his right wrist.

Dra was dimly aware as his right arm let go of a brief flare of pain that cut through the numbness. He managed to push himself into a sitting position and supported himself on his left hand, his right arm hanging limp at his side. His maille felt too tight and constricting. He felt like an oven was in his chest. Panting, Dra looked over to where the wolf-demon Gwanc lay and started in shock. There was no creature there any longer. What remained of the wolf creature was now a blackish-grey pool of twirling shadowlets that streamed upward into the fading light of the early evening. He stared at the shadowlets as they streamed upwards and away. When naught but a few tendrils remained, Dra turned to look for the other wolf-man-thing he had killed. Where it had lain, there was no trace. All traces of it had disappeared.

Dra stared in suspicion at the spot where the other wolf-thing had died for a moment. It would not be good if that thing were still alive and could come after him and Haelder....

Haelder!

Dra twisted around, leaning to the side to look for his friend, subconsciously supporting himself as he turned on the stump of his broken wrist, which flared a painful message that was not received. He saw Haelder lying a few feet from him, pale as milk, lying in a pool of bloody mud, unmoving.

Dra began to crawl through the muddy earth, clawing with his left hand and pushing himself with his right arm. He could not control his fingers anymore, so his grip was claw-like at best, and he used his right elbow to dig in and push himself. He thought his knees moved, but everything below his chest was a cold void. He got two pulls forward, and then all the strength went out of his body. He felt so tired and so hot. His mind was sluggish, and his head ached something fierce. He panted for air but felt like he could never really draw a full breath anymore.

And he was so damned thirsty! Why was he so thirsty? Must have sweated too much with that lion he fought. Both lions, actually…

What lions? There were no lions here…. In …. Where was he again? Brittany?

Dra shook his head again, trying to clear it, but in doing so, he lost his tenuous grip on balance and fell over onto his broken wrist. Couldn't feel it, but he knew it was broken. Didn't hurt, though, so that was a relief.

It was nice there, in the cool mud. Dra felt so weary. He would check on Haelder in a moment. He just needed a short rest. He was so *tired*.

He turned his cheek to the soothing coolness of the earth, his heart slowing, and Gwyleidd-Dra closed his eyes.

Twyll had made the first turn in the descent after passing through the rocky scree that demarcated the edge of the grass-pocked clearing from the pathway down the Steps of a Thousand Cares with an agility that belied his form. Maddau made after him like the dawn's light chasing away the last whispers of the night's darkness. Faster and faster, Maddau ran. His pack banged against his side in a staccato pace, accenting his steps. In a long time past, pilgrims would descend these steps, meditating on the worries and cares that distracted them from pursuing the purity of their spirits. Now, as Maddau's feet pounded the stone of the once clean and well-cared-for steps, he was oblivious to the neglect that had caused scraggy weeds, dirt, and rocks to litter the cracks between the steps. His only worry and care was getting the Relic to the Temple.

But first, he had to catch up with Twyll.

It was the same as when they had been boys, freshly painted with the Light's Charge in their youth. Twyll had always won the race down the steps to the Temple. The Steps of A Thousand Cares were not truly a thousand steps, but only eight hundred or so. Still, Twyll was always keen to keep his lead and did so even now, jumping down from one ledge to another to build the gap between himself and Maddau. Convinced of his lead, he turned back to see how far Maddau trailed him. What he saw brought him to a skidding halt.

Maddau was two turns of stairs back on the pathway above him. Looking further back up the zigzag turns of the Steps of Thousand Cares, Twyll saw Lymder was close behind Maddau, and right behind him was Gor-yfed, brandishing his flail. Twyll watched as the Cotheda chevalier slung his arm forward, bringing the chain and the spiked ball-head into Lymder's right leg.

Lymder was descending as fast as he could, chasing after his Captain and the First Knight. His heart screamed with the knowledge that he was leaving Dra and Haelder to die. But they had to get the Relic to the Temple. And Gonestrwydd had given orders. He must obey. It was nothing but emotion anyhow, but it was… Dra. Dra would be dead. Haelder, too.

Maybe they would survive, he reasoned to himself as he rushed down the steps after Maddau. He could barely see the edge of the Captain's cloak and could only sometimes catch a glimpse of Maddau's road-dirt-dulled reddish hair as he made the turns in the descent much faster than Lymder. He was trying to convince himself that Dra—and Haelder—might survive this encounter with the Dark Lords and he *could* see him—them—again when this was all over. It was not at all a convincing argument, though, and just as Lymder was trying to believe further that they would all be together again when… when whatever was going to happen was over, he heard a high, keening shriek. Lymder turned back to look, and his legs went out from under him. He fell backwards, turning as he fell, and saw the malignantly gleeful eyes of a Cotheda chevalier barely moments away from crashing into him. Lymder screamed.

Maddau heard a shriek followed by a terrified scream behind him and slid to a stop on the pathway landing he had just stepped onto. He scanned up the steps behind him and saw Lymder lying in a crumpled heap one stairway above him, a Cotheda chevalier looming over him and brandishing a long staff with a spike-ridden ball and chain on the end. Maddau turned, and no sooner had he placed his foot on the first step than he was roughly pushed aside. Twyll had bounded up the steps, sword in hand, and arrived at the landing where Lymder lay. His blade flashed in a precise arc, aimed to deflect the Cotheda chevalier's blow.

The flail hit Twyll's sword with a hollow vibrational *TEHIING* sound that caused Maddau's teeth to clench. He had arrived at Lymder's body and was relieved to see his friend was still conscious. Lymder was grasping his right leg above the knee with both hands. Blood welled from a large gash on the side of the joint and was oozing through his pant leg to spatter onto the steps below. Maddau could see the leg was starting to swell.

"LYM! You're alive! Are you hurt?" Maddau could see he was hurt but was worried Lymder had hit his head in the fall on the stairs. *The Steps of a Thousand Cares...* Maddau's confused brain mused as he studied Lymder's face. *Now I have one more Care to carry...*

"Bastard hit me in the leg!" Lymder gasped.

"Can you walk?"

"Dunno... I... Help me up, Captain!"

Lymder tried to stand, using Maddau's shoulder as support to lift himself. His left leg held well enough, but when he tried to stand on his right leg, the knee buckled at the joint, and he yelped in pain. He would have fallen again had Maddau's arm not kept him standing.

Twyll's sparring blow had stopped Gor-yfed's attack cold. When the Cotheda chevalier saw who had defended the Koteli he had attacked, he keened and withdrew in a violent stream of shadowlets to a safer perch, two stair turns above the Koteli. Twyll regarded them with an intensity that was almost tangible.

"Maddau, take Lymder and make for the Temple."

Maddau looked up, incredulity writ large upon his face. "Lym cannot run, Twyll! His leg—"

Twyll turned, and the look in his eyes caused Maddau's tongue to shrivel upon itself. He saw a shimmering light flicker around Twyll's face as he said, "You'll have to run if you're to survive, Madds. I'll hold them off here as long as I can, but spare no movement. The Cotheda are upon us. If they take us now, they take the Relic, and the Light will be lost!"

"But..."

"RUN!"

Before Maddau could argue—or even answer—Twyll turned back and bound up the next flight of steps to where the shadowlets were clouding together again. There seemed to be even more of the shadowlets forming into a large, dark cloud on the upper landing.

Maddau grasped the gasping Lymder firmly under his right arm and began guiding them down the steps at a quick, hobbling trot.

He heard Twyll screaming something and a rasping answer scraping across the air, but he did not look back as he and Lymder descended the stairs.

The last turn of the steps brought the gates of the Temple de La Sagesse into view. Lymder's shifting weight made descending the last part of the steep cliffside steps perilous, and he hobbled along as quickly as possible while Maddau supported his weight. The gates of the Temple lay thrown open, with the expanse of the low prominence before the entryway hemmed in by craggy teeth of rock that allowed seawater to splash in from the ebbing and swelling tides to form little pools in the Dragon's mouth. As Maddau and Lymder hopped and hobbled down through the gates and started to cross the prominence, a whooshing noise closed in on them from behind. Maddau turned his head to see that Twyll had rejoined them.

"How did he get here so fast?" Maddau wondered. "And I didn't even hear him approach."

Twyll met Maddau's gaze and nodded to him. Without a word, he slid his shoulder under Lymder's left arm and helped to prop him up as the three moved across the final half of the prominence and into the doorway of the Temple.

As they crossed the threshold, Twyll set Lymder back down on his own legs, still supported by Maddau's help, and turned to them.

"Twyll," Maddau began.

Twyll shook his head. "There's less time than you think. I've held them off, but they are right at our throats, Madds. Whatever you have to say, save it. Get inside. Find the Sages. Save the relic."

"But Twyll,"

"Go!" Twyll turned to look at him with a furious glare, and a shadow fell across his face as he pointed towards the outer chamber of the Temple. His pointing fingers seemed to vibrate with an imperative force, and Maddau shrank again beneath the weight of Twyll's gaze. "I'll keep them from getting inside. You must get the relic to the Sages!"

"Captain," Lymder whispered. "Maybe we ought to do as he says?"

Maddau looked with uncertain unease between Lymder's agonized wince and back to Twyll's forceful glare. Feeling that he had no choice, he shifted his shoulder under Lymder's arm to support him and turned to move the two of them into the outer chamber.

Twyll watched them leave, and when he was certain they had entered the Outer Chambers, he turned to face the doorway of the Temple. He stepped onto the threshold of the doorway and planted his feet. He crossed his arms and relaxed into a leaning stance to wait. He did not have to wait long.

A few moments passed, and he saw the sparkling dark glitter of shadowlets quickly flashing along the path down the Steps of A Thousand Cares to the prominence of the Temple. The tide was coming in, and the sea flashed a dazzling array of patterns of Light across the prominence, turning the sand to gold. The shadowlet streams approached the gates to the Temple, and there flashed into being the familiar shapes of Cyndaredd and Gor-yfed.

The two Cotheda knights began to cross the prominence. A flurry of clouds passed across the sun, shrouding the prominence and gates in shadows that heralded the Cotheda's advance. They approached the entryway and stopped when they saw Twyll standing there.

Cyndaredd and Gor-yfed both dropped to one knee.

"Commander," Cyndaredd snarled. "It has been a long time."

"Indeed," Twyll answered. "You have failed in my cat and mouse game to obtain the Relic for me, but we have managed well so far, have we not?"

"You could have let us have it! Why did you not just take it for us?" Gor-yfed spat.

"And bring down the full regiment of Light-worshiping dogs on our heads? I think not," Twyll snapped, staring at Gor-yfed, his eyes glowing an icy green. "Need I remind you that our ranks have been weakened over the years? That we can ill afford an outright clash?"

Gor-yfed bowed his head and remained silent. He did not want the Commander's ire visited upon him.

"What are your orders, Commander?" Cyndaredd hissed with a sharp glance at Gor-yfed. "We await your words."

"Fall back," Twyll snapped. "Return to our base. We've no need to remain here. I will obtain the bauble from the Light worshipers and present it to our Dark Masters upon my return."

"And what of the two Light whores that escaped into that tarnal adytum?" Cyndaredd seethed.

The air around the shadowed entryway seemed to darken. Twyll narrowed his eyes at the implication of his incapability, a fresh anger bubbling in his chest and spreading the heat of hatred throughout his heart and mind.

"Do you mean to tell me, Vice Knight, that you think I am incapable of dealing with two injured whelplings of the Light bitch?" Twyll inquired in tones of deep ice, eyeing Cyndaredd's face.

"N-no, Commander!" Cyndaredd spat violently. "I would never mean—"

Gor-yfed looked up, the fear writ large upon his pinched-in, blackened, and scarred face.

"Good," Twyll replied, the cold terseness in his voice seeming to cause the air to shiver around them. "Then we shall look upon your querying as mere concern, and nothing more then? Not…insubordination?"

Cyndaredd bowed his head, gritting his teeth and acquiescing to his Commander's words.

Gor-yfed bobbed his head up and down as he began crawling back-ward. "Of course, Commander! T'was only for concern of yor person! Yor vury val-oo-ble - cann't be lost… ye-know?" He slid backwards, the greaves of his armored legs leaving deep scratches in the worn stone.

"Of course, Commander," Cyndaredd hissed with savage terror as he, too, began crawling backwards, mimicking Gor-yfed. "I was only worried for… for your safety. We'll take our leave and fall back to the base, as you say."

"Wait!" Twyll barked.

Gor-yfed and Cyndaredd froze, still crouched on the ground.

Twyll stepped from the doorway onto the Prominence. The sun's previous appearance had given way to massing coils of black storm clouds.

Twyll approached Cyndaredd's prone form and leaned over him. He passed his hand over the Vice Knight's back and murmured words in the speech of the Dark Eternalia. Cyndaredd's body twitched, and the handle of his blade appeared on the side of his hip. Twyll reached forward, grasped the handle, and pulled it out in one swift movement. Cyndaredd's torso jerked to the side, shadowlets spilling from his form and puddling on the Prominence beneath him. He dared not move while his Commander brandished his blade over him. Twyll held the blade aloft, studying it in the dim light of the day.

"This will prove useful enough, I think. Now go," Twyll said, with flat emphasis. "Begone."

He watched as the two Cotheda knights began to stream into spiraling streams of glittering shadowlets: first from the edges of the armor, then from the joints of the bodies, and finally from the main body parts themselves. Spiraling and glittering away into the light of the day, which came flooding back to illuminate the Prominence to the Temple as soon as their presence was mostly gone. When he was certain the Cotheda had left, Twyll sheathed Cyndaredd's blade into his belt and stepped back from the threshold to inspect the doorway. Just to the left side, he found a large, flat, rounded stone whose intended purpose was easily evident: to be rolled across the doorway as a seal against those who would gain entry to the Temple. Twyll walked over and traced his fingers along the outer edge of the stone. It burned hot against the brush of his fingers, and he pulled them away, sucking in a harsh gasp of air as he did so. Light briefly illuminated the edge of the round stone door, and the symbol of wisdom, inscribed in the door so far in the past that the once deep grooves of the insignia had long worn away to be almost smooth, lit up with a brief glow. So, it was to be thus…. the place knew his nature, even if the others did not yet, and the ward of the Light that lived within the door would not abide his touch.

Twyll put the tips of his fingers to his mouth, blowing on them and shaking them in the air before his face to cool the pain. He studied the door. It needed closing to keep in as much as to keep out, and he had little time. So how to manage?

He unsheathed his own sword and studied it. The silvered metal of the blade itself could be useful, but the curve of both the upper and lower edges prevented any proper hand placement that would not result in a nasty cut. Twyll frowned at his blade and then dropped it on the floor in disgust. *Useless!* The sword fell to the ground and bounced once with a hollow, metallic *TING*. He reached for his other hip and pulled the Cotheda blade that had come from Cyndaredd from his belt. The jagged path of the blade's edge made it even less suitable as a barrier between the ward and his hands. He looked doubtfully at the stone. He *could* use it to attack the ward and might even break the energy of the seal that protected this place. But to counteract this ancient spell of the Light would be long work, and he had to find Maddau before he sealed the Relic away. He was about to toss Cyndaredd's blade away after his own when it occurred to him that he was supposed to have vanquished the Cotheda in an epic battle, sacrificing himself for the cause of the Light. To show up without a hair out of place did not fit the narrative of his predicament. Cyndaredd's blade might have some use after all.

Twyll placed the wicked point of the blade against the shelf of his cheek, gritted his teeth, and pulled down and toward his throat, twisting the handle as he did. The result was an uneven slash beginning at his cheekbone and ending near his jaw. Tiny spirals of shadowlets oozed out and effervesced into the air from the wound. Twyll covered it with his hand for a moment, willing the shadowlets to hold inside himself while the blood welled within the cut and oozed down his face. He knew the wound would remain for a time, being that it was made with a Cotheda blade, and weapons of the Dark were the only ones that could do lasting damage to the Cotheda.

Now that I look the part of the injured knight, I need to close this door.

He glanced around the tight enclosure of the entryway. Minor detritus that had made its way into the entryway over time: rocks, shells, the random scat of an errant bird, scraps of cloth, and some driftwood that had been dropped before crossing into the Temple's Outer Chambers.

Wood?

Twyll reached down and grabbed the driftwood from where it lay near the threshold to the entryway. It was a large chunk of the trunk from some faraway tree. At about the span of his forearm and the thickness of his hand, the wood was pitted from the burrowing of many insects or birds. He gripped it with a firm hold on either end and brought it down hard across a quick upthrust from his knee, causing it to splinter into two pieces.

Holding a piece in each hand, Twyll grinned with malicious glee at the door. *This will do*, he mused after studying the door for a moment longer.

He stepped back over to stand behind the left side of the doorstone and placed both hands on the outer edge of the stone, with the driftwood separating the skin of his hands from the doorstone. It worked! He felt no pain as he was not touching the accursed ward that lived within the door. His grin widened even more into a grotesque rictus, showing more teeth than a normal man would have, and he began applying pressure to the wood. It cracked and made soft popping noises from beneath his hands, but held all the same. Little by little, and with agonizing slowness, the door began to move.

Maddau managed to maneuver a limping Lymder through the entryway and into the Outer chamber. The room was much larger than the entryway, and although dimly lit from vents to the outside that cast little light, Maddau could see that it was paved with soft stone from the caves the Temple was built into. Just before them was a short set of three steps, bookended by two great pillars, that led up to a wide, open area supported by vast columns. From there, three large doorways opened into dark caverns beyond. Shadows pooled in various areas of the floor, often congregating around supporting columns. A large stone block from overhead had fallen and broken upon the steps in the middle, casting dark pools of shadow that seemed to spread across the steps. In his memories of the dim time of his youth, Maddau had seen the Sages converse with pilgrims who came to the Temple here, evaluating their ability to ascend the Promenade d'Aspirantes, traveling to the Inner Chamber, which housed the Sage's dwellings, or counseling those working on the Challenge of the Light.

"It seems bigger than I remembered," Lymder whispered.

Maddau nodded. "Quieter, too."

"Where do ye think the Sages…?" Lymder trailed off.

"No idea," Maddau whispered back. "But they must be here… somewhere… if they're still alive," he finished, a grim foreknowledge bubbling in his tone.

Lymder looked at him with uncertainty and fear in his eyes. They had known that this would be a possibility; the Sage of Veneration had been said to have escaped a horrific experience. Since the Sages rarely left the Temple, it could only have meant that something had happened at the Temple. But to imagine the Sages dead. To imagine the Keepers of the Wisdom of the Light no longer being there. It was too much. He shook his head.

"Maddau…Captain… I—"

"Let's go, Lym," Maddau responded, still whispering. The ominous quiet of the room seemed to demand it. "We must find out what happened here and help. If there's anyone here that's left to help," he finished, deliberating the words as he spoke.

They moved towards the steps, taking care to step to the side of the large white rock that blocked the central part of the steps. As they walked around, Lymder looked down and sucked in his breath hard. "Captain!"

"What?" The fear in Maddau's voice spiked across as irritation in his tone.

"L-Look!" Lymder pointed down with his right hand. His left hand, wrapped around Maddau's shoulder to hold on to his support, spasmed into a claw. "Look!"

Maddau looked where Lymder pointed. What he had taken to be a large, broken, white rock from the overhead lentil was the calcified body of a Sage, lying head down across the steps. White salt-like deposits were growing up around the man's body, and his hands were thrown out so that he made an inverted T shape on the steps. What Maddau had taken to be shadows were black ichor that had seeped into the soft sandstone, staining it with what had once been the man's blood.

"Captain…is that…. a Sage?" Lymder's voice was the barest vibration in the currents of air that blew in the stillness. He stared, transfixed by the broken and stone-like figure on the steps.

"He was once," Maddau whispered back.

"What 'appened to him? What 'appened 'ere?" Lymder's voice was robbed of its normal stoicism and thickened in disbelief and terror.

"That's what we have to find out, Lym." Maddau looked around, freshly aware that what he had taken to be other pools of shadow along the low spots of the floor were odds-on more stains from the blood of the Sages. He felt relief when he saw no other rocks or stones large enough to be Sage bodies in the rubble littering the room. "We'll need to explore the other areas. Maybe we'll find someone."

"Someone living..." Lymder's voice was even softer.

"Right. Someone who can—"

A loud *BOOM* echoed from the entryway behind them. Maddau spun around, pulling Lymder with him to stare at the doorway they had just come through. A cloud of dust and dirt blew in through the doorway, spraying their faces with tiny, stabbing, needle-sharp pieces of rock. The dust coated their throats, making them cough and splutter, and flew into their eyes, causing them to water.

A shadow separated itself from the gloom of the hall beyond the doorway. Squinting through his leaking eyes, Maddau could make out the shape of a man through the clouds of dust. He recognized the shape of Twyll stepping through the entryway and into the Outer Chamber and was conflicted by the intermixing feelings of relief and an unmistakable, yet undefined, dread.

"Twyll," he called out as the man stepped into the room.

Lymder looked up and saw glowing green eyes fixed on them. He stiffened in fear, then began to relax when he saw it was only Gonestrwydd who had arrived. Only the First Knight, whose normally shining green eyes looked old and tired in the dimness of the room.

Yet for a second, they had been glowing. Lymder was very sure of that. He stared hard at the First Knight's face.

Twyll's voice was broken. "I've turned them back... for now. The Cotheda...I...closed the door. They cannot get through. I think...I think... we'll be safe here."

Maddau shook his head. "Light keep ye, Twyll. You could have been killed!" He paused, studying Twyll's face. "You've been hurt."

Twyll gave Maddau a tired smile. "I think I'm a match for two whelplings of the Dark, Madds, although one of them did give me a good run. It was almost a close match..."

"What was that loud crash?" Lymder ignored Gonestrwydd's commentary and continued to stare at his face in fixed concentration.

Twyll met Lymder's interrogative stare for a moment and sensed a developing suspicion under the inquisitiveness. "I had to move the door. It would not shift on its own. I had to force it, and it fell across the doorway with a loud crash." He met Lymder's eyes for a moment longer and then turned back to Maddau in an effective dismissal.

Maddau smiled back at Twyll, the relief blooming fully now and overtaking the whispers of dread that had been rising in his mind. Lymder, aware that he had been rendered inert in the conversation by Gonestrwydd's dismissive air, clutched tighter to Maddau's shoulder and muttered to himself. "I 'member that door was always the easiest to move in the evenings."

Twyll glanced at Lymder again as Maddau turned and began leading them back to the body of the Sage.

"You forget, Lym," he said, so low that Lymder barely heard him. "The Dark ones have damaged this place. Things are not as normal as they appear, here."

Lymder stared at Gonestrwydd again, unable to cap the growing fear that was hugging his heart.

Something is not right here, he thought.

And it's less now that the First Knight has returned to us.

Chapter Ten

Betrayal

Twyll glanced at the remains of the Sage on the steps as they moved into the Outer Chamber and towards the three gated portals from the room, even as the others averted their eyes. The Sage, whose body was covered with stony deposits and desiccated from the salt air, was almost unrecognizable in this state. Twyll thought he could see the symbol of Mercy peeking through some of the salt-smeared blood stains on the Sage's shirt, but he could not be certain.

The Koteli knights crossed the Outer chamber, avoiding the shadowy stains of what had proven to be blood that had collected in the lower parts of the stone-paved room. Insects had made their presence known and, at some point, had departed. The occasional faint buzz of flies could still be heard near the spots of spoilage.

Twyll and Maddau helped Lymder to the center of the room, where they paused.

"It looks like we should split up here," Twyll said, eyeing the three gates.

Maddau and Lymder looked at him. Twyll felt their gaze and flushed a bit. "Come, now. It's not like that," he offered. "There are three different passages here, and there are three of us. We need to find the Sages and secure the Relic. It will be quicker if we split up," he finished weakly.

His voice echoed back to them in the empty room: "quicker…"

"And reach our doom faster," Lymder intoned, his dry voice also echoing back to them: "doom…"

"Twyll…" Maddau frowned. "Lym can't walk without help. And splitting up increases our risk. What if we're attacked?"

Twyll shook his head. "The Cotheda are done. They cannot enter here! You know so yourself. The wards of the Light will not suffer any who bear the Darkness in their soul. We are safe here!"

"And what of the Sages? They were safe, too, right?" Lymder inquired. "Seems they fared well, in all their… *safety.*"

Maddau's frown deepened at Lymder's words. "Truly, Twyll. What if whatever killed that Sage is still here?"

Twyll flapped his hands in exasperation. "What do you want, Captain?" He snapped. "Shall we just stop here and await our doom like good little sacrifices to the Darkness? Is that it, Madds? Did you bring us all this way just to sit here and give up because you're scared?"

Maddau blinked, hurt. "No, but I—"

"Fine!" Twyll snapped. "Let's be done with this, then. I will go with Lymder. I'm the better swordsman, after all, and I can protect him better than you! You will go to the eastern room—the Challenge of the Light, was it? Check there for any Sages and bring all you find back here."

"And where will we go, First Knight?" Lymder asked, his voice stony as he stood up and unwound his arm from Maddau's back.

"We shall go to the Inner Chamber…. That's… over there." He pointed to their left. "It's where the Sages' lived. We shall check their rooms and see if there is anyone still alive who needs help, or who can help us."

"And then?" Lymder prompted.

"We'll meet back here!" Twyll glared at them. "By the Light! Must I spell this out? You are Koteli Knights. The way forward should be evident! Then we will proceed together with the Sages to the Promenade D'Aspirantes and secure the Relic!"

Maddau's frown had lessened a bit. "But why don't we do that first?"

Twyll's frustration was almost palpable. "Aagh! Because Madds! If there is some ward or trick to secure the Relic, don't you think we'll need the Sages' help to bypass or enact it? We'll need to get them first!"

Maddau was not convinced, but what Twyll said *did* make a crazy sort of sense. He sighed.

"Lym?"

"Aye, Captain," Lymder said. "I dun like 't'either, but it seems we have little choice." He offered his right arm to the First Knight, who leaned under to support him. "I guess we be goin' t' the Inner Chamber, Gonestrwydd?"

Twyll nodded, his face a mask of resigned consternation that had erased the frustrated annoyance dancing across it moments before.

Without a word, Twyll gave Maddau a curt nod, then turned toward the western doorway. Maddau watched the two men pass through the archway. A dark curtain of shadows fell around them, obscuring them from view. He waited a moment longer to see if either of them would turn back, but they were gone. He sighed and turned towards the doorway that led to the Challenge of the Light. Peering inside, he could just make out the thin corridor that led to the trial by which one proved the purity of their spirit to the Charges of the Light. Taking a deep breath to steady himself, he stepped across the threshold.

It seemed an age since he had trod the quiet halls of the Temple. Now, as Maddau walked the dark corridor to the Light's Challenge, it was even quieter. Before, there had always been the quiet buzz of conversation, faint music, or prayerful song. Now, there was just silence—the heavy silence of carnage and death. The shrieking silence that came in the wake of the Dark.

Maddau shivered. The lighting had always been low here, but before, it had been augmented by candles or torches spaced equally down the corridor.

Now, it was totally dark. Three hundred paces brought him to the room where aspirants to the Challenge of the Light would face the darkest parts of their hearts. He could feel the constricting squeeze of the corridor give way as he stepped into the Challenger's arena, despite not being able to see any discernible change in the darkness that surrounded him. He took several strides into the room and stopped, listening in the suffocating gloom. In the distance, he heard the quiet, intermittent drip of water somewhere on the far side of the room. Other than that, there was nothing. He opened his mouth to call out and stopped. Something felt off—like the wrong vibration of the air around him. His parched tongue flicked out to give what moisture it could to his dry lips, effecting no real change but giving him the impression of control just the same.

He waited, listening to that wrong vibration of the air around him. Listening for, well, anything. Anything aside from the drip… drip… drip…. of water in the distance.

What if that's not water?

Well, what else could it be? He chastised himself for creating catastrophes where there were none. This cave jutted out over the sea. It's only natural that water finds its way in here. Let us not see storms when there are only clouds.

You are not in the part of the cave over the ocean…. That's where Twyll and Lymder went. You are in the part of the Temple that is deep within the rock. There should be no water here.

Well, water could still find its way in. Maddau's reasoning with himself was weakening.

What if it's blood?

How could blood be dripping so much in here? He scolded himself harshly for catastrophizing again. This was truly too much. He needed to get a hold of himself.

Before he could listen to his better judgment, he called out, "By the Challenge of the Light, I am Maddau, the Captain of the Koteli! Is anyone in here?"

His voice echoed off the stone walls, bouncing mockingly back to him from the farthest reaches of the room. "*Anyone in here? Anyone here? Here?*

When the echoes had died down, silence resumed its heavy pall. He tried again: "Hail, Sages! Call out if you are in need of help!"

Hail Sages…. Hail…. Hell…

In need of help…. Need…. Help….

Help…

He paused again, listening for the echoes to die away. When the nothingness in the room resumed, he sighed. It seemed like there was no one there.

No, that was not right. Not quite no one. There was the continued intermittent dripping of water (*blood!)* from far off. But now there was something else—a soft scraping noise from the furthest corner of the room.

Maddau held his breath. It came again—a soft scrape—as though a foot was being carefully placed to make the least amount of noise possible. There was someone or some*thing* in here with him. And it was drawing nearer. He began backing slowly towards where he thought he had entered. He slid one foot back, lightly brushing it along the floor, and then the next in the same manner. Four steps back, and he should be close to the distance he had crossed when he entered the room. He slid his foot back again, and his heel and ankle bumped into something both soft and very hard at the same time.

Maddau froze. His eyes opened very wide in the darkness, and he looked down and behind him, straining to see what his foot had bumped into. Trying desperately to see what had not been there before when he strode into the room with reckless zeal just moments ago.

With glacial slowness, he carefully pulled his foot forward and away from whatever it was that he had kicked by accident. He could feel the thing, which had yielded a bit when his heel struck it, lean after him as though it were following his foot.

What if you just stepped on the body of a Sage?

No. That could not be!

You know, like the one on the stairs in the outer chamber?

Another sound became apparent to Maddau then. A wheezy panting that rose and fell with the pounding of the blood in his head. It was his own ragged breathing, he realized, and he could no longer hear the scraping or dripping sounds. He was so concerned for the thing he had encountered that he had ceased to be concerned for the other entity or entities in the room.

He grasped frantically for the reins of control in his mind and slowed his breathing. He placed the heels of his palms over his eyes and pressed in lightly, as though to block out any light that could creep in, despite no light being in the room.

Breathe in. Hold. Breathe out. Hold. Repeat. And repeat again. And again.

Slow. Soothe. He closed his mind against the screaming fear that gibbered away at his concentration and focused on what he could hear. There it was again. The faint sound of falling liquid from far away: drip.

Drip. Drip. Drip. Scrape.

There! Closer now—the sound of careful foot placement as something advanced.

Maddau opened his eyes wide in the darkness. Still, he could see nothing but the wild-colored starry shapes that were always there when he put pressure on his eyes. It sounded close now, perhaps two arms breadth away. How did it get so close so fast? Maddau inhaled sharply, turned on his heel, and ran in the opposite direction—back in the same path that he had traveled to get to the corridor back to the Outer Chamber. Without consideration for the darkness, he moved at full speed in his desperation to get away from whatever was stalking him in the Challenge arena.

And rammed his shoulder straight into the stones that built the archway of the transition to the corridor. His head whipped to the side from the impact, and he saw a swirl of colors in his jumbled thoughts. He bounced off the doorway, fell against the wall of the corridor, and slumped down onto the floor, grasping his left arm. He could not feel his shoulder or his hand; they had gone to sleep from the impact, and nothing but the ticklish bug bite feeling resonated on his left side.

Maddau propped himself up with his right arm, supporting himself against the wall of the corridor, and took stock of his situation. There was absolutely no feeling in his left side except for the tickle-tingle of agonized nerves. He was panting rapidly, and his heart pounded in his chest. He felt, where he could feel, as though his body was quickened to move, yet he could not focus except in short intervals.

Scraaaaaappeeee....

He froze. There it was again—the sound that indicated whatever else was in the room was drawing nearer.

Scraaapeee...scrape!

He turned his wide, terrified eyes back towards where he thought the corridor ended and opened into the room of the Challenges, conning the dark void that spanned his vision for whatever could be producing that noise. But he saw nothing, and somehow that was worse than seeing something emerge from the darkness.

He began pushing himself backwards against the wall, one agonizing arm span at a time, propelling himself with his right leg. The left side of his body still would not respond, and it hung with limp regret against him as he moved, flopping this way and that. Keeping his wide eyes facing in the direction of the noise, Maddau gave no heed to his own noisemaking as he busily made his way backwards down the hall. It made no difference. After all, whatever was in there with him already knew his location.

Lymder remained silent as they made their way down the pathway to the Inner Chamber, where the Sages dwelt. It was a short course, but their progress was slow even with Gonestrwydd's support and lithe movements. At the end of the corridor, the Inner Chamber opened up before them into a large, sunny room. Twyll stepped into the room, Lymder hopping along beside him, and they both stopped, gazing about the room.

Long, thin holes had been cut through the cave's stonework to the outside world, allowing the sunlight to filter in and reflect off the cavern walls, filling the room with a soft and mellow light. Deep oblong shapes had also been carved out as benches for the Sages to sit upon or higher up to form recesses for sleeping. In the center of the room were two long benches where the initiates of the Light would while away their time under the tutelage of a Sage mentor. Lymder smiled at the familiarity. It brought back gentle impressions from his boyhood that smacked of nothing more dangerous or untoward than a chair left out of place in a schoolroom.

His smile curdled as he gazed about the room. Reality bled through and marred the memories of his youth. Darkened splotches dotted the floor and covered the resting slabs. Each recessed resting area held a still, calcified form whose head was tilted back towards the entrance the men had just come through. Lymder stared in horror at the scene, dimly feeling Gonestrwydd's arm slip from underneath his shoulder as the First Knight stepped back. From the corner of his eye, Lymder saw Gonestrwydd's hands reach up to cover his mouth, and he became aware of a faint retching noise coming from somewhere in the room.

The tilted heads were all angled to look towards the entrance, but there were no eyes in the sockets of those heads. The mouths were all agape as though frozen in agonized screams, and the hands of these poor shapes were curled into ragged-looking claws that were pulled up against their chests. Beneath each of these was a large, black stain.

Almost all the recesses were filled, save three. Lymder stared around the room but could not see any trace of the missing forms.

"Gonestrwydd," he whispered.

"I see them, Lym."

"It's… it's the Sages, isn't it?" Lymder whispered, transfixed by the horrors he saw.

"It does appear to be so."

"What's 'appened t' them?"

"They appear to be dead, Lym." Twyll's voice was flat.

Finally, Lymder looked around at the First Knight. Gonestrwydd's face was pale, and he held one hand in front of his mouth as he regarded what was left of the Sages of Light's Wisdom.

"Gonestrwydd? How could this 'appen?"

"It appears they were killed."

"I SEE that!" He snapped in a fury of fear. "By what? By whom?"

"I would wager… the Dark. The Cotheda"

"The Dark? But how? *How* Gonestrwydd? HOW?"

Twyll sighed and shook his head. "The Cotheda have many tricks up their sleeves. It is not so hard to tempt the weak-willed. And those self-righteous prigs that dwelt here were not known for their iron-clad wills…. unless it was for forcing their will upon others," he finished, a bitter note rising in his voice. "I only hope that their deaths were—" He stopped, realizing that Lymder was staring at him, a shocked understanding creeping into his eyes.

"Ah, well, I let my mask slip there, didn't I?" Twyll smiled. "I guess it's almost done with, so I'm not worried. Can't keep to being the good *Gonestrwydd* all the time, now, can I? Not when I'm so close now—when *we're* so close."

Lymder shook his head. "Gonestrwydd"—His voice was soft, almost a whisper—"what are you saying? You can't…you can't have been part of… of this!"

Twyll's smile became a grin. "Indeed, Lym."

Lymder looked around the room, distress coloring his every movement. The Inner Chamber, for all the carnage that filled it, was strangely empty of much else. There was nothing to reach for as a shield, nothing to use in defense. He had lost his weapon in the clash with the Cotheda on the Steps of a Thousand Cares. He was defenseless.

Twyll watched as the realization dawned on Lymder that he had come to this place of slaughter, defenseless and of his own volition, and was now in the presence of the architect of his demise. He finally ceased casting about for any form of assistance, and his eyes returned to Twyll's face.

There was a defeated air about the man; he was fearful and disbelieving.

"Gonestrwydd, ye can't've been party t' this," Lymder whispered. "I cannet believe it of ye."

An ugly snarl twisted its way across Twyll's mouth. He stepped forward, raised his right hand, and pushed Lymder's chest hard. Lymder's weight shifted to his right foot to support him, but the traitor leg buckled, and he fell back, sitting hard onto the ichor-stained, unforgiving stone floor.

He gasped for breath and tried to pull his left leg underneath him to stand as he called out, "Captain!"

Twyll stepped forward, planting his foot on Lymder's chest and kicking the man back down to the ground. Lymder landed hard again, on his back this time, knocking the air from him again. "No, no… none of that, Lym. Let's face this with honor, now. No calling for someone to come rescue you. Your charge is Discipline, so have some self-control!" Twyll placed his foot down on the prone Lymder's chest and leaned his weight into the man. Lymder coughed. The weight of the First Knight was making it difficult to draw breath.

"Gonestrwydd…why…," he wheezed.

The snarl on Twyll's face writhed into a mask of fury.

"I hate that name! Hate it! HATE IT! I have ALWAYS hated it. That never was my name. It's a stupid title of the Light's brainwashing! They were trying to change who I was—trying to take from me the power that I ALWAYS had! My name is Twyll. It has ALWAYS been TWYLL! Remember it! Know my name, and believe it is WHO I AM!!"

Lymder stared up at Twyll's face, understanding shining clearly in his eyes. "*You… DECEIVER!*"

He stamped down on Lymder's chest again and again. Each stomp of his foot cracked his ribs. Blood droplets flew up as the air was forced from his lungs again and again. Lymder's head cracked back against the floor as Twyll stomped him to death, and blood began to flow along the stone floor. Soon, it would dry to a horrid black stain.

Just like the others, Twyll thought, staring at the reddish pool forming under Lymder's head.

Lymder lay still with Twyll's foot still firmly planted on his chest. Tiny hitching movements could still be seen as the man's pulses slowed down. Twyll stared at the knight. Had he not used the hated name, Twyll might have killed him with a gentler hand. He might even have taken his time and drawn things out. Lymder had always been suspicious of him; of this, Twyll was sure. He had looked at him with suspicion for days now. Twyll had known he'd have to deal with Lym at some point. Regardless, time was short. Maddau would soon be done playing with the wolf of the Dark that stalked the halls of the Temple, and he needed time to convince him to join the Darkness and hand over the relic. It was all moving too fast as they approached the end of the game, and he still had so much to do.

The quietest of squeaks permeated his thoughts as the dying knight beneath his foot tried to draw a deeper breath. Twyll looked down upon Lymder's bloodstained face and sighed. It had been an eternity since he'd debased himself by feeding on the Light, a thing he had deferred to avoid any changes in his form that might have given him away while he was amongst the Koteli. Now that that time was coming to an end, he could allow himself the tiniest slip into the pleasures of the Dark Eternalia.

Twyll leaned down, feeling his weight—the weight of Darkness, of Deception— crush into Lymder's chest. He stared down into Lymder's face and firmly gripped the man's chin with his right hand, forcing the slackened mouth open. Twyll leaned in close and opened his mouth, curling his tongue into a long, protruding tube. He began to pull through this tube, and a staticky hissing noise filled the air. In response, a faint and flickering light began emanating from Lymder's mouth, eyes, nose, and ears. The glowing light flitted up and was sucked into Twyll's mouth through the tube of his tongue, much like a dancing trail of fireflies. As the light was pulled away, Lymder began to rapidly age: his hair fell away in gossamer fluffs, deep wrinkles carved their way into the rapidly drying and peeling skin, dark spots began to surface on his scalp, and his lips puckered and pulled in towards his teeth as if his mouth was too small for its opening.

In the space of a few moments, the last of Lymder's light had been swallowed by Twyll, and all that was left on the ground beneath his foot was the calcified husk of what had once been a Koteli knight.

Twyll stood and removed his foot from the indentation it had made in the desiccated chest. When he pulled his foot back, the corpse shifted and the head shifted to the side, giving the corpse the appearance that it was looking back into the room towards the upturned faces of all the other corpses in the room. Twyll chuckled at this irony. An aura of darkness and orphaned shadowlets swirled about him as he fed, then faded away, leaving in its wake an air of youthful grace.

His left cheek itched a bit as the remaining orphaned shadowlets began spiraling up the open edges of the wound on his face, knitting them back together. A moment later, the shadowlets disappeared into the air, revealing the smooth, unmarred skin of Twyll's cheek.

"Be a good boy now, Lym, and keep an eye on those Sages for me."

Still chuckling, Twyll turned away from Lymder and began walking back down the corridor towards the Outer Chamber.

Maddau had backed himself into the Outer Chamber and was propped up with his back against one of the wide stone columns that supported the overhead structure of the room. His gaze never left the entryway to the corridor of the Light's Challenge. In the darkness of that corridor, two yellow eyes gleamed, watching him. He stared back, unmoving, even when he heard a faint cry come from the Inner Chamber.

Perhaps they've found the Sages, Maddau thought. *Now someone will come to help me!"*

Still, he did not move. If he watched those eyes, and if he was still, they did not move either and only watched him in return.

Footsteps were hurrying from behind him.

The steps slowed as they approached.

They can't see me, Maddau realized. *I'm hidden behind the column.*

"Madds?" whispered a soft voice across the room. "Are you there?"

It was Twyll.

"Here, behind the column," Maddau called back, matching Twyll's whisper. "There's something in here with me."

He heard the footsteps begin again, this time slower and more deliberate. The sounds of a fighter who was unsure from which direction the next attack might come. The steps drew closer, slowing down even more.

"Almost to you." Twyll's voice was quiet, firm, and reassuring in the dim light of the Outer Chamber. A moment later, Twyll dropped to one knee beside him.

"Maddau, are you hurt?" Maddau turned to look at Twyll's smooth and unmarred face. He looked as though he had just awoken from a relaxing nap.

Hadn't there been a wound on his face?

"Only a little dazed… My left side is a bit… unstable… right now. But I think I could walk. I have feeling in it again."

Twyll did not ask how or why Maddau had lost feeling in his left side. He simply slid his arm around Maddau's shoulders and, in one fluid movement, stood them both up. The fresh addition of weight on his weakened side caused Maddau to stumble back against Twyll's comforting arm, which tightened around his shoulders, supporting him until he regained his balance.

"You said there was someone here with you?" Twyll peered at Maddau's face, concern deepening his voice. "Did you find a Sage?"

"No, it's there." Maddau pointed to the shadow-festooned corridor from where the yellow eyes had been watching him.

There was nothing there.

Twyll looked into the corridor for a second, then looked back at Maddau. "Madds, it's… it's just an empty hallway."

Maddau's head jerked back to look at the corridor, and he saw it was as Twyll said: the corridor was still shrouded in shadows, but there were no eyes peering at him. It was empty.

"But there's something there, Twyll. I swear it! It's been watching me ever since I got back in here!"

Twyll looked to the darkened corridor for a long moment, then back to Maddau again, worry clouding his voice.

"Madds," he said, his voice soft and careful, "it's pretty dark in there. Did you fall?"

He looked at Twyll. The concern was obvious in Twyll's eyes, and the careful way he spoke made it clear he thought something was wrong with Maddau's mind.

"You're thinking I hit my head, eh? You're thinking I've lost my mind?"

"No, it's not that, Madds. Honest." Twyll smiled to himself at the irony. "It's just… there's nothing there."

"Nothing there *now*."

"Ye-yes, of course. Nothing there now." Twyll licked his lips and glanced back towards the corridor again. "Perhaps we should… ah… relocate… then?" He saw Maddau watching him and looked away. "In case whatever *was* there comes back."

Maddau pressed himself back against the cold stone column and braced his right leg beneath him. Twyll reached forward to assist, and Maddau shoved his hand away, pushing himself up in the process. He tentatively balanced his weight on both legs and was relieved to find that the left leg held without buckling. Maddau looked pointedly away from both Twyll and the corridor entrance. "I s'pose we should go to the main chamber, where the Promenade is. I think that's our next step."

Twyll studied Maddau as he looked towards the last archway in the room. He was able to stand and balance, despite commenting about having lost feeling in one side of his body, and was alert enough. As well as being apparently quite irritated, Twyll noted to himself.

"Madds…"

"Let's go, Twyll." Maddau started forward. His left foot dragged a bit on the floor, evident by the faint scraping of the ball of his foot against the stone floor as he made his way, with stilted steps, across the room. Twyll followed.

When they reached the door to the main chamber, Maddau stopped. He turned his head slowly to look over his left shoulder. "Twyll?"

"Hm?"

"Where is Lymder?"

Twyll halted mid-step and cleared his throat. "He's still in the Inner Chamber."

"And why is that?" Maddau's tone had taken on an authoritative cant.

"He's… seeing to the Sages."

Maddau turned to look fully at Twyll and saw the faint flicker of an aura about Twyll's profile. "You've found them, then?"

"Aye, we found them. All the ones that were missing, at least." He found it hard to meet Maddau's gaze.

"And? What of them?"

"They're not able to assist us, I'm afraid. They're all quite injured."

"Truly?" Maddau blanched. "Are any of them—"

"It will be fine, Madds," said Twyll overriding him smoothly. "There's nothing we can do for them at this time. We must finish our task. Then we can go see the Sages."

Maddau studied Twyll a moment longer, seeing the aura of honesty play about his friend. "And Lymder elected to stay behind?"

"It was my decision, since he is also injured and would only slow us down further." Twyll finally met Maddau's gaze fully. "Do you fault me?"

Maddau looked at him, a mixture of pensive consternation and a faint feeling of unease coloring his faith in his friend. "No," he said after a while. "I don't fault you. You made the decision you had to in order to achieve the outcome we seek. You always said that the end justifies the means, does it not?" He turned back towards the door. "Come. Let us complete this cursed task and be done with all of this. Maybe then we can talk. I have some questions, Twyll."

"Aye, Captain." Twyll's voice was almost ceremonial as they passed through the archway and into the main chamber. "We have many things to discuss."

Maddau stepped across the threshold and stopped, surveying the room. The main chamber of the Temple was a sprawling affair. Large, square blocks of stone made up the floor, and the walls were carved into the very sides of the cave itself and were decorated with a busy intaglio of symbols, names of the pilgrims who had traveled far to study here, statements of wisdom, and symbols of inspiration. No columns held up the high ceiling, which was carved into the overhead cliffside. Small holes had been meticulously cut to allow for natural skylights to light the room, along with the intrusion of the occasional seabird, who found the recessed light holes prime nesting spaces. Bisecting the room were a set of seven tall steps, mimicking the entryway from the outer chamber, the Promenade d'Aspirante, that held the final test for those seeking to dedicate themselves to the work of the Light. Each step held a challenge to one's mind-state as an evaluation of the spirit of the Aspirante. The room was wholly empty and filled with a booming quiet, characteristic of a long-abandoned room.

Seeing no movement and nothing to indicate a need for his attention, Maddau started towards the steps. His steps left imprints on the thick dust that coated the floor.

"Maddau," said Twyll, his voice hushed in the room's solitude. "You said you had questions?"

"Mhm."

"Well, what are they?" Twyll asked, apprehension picking at the edges of his voice.

"We'll deal with that later, Twyll. Now we've almost come upon the end of our task—of my task." Maddau had reached the steps of the Promenade. He paused before the first step.

"I'd like to know before we proceed farther." A bit of iron had crept into Twyll's tone.

Maddau placed his foot upon the first step: the analogue of Purity. As his foot made contact, a faint blue light infused his mind, and Maddau suddenly remembered a time before, what seemed like a man's age past, when he had awoken in the still, quiet hours of the barracks morning with a burning desire both in his mind and his body. He had been dreaming of travel, and his mind had turned to his favorite subject at the time: the Brehines, and his hands had begun the busywork of settling his spirit with its needs. He'd no sooner started when the memory of her reproachful eyes stilled his movements. What would she, with so much heavy weight of worry and responsibility, think of him should she know of his debasement of himself on her behalf? Her regal air made his awakened needs seem like pale desires compared to her esteem for him. He wanted her regard, her esteem, and not at all her scorn. This, what he was doing now, would earn only scorn. He was sure of this in his secretest of hearts. His hands pulled away of their own accord, and feeling cold and unfulfilled, he rolled himself out of his pallet and trudged out the door into the filmy morning light to relieve himself.

The scene was engulfed in the bluish light, and Maddau was aware of his presence on the first step of the Ascension. He took a deep breath and stepped fully up onto the plateau of the step. He glanced back as he raised his foot to broach the next step—and the next test. "Come, Twyll. We can speak once we've ascended the steps."

"Maddau." Twyll watched in consternation as Maddau worked the last of the trials in the Temple. "I would rather us discuss now." A wheedling note crept into his tone, overlaying the iron that was still there.

"No, Twyll. I want to see this through. Then we can talk, and… we can… we can see… what there is to become of this. Come along now. I'll not wait longer."

"Maddau, wait!" Twyll cried out.

Maddau stopped, still facing towards the Hall of the Hallows with his back towards Twyll. "Yes?"

"You… you cannot ascend any further!" Twyll gasped in panic.

"And why not?" Maddau raised his foot to place upon the next step.

"Because… because… because you're tainted!" Twyll spat out, then sucked in breath. His knuckles flew to his lips with such force that the impact caused his upper lip to split against his front teeth as he moved to cover his mouth in shock from what had just issued from his lips. Blood began to drip a trickle down the side of this mouth.

Maddau looked back at Twyll, locking eyes with him, and deliberately placed his foot on the step. As Twyll watched, a yellowish flickering flame of the Light engulfed Maddau's form in a brief sparkle, then died away. At the pinnacle of the flame's brightness, Maddau closed his eyes as the intensity of emotion and memory moved through him. As he completed the test, he opened his eyes again, resuming Twyll's gaze.

"Tainted. What do you mean *tainted*?" Maddau's stare was intent and penetrating. Twyll held his gaze for a moment longer, then dropped his eyes.

"I... I saw...."

"You saw what, Twyll?" His tone was even and smooth, but there was a dark undercurrent flowing beneath the calm exterior. Twyll licked his lips, tasting blood. "I ... saw that you... Planeswalked. I was dreaming... and I...saw it." He rushed to finish. "Maddau stood still, regarding Twyll for a moment, evaluating him.

"I wasn't trying to...to spy on you...on anything," he stammered. "I just... I was Dreamswalking... and saw...you... there."

"And that makes you think I'm tainted? Because you saw me... in a dream?" Maddau smirked. "Really, Twyll. I expect better of you." He turned back to face the steps.

"I saw you. Do not play coy with me! I saw you parleying with the Dark Lords!" Twyll shouted.

Maddau froze again. "What is it exactly that you thought you saw?"

"The Dark Lords offered you their hands, and you accepted their gifts! Only one who has known the gifts of the Dark can actively Planes walk. We have known this from the times of our training. I know it was you, Madds! I SAW YOU!"

"I have never actively Planeswalked, Twyll." He turned to look back at his companion. "I have Dreamwalked, to be sure. We all have. All who bear the charge of the Light are allowed to Dreamswalk." He paused. "But only one who could traverse the Planes would be able to see another walking their Dreams."

Maddau's voice trailed off as he stared at Twyll. A strange certainty about why Twyll was delaying was growing in his mind.

"You cannot go up there, Madds…" Twyll's voice was now raw around the edges, with fear and desperation coloring his tone. "Please…."

"You have yet to tell me why. You say I am tainted but cannot explain how other than "you saw it in a dream," but I tell you I have never actively Planeswalked." Maddau placed his foot on the next steps of the Elever and was engulfed in a flash of green light. As the aura faded, he looked back at Twyll again and stepped up. "You also claim to have seen me, which would be Planeswalking on your part, Twyll, which you have also not explained. Don't you think you owe me some clarifications here if you expect me to delay my Charge any further than it has already been?"

Twyll stared at Maddau, bloody lips quivering and dark tears brimming in his eyes. "Please, Madds." His voice had become husky from the strain of shouting. "I need you here, with me. Please. We need to…to talk…to… *discuss*…some…things."

Maddau shook his head and placed his foot on the next step of the Elever. A blinding silver light surrounded him, and he began to shiver violently. The trial lasted longer this time, and he was sweating when it released him, bent over with his hands braced against his knees.

Twyll involuntarily took a step forward when he saw Maddau brace himself. "Maddau."

Maddau stood up and wiped the moisture from the planes of his cheeks, where tears had begun to trickle down.

"No more, Twyll," he said with hoarse determination. "If you'll not accompany me, then I'll finish this alone." He lifted his foot, the weight of which seemed heavier and heavier with each passing trial, to ascend the next step.

"NO!" Twyll screamed. He sprung forward in an ungainly hopping motion, his hand grabbing the tattered edge of Maddau's tunic. He gave an enormous tug downward as he landed a mere breath from the edge of the first step of the Elever, careful to avoid it. Maddau felt a ferocious pull against his shoulders and thrust his chest forward, pushing his head down to counteract the force pulling him back. For a moment, the opposing forces held: Twyll pulling him back and Maddau pulling himself forward. Then there was a tearing sound as the thready fabric of Maddau's tunic, already weakened from sweat and endless washings, gave way under his arms and at the seams holding the collar piece around his neck. The back of the tunic ripped away, and he was thrust forward under the unmitigated weight of his own force. He tripped up the last two steps, falling forward through brilliant explosions of Light that blinded him. Horrifying visions filled his mind as the last two Trials combined themselves and overtook him, wrenching his body in agony as he fell forward through a space he could not see and for a time he could not measure, until it finally ended when his frame collided with the hard, unyielding stone of the Digne-couloir. A small, triangular segment of stone had fallen from some unknown shifting in the cavern overhead, and Maddau's left brow found it well when he landed. The impact gave off its own blinding light, this time only inside his head, that boomed violently through him and overrode any lingering horrors from the Trials, driving them right out of his concern. Maddau shrieked, his voice a hollow echo in the main chamber as it ricocheted off the walls, and covered his forehead with his hands. He curled into a ball on his left side, clutching the relic to his chest and shielding his eyes and the impact area as he dry-heaved from the pain. Blood dripped through his fingers and fell onto the stones of the Digne-couloir.

Twyll had held Maddau steady, preventing him from taking another step up the Elever, until the weak fabric of Maddau's tunic ripped at the seams, causing him to overbalance and fall onto the Elever.

But now Maddau was up there.

Alone.

And in pain.

Twyll had to reach him.

Had to get the Relic.

Had to get to Maddau.

Had to.

He could see, as he moved towards the unforgiving stone steps with increasing slowness, that each step seemed to glow with its own inner light: blue, orange, yellow, green, silver, red, and purple. They seemed to pulse brighter the closer he got. He readied himself and leapt forward.

As Twyll crashed into the steps of the Elever, a blinding rainbow of light surrounded him as all the Trials leapt into his mind at once. A loud roaring sound filled his ears, and Twyll was thrown back from the Elever with a violent force that sent him sprawling through the air. He landed, face down, in the dirt of the Promenade D'Aspirante, panting and bleeding in equal measure. The steps of the Elever continued to glow briefly in their colors of the Trials, then faded back to stone.

For a few moments, there was no sound in the room but the quiet shushing of the waves as they met the beach outside and brushed the walls of the Temple and the hollow-sounding chatter of the seabirds who made their home in the caves. Maddau gradually became aware that he was lying on the cool stone way. His back was cold, and blood had pooled around his temple, which was now sticky to the touch as it dried. He licked his parched lips and found the taste of blood as well as salt from the grit of the floor. He lifted his head and spat, trying to clear his mouth from the metallic taste of blood, and sat up. The world seemed to move in and out of place around him for the briefest of moments, and all the edges of the shapes seemed soft and out of focus. He squinted his eyes and braced his hands on the floor as he looked around. He was on the Digne-couloir, the topmost level of the steps of the Elever. He had passed the final tests, albeit unwittingly, when he had been overbalanced by Twyll, and... *there had been a ripping noise...,* he thought. His free hand went to his back, and a pained smile wormed its way across his face. *That explains the ripping noise and the cold back.* His tunic was torn... but that meant...

Maddau looked down the steps to where Twyll lay, face down, on the Promenade D'Aspirante. Blood was smeared on the stone around Twyll's head, and he lay still. Maddau stared. Twyll should have landed on the Elever. That he was so far away meant that the Trials had…. They had…

"Twyll," Maddau croaked. "The Trials…rejected…. *You*?"

Tears began to flow as he finished this statement. Just to ask the question was enough to break through Maddau's final resistance to the knowledge that had been growing in his heart, despite his mind's refusal to see it.

It was not he who was tainted…. For he had passed the Trials, even with all it had cost him.

It was Twyll.

Twyll twitched at the sound of Maddau's voice. After a few heaving breaths, he lifted his head and looked at Maddau, who was crouched on the Digne-couloir. For a moment, Twyll was sure that Maddau had been surrounded by the others of their regiment, all encased in a halo of silvery light, up there on the top of the steps. Then his vision cleared, and he could see it was just Madds up there, alone and with no special aura. Maddau seemed to be listing to his right side, and the left side of his face was a mask of blood stemming from a black, triangular shape that had been cut into his left brow. Twyll knew that shape—it was the cursed mark the Sages were branded with when they ascended to their Light duties. "Wha…Madds!... Wha-wuzzit?" he panted, still unable to keep his air from the force of the impact or to remove his eyes from Maddau's face. "What?"

"Did the Trials reject you, Twyll?" Maddau's face was resolute, despite the tears streaming down his cheeks. His voice trembled. "What happened there with you?"

"No… it was the… impact. Yes… the impact… from your Trials, several at once, now… that was forceful, eh?" Twyll licked his lips again, smearing the blood that had coated the lower half of his face. "I'm fine."

"Then join me here, Twyll," Maddau whispered, his voice echoing hollowly in the room. "Prove it and join me now." He raised the hand that was not clutching the pack with the relic and offered Twyll his hand as a silent plea.

Twyll looked at Maddau's outstretched hand and then at his face. He could see the tears brimming in his eyes and overrunning his cheeks to drip onto the front of his cowl. Twyll licked his lips again, torn between desire and fear.

Maybe, for just this one… last… time… it will let me through. Maybe… just so I can be with him again… for a moment.

With these thoughts and the whirling, screaming voices of the Darkness spinning about in his mind, Twyll approached the Elever. At the base of the steps, he took a deep breath, closed his eyes, and stepped forward onto the step of the first Trial.

Chapter Eleven

One Final Test

Maddau stared at Twyll, desperate to believe in him again. The angular planes of his earnest face were smeared with dirt and clotted blood. Below the tendrils of hair dried amongst the caked detritus on his face and covering one eye in careless abandon was the familiar comfort of a lifetime of companionship and shared memories, but the cold light behind his pleading eyes intimated a strangeness that Maddau did not know. A *separateness* that spoke not of his Twyll, his beloved friend and closest confidant, but of an entity with its own agenda. Its own agency. An entity that moved through Twyll.

And it was not one that Maddau knew.

The mocking and silent laughter that had been drowned out once he ascended the steps seemed to whisper in his mind again. *Not know…?*

Oh, but he did know. Yes, he did. He did not want to, but he did.

Twyll gazed up at Maddau. It was only seven steps from the promenade d'Aspirante, where those who wished to enter the temple could gather and walk the living meditations to the Digne-couloir, where those judged worthy could enter the Hallows of the Temple. Once, Twyll had been worthy, but that had been many years past. Before his break with the Sages and before he had met Llygredd. Now...

Twyll placed his left foot on the first step of the Elever, the ascensions, where the aspirant was to meditate on the death of his mind-self. His foot contacted the unassuming, carved stone step. A memory sprang into his mind, overtaking his sight and blotting out all traces of the Temple around him.

Rough sacks, empty of the previous foody occupants, were piled against an isolated slab of rock outcropping from the cliff, not far from the Temple. This time of day was too hot for fishing, so they would not be seen. The cry of seabirds rang out in the salty air.

His hand grabbed a soft, woolen garment embroidered by hand with all the regency of the Light's Sages and shoved it sharply up past her hips. The other hand curled around her back and drew her close. The smell of her, ribald and earthy sweat overlaid with the ceremonious oily notes of Temple incense, flooded his nose.

Gwirionedd's laughter whispered in his ears as he fumbled with her garments and pushed himself upon her. Her laughter had a scornful tinge to it as he tried to prove himself to her again and again.

And failed.

The awful feeling of betrayal of himself as his fervor melted away before her intimidating eyes and mocking grin. Clouds blotted out the sun, and a cold, blue shadow fell on his shoulders, chilling him. He felt small.

He pulled away from the memory in disgust and self-loathing, recoiling from the meaning of the experience and the shame that came with it.

A shearing cold arced up through his sole, ignoring the layers of cloth, leather, wool, and metal that separated his callused archway from the step itself. The cold wrenched through him, and an immense contractive reaction that was both numbing hollowness and pulsating aches centered between his eyes but above his mouth began to pound into his head. With each heartbeat, it pounded. With each breath, it pounded. And with each second, it ached—an ache that echoed through the cavity of his mouth and down his throat. His hands spasmed into clenched fists and flew to his eyes to wipe away the tears trying to escape. He gritted his teeth against the pain and yanked his foot away from the step, staggering backwards in a large, ungraceful lunge that brought him to one knee.

He knelt there, prostrated at the base of the Elever, panting. He was careful to place his hands on the lowest level and not touch the first step as he braced himself. Tears and saliva carelessly dripped down onto his hands as he gasped for air. His mind ached with the fierce, pounding pain that pulsated still in his temples and reached tendrils of fiery agony down the planes of his face, across his scalp, down his neck, and into his shoulders.

Maddau looked down at him, concern writ large on his face, but made no movement.

The reluctant and slow understanding of what it meant that Twyll could not pass the trials of the ascension was starting to unfold in his mind. Whatever he had done, whatever he had let inside, whatever he was now, the Temple's protective guards would not let him in, and that could only be because….

He sucked in his breath. "You've betrayed your charge, Gonestrwydd."

His words hung in the air with a deadly finality that conveyed the authority and condemnation of his station. Not with the rage and righteousness of an outraged leader, but with the sadness and reluctance of an ultimate understanding that was somehow much, much worse.

Twyll looked up at Maddau's words. He could barely see, but Maddau's form, surrounded by a wavering white light, was blurry through the tears that continued their course. Maddau looked as though he was behind a wall of water. As he stared, the light seemed to surround Maddau's form and obscure him from sight. Twyll raised his right arm in a pleading gesture and croaked, "Maddau, please…help… me…"

Maddau winced. The weight of the relic, as light as though his pack was filled with air only moments before, now hung heavy on his back as though pulling him back towards the Hallowed Hall. He regarded Twyll. He could see clearly now the veins of the Darkness running under his skin and slowly steaming off him like sweat in the cold. The Darkness had begun to fill in around his eyes, but Maddau could still see Twyll's dull green eyes staring through at him. The veins under his skin shone through with the Dark, and slowly it began to bleed into the surrounding tissue, leaching into his skin and staining it a nasty, ashy grey as it spread. His body seemed to be rotting with Darkness from the inside as Maddau watched.

"Maddau..." Twyll's voice had thickened, and it seemed a hundred howling voices had been added in chorus underneath. *"Please...."*.

Reluctantly, Maddau lowered the pack to the ground in the archway of the Digne-couloir. The few short steps of the Elever were the distance of maybe half a man's measure, but in the intensity of the moment, it might as well have been across an ocean in another land. Maddau could feel the pull to fulfill his duty nagging at him. Stopping to assist Twyll would be to willingly walk back into the reach of the Darkness he had denied by his ascension of the Elever.

But it was Twyll. He could not leave Twyll.

Not his Twyll.

Not like this.

His fingers released the strap on the pack, and it slid to the floor with a soft *clink*.

His feet moved before his mind registered his intent.

Each step gave him no impact at all, and he felt nothing as he descended the Elever. Seven short steps, and he was at Twyll's side. The stench of the Darkness that roiled off of Twyll was not something he smelled with his nose, but an offense he felt in his heart. He reached into the miasma of corruption enveloping Twyll, placed his hands under Twyll's arms, and with a heaving jerk, lifted Twyll to his feet. Twyll wrapped his arms around Maddau, leaning heavily on him. Twyll had always been taller than him, despite his slighter build. Now, as he leaned upon Maddau, his presence was overwhelming, and Maddau felt smothered as he supported the taller man. Twyll not only relied on Maddau to stand, but he had also somehow draped his arms around Maddau's shoulders and wrapped him in a clinging embrace. Maddau grunted as he shifted position to support Twyll more fully and fought to remain upright.

"Madds." Twyll's voice still sounded as though there were so many screams filling his words, though they were but a whispered hiss. "Thank you."

The sound of his voice curled up at the edges in an almost muted, horrified glee, and Maddau jerked back from Twyll's embrace to stare up at his face.

Twyll's eyes were two green pinpricks in the swirling dark that had filled the sockets in his face. The Twyll he had always known was gone, and the cold, howling madness of the presence of the Dark was the only thing visible in those eyes. Maddau stared into the face of this Twyll-thing, and it spoke again, the sides of its mouth moving in a disjointed yet horrid synchronicity.

"Thank you…so much…for not leaving me." Now its voice was overlaid with the buzzing of a million flies feasting on the rot of Twyll's soul. In one fluid movement, almost too quick to track, Maddau watched as the left arm pulled back, grasped a dark shape protruding from the waist edge of its mailed shirt, and withdrew a blackened, serrated short blade with a forked tip. Maddau had time enough to see that the jagged and chipped blade looked as though it had been recovered from a fire before it was thrust forward. It neatly plunged between the fitment of his chest mail, through his vestment, his overtunic, and his shirt, into the V between his ribs, skewering his stomach.

Maddau's body contracted around the offending intruder, and as he did so, the Twyll-thing forced it further up, twisting it. Hot, acidic agony spread in his guts and chest. Instinct took over, and Maddau grasped at the hilt of the blade with his free hand as the hand that had previously been supporting Twyll grasped for purchase on the Twyll-thing's body. The momentum of the attack caused him to stagger backward. Maddau's foot, searching for stability, stepped back on the first step of the ascension of the Elever.

His foot made contact, and the Twyll-thing let him go, allowing Maddau to collapse backwards onto the Elever. A whitish halo began creeping in at the edge of his vision, but Maddau could still clearly see the pinpricks of green in the black of the Twyll-thing's eyes as they followed him as he fell back. He could see the Twyll-thing's face receding as he fell, and he knew he was falling down to the Elever, but he had no sense of falling or of impact. The world around him was experiencing a groundshaker that caused his vision to shift violently to the side, and a spreading cold informed his muddled thoughts that he must have landed on the Elever, but there was no real sensation outside of the creeping chill. He could no longer see the Twyll-thing's eyes, as he was now facing the promenade d'Aspirantes and lying on his side, crumpled against the steps. A hollow, drawing feeling in his chest had replaced the acidic pain that had first presented with the…. when he had been….

The whitish halo had encroached from the edges of his vision to now obscure most of his sight, and a darkness was beginning to infiltrate the light. It was as though he was falling backwards down a dark tunnel. Thankfully, this darkness was empty, Maddau realized. It had no agency, and it did not care.

As his eyes closed, Maddau thought with real relief how wonderful it was that this darkness that spirited him into oblivion did not care about him. Not at all.

The Twyll-thing watched as Maddau crumpled to the ground before him. Maddau's head rested upon the top of the Elever, with his chin jutting into the air and clearly exposing his throat as though it thirsted to be cut. But there was no need for that now. This pathetic, pure cow, which would have been the ideal vessel to obtain the cup of disgrace and make the ascension of the champion of Darkness all the more perfect, had shaken off the mantle of Darkness once. Reacquiring control of the pure cow's mind would be a simple child's exercise now that his life was ebbing away and his Light faltered. Keeping him alive long enough to turn him into the Dark champion would be only slightly more work. But while this would be an irony of the most delicious sort—to corrupt the Light's last champion for the work of the Dark Eternalia—it was no longer worth the time. It had converted this being, impure as it was, to the task at hand. All agency and desire within had been destroyed, and any inclination to work for any other goals than the goal of the Dark Eternalia had been quashed. Only the Dark Eternalia and its needs remained.

The Twyll-thing lifted its left foot and placed it on Maddau's right hip. As it shifted its weight forward, using Maddau as its bridge to reach the Temple's sacred hallows, the crushing weight applied to the joint of Maddau's hip created a popping crunch as the bone in the joint gave way. Maddau's face pinched inward, but his eyes remained closed as his mouth dropped open. A pitched wail issued forth from the limp form.

"Still alive?" the Twyll-thing buzzed. "Then you will live to see Our Ascension into the Dark."

The Twyll-thing stepped forward and onto Maddau's chest. Maddau's face contorted into a snarling squall of agony as the crackling of ribs giving way under the weight of the Twyll-thing shifted the blade embedded in his gut. The pain had a clarifying effect and halted the silent descent into oblivion. Maddau's consciousness returned to the present moment, as though the ending of his life had been slapped away, and he opened his eyes. Forcing his attention away from the ball of agony in his chest and now his hip, he looked up to see that the Twyll-thing was using him to get past the wards of the Elever. Another trick of the Darkness, he realized. It had tried first to use and twist him to its own designs, to turn him into its own agent, and to take the relic for the Darkness. When he had thrown off the horrible corruption of his soul and blighting of his mind through the intervention of the Sages of the Past, the trials of the Elever, and ascended to the Digne-couloir, it had used his last weakness, his love for Twyll, to bring him down. If it could not use him to achieve its means, it would achieve them over his lifeless body, evidently.

I'm not lifeless just yet! Maddau growled to himself and looked up. The Twyll-thing had forgotten him; its gaze was fixated on the pack puddled on the floor in the entryway to the Temple hallows. At the approach of the corruption of the Darkness, a pealing and melodious bell-like sound was beginning to ring forth from the pack containing the relic. The Twyll-thing shifted forward to take the next step off of its Maddau-bridge and onto the Digne-couloir. It ran its tongue, which had become strangely elongated and conical, like an animated rootlet, out of its mouth and around its lips. Saliva oozed out of the corner of its mouth and dripped down in a patter of shadowlet masked droplets onto Maddau's face. The drops landed on Maddau's jaw and sank into his skin, burning like acid. He ignored this irritating pain and reached forward with his right hand to grasp the Twyll-thing's calf where it met the ankle. With his left hand, he braced himself against the third step of the Elever, the test of Charity, and in one heaving moment, he sat up and at the same time twisted the ankle in his grasp hard to the left with a surging, fierce strength.

A faint memory of his boyhood flashed through his mind, flaring in the briefest pictures of him sharing the only food he had with a younger sibling. The memory was so old and tattered from ages past that it was there and gone in the glow of the Elever test.

Then, wrenching forward, against the agony of the blade in his stomach twisting in, against the shifting of the broken ribs, and against the grinding of the crushed joint of his hip, against the unimaginable weight of the Twyll-thing and the evil intention of the agency of the Darkness behind it, Maddau sat up, a scream tearing itself loose from the depths of his soul, unknowing in the process.

The Twyll-thing lost its balance as its bridge revolted against it and fell backwards, landing on the promenade in a graceless sprawl. Its head hit the large stone plates with a hollow thunking sound.

Maddau collapsed back onto the arm propping him up against the steps, barely conscious. He could see, through his twitching eyelids, a hazy view of the Twyll-thing lying on the ground before him in a tangle of limbs. A darkness was pooling beneath its head, but whether that was blood or the ichor of the Dark, he could not tell. He strained his arm and body's weight against the stone steps, feeling none of the effects of the tests, for he was beyond all in his extremis and actions. Slowly, ever so slowly, he lifted himself up one step and then rested on his good left hip, panting, while he regained his strength. Then slowly, slowly, he lifted himself again. The arm over the broken ribs would not support him, and his sword arm would be useless after so much strain.

Slowly… slowly…. A little bit higher…. And another step. Rest. He tilted his head backwards and peered at the Elever. Through the whitish hazy glow that was encroaching upon his sight again, he could just make out three more steps above his head to make it to the Digne-couloir.

The world began to fade away, a little at a time. He could feel a cold hollowness slipping away from his chest, and his body seemed to not be there below his hips. The hips were there, though. He knew that well because of the pain—the damaged bones were singing a high chorus like the boys in the field during reaping season.

The pain! If he could use the pain to clear his head, he could at least make it to the relic and protect it from…

He swallowed thickly, a sharp, metallic taste coating the inside of his mouth with a slickness that was more than spit. What he would have to do was… unthinkable. He was not sure he could. He looked down at himself, a gory mess of blood-blackened clothes, armor, and wounds that were invisible yet hot within him. He was sweating with such intensity from the pain that he felt like he was swimming in his tunic.

He tentatively cupped his hand on his right side. The heat radiating from his ribs was tangible even beyond the thinning cloth of his overtunic and vestment, and the pain in response to his touch was immediate and pulsing. The damage there was bad, he knew, and even his light touch was enough to immediately bring awareness to the area and the rancid, spreading heat. It would suffice for just the lightest impact to keep him clear. Any more might bring him closer to crossing the veil of this existence into another plane. That inevitability was closer now than ever before, but there would be time enough to deal with it when it came.

He raised his hand a span away and readied himself. Turning his face away from what he would do, he closed his eyes and gritted his teeth. It was time.

Maddau stayed in this position, waiting. He knew he was ready, though he would never be ready. It was but a moment's action, then it would be done, and he could be clear enough to focus…. To move. It would not hurt too much, except that it would be horribly too much. It was just another small ache on top of everything else, except in the anticipation of the moment, it was beyond huge. It was enormous. It was monstrous. The fear of the pain stemming from his actions was unmanning and not fit for the Captain of the Koteli, and he was riddled with it.

Chuff.

A small sound intruded into his cocoon of anticipatory torture. Maddau opened his eyes and looked up. Peering past the lengthening white tunnel surrounding his vision, he saw the Twyll-thing's body twitch, and another small sound escaped as its hands scraped against the floor: *Chuff.*

"No…" Maddau's cracked and dry lips formed the word as it slipped silently from him. "NO!"

The Twyll-thing twitched, its feet kicking against the floor without direction. It sat up in one flopping movement. Its upper body hung limply on its spine like meat rags on a hook. Its head had an awful, flattened shape on the back from where he had landed on the stones. With sickening slowness, it turned its face towards where Maddau lay. The distance between where Maddau lay on the Elever and where what had once been his Twyll lay on the promenade was perhaps the span of a tall man's height, but as Maddau watched the thing's twitching movements, it felt both like an ocean's distance away and closer than a breath apart.

When the thing's… head fully faced Maddau, an unwitting groan slipped from his puckered lips. The flattened side of its head extended to the face, leaving a large, voided plane over the top of what had been its right eye. But for the eyes, there was no Twyll left in them. The green of his vibrant spirit was gone, and there was nothing but dripping black ichor left in those hollowed sockets. Black tears of Darkness bubbled down from where Twyll's eyes had been and left ragged trails in the skin of the abomination's face, which had begun to sag and pull to the side under the weight of the impacted skin.

A high-pitched keening filled his ears. Without thought, his hand slammed down upon his injured side and clenched. The keening noise cut off as he gasped for air from the staggering shock of the impact. Pain speared him like a fish from the water, and he wriggled like the same, unable to extract himself from the tenterhooks that sank deep within him. The effects, however costly, were immediate. His vision cleared as blood slammed into his head, providing a rush of agony and focusing his mind. His heart sped up, and he began panting, trying to fill his damaged lungs with air to accommodate the injury. Little flecks of blood sprayed from his lips. Sweat began dripping from his brow, and Maddau began pulling himself up the Elever's last steps.

The abomination of the Darkness that had once been his childhood friend leaned to one side and clumsily placed one foot beneath itself. It extended the leg in a stilted motion and pulled the other leg underneath it to stand. It moved, not in the way a person with an understanding of balance and falling would do—with care not to lean too much one way or the other to keep upright—but with a wooden pulling of limbs and arranging of forces. As though it understood the need for structure and support but not the rationale as to why or the consequences lacking that.

It balanced precariously upright, hewn over as though stooping, and placed its hands on the ground before it. Snapping and rending sounds began to emit from the body of the abomination. Maddau's horrified eyes jerked back to focus on the thing.

It was…rebuilding itself. Its body structure reshaped to be on all fours instead of upright on two legs. The head that had once held the well-known visage of his friend Twyll was now rotated so that when it looked up, the mouth was on top, the nose, flattened in the fall, was all but pushed into the face, and where the eyes had once been, there were now empty black holes from which the ichor of darkness dripped freely. The bloodless pallid lips skinned back from the teeth, which displayed in a hideous donkey-like bray, and the tongue dropped down and elongated out, splitting into two singular and seeking worms. The abomination shrieked at him. It was the face he had seen in Holaf Tavern.

That could have been me, Maddau thought in numb horror. *Had I given in, that could be me right now.*

IT STILL COULD! The silent voice of the Darkness roared into his mind, echoing from nothingness and booming from the cavern around him.

YOU SEE THE POWER WE HAVE. THE LIGHT BEARS NO ABILITIES EVEN CLOSE TO THIS! YOU WANT THIS POWER FOR YOURSELF—TO BE A TRUE COMMANDER WITH THE ABILITY TO MAKE ALL BOW BEFORE YOU! TO MAKE ALL FEAR YOU. TO MAKE ALL RESPECT YOU. THIS IS THE GIFT OF THE DARKNESS: TRUE, UNRESTRAINED POWER! TAKE IT FOR YOUR OWN!! A MEANINGLESS BAUBLE IN EXCHANGE FOR EVERYTHING YOU'VE WISHED FOR— EVERYTHING YOU WANTED FROM THIS BODY!

GIVE US THE BAUBLE... THE CHEAP TOY OF THE PRETENDERS TO THE RULE OF POWER... AND WE WILL MAKE YOU A GOD!

Maddau closed his eyes against the disgusting, yet somehow attractive, siren's song trying to pound its way into his heart and mind again. He could feel the cold steps of the Elever pressing against his back, playing no part in the silent battle he was fighting for control, yet somehow comforting in their immobile presence all the same.

"*Give it to me, Madds.*" Twyll's voice cut softly through the echoing cavern, causing Maddau's eyes to jerk open in shock and surprise. "*Just give it to me, and everything can be like before. You'll command the knights, and I'll be by your side. Just like always. We don't even have to talk about this.... little excursion. We can pretend it never happened and go back to being together like always. You know I'm always by your side—you know that, right? How I always made things better when you made a misstep? This is one of those times.... A little misstep! I can make it all better, Madds, I promise! Just give me the bauble...*"

Maddau stared down at the abomination. From its dripping hole of a mouth echoed Twyll's voice, as if it had been Twyll speaking to him in the barracks back in Caer y Twr. But it was not Twyll speaking, he knew. There was no more Twyll left in that thing... no more Twyll left in the world. In this plane or the next. He could feel hot tears on his cheeks for this knowledge and could do nothing to stop them. He closed his eyes, turned his face away from the abomination, and placed his left hand on the highest step of the Elever, the one that led to the Digne-couloir, and pressed down. The reaching movement stretched injured parts of his body, causing him to pant like a dog. The sweat streamed down his face and dripped onto the stone below him. He could hear, over the roaring blood in his temples, a scratching sound. One final lift, and he was sitting on the top of the Elever. The scratching noise grew louder, maddening in its obscurity, and Maddau, eyes still closed against the horrors the Darkness had wrought upon his Twyll, lay back on the cold stone of the Digne-couloir and began to push himself with his one good arm and one good leg backward, towards the pack and the entrance to the hallows.

The scratching stopped.

The abomination had ceased to crawl towards the Elever and now stood, watching Maddau's exhausted progress. The realization that it would not get the bauble—that it was out of its reach—was dawning upon what now passed for its mind, which was really only a barely controlled consciousness. It sprinted forward, intending to overtake Maddau's form and take the relic for itself. The first touch of the Elever slammed it backwards with an intense rebound that threw it back almost to where it started. The steps of the Elever glowed bluish white, then returned to their unassuming stone. There would be no traversing the Elever for this creature; the wards of the Light had been well crafted in the event of such an encounter. Even so, the abomination of the Dark understood that there were ways around such things. The Darkness had always been crafted to work around the edges of the Light.

It turned and began shuffling towards the center of the Promenade d'Aspirantes.

Maddau reached for his pack. He picked it up with his good hand, but the strength was gone from his arm, and his fingers splayed, betraying him as he tried to lift it. The relic fell out with a hollow *PONGK* and lay gleaming with dull light on the stone. He placed his fingers around the stem, forcing them to close one by one, before he attempted to raise it again. The instant his hand connected with the metal, he felt an energizing relief spread through his hand, returning the strength he had exhausted, and flowing through his arm and into his body. He could hear a faint and strange chiming music that seemed to overlay the air, and he momentarily forgot the various insults his body had endured. A blanket of calmness radiated out from the relic, speaking to him in a similar way that the Darkness had, yet very differently. He knew he had succeeded in overcoming the Darkness' final attempt on him. He understood, in a strange way of knowing, that this was where he would stay. His injuries had been too much, and he could not overcome them, but that was ok—expected, even. Had he not thought, just a fortnight past, that he would be sacrificed for Abertha to obtain the relic? This was simply the ending coming to fruition, only in a different place and time.

Once he had placed the relic in the Hallows, he could finally rest.

As Maddau raised the cup, the Abomination could sense the presence of the relic of the Light. Unshielded in this world—and it hurt! It hurt so much—this presence of Light without cover, without amelioration, without restraint. It began to howl and shriek in tones that vibrated the stones surrounding it. The cacophony of millions of souls given over to the Darkness, howling in agony as one. The stones began to move, vibrating in their places, causing cracks and small chunks to fall in showers of dust and sand.

The noise grew louder and louder still. Large pieces of rock began to fall from the ceiling of the cavern, and the large laid stones of the promenade began to kick up at angles as the sand below shifted. Plumes and small, swirling dust demons began erupting from the cracks.

The abomination stood up on its rear legs, threw its arms out and its inverted head back, and roared the chorus of millions of voices of fear, agony, terror, and despair. And Fury.

Huge chunks of the cavern's ceiling began raining down. Boulders fell onto the Elever, smashing the steps into a shattered ruin. Large chunks of rock fell onto the promenade and bounced around the abomination. One chunk of rock crashed into the promenade and bounced back, smashing into the abomination's leg and taking it off below the knee. The mangled and twisted flesh of the joint dripped blackened streams of ichor and shadowlets into the air instead of blood.

The shrieking howling fury of the Darkness shook the remains of the Temple entryways, causing it to collapse in on itself in a pile of rocks and ruin; the detailed carvings done with such care and joy over centuries of occupation fell from the archways and shattered on the paved mosaics of the entrance. A piece of the carved ceiling over the Digne-couloir shook loose and landed with a hollow boom across the entrance to the Hallows, cracking into multiple pieces in the process and destroying the entrance into the Hallows of the Temple.

The abomination ceased its howling to watch the Digne-couloir and the rubble-strewn hole where the entryway to the Hallows had been. Rocks and sand continued to rain down around the creature that had once been the First Knight of the Koteli, and the echoing wails of those who serve the Dark Eternalia continued to swirl around the ruined Temple cave.

Debris shifted down around the remaining first step of the Elever, and rocks continued to fall at regular intervals, but there was no movement from the entrance to the Hallows. A thick tenseness of silence had filled the Temple promenade.

The abomination craned its inverted head around on the twisted-meat rope of a neck, looking for signs of movement, signs of action, signs of *life*. But there was nothing moving except the falling shifts of sand and rocks from the damaged ceiling and the occasional bouncing stone that landed on the ruinous heap.

It waited. The body still moved through the process of breathing, though there was no reason to do so. The thing it was no longer had a need for breath. It was no longer alive. The life force that animated the abomination stemmed entirely from the Dark Eternalia.

The chest expanded in the simulation of inhalation as it listened, and streams of shadowlets and drips of the ichor of the dark fell to the shattered paving stones of the promenade and oozed into the cracks between the stones.

NO MOVEMENT.

NONE.

THE PURE COW IS DEAD.

THE STUPID TOY OF THE LIGHT IS GONE! CRUSHED BENEATH THE ROCKS OF ITS HIDING PLACE.

CRUSHED! DESTROYED! GONE. FOREVER!!!!

Gone… yes…. But… it *could* be recovered…

If it wished to do so.

But for now, it was to ensure that no one would disturb this place.

I HAVE WON!!! It cackled with a mad shriek. It threw its inverted head backwards, mouth raised to the ruinous remains of the top of the cavern, and screamed its triumph in a long ululating cacophony of the mad and gibbering voices of the Dark.

As it howled, the edges of the abomination began to bleed away into streams of shadowlets that flew through the seams between the rocks and sand that filled what had been the entrance into the Temple. The swirling shadowlet breezes streamed out through the rubble, coalescing together into a larger funnel of darkened smoke, and whirled up the sand inlet, dispersing into the larger pools of shadow that held court under the steps leading down the cliff.

Maddau had made it through the entryway to the Hallows when the world began to crash in around him. He had heard a horrific scream coming from the promenade but could not understand why the Twyll-thing had ceased to chase him. Then the ground shaking began, and when the first section of the tiled ceiling in the hallway clattered down around his head, Maddau finally understood. It meant to bury the relic here. And to bury him with it. If it could not obtain the relic, as the wards of the Light were still active here to protect it after all this time, then it would destroy the whole place, him included. And then return when the wards were destroyed to retrieve its prize.

He had to do something while he could still draw breath. He tried to fill his lungs with air and coughed back a spray of blood as a sharp stabbing in his chest changed his mind with ferocious speed. He tried slowing his breaths to shallow, panting gasps in an effort to get the depth of breath for which his lungs clamored. His heart pounded, and he could feel his pulse echoing all through his body, but there were additional points now that echoed back somewhere below his chest in a hazy, but very there, ache.

The delicately carved sections of the overhead facade had all fallen and shattered on and around him, and the fallen molding of the arched entryway had blocked the entrance. He was trapped in the hallway to the Hallows.

And he was alone. Of this, he was certain.

The Twyll-thing—the abomination that Twyll had become—was gone. It had left. Probably when certain of his demise.

His… and the Relic's….

In the splattering of light that crept its way through the rocks and falling sand blocking the entrance, Maddau could see that the shadow-shrouded hallway to the Hallows, while littered with broken tile and rocks, was still mostly intact. One of the facades on the west wall had crumbled into a pile of sharp-looking pieces, and the wall itself was cracked in half a dozen places, but it looked like he could get through the hall, he thought.

Another rumble came from overhead, and something crashed to the ground outside, making the stone floor way beneath him tremble. More debris and dust fell around him, and the light filtering into the hall became dimmer.

He could make it down the hall if he wasted no time, he amended.

Maddau began pulling himself along the debris-strewn floor: first with one hand placed firmly, then with the foot planted to provide propulsion, then extending the leg and pushing. Pause. Repeat.

He placed his hand down on a protruding sliver of tile and felt it slice deep into his palm.

Maddau could feel something between a yelp and a sob building up in his chest as he carefully examined the heel of his hand in the fading light for the offending shard. This would be another pulsing point he felt with each hammer of his heart. He felt more than saw the hilt of the tile shard and, in one swift movement, yanked it out of his hand. The quick movement and re-rending of already damaged flesh forced an unrestrained yelp from his throat, and the quick expulsion of air brought with it more blood. Not just flying around on the wings of his breath but starting to well up in the back of his mouth, making him cough, and dripping down his lower lip and chin.

So much more blood now.

He felt like the ground beneath him swayed as he strove to keep moving forward. It was shifting each time he placed his bleeding palm on the ground. Maybe the ground was quaking from all the damage to the Temple?

Maybe the world was falling in on itself now that the Darkness had won?

Maybe what he did here in these last fragmentary moments of light no longer mattered.

Maybe *all* that mattered was what he did here, in these last fragmentary moments of light.

He pulled himself another arm's span forward, and the sobbing-yelping sensation pulled up from his chest again to nest in his throat. His mouth filled with the acid taste of saliva and blood.

Maddau gagged, and his mouth dropped open, spilling blood and a strangely dark fluid across the floor in front of him. It splashed onto his left hand, burning his knuckles where it landed.

The room around him tilted pendulum-like, left and right, and he lowered his chin to his chest, gasping and sobbing for air, eyes closed.

No good. Even with his eyes closed, he could feel the room swaying wildly about him, making his fluids crawl up the back of his throat again. Soon they would bubble out of his mouth and back onto the floor of this once sacred place of the last Temple of Sages. Once a place of learning…a holy place of training for the Koteli…. a sanctuary for those touched by the Light….

"Now it would soon be his tomb."

The words lanced out at his heart from the darkness surrounding him, arriving fully dressed in the despair of absolute and unassailable knowledge.

But how, and from whom? The Darkness could not be here with him in these desperate last moments of his life? Surely not. Yet here he was…. In darkness…

This darkness, much like the respite he had had faded into during his battle with the Abomination, had no agency, though. No malice or menace to it. It was simply the absence of any illumination—quietly still.

From where, then, had those words been issued?

It took more than one panting moment to realize that the words had not, as it had seemed, come to him from the darkness surrounding him. Instead, those words had reached his heart from his own lips before his mind had even realized what it knew to be true.

Yes, he would die here. This was the goal of the Dark Eternalia: to bury him and the Relic within the ruins of the Temple. And then, when the last agent acting on behalf of the Light, the last of the Koteli, was dead, to retrieve the Relic and bring about the Grand Ruin of the world…on all the Planes.

But there was one thing he could do, he realized. The true purpose of the Temple had been as a safeguard for the Relic and the Koteli, much like the mechanisms in the Caer had been what seemed like a lifetime ago. The ancient wards had saved him from the abomination of the Dark Lords and the designs of the Dark Eternalia. And despite the actions of the Twyll-thing in bringing about the ruination of the Temple, the wards had held.

They had held. And in this, it had given him time to sequester himself in the hall in which he now lay, prone and alone. But safe from the abomination and yet alive.

Maddau knew he could activate the last of the old wards to protect the Relic. It was not too far down this hall, though he knew not the mechanism. He could figure it out; he had to try.

He began to pull himself forward again: hand placed firmly, then foot planted. Extend and push.

He got busy moving.

The work of fifty shifts forward had brought him to what he sought. Maddau knew not how long it had taken him; time had become thin here. He knew he had retched twice more, the last time about 38 shifts in, and something seemed to have torn inside him with the last heaving. More blood than he had ever seen had spilled out of his mouth, and now his chest and the rags of his tunic were drenched with his own fluids and juices. It was a horrific feeling, and the smell wafting up to him made him more nauseous still. He had fainted, he guessed, for a short period of time after the last heave. He surmised this only because he had awoken with his forehead resting on the back of his hand, his check pressed into the cool dirt that used to be the floor ways. He had pushed himself up and kept repeating his movements, despite the world dancing around him every time he moved.

His ribs and chest were a hot ache now, loudly pounding in his temples and with no ebb to the dry spasming of his nerves, and he could no longer feel anything below his belly. It was as if he had been cut in half and left his legs and ass back on the Promenade.

But finally, slow sliding drag by slow sliding drag, he had made it to what was the last vestige of safety within the Temple. At least, he hoped it was.

A small pedestal, much like the one in the Caer, if it still stood, but much, much older, stood in a recessed alcove of the passage. Unassuming and barely visible in the dimness of the hallway of the Hallows, Maddau could more sense the feeling of power emanating from this old cluster of stonework than see it. He squinted meanly in the dimness but could only make out the barest of outlines. But it was when he closed his eyes that the shape of the power before him screamed its presence into his mind, and he was uniquely aware of a muted, yet very real guardianship… no… a Guardianship…. A presence so real and so there, its very energy screamed protection at any cost.

At all cost.

And there it was—Maddau finally understood. This was, indeed, what he had been charged to do from the very beginning. It was his charge, as the Captain of the Koteli, to give his life for the obtainment of the Relic.

It was not what he and Abertha had thought a lifetime ago, in the sacred room in the Caer, when she had given over her life to defeat the ward.

It was here, in the darkness of the Temple de la Sagesse. Where he would give over his life to enable the ward.

It was as it had always been: a life given over to protect something with a Guardianship that was not of this world…. not of this Plane. And in order to bring it back into this world, this *plane*, a life must be given over again. That was the amount of energy needed for each transaction; this amount, and no other, Maddau understood.

He had no idea how exactly he understood this, but it seemed to be there, full-blown, filling him with this necessary knowledge for him to fulfill his task.

He had no idea how this process, this contract to exchange a life's energy for protection of something so valuable beyond compare, had been made, but somehow a contract had been made and this price, which was so incredibly high, had been agreed upon.

Maybe The Teacher had been the one…?

And it really didn't matter how the contract had been struck. That was not his purpose here—to inspect sacred bonds agreed to by others—that he had been chosen to fulfill.

It wouldn't matter at all in a few moments, anyhow.

The lack of fairness in this situation had not escaped him. That so many had been required to give so much and pay such high prices for others' actions seemed like an unbearable burden. He had not even been asked or advised of the true price of his charge. None of them had! No one had truly known what their actions would cost!

Would he have taken on this unspeakable price to pay had he been told what it would truly entail? What would it truly cost him? That it would cost him Abertha and all the Koteli knights?

That it would cost him Twyll? And that Twyll was gone…. forever?

That answer was a clear and resounding *NO!*

And maybe that was why. Why none of them were told. He had known more than the rest as their Captain, to be sure, but even he had not been aware of why…. Not until now.

Now, when it no longer mattered. The oaths had been struck, and the contracts had been signed by others long gone to be paid out with the blood of those living today.

And here he was, as foretold. The last of the ones left alive who could pay over the cost of this foully necessary contract. For as long as he was still living, which would not be for too much longer, if the growing and pulsating tearing in his chest was any indication.

Oh… but it hurt. It *burned.*

Head lowered and eyes still closed, Maddau could see the mute outline of the Guardianship's power glimmering like a blue fire in his mind's eye. The silent offer to complete that which had been augmented long ago.

He understood that he did not have to. If he wished, he could just lie down and let go. The relic would be fine here, perhaps. Someone could find it… Maybe one day a passing peasant's child would unearth it when all the wards were dissolved and nothing of his bones even remained but dusty flecks in the light's grasp. They would probably play with it like any other toy. Possibly even be able to sense its power and worth. Or perhaps they would just play with it and then throw it out with the day's scraps.

The relic *might* be fine. Maybe the Darkness would even forget about it.

Except that the Darkness never forgets. Or forgives.

He understood this. *Just look at what it did to Twyll.*

He could not, in good conscience, let the Relic lie there and cast its fate upon the *hope* that it *might* be safe here, in the darkness of the ruins of the Temple.

He would not be able to live with himself, knowing that others had paid the highest price to see it safely home, and he had left it to chance.

Not that he would have to live with himself, ultimately, for very long.

He barked a dry and near-silent laugh in the encroaching darkness. Did he actually laugh? Or was that all in his mind?

Did it even matter anymore?

No, he decided. It did not.

He knew what he had to do—what he was meant to do all this time and all these long years.

The right thing to do.

Even though no one would ever know.

No longer worrying about opening his eyes, as he could see the presence of the Plane's Guardian outlined on the pedestal clearly in his mind, Maddau lifted the Relic—it had been so heavy before but now felt like nothing in his hand.

He placed his left hand on the corner of the stone pedestal's base. There was no impact as he made contact. The stone felt worn and smooth, perhaps thousands of years old. Beneath the calluses on his palm and fingers, Maddau could feel the tiniest hint of lines, indicating that at some point this stone had been carved. The touch was warm beneath his fingertips and somehow comforting.

With his right hand, he placed the Relic on top of the pedestal. There was a hollow, metallic *clonk* as he set it down on the cornice capping the pedestal, and there he held it in his right hand while his left gripped the corner of the foot. The circuit was complete, and the contract was filled in with this name.

And now to sign it with his life.

Maddau sagged forward until his head rested against the strangely warm stone. Unrealized tears slipped from beneath his closed eyelids and danced, dangling on his lower lashes, until they fell against the worn and time-eroded surface, where they were instantly absorbed, leaving no trace that they had ever existed at all.

He knew, with no instruction, that it would not matter how he enabled the ward. And despite his dying here, of which so little time was left for the immediate warrantless cares of life, he took just a moment to mourn in silence what his life could have been: a family man—co-ruler beside Abertha, perhaps? Some other sort of soldier, dying on foreign soil in an undeclared war that only aged rulers understood? Perhaps. Traveling the world with Twyll as vagabonds, perhaps? All these possibilities of what could have been, and so much more, that now would never be. And all necessitated by the need to protect the world from the machinations of the Dark.

His heart had slowed, and his breath felt heavy in his chest. He felt a strange lightness fill his body, and with it came a wavering feeling of nausea. He felt like the hall around him was spinning away.

Another tear, this one selfish and known, filled with regret in the way the others had not been, for himself and himself alone, slipped over his lower lash line and traced its way down the crags and lines that had etched their way into his face over these long days. It trembled in a bulging half drop on the precipice of his upper lip and then jumped to the scraggling, foresty presence of a week-old beard. This last vestige of the regretful dreams of his life slipped through the roots to dangle at his jawline, tracing along the curve of his chin for just a moment before dropping away. As it released its tenebrous hold on his skin and fell into the chasm between him and the stone pedestal, Maddau let go of the Relic.

In the growing gap between the tips of his fingers and the darkened, brassy-gold curve of the half-plate metal supporting the Relic, a scalding and booming silent white light filled his conscious mind, overrunning what remained of his senses and subsuming everything.

The final Ward had taken hold, and the Planes Guardian assumed its watch.

Dywedais i'r hyn a ddywedais

Song of Dancing Light

What does all this mean?
The Spaces in between –
What braids the ropes for ties that bind-
The saving grace of mortal-kind?
That which dances with the Dark-
Illumination as the Spark-
Battling below and above
The wars spanning ages of old.
The Saving Grace is only love.
And Love's Forgiveness, as foretold.

Epilogue

The grey-blue water lapped against the wooden pillars of the crude dock. In the distant fog, the form of a ship materialized from the nothingness. As she moved, the fog peeled away to show the humble front end of a medium fishing vessel, whose single sail hung limp in the wet air. The boat nosed forward with ponderous slowness until it reached the end of the old wooden dock. Voices emerged through the fog, quiet and terse, arguing in the jagged tones of a foreign land. The prow drew abreast of the end of the dock, and a short, stocky man climbed over the hand-helds and dropped with deceptive light-footedness onto the dock end. The aged and sun-bleached wood creaked beneath this new weight. The squat man raised his arms towards the boat's hand-helds.

"Giv'us 'ere 'im!"

Murmurs came from within the boat, and then a thin, bandaged leg reached over the hand-helds.

"Easy does'er, Cap'n," The squat man said, reaching to grip the leg under the thigh, where the bandages revealed worn canvas trousers, to support the body exiting the boat. "I'v'n got'chu"

"I am no Captain!" A quavering voice floated down to him, thin and reedy.

The sailor rolled his eyes as he helped the knight settle onto the dock. The figure hunched before him, wrapped in dirty, stained bandages on all limbs to each end. Even the man's face was wrapped with the stinking and dirty wound dressings, leaving only the mouth and chin visible. He could see horrid shadows beneath the edges of the bandages, perhaps where the wounds had healed badly. The mouth was visible only as a slit in the lower face, as the lips were so pale as to almost be white, as though faded from the face.

Must've lost almost all 'is blood in some battle, the Sailor thought, distaste coloring his mood.

The sole identifiable aspect was the ragged cloak the man wore, with the heraldry of the Koteli knights on the back and the emblem of the Captain on the shoulder. Even that had been through an ordeal, as it was ragged along the edges and tied at the man's throat in a knot, as if the clasps had been ripped off and lost.

"Rite, Cap'n. Let's get ye settled. 'Sa long way'te Caer foot'in it." The sailor grasped the frail knight's shoulders with surprising gentleness and steered him from the dock and towards the land.

"I am not…!" the weak voice began again.

"Yes'ah, we know." The sailor pulled the knight along without looking back.

A stinging bug flitted in and around the uncontrolled tousles of the boy's curls. Said boy slouched with irritable boredom against the battered and hanging gates of the outer wall. He waved at the bug with languid annoyance, bothered by its presence but not enough to do more than bat it away. Tired voices in the tones of several men brought his attention round from his bored musings. He looked up to see four men cresting the hill. Three were dressed for a life at sea. They were helping a fourth, who was dressed as one who had suffered a grievous injury, wrapped in torn and tattered garments and dirty, unwinding bandages. The seafarers half helped and half carried the injured man along the path as the quartet approached the outer wall. The tousled youth stood up, shaking his hair and, thereby, the biting bug out of his eyes.

"Hold it! What brings us this t'day?" he challenged.

The four men stopped, blinking at the youth who blocked their way through the gate. The shortest of the seafaring folk, a squat man with a darker countenance than his companions, squinted at the youth and smiled, showing a massive grin of all four teeth. His voice was a deep and husky baritone.

"Let's us pass, child of the fields. We've a person of great import t'Brehines, ya?"

The youth's eyes flitted across the men, suspicion filling his tone. "Who's of such import, eh?"

"Koteli Cap'n. Back from th' Temple."

The boy froze, staring at the bandaged man. The Koteli Captain? Back from the Temple? Where the Sages lived…back from…whatever… war had been waged against the Cotheda? But why was he bandaged so? And where were the others—the rest of the regiment? His mind reeled with questions, but nothing was coming from his lips.

The four men drew closer, ignoring the gawping, tousle-haired youth, and passed through the remains of the outer gate. They ignored him as though he were a decorative statue.

The boy's eyes followed the injured man in awe, marking his slow progress down to the minute detail of his dragging, ragged cloak.

"My Lady!"

"What brings you?" She stood in the main hall, surveying the repair work being done over the hole in the roof. It had appeared, she was told, sometime during the Cotheda attack. The old man knelt low before her, anxiety shining keenly upon his face.

"Men approach, my lady. They say they bring a man of great import here."

Her brow wrinkled. "Of great import, you say? Hmm, bring him forth, I guess. Let's see who is of such import."

The old guard staggered to his feet and hobbled to the inner hall as fast as his old legs would carry him. Moments later, a squat and swarthy man entered, leading a bandaged, bedraggled, and tattered knight in a ragged cloak behind him. The guard brought them closer but stopped a man's span away from them.

"Kneel before her Ladyship, Brehines Anwadaledd the Reclaimed!"

The swarthy man knelt clumsily at the guard's admonishment, but at the sound of her name, the bandaged man's head jerked up. He moved his head back and forth, as though he were trying to peer through the wrappings covering his eyes.

"Lady Anwadaledd. You've truly returned to us?" The reedy, quavering voice pitched even higher, and a trembling hand arose from his side to paw at the air as if of its own will, searching the air before him for her presence.

The sailor and the guard stared at the bandaged man, shock silencing them for a moment at either his actions, his tone, or his words. Anwadaledd was unperturbed and stepped closer, closing the distance between them. She raised her own hand and gently cupped the bandaged hand and seeking fingers that waved before her face.

"The Koteli Captain. Captain of the Brehines' Guard," she murmured. "You've returned to us. We are most blessed with your return, Light's Guardian Madd—"

"No!" the shrill voice hissed, stopping her mid-word. "I… I am not… not… the Captain."

Anwadaledd paused, taken aback. "Then… with whom do we speak here… in the Captain's cloak and in Knight's attire?"

"I… we… *I* am… First… of the Knights. The First Knight."

"I see." Anwadaledd's smile warmed through her voice, and she held the fragile fingers more firmly.

"We welcome you home, Gonestrwydd, First of the Koteli Knights."

Summary Character List

Maddau – Captain of the Koteli Knights, Knight of Mercy

Gonestrwydd / Twyll – First Knight of the Koteli Knights, Knight of Honesty / Commander of the Cotheda Chevaliers, Chevalier of Deceit

Burdeb – Koteli Knight, Knight of Purity

Olwygg – Koteli Knight, Knight of Veneration

Haelder – Koteli Knight, Knight of Humility

Lymder – Koteli Knight, Knight of Discipline

Gwyleidd – Dra – Koteli Knight, Knight of Kindness

Cynddaredd – Cotheda Chevalier, Chevalier of Fury

Gwanc – Cotheda Chevalier, Chevalier of Greed

Malchder – Cotheda Chevalier, Chevalier of Pride

Gor-yfed – Cotheda Chevalier, Chevalier of Temptation

Blys – Cotheda Chevalier, Chevalier of Lust

Cenfigen – Cotheda Chevalier, Chevalier of Despair

Abertha – Brehines of Caer y Twr, Second Daughter of Beli Mawr

Anwadaledd – Sister of Abertha, First Daughter of Beli Mawr, Former Brehines of Caer y Twr.

Teacher – Mentor to the Gwaedreiol line, person unknown

Gwirionedd – Sage of Honesty

Castale – Steward of Caer y Twr

Ronanus – Owner of Santus Ronanus farming township in Brittany

Jantielle – Wife of Ronanus

About the Author

M T Lynx is the author of the Project AGOSHA series and the Myths of Endolia series. After achieving a baccalaureate degree in Engineering and completing a long career in Project management, MT felt it was time to begin putting to print the fantastical tales developed as a creative outlet over the years. MT enjoys travelling to new places, writing, playing D&D with friends, keeping up with the latest video games, and is often managed by two feline overlords.

More information about the author and books can be found at
www.MTLYNX.com

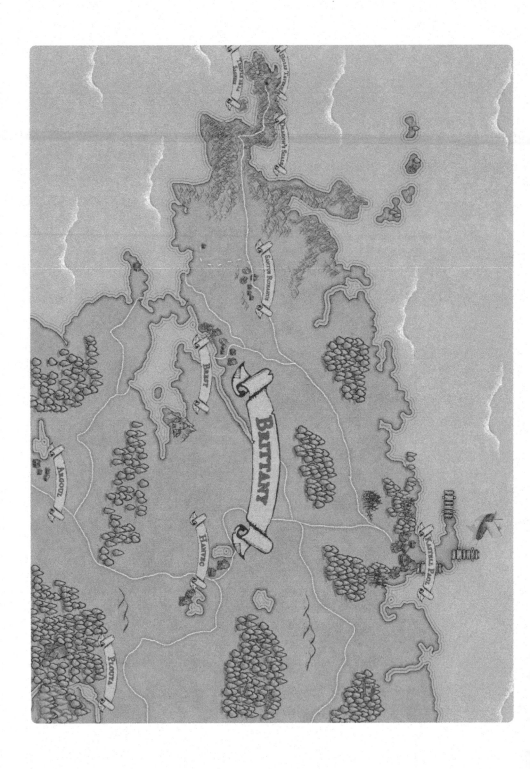